"I hav

ate, last

The t

her ear.

She s

very big mistake as it turned out. With her rational mind, she'd meant to deny his request. But he hadn't put any space between them and she brushed up against him as she rotated, sweeping hip, thigh, shoulder and breast across muscular corresponding body parts. Once she was fully around, their mouths were only inches apart and his eyes . . . God, his eyes. For once in her life, her fine intellect didn't stand a chance against the urging of her senses. She knew she should send him away. She could do that. She could. But if she did, she'd never know what it was like to be made love to by this man. And she very badly wanted to know.

Books by Susan Andersen

*Published by Kensington Publishing Corporation

Obsessed

Susan Andersen

ZEBRA BOOKS
KENSINGTON PUBLISHING CORP.
http://www.kensingtonbooks.com

ZEBRA BOOKS are published by

Kensington Publishing Corp.
119 West 40th Street
New York, NY 10018

All Kensington titles, imprints, and distributed lines are available at special quantity discounts for bulk purchases for sales promotion, premiums, fund-raising, educational, or institutional use.

Special book excerpts or customized printings can also be created to fit specific needs. For details, write or phone the office of the Kensington Special Sales Manager: Attn.: Special Sales Department. Kensington Publishing Corp., 119 West 40th Street, New York, NY 10018. Phone: 1-800-221-2647.

Zebra and the Z logo Reg. U.S. Pat. & TM Off.

ISBN-13: 978-1-4201-1715-8
ISBN-10: 1-4201-1715-7

First Printing: October 1993

10 9 8 7 6 5 4

Printed in the United States of America

Dear Reader,

Back when I was a rookie writer, brevity was not my strong suit. I made the usual beginner's mistakes and rambled a bit, especially in the early chapters where I was still feeling my way. While I was unable to correct those sophomore blunders in this book, the story still kicks you-know-what (in my not-so-humble opinion) as it's about family, love, trust—and the darker flipside when trust is withheld. It's about disturbed minds, close calls, and near misses. And the push me/pull me between men and women—the fascination for which, I gotta tell you, I've yet to find an end.

Can I be more specific, you say? Heck, yeah. Not only can I, but never let it be said I haven't learned to pare down my sentences since back in the day. So here's my shot, in short, at what OBSESSED is all about.

A doctor from a big, nosy family who works in Seattle's busiest emergency room.

The cranky, macho cop who moves in next door to her.

A bowl full of condoms and erroneous conclusions.

Sex. Jealousy. And the decisions of a man and a woman to stay out of each other's way.

Until the serial rapist the cop is hunting pulls the pretty ER doc into his madness, and turns those decisions to dust.

Then things start to get interesting.

Happy Reading,
Susan

This one is for the family;
Dedicated with love

to
My brothers Ken and Ron
Who aren't nearly as obnoxious as they used to be

to
Auntie Jean and Uncle Chuck
Who know a little something about homemade soup
and handcrafted bears

and to
My cousin Colleen
With whom I can pick up a conversation like it was
yesterday even if it's actually been a very long time

Not to mention
All the rest of my sisters-in-law, aunts, uncles and
cousins, nieces and nephews
Whom I'd list by name, if there weren't so many of
you

. . . Susie

Prologue

It was another full moon; he felt invincible and full of purpose when he set out. Everything went like clockwork at first, too, just as he'd expected. It was, in fact, a downright shame that aside from ole Bess there was no one around to witness his performance. He was brilliant—anyone seeing him would have had to admit as much.

Then things started to go sour. For a while there matters got a little dicey before he finally managed to get a handle on everything. It was his show, though, all the way; so naturally it worked out just fine.

It even got interesting . . . and all's well that ends well, he always said.

He wasn't a killer, but that night he teetered dangerously close to becoming one. Not that he harbored any particular moral objections to murder; he simply didn't get his kicks that way. No, for him it was the thrills derived from hurting and terrorizing; he'd opt for those any old time, reveling as he did in his victims' fear. He loved to hear the high edge of hysteria that colored their voices when they begged; to see their eyes stretched by terror as the cool point of his knife caressed their throats, their faces, their breasts; to feel the futile resistance of feminine muscles violently breeched. Kiss the girls and make them cry—Georgie Porgie was his kinda guy: a man with a righteous attitude. To curtail the enjoyment by killing seemed to him unnecessary, pointless . . . hell, almost redundant. Give him a good old-fashioned slaughter of the emotions any old day. It wasn't for nothing that he left each of his ladies with a permanent little memento. He knew that deep down they all wanted it anyway: he merely did his best to accommodate them. He wished all his victims a long and fruitful life—years and *years* in which to remember him.

But that night something went wrong.

He was in the midst of carving his trademark heart in sweet Bess's chest when he realized she had passed out. "No, no, no, sweetheart," he murmured. "This will never do." He gave her cheek a smart tap with the flat of his fingers. "Wake up, babe," he ordered. She remained unconscious and he slapped her again impatiently. "C'mon, c'mon; I ain't got all night. Nobody likes a party pooper, sweetheart, and if I have to go hunting for the household ammonia . . . well, it's gonna be used for more than just bringin' you around." He glared pointedly at the half completed, bleeding wound on her chest.

It wasn't until he looked up at her face again that he realized her lips were turning blue.

"Shit!" He leaped to his feet and stared down at her. Using his teeth to rip off his surgical glove, he fumbled for a pulse beneath the curve of her jaw. Once located, it beat with an irregular, thready rhythm beneath his fingertips.

Damn her! This wasn't supposed to happen. He was supposed to help her get dressed, kiss her goodnight, and then leave, savoring the power.

In an unaccustomed panic, he hastily tucked himself back into his gaping fly and glanced about wildly as he zipped and buttoned to make sure he wasn't leaving anything behind. He recovered his knife from the mattress where it had fallen, removed Bess's blood from it by wiping it on the sheet, and then stuffed it into its sheath.

He strode swiftly from the room, using the removed glove to turn the doorknob. At the front door he paused to collect his wits, drew in a deep breath to steady his racing pulse, and then checked his clothing over to make sure it hadn't been marred by the slut's blood. Pressing a clenched fist hard against his sternum, he struggled to contain his fury.

Damn that little bitch! She'd ruined everything. As a rule, he could count on his anger to build slowly over the course of a month, until it reached a zenith when the moon rode full in the night sky. By that time the predator to whom his body played host had usually generated a wrath so fierce it left him feeling as if he'd blow apart if something wasn't done. The instant the timing was right, he purged himself of it. He picked out a likely looking target, followed her home, forced his way in, and unleashed on her the black rage that had been building inside him all month. Then he felt good for awhile. He felt released, calm again.

But the fury that had drained in the sweet aftermath of his attack on Bess was back in force now. How dare she wreck his hard-earned tranquility this way? Hell, she'd wanted it—they all wanted it. Women were sluts. A man merely had to observe the way they were forever wiggling their butts and their tits in his face to know it, had only to see them showing off their bodies in their skimpy summer clothes. Bess was no exception.

Now that she'd gotten her just desserts, however, she thought she could deny her own culpability by turning her toes up. Well, if she thought for a goddamn instant that by dying she could make it all his fault, she was sadly mistaken.

He cracked open the front door cautiously and looked both ways before stepping out into the hallway. Bypassing the elevator, he pulled open the fire door to the stairwell and slipped through. As he clattered down the stairs, he pulled off his ski mask and stuffed it into his hip pocket. Shoving unsteady fingers through sweat-dampened hair, he swore viciously under his breath.

The disguise had to go; it was too damn ludicrous for words. Here it was a breathlessly hot night and he was running around in friggin' *wool*. Before the pressure within him built once again to uncontrollable proportions, before the voice in his head drove him out into the next full moon, he was damn well getting himself a cooler disguise.

Out on the street, he controlled an uncharacteristic impulse to run and forced himself to stroll along with studied nonchalance. There was a dumpster halfway down an alley at the end of the block and he tossed his disposable gloves into it. Stepping back onto the sidewalk, he studied his surroundings to make sure his presence had gone unnoticed. A pay phone on the neon-washed arterial an avenue away caught his attention. He hesitated.

He didn't know what the hell was the matter with ole Bess, but he didn't want her to die. Where was the fun in that? She had a responsibility here— she was supposed to remember him. It was gonna be one fuckin' short memory if he allowed her to up and croak, and from the looks of her that was exactly what she was going to do if she didn't get some attention.

He covered the distance to the phone, fished a quarter from his pocket, wrapped his T-shirt around the receiver to keep his fingerprints off it, and dialed 911.

Okay, he thought as he hung up a few moments later, *you've done your good deed for the day. You have been, in fact, a regular goddamn boy scout . . . Now get the hell outta this neighborhood.*

He fully intended to do just that, to melt into the quieter side streets and slip unseen through the darkened residential district to the place where he'd parked his car a safe distance away. Then as soon as he'd driven far enough from the scene of the crime, he meant to stop by the first bar he came upon for a tall, cool drink to celebrate a job well done.

His curiosity, however, proved to be stronger than his ever-vigilant caution. He found himself drifting back toward Bess's apartment house, lured by the swirling lights and wailing sirens of the emergency vehicles that careened off the arterial and roared up the darkened side street.

He wasn't the only one drawn to the scene. The excitement of sirens destroying the silence of the night had brought out a considerable crowd from the neighborhood. It was simple to blend into the gathering spectators, and when the voices eddying around him asked each other what was going on he was hard pressed not to fill them in on all the delicious details.

The paramedics were in the building for what seemed to him an inordinately long time, but eventually they rolled Bess out on a portable gurney. Much to his disappointment, she was covered to the shoulders with a white sheet that effectively hid his handiwork. An oxygen mask was strapped over her nose and mouth, and an IV bag hung from an overhead hook and rocked with the motion of the gurney.

He overheard a paramedic telling the patrolman who held back the crowd that Bess was still in critical condition as he and his black partner bundled her into the Medic I truck. When the cop inquired where they were taking her, the paramedic called out the name of the best-known trauma unit in town. The doors of the vehicle slammed shut and it roared into the night. With nothing left to look at, the crowd began to disperse.

He knew then he should call it a night and go get that drink. But somehow, once in his car, he found himself driving at top speed to the hospital. The paramedic had said Bess was still critical. He needed to know she was going to live. She *had* to live, dammit . . . to remember him. To relive his mastery over her again and again.

The emergency room was bright, noisy, and busy. Bess's rapist took a seat in the crowded waiting area but quickly grew impatient when he was unable to see anything. He hadn't come all this way just to sit here twiddling his thumbs—he wanted to know what was going on. Getting up, he drifted through the corridors, craftily avoiding contact with any hospital personnel who might tell him he was in a restricted area. At an intersection of two corridors, he came across a large, wheeled canvas cart pushed up against one of the walls. Liberating himself a pair of surgical scrubs from the soiled laundry within, he donned them as protective camouflage and moved on.

Eventually he located the cubicle that held Bess. The curtain wasn't fully drawn and he could see through a gap to the medical team working on her. Finding a nearby vantage point, he positioned himself to remain inconspicuous while retaining an unobstructed view.

Attention fully captured, he stared at the physician in charge. A lady doctor no less. He studied her with interest.

Not at all his cup of tea, of course; he could tell just by looking at her that she was one of those strong-willed, authoritative types. He liked women who were weak, submissive, and easily intimidated.

Nice tits, though. And great legs. She was way too tall, of course, and too bad about that hair. He had never seen the point of red hair. Well, hers wasn't really *red* red—what did they call that deep copper color, strawberry blonde? No, that couldn't be right; there wasn't any blond in it. Well, regardless of its name, it was still too red for his taste. He preferred his ladies dark . . . like little Bess there, lying so still.

Nevertheless he found himself watching the doctor with increasing absorption. He'd never cared for strong women, but there was something about this one that tugged at him. Watching her bend over Bess, directing low-voiced orders to the staff around her, he wondered if perhaps it wasn't simply a matter of her being a provider in the health-care profession. He'd had an aunt who was an LPN and she'd treated him pretty good during the worst period of his life. She'd treated him, in fact, better than any woman in his life ever had. Not that the Doc here looked anything like Aunt Flo. Still, there was *something* about her, and when she stepped out of the cubicle to consult with another doctor, he found himself relinquishing his vantage point and strolling casually past her. From the corner of his eye he read the little name tag pinned on the breast of her white lab coat. I. Pennington, M.D. it said.

There was a water fountain located just beyond the conversing physicians, and he bent over it, sipping slowly until she returned to the cubicle and the other doctor left. Then he took up his post once again, and as he continued to watch her his fascination grew.

A nurse suddenly tugged the curtain fully closed. Afraid of courting discovery by staying in one place too long, he was just on the point of drifting away when the detective arrived. Oh, sure, the cop was dressed in plain clothes—jeans and running shoes no less—but the watcher wasn't fooled, not for a goddamn second. He could smell a cop a mile away.

Dark and towering, this one came barging onto the scene, just another aggressive, bullshit cop making demands that brought the tall red-headed physician out of the cubicle. They were too far away for the man observing them to overhear their conversation, but it wasn't difficult to figure out what was being said. His lip curled in disgust.

He knew all about cops and their arrogant ways, and this one looked typical. He looked, in fact, even more overbearing than most . . . and that was saying something. Bess's attacker didn't have to actually hear the conversation to know the detective was aggressively badgering the doctor for information. God, he hated cops. In the end, they always bullied people into giving them exactly what they wanted.

The doc, however, surprised him. She stood her ground, brushing the detective off with swift, unsmiling efficiency, and then she returned to the cubicle, leaving him to scowl after her departing back. Not surprisingly, given the inherent pushiness of police the world over, the detective immediately bulled his way into the cubicle after her, but he was back out in the hall again in record time. He stood there for about two seconds before he stalked off down the hallway.

A strong surge of affection suffused the hidden observer and he immediately forgave the doc her height, her hair color . . . even her air of authority. Oh, this was just too fucking perfect. His doc had gotten the best of a goddamn cop. Hell, not only gotten the best of him, by God—she'd actually managed to royally frustrate the guy in the process.

He knew he'd better move along now before he risked drawing the cop's attention to himself. He didn't underestimate the tenacity of cops when there was something that they wanted . . . and this one looked particularly unlikely to give up without a fight. Taking care, the silent observer navigated the hallways, hugging his near-perfect content-ment to his breast.

The doc was all right, he thought. Hell, she was more than all right; she was a goddamn miracle worker. She'd cured him of his corrosive anger, and that was not a negligible endeavor.

Wrapped in a cocoon of warm euphoria, he decided he just might be in love.

Chapter 1

Three weeks earlier

Ivy Pennington was becoming upwardly mobile today and several of her cousins had turned out to lend their assistance getting her moved. They arrived with the dawn at her old apartment above Aunt Babe and Uncle Mack's garage.

Ivy had packed her coffee maker the night before and much to everyone's disgust couldn't remember into which box it had been stuffed. Yawning and bleary-eyed, her helpers stumbled up and down the exterior staircase in the early morning chill as they emptied out her apartment, loading her possessions into Sam's truck, Terry's van and Ivy's car. When the last swear word had faded, the last stray item had been tucked into a free corner in one of the vehicles, they formed a convoy and pulled out of the driveway. Their only stop was at a drive-through window at McDonald's for coffee, and by the time they reached her new apartment, everyone had finally started to come alive.

Ivy, Sherry and Jaz unloaded labeled boxes, the lighter pieces of furniture, armloads of hangered clothing, and the one plant Ivy had managed not to kill. Sam, Davis, Terry, and Sherry's husband, Ben, handled the heavier furniture. They had to make several trips from the vehicles to the apartment and high spirits rapidly began to replace the sleepiness with which they'd begun the day. As was usual when they got together, their conversation rapidly degenerated into a lot of noisy, good-natured squabbling and boisterous laughter.

Ivy's belongings were banged around with careless abandon, bounced like so many bumper cars off walls and doorways. Her pride and joy, however, her brand new, tapestry-upholstered hide-a-bed couch, they treated with kid gloves. Everyone knew how long Ivy had had to save to buy it.

She stroked its rich fabric affectionately and directed Davis and Terry in its placement, making them move it three separate times in her search for the perfect spot to display it to its best advantage. The men set it down in the third location with an air of finality, and exchanging a glance, flopped down on its cushions. Ivy stood back and eyed the couch's position critically, undecided if it looked better where it was or against the wall where they'd tried it a moment ago. She opened her mouth, but Terry correctly read her intention and forestalled her.

"Forget it, Ivy," he advised her with calm finality. "We aren't moving it again. Sucker weighs a ton and it looks just fine right here."

Ivy gave him a look she had patented when she was about twelve years old. Terry all but yawned, plainly unaffected, so she transferred it to Davis. He'd always been an easier touch anyway.

He shifted uneasily. "Don't look at me like that. I hate it when you do that."

Terry grinned. "It's her I'm-the-cutest-puppy-in-the-pound-and-they're-gonna-gas-me-any-minute look." He made his voice a high falsetto. "Save me, Davis. Save me!"

Ivy wanted to laugh, but she knew she had Davis on the ropes, so she intensified the soulfulness of her expression instead. Now if only she could dredge up a tear or two . . .

"Knock it off, Ive," Davis demanded. "I mean it. It's not gonna work; I quit fallin' for that big-eyed look when I was about fourteen."

Sam strolled in from the kitchen clutching a pair of long-necked beer bottles in each hand. Passing them around, he directed a smile of brotherly maliciousness at Davis. "Wasn't that the year you decided you were gonna marry Ivy when you both grew up?" He flopped onto the couch between his brother and cousin, and Ivy knew she could kiss goodbye to any hope of having them move it for her again. There had been a slim chance she might have swayed Davis, in which case Terry might have agreed to go along with it, but Sam and Terry combined? Not a prayer.

"Yes," Davis replied, giving his brother a sour look. "It was; thanks for remindin' me. You broke my heart that year when you told me first cousins couldn't marry because their babies would all turn out to be drooling idiots."

"Sam, you didn't!" Ivy sank cross-legged to the floor in front of them. She took a sip of her beer and gave her cousin a wry, one-sided smile. A strange expression on Terry's face momentarily caught her attention, but Sam's reply recaptured it before she could pin down or interpret its meaning.

"Hey, I had it on the best authority," he said

with a shrug. "Inbreeding weakens the genes. Besides, the way *I* remember it, Davis, your heart didn't remain broken for long. You consoled yourself within the week with little Judy what's-her-name."

"Helman," Davis clarified. "Judy Helman."

"Hey, I remember her!" Jaz exclaimed, walking into the room. She handed Ivy a pillow and tossed one down on the hardwood floor for herself. Ivy rolled up on one hip and slid the pillow beneath her buttocks while Jaz settled onto her own beside her. "She was the first girl in the fifth grade to wear a bra. God, how I envied her."

"At my school that would have been Beth Johnson," Ivy said. "Big Boobs Beth, we called her. At least the girls did. I think the boys called her for dates—or whatever the fifth grade equivalent is."

"Hey, what's going on in here?" Sherry and Ben came out of the bedroom and walked down the short hallway. "You lazy bums! Are Ben and me the only ones still working?" She stopped in the living room entrance and stared down at her cousins, her hands propped on her plumply rounded hips. "And you're drinking *beer?* Good God, you guys, it's barely noon." Then she shrugged. "Oh, what the hell—gimme one too. We've been workin' our tails off since daybreak."

"They're on the door in the fridge," Sam informed her. "Grab one for Ben while you're at it."

"Get me one too," Jaz demanded.

"Sammy and Ben set up your bed, Ivy," Sherry called from the kitchen. "I made it up with the sheets and a blanket I found in one of the boxes." The beer bottles on the refrigerator door rattled as she slammed it closed. "I couldn't find your comforter, though."

"Thanks, Sherry," Ivy replied and smiled up at her cousin as she rejoined the group in the living room. "It's got to be around here somewhere; it'll surface once I get everything unpacked."

Sherry handed a sweating bottle of beer to her husband and one to Jaz, then took a seat in Ivy's overstuffed chair. "This is gettin' kinda shabby, babe," she informed her cousin as she ran a hand over the worn fabric. "I never noticed that before." She looked up from the thinning material and gave Ivy a crooked smile. "I suppose it's the comparison to your brand new couch."

"It's pretty ratty," Ivy agreed gloomily. "But for the time being it's just going to have to do. It'll be six months at least before I can afford a new one."

"And you haven't rushed right out to charge one anyway?" Ben marveled with ironic incredulousness. "Are you positive you and Sherry are related?"

His wife nudged him with her toe. "Funny, Ben. Extremely droll."

"I have student loans that will take me a good five years yet to pay off," Ivy told Ben. "And payments for my new car—not to mention higher insurance rates now that I'm no longer driving a thirteen-year-old rust bucket." She waved her hand, indicating the apartment. "*And* malpractice insurance *and* higher rent. Just the thought of another debt makes me break out in a cold sweat."

"Could you afford seven or eight yards of material?" Terry inquired. "I could probably reupholster it for you. I did a fairly decent job on the seats in my van."

"Oh, Terry, would you?" Ivy's smile was radiant. "That'd be so great. I love the lines of the chair and I think the structure is sound enough; it's just the fabric that's a mess. You'd really do that for me?"

"Sure. Consider it my housewarming present."

He grinned. "After all, we can't have the family's only doctor living in shabby squalor, can we?"

Davis snapped his fingers. "Hey, speaking of housewarming presents . . ." He hopped up and left the room. Ben immediately crawled up off the floor to steal his seat.

Ivy's eyes lit up as she glanced around at her cousins. "You guys bought me a present?"

Sam and Terry smirked. Sherry groaned theatrically. "I swear to God, Ivy," she earnestly assured her cousin, "I tried my damndest to talk them out of this."

Jaz grinned like a cat in the creamery and butted her shoulder against Sherry's calves. "C'mon, Sher, don't be such a prude," she said. "You know it's a great present."

"Uh-oh," Ivy murmured. Anyone familiar with Sherry knew she was far from prudish. It therefore stood to reason that if whatever this gift was had given *her* second thoughts . . .

"No, really, Ive," Jaz assured her. "You're gonna love it. Trust me." She stared at Ivy with large, guileless eyes. "It's *exactly* what you've been needing—and I got that straight from the horse's mouth."

"Trust me, she says." Ivy eyed her cousin suspiciously. "Why is it whenever I hear those words, trust is the very last thing I have the urge to do?"

Jaz merely grinned. "Beats me."

Davis returned to the living room and extended a package to Ivy. "Here you go, Doc," he said. "Happy housewarming, from all of us."

She thought for a moment they'd bought her a bowling ball, which would be odd, since she'd only been bowling perhaps three times in her lifetime. But as it turned out, the shape and size were misleading, for her gift was much lighter than it appeared. Sitting cross-legged on the floor, Ivy rested the present between her thighs and simply admired its wrappings for a moment. It was festively done up in irridescent tissue, gathered at the top and secured by a bow with flowing streamers. Glancing up at her cousins's attentive faces, she smiled and then picked the bow apart. She set it aside and unfurled the gathered tissue.

At first her eyes refused to believe what they were seeing. Then a choked laugh escaped her. "Oh . . . my . . . gawwd."

She removed a round crystal vase from the wrappings. That was where the *conventionality* of the gift stopped and her cousins' sense of humor took over. They had filled it to the brim with condoms of every conceivable brand, color, and style. Looking up, her eyes caught Jaz's. "Horse's mouth, my ass. When I said I might finally have time for a relationship now, Jasmine, I was thinking more along the lines of one man, not the entire fifth fleet."

She silently cursed the heated color she could feel climbing her throat. She was more amused than embarrassed by her cousins' gift and God knew that after everything she'd seen in med school and on the work lanes at the trauma unit, one would reasonably expect she'd have lost the power to blush by now. But no such luck, dammit—she still turned color at the drop of a hat, a hated legacy passed down by generations of thin-skinned ancestral redheads. And naturally her cousins could be counted upon not to let the fact pass without comment . . . not when pointing out each other's inadequacies was such a popular family pastime.

No sooner had the thought crossed her mind when Sam commented on her high color to the group at large. They heckled her mercilessly.

She fanned her hot cheeks and gave them a lopsided smile. "Trust you guys to pass on the toaster oven." She held out the vase. "Party favor, anyone? Please. Help yourselves to a handful."

They were all laughing and talking at the same time when Davis started tapping out a tempo on the hardwood floor. He looked up at Ivy. "I know the real reason you picked this apartment," he said. "And it wasn't just for its good looks, was it? You rented it for the acoustics." He began to sing an old fifties Motown tune and one by one everyone except Ben joined in, immediately falling into their accustomed harmonies.

Ben was content to lounge back on the couch and watch them with wry amusement as their voices soared in the high-ceilinged, hardwood-floored room. Damn, this is a strange family I've married into, he decided without regret. Then he smiled to himself as he listened. Actually, this was fairly par for the course whenever they got together and he shook his head in rueful admiration, knowing they were just getting warmed up. Once they broke out the harmonies, it was hard stopping them. Sherry told him they'd been singing together, mostly a cappella, for as long as she could remember and he had to admit they were damn good at it. It was entertaining—that was guaranteed, but it sure as hell could be disconcerting to have a roomful of people just spontaneously burst into song around you.

Singing? Now they were *singing*? That did it. Vincent D'Ambruzzi tossed back his tangled bedcovers and stormed to his feet.

For the past two hours he'd been growing progressively tenser as he'd listened to the thumps and thuds emanating from the apartment next door. More annoying still had been the loud bursts of raucous laughter echoing both out in the hallway and through the adjoining apartment walls. He'd put up with it, holding onto his temper, but enough was enough. Just when he'd thought they were finally beginning to settle down, they'd managed to come up with something to push him right past the threshold of his tolerance. He'd had less than four stinkin' hours of sleep this morning and was in no mood for this shit.

Pulling on the first thing his hand encountered, a pair of skimpy red nylon running shorts, Vincent winced as he bent over to tug them up his long legs. There was a pressure building behind his eyes, which he knew from experience was the precurser to a royal pounder of a headache. Sleep would make it go away, but sleep seemed to be the one remedy the rowdy crew next door was determined to deny him.

Well, he'd see about that.

It wasn't until he'd already pounded with irrevocable, thunderous hostility on the neighbor's door that he was struck with second thoughts. Oh, shit, why hadn't he simply pulled the pillow over his ears? It probably wasn't even all that early—he hadn't thought to consult a clock. And the singing wasn't actually all that loud; it had merely been the final straw to the increasingly annoying pandemonium preceding it, a racket which had left him twisting and turning in a futile search for a few hours of undisturbed rest. Vincent rammed his long fingers through his hair and started to turn away. But it was too late; the door behind him opened.

"Yes?"

He sucked in a deep breath and turned back, his fingers still snarled in the thick heir above his nape, his elbow jutting ceilingward.

Ivy felt herself gaping and had to make a conscious effort to close her mouth. When the pounding on the door had commenced, she had automatically surged to her feet to answer its commanding summons. She had not thought to visualize the caller in advance of opening the door, and as she stared at the man on her doorstep she dazedly imagined that was probably just as well. For even if the idea had occurred to her, her imagination certainly never could have conjured up anything remotely resembling this hostile, nearly naked man.

He was taller than she by three or four inches, something of a rarity in itself as she was just shy of six feet tall and thus tended to stand eyeball to eyeball with the majority of the men she met. And he was dark—very dark. It was his coloring, she thought, that most arrested her attention—she was momentarily mesmerized by the sleek tangle of black hair in his armpit; the inky thickness of the hair on his head; his thick black brows. His eyes, too, were black and he had ebony eyelashes so dense they tangled in the outer corners. His jaw had what appeared to be a permanent dark shadow beneath the skin, his arms were feathered with black hair from elbows to wrists, and there was a thick cloud of hair on his chest that started at his collarbones and ended at the bottom of his pectorals, tapering to a silky stripe that bisected his abdomen and swirled around his navel before it disappeared beneath the waistband of those tiny red shorts.

She gave herself a mental shake. *Good grief, Ivy, it's summertime—deep tans aren't exactly unheard of this time of year.* But she instinctively felt this man's coloring wasn't a product of hours spent at the beach. It might be slightly enhanced at the moment by the summer sun, but she'd lay odds his natural skin tones were a deep olive. There was a rather Mediterranean look about him overall—a large,

Roman nose, which was curiously flattened at the bridge, angular cheekbones, a full mouth.

He possessed one of those bodies that probably looked on the skinny side when it was clothed . . . but unclothed? There was certainly nothing weak or soft looking about it now. The little red shorts didn't disguise a whole hell of a lot and in the few seconds that she stood there, dumbstruck, simply staring at him, Ivy got an eyeful of the flat, ridged stomach, the powerfully developed chest and long thighs, of the solid mass of calf and bicep, the wide shoulders. Every blessed inch of it looked as hard as aged madrona.

Ivy shook her head slightly as if to clear it of the man's overpowering effect. All and all, he was quite a shock to the system, but he certainly hadn't stopped by just so she could admire his coloring and body. He appeared to have some sort of a problem. Ivy, being a neighborly woman by nature, gave him a warm, friendly smile. "May I help you?"

Vincent tried to smooth out the scowl he felt pulling his eyebrows together above the bridge of his nose. He gripped the knotted muscles in his neck between his fingers and thumb, massaged fiercely for a moment, and then dropped his hand to his side. God Almighty. Why hadn't he stayed in bed? Somehow, she wasn't at all what he had expected when he'd stormed from his apartment. "Uh, listen," he said. "I'm your next door neighbor—"

Ivy immediately swung the door wide and her smile grew even warmer as she shifted the bowl she held to her hip and stepped back in welcome. "Hello!" she exclaimed. "How nice of you to stop by. Please. Come in."

Vincent took an involuntary step forward in response to her cordiality before he caught himself and halted. Oh, hell, nice, she says. He stared at her helplessly. It wasn't an emotion he was accustomed to feeling and he didn't particularly appreciate experiencing it now. On the other hand, he was at a bit of a loss as to how to proceed. The pressure behind his eyes grew stronger.

Why the hell had he acted so impulsively? It wasn't at all like him, and now that it was too late he remembered why. Impulses tended to land him in a world of hurt; they always had. He'd come storming over here to reacquaint his new neighbor with a few basic courtesies she and her friends had apparently forgotten, and what had happened instead? He'd been greeted at the door by big, green, friendly eyes, by a pretty, welcoming smile, and now he hesitated to give offense.

This tall, amiable woman inviting him into her home projected an impression of warmth, due perhaps to the warm tones of her coloring. She had straight, swingy red hair that ended in a blunt cut at her collarbones; rubicund color in her cheeks and lips; and a smattering of rosy freckles that scattered across the bridge of her nose and her cheekbones and sprinkled the exposed portion of her chest. Her eyes and smile made her seem very friendly, very approachable. And standing this close, he couldn't help but notice that she also smelled extremely . . . female.

It came out of the blue and caught him off guard—the shaft of sexual craving that speared straight to his groin. He was an abstemious man ordinarily, it had been a very long time since he'd last been even remotely attracted to a woman in a carnal sense. He stiffened with automatic defensiveness, unwilling to feel any sexual awareness now. Yet he was unable to prevent his eyes from taking a swift, visual survey down her body. And he liked what he saw, he liked it very much . . . right up until the moment his eyes stopped dead at the crystal bowl brimming with condoms that she hugged against her hip in the crook of her arm.

Oh, Christ. He stared at the jumble of condoms and nearly choked on the ice-cold rage that exploded in his chest as visions of The Bitch filled his mind. Get a grip, he fiercely demanded of himself, blinking away the memories. This isn't LaDonna, Vince—get that through your head. Hell, you don't even know this woman, so what's it to you what a complete stranger chooses to do with her private life? It doesn't matter. It doesn't. Only . . . what was wrong with him that the only women to physically attract him always turned out to be sluts?

Every last vestige of sexual desire departed as swiftly as it had appeared.

Ivy had drawn enough male attention in her life to be aware of her neighbor's interest and of the thawing of hostility in those jet-black eyes. She experienced a reciprocal flush of awareness and the first small pulse of a sexual excitement of her own. She even felt a little surge of gratitude toward him, for it was difficult to remember the last time she'd been aware of her own sexuality. She couldn't help but appreciate the person reminding her of it now. This was beginning to appear most promising: a new home *and* an attractive new neighbor.

It was therefore a shock when his eyes suddenly snapped up to meet hers again. His dawning interest had disappeared as thoroughly as though it had never existed outside the bounds of her own imagination. His eyes were dark and cold again, containing even more animosity than they'd originally displayed. Considering she hadn't slapped eyes on the man until two minutes ago, Ivy was stunned by the depths of feeling she experienced. It seemed absurdly disproportionate to the circumstances.

"I won't come in, thanks," he said coolly. His eyes dropped to the round crystal container of condoms, briefly flashed to Ivy's cousins in the living room, then returned to meet hers once again. "I wouldn't want to interrupt the group activities."

She glanced at her cousins herself and then down at the gift they had given her, wishing she'd had the sense to set it down. It had still been in her lap when the pounding on the door had started and she'd automatically carried it with her when she'd risen to answer it. She could scarcely believe she correctly understood what he seemed to be implying, but when she looked back at her new neighbor her own eyes had nevertheless lost their warmth.

"I beg your pardon?" she said in tones of frosty civility. One eyebrow arched disdainfully. "Perhaps you'd care to define what it is you assume those activities to be?"

"Listen, lady, I think your little bowl there says it all. What you do in the privacy of your own apartment is your business—"

"I'm thrilled you realize it."

"—I'm just not interested in coming in and joining the games, okay?" Vincent stepped back out into the hallway and Ivy, dropping all pretense of politeness, took an incensed step after him.

"I think you've got things a little backward here, Slick," she snapped and then pointed out frigidly, "I'm not the one who showed up on your doorstep wearing nothing but my underwear." What a self-righteous, tight-assed, presumptuous prig! She could dispel his erroneous assumption with a few brief words, of course, but she wasn't in the least inclined—she didn't owe this jerk any explanations. Who on earth *was* he, anyway—the moral arbiter of the fourth floor? "Frankly, buster," she said with a spurious calm she was far from feeling, "I find you delusional beyond belief. Nevertheless, let me give you a little friendly advice." She looked him up and down pointedly. "The next time you get the urge to preach to someone, put your clothes on first. It will make the sermon much more effective."

Vincent held onto his temper with an effort, which was much more difficult than it should have been. "I came by to ask you to hold it down," he said with stiff formality. "I worked late last night and you've made sleep all but impossible this morning with all the racket you've been making."

Then he lost it. "And if you don't like what I wear, don't roust me out of bed and you won't have to see it!" He rubbed at the headache pounding in earnest now behind his eyebrows and tried to get a grip on his anger. He'd been a cop long enough to know it was the least productive emotion in a confrontation. It was also, he discovered when he caught her looking him over as if he were a particularly repellent slug, not that easily dispelled. Thoroughly out of sorts, he snapped, "From now on, why don't you and your little friends do everyone a favor. Go practice your damn singing in whichever bar it is that pays your salary." Without awaiting a reply, Vincent turned on his heel and walked away.

A high-pitched squeal of rage escaping through her teeth, Ivy slammed the door behind him. Breathing as rapidly as if she'd just run an uphill 10K, she turned to find her cousins had all fallen silent. They were staring at her with varying degrees of shock, incredulousness, anger, or amusement, depending on their particular personalities. "Do you *believe* that jerk?" she demanded.

"Um," someone murmured.

"Real friendly individual, wasn't he?" murmured someone else.

Long after her cousins had left, Ivy kept reliving that bizarre confrontation with her neighbor. Her undiminished anger kept her moving full speed around her apartment, unpacking box after box, finding new places for her belongings and arranging the small pieces of furniture that had been carried in earlier and set in the middle of whichever room her cousins guessed they would most likely belong. An unexpected bonus of all that leftover ire was that she set her new home to rights in record time.

When she finally began to calm down, she felt a little ridiculous for letting him get to her that way. She had her share of temper; it had been inherited right along with the red in her hair. But years of med school, an internship, and a three year residency in the city's busiest Level One trauma center had knocked most of her quick temper out of her. She would have never made it past third year medical school if she hadn't learned long ago to control most of her emotional reactions. And it had been years since she'd allowed herself to care about the opinion of a total stranger. She didn't know why her new neighbor's obnoxious presumption had rubbed her so raw. Ordinarily, it simply would have made her laugh before she shrugged it off.

Well, all right, she admitted as she organized the bathroom, she did know. She knew perfectly well. That horse's ass had managed to awaken her long-slumbering sexuality and now it was screaming for attention with no relief in sight. *Damn* him! He'd started her libido humming only to turn around and figuratively speaking—slit its damn throat.

She'd had her sex drive in mothballs for a long time now, and this was the year she had planned to finally take it out of storage. Naturally, she hadn't expected it to happen overnight, but neither had she expected to be kicked in the teeth and accused of God-knows-what perversions the first time she felt a spark of interest.

It had been ages since a man had caught her attention. She'd had a couple relationships in college, but nothing in the long run that could compete with her ambition to become a doctor. Once she'd begun med school, it had been even harder to sustain a serious attachment, for sooner or later the men she saw inevitably got jealous over the time and energy she poured into her developing career. They expected her to be equally—or better yet, more—devoted to their needs. As soon as that particular argument reared its ugly head ("If you'd put as much effort into *us* as you do to your damn medicine!") Ivy always knew it was the beginning of the end. For she had wanted to be a doctor since she was fifteen years old, and if the man with whom she was involved knew her so little as to suggest she give up her long-held heart's desire simply to cater to his comforts, then he obviously wasn't right for her in the first place.

So she'd repressed her sexuality, and if the truth were known for the past few years it hadn't been all that difficult to do. Internship had been one long, sleep-deprived stretch in which she'd managed maybe three casual dates in twelve months; and her residency hadn't been appreciably better. Working twenty-four hours on and twenty-four off, she'd generally considered herself lucky to squeeze in time for an occasional lunch or dinner with one of her cousins before she stumbled home to bed. The few nights that she'd both had off and could manage to keep her eyes open, her social life had consisted primarily of joining various relatives at Uncle Mack's bar for a beer and a sing-along.

So, big deal, she was ripe for a relationship. That probably explained the sudden lust she experienced for that idiot next door. But it sure as hell didn't give him leave to pique her sexuality with one hand, only to squash it with the other. There was no excuse for the things he'd said; as far as she was concerned, his attack on her had been unprovoked. She would, however, grant him one extenuating circumstance—the innate mouthiness of her family.

She had grown up in the bosom of a close-knit extended family in which there were precious few secrets. *Nobody*, with the possible exception of Terry, seemed able to keep anything to themselves for any length of time. Most of the time that wasn't a problem, for her family was warmly interested in the happenings of others. Never were they malicious, and their inbred curiosity did promote a sense of intimacy and belonging that was hard to deny. There were times, however, when it could be a downright interfering curse.

Not for a moment did she doubt that it was the conversation she'd had with Jaz a few weeks back that had given birth to her cousins' offbeat housewarming gift. She had been rhapsodizing over finally being able to establish a work routine with regular hours—or as regular as it ever got when it came to trauma care. She'd further ventured to express that, maybe, for the first time in what seemed like forever, there was even an eventual chance as well of actually developing a steady relationship with a man—a relationship which she'd finally have time to devote a little effort to. And that, she'd told Jaz, was bound to have better odds for success than anything she'd managed so far.

If she'd had any sense, she would have stopped

right there. Instead, she'd set herself up with her very next words. "And sex!" she'd said. "My God, Jaz, do you have any idea how long it's been since I've participated in even the most innocent sexual activity?"

Jaz had probably mentioned it to Sherry, who had probably mentioned it to her brother Terry, who probably *hadn't* mentioned it to anyone, but then Sherry wasn't known to keep things to herself and was sure to have mentioned it to someone else, who had probably mentioned it to . . . well, the list went on. And before you knew it: a lifetime supply of condoms.

Much as she hated to concede anything, she would admit that it might have been disconcerting for her neighbor to be greeted at the door by a woman gripping a container filled with enough protection to render the entire personnel of the USS *Constitution* safe. Had their roles been reversed, she, too, probably would have been taken aback. She was even prepared to find it understandable if he had concluded that she must lead a busier sex life than most.

What she didn't understand was how he could have taken such a wild leap beyond that conclusion. How many people would see a bowl of condoms, look into a room of fully clothed people, in an apartment obviously just being moved into, and immediately assume they were gearing up for an orgy? An orgy, for God's sake! If you asked her, *his* sex life must be a hell of a lot more interesting than hers had ever been.

Somehow, though, she doubted it. Not that he wasn't loaded with latent sexuality—she didn't even attempt to fool herself into believing otherwise, for she'd felt it too strongly. But even if she could set aside the prejudice he'd managed to instill with his obvious disdain, there was just something too disapproving and rigid about the man—as if he kept himself on a very short leash.

And did the guy have a problem with contemporary sexual mores, or what? She hadn't been mistaken about his interest in her—it might have been fleeting but it had been real. What had killed it stone dead, without a doubt, was the implied promiscuity he'd read into the sheer number of condoms in her possession. Well, perhaps, since he didn't know her, he could be forgiven that assumption. But if he expected to find a thirty-year-old virgin in this day and age, she was afraid he was doomed to disappointment. And more to the point, even if she had been the kind of woman that he so clearly assumed her to be, she'd been in her own apartment, with the doors closed, minding her own business. So, really, what the hell business was it of *his?*

Vincent spent the next couple of weeks asking himself the very same question. It took him that long to concede that maybe he had made an ass of himself by jumping to all the wrong conclusions during his encounter with the woman next door.

His continuing curiousity about his new neighbor irritated him no end. It was not at all like him. For example, he shouldn't give a damn what her name was, yet he'd gone out of his way to discover from her mail slot that it was Pennington.

Okay, that was understandable.

What was not was that damn computer check he'd run on her the day after they'd ridden the elevator together. He knew damn well she wasn't a prostitute, but that hadn't stopped him from checking for an arrest record.

To top it off—as if that hadn't been cretinous enough—he'd gotten caught at it.

* * *

He knew he was acting like an idiot even as he scanned the computer screen. He was a detective in the Special Assaults Unit of the Seattle Police Department, and this was not an acceptable use of his time or the department's resources. But in his mind's eye he kept seeing that smile of hers in the elevator early this morning, and it prodded him to continue the search he'd begun.

He hadn't even noticed her when he'd first stepped onto the elevator. It had been a long, frustrating night and he'd been exhausted, desiring nothing so much as a solid eight hours of uninterrupted sleep and knowing there was no way in hell he was going to get it. He'd entered the elevator and reached out to punch the fourth floor button, only to notice it was already lit. Rubbing his tired eyes, he'd turned his head, and there she'd been. Leaning against the opposite wall, wearing a short skirt and modest-heeled pumps, her long legs crossed at the ankle. She'd stared at him with unblinking, green-eyed solemnity.

He'd wanted to ignore her altogether, but his eyes kept returning to her legs. He couldn't seem to help it; they were exceptionally fine and in that short skirt they were damn hard to ignore. She'd caught him dead to rights looking at them. He had glanced at her face following a brief survey of the shapeliness of her ankles, calves, knees and thighs, only to find her steadily observing him.

That was when she'd given him that smile, and just the memory of it was enough to make his teeth clench. It had been so damned knowledgeable, that smile, so carnal. As if she'd looked right inside of him and said, 'You may think you're mighty righteous because you've been celibate for a few years, but you don't fool me for a minute. I know exactly what you'd like.' She had then looked him up and down with one brief sweep of her eyes; then her lashes had dropped closed, and her lips still curled upward in that knowing smirk, she'd ignored him until the elevator had come to a stop on their floor. She'd pushed herself upright, swept past him without a word, and disappeared into her apartment.

"Hookers?" Vincent's friend, Keith Graham, stopped behind him. He leaned down to read over Vincent's shoulder. "What are you working on that involves hookers?"

"Nothing." An intrinsically honest man, Vincent didn't even consider lying. He pushed back from the terminal and swiveled around to face his fellow detective. Feeling like an ass, he told Keith what he'd been doing . . . and why.

"Jesus, Vince," Keith muttered when he'd finished. Leaning against an adjacent desk, he crossed his arms over his chest. "I don't know whether to congratulate your hormones for finally clawing their way out of that cage you've had them in, or start worrying that you've had them boxed up so long they're starting to short-circuit your brain."

"She said I was delusional."

"Well, Jesus, son, I don't wonder. Put yourself in the woman's position for a moment. Sounds to me as if she had some friends helping her move in and you jumped to some pretty hasty conclusions just because she was cuddling a couple condoms."

"Couple, hell! There must have been a gross of 'em!"

Keith squeezed the bridge of his nose between his thumb and forefinger, eyeing his friend in puzzlement. "People collect all sorts of weird shit, Vincent. You know it; I know it. Even if she planned to use them all in an evening, it's still a considerable leap from being an oversexed amateur to a pro for hire."

"Yeah, okay, I know. She doesn't have a rap sheet, and I guess I didn't really expect to find her in the files anyway." Vincent smiled up at the pretty blonde detective who appeared at his side to ask if he was finished with the computer. He set the screen back to the main menu, pushed the chair back from the terminal and arose, offering it to her. Moving over to his desk, he said in a low voice, "I think I'd like her to be a hooker, though, Keith. Then I could write her off. She has this way of *looking* at me that messes with all my convictions."

"Maybe that's not such a bad thing," Keith replied. He considered his friend thoughtfully. "Not all women are like The Bitch, Vincent."

"Oh, please." Vincent struggled to tamp down his rising irritation. He did *not* want to talk about his ex-wife. "I know that, okay? I see the victims just as often as you do."

"You know it intellectually, maybe."

Vincent's black eyes were suddenly cold and impenetrable as he stared at the man he considered his closest friend. "Meaning?" he demanded, sure he wasn't going to like this.

He was right.

"Meaning," Keith stated bluntly, "LaDonna Baxter D'Ambruzzi Whatever-the-hell-she's-calling-herself-these-days did a damn fine job of stunting your emotional growth, son." He hesitated a moment, then decided to say what was on his mind. "She didn't just sleep with half your friends, Vincent. She fucked with your mind."

Chapter 2

Vincent stilled. "What are you trying to say, Keith?" he demanded in a low voice. "You think I'm twisted now? Dangerous, maybe?"

"If you mean do I think you're likely to go off the deep end and suddenly start taking pot shots at strangers from the top of a building, then no, man, you know I don't." Keith draped a leg over the corner of Vincent's desk. Half sorry he'd started this, he rubbed his hands over his face. Well, he was in it now and it probably needed to be said anyway. Might as well unload it all now before the whole damn unit started trooping in. He took a deep breath and looked Vincent in the eye. "I do think, however, that ever since you caught on to The Bitch's tricks, you've had a fairly abnormal view of women in general. Anna worries about it, too. And before you say it, I already know you're a professional, Vince. I'm not talking about your dealings with women in a work-related capacity. I'm talkin' socially."

"Just because I don't pounce on every piece of tail that twitches my way?"

"You don't even *look* at that twitchin' tail, son."

"Oh, I look. I just don't touch. And before you start worryin' that my bottled up testosterone is gonna explode me into a psychopathic frenzy someday, I'll tell you straight out that I regularly take myself in hand . . ."

Keith grinned. "So to speak."

Vincent relaxed fractionally and gave Keith a lopsided smile in return. "Yeah, well, in this day and age, you gotta admit celibacy's not an unrealistic alternative. It beats hell outta the Russian roulette I played with sex when LaDonna and I first split."

"Okay, I won't argue that." Keith remembered that time well, and if you asked him, one reaction seemed as extreme to him as the other. He let it pass. What really worried him or made him hopeful—he couldn't quite make up his mind—was Vincent's unusual reaction to this Pennington woman. "But, tell me the truth," he invited. "Do you honestly think that it was reasonable to assume your neighbor might be a hooker simply because she's not adverse to displaying her legs and givin' you the once over?"

"Then what the hell was she doin' coming home at that hour of the morning?" Vincent felt like an ass even as the words left his mouth. Christ Almighty, he had questioned the rationality of what he was doing himself, and still he kept trying to defend his position. The incredulous look Keith gave him didn't help.

"Maybe she works swing shift, son," he said. "Maybe she had a date. *Maybe* she's wondering what *you* were doing comin' in at that hour." He cracked a couple knuckles and regarded his friend intently. "Jesus, Vince, get a grip. For all you know, the woman could be a brain surgeon! This isn't a teenager we're talkin' about, is it?"

"No." Vince pictured her, resenting the ease with which she sprang to mind. "She's probably twenty-six, twenty-seven."

"Then don't you think she's entitled to a sex life? Women *can* have them, you know, without turning pro or being sluts like LaDonna. There's not a whole helluva lot of 'em out there ever reach that age with their virginity still intact. Anna's wasn't when I met her and I wasn't fool enough to expect it to be."

"Okay, okay—I get the picture. You think we could get to work now?" Vincent picked up a pencil and stared at its pink eraser tip as he tapped it irritably against the desk top. He halted the action and held it in both hands, just staring at his thumbs where they met on the pencil's underside. Suddenly he snapped it in two and looked up at Keith. "I know you're right, Keith, all right?" He threw the pieces in the trash can and shoved his long fingers through his hair. "I've been having the same damn conversation with myself for the past two weeks."

"You have?" Keith looked down at him. "Oh. Well, okay then. That's good."

"Good," Vincent repeated flatly and shook his head. "I'm glad you think so. I had a perfectly satisfactory life before the advent of Ms. Pennington, you know, but now . . . hell, I don't know. It seems to be falling apart on me. I thought I had it all together—the career stuff, the life stuff. I was doin' all right. But ever since that woman moved in . . ." He shook his head. "Dammit, I hate it that I'm so aware of her, but I can't seem to shake her image loose." Rolling his shoulders, he dug his fingers into the knotted muscles at the base of his neck and swore softly under his breath.

"What's so terrible about being aware of a pretty woman?"

"Think about it, Einstein. You know my history." When Keith simply looked at him patiently, Vincent blew out an impatient breath, knowing he was going to have to put it into words. "Maybe you're right; maybe The Bitch did permanently screw up my perception of women. Conceding the possibility doesn't change anything, because I still can't handle the thought of panting after another woman who indiscriminately sleeps with any man who gives her the eye. I just can't—not after life with LaDonna." He shook his head with rueful irony. "Christ, Keith, why don't I ever seem to be attracted to women who are nice and repressed?"

Then he laughed, a short, humorless exhalation of breath. "On the other hand, it's not inconceivable that I've been dead wrong about her from the first, is it? In fact, it's highly probable. I didn't honestly expect to find a rap sheet on her, but I'll tell ya, Keith, I was hoping she'd have one as long as my arm. For soliciting, for corrupting minors, for—I don't know, something nice and sordid. It would have been so much easier that way. Hell, after LaDonna, it wouldn't take me five minutes to get my mind off a woman like that." Elbows on his desk, hands raking his dark hair off his forehead, Vincent stared up at his partner. "Not to mention that if she turned out to be a hooker I wouldn't have to regret what I've already blown. Because Pennington could be Snow White, couldn't she? Not that it matters now. My mouth has already seen to it that I'm screwed."

"Screwed, blued and tattooed, son—I see your point." Keith slid his leg off Vincent's desk and stood. The look he leveled at his friend was half amused, half regretful. "Inflammatory accusations do tend to torch those bridges behind you, don't they?''

Ivy's ears should have been burning, but she was unaware that she was the subject of a heated debate. Her new neighbor had already bent over backward to make his opinion of her glaringly apparent and having done so, she wouldn't have expected him to spare her so much as a thought again. Even last night when she'd caught him eyeing her legs, he'd followed it up with a look so sour she could've made lemonade out of it. He'd appeared so stern and disapproving that she hadn't been able to resist vamping him a bit.

She wondered what had happened in his life to make him so puritanical, willing to bet he hadn't always been that way. But she wasn't going to waste a lot of time worrying about it. She was too busy enjoying herself.

Caught up in a rush of near euphoric contentment, she was happy in her new apartment, ecstatic in her occupation. Okay, her love life was still on the barren side, but at least with the memory of her residency fading behind her there seemed to be an abundance of extra hours in every day. And for the moment at least she was more than willing to settle for that.

She loved her job. She was doing much the same work that she'd been doing for the past two years, yet there was a surprising new element of freedom she hadn't thought to anticipate. It was unbelievably liberating to be treated as an equal by the other doctors.

She had proven her competency over and over again through the years, to herself, to others. Yet somewhere deep inside she had harbored an awareness that she was still a student. For years she'd had an M.D. after her name, but it had lacked any shred of real authority. She had always been accountable to a higher power: senior resident, head of the department, chief of staff, someone. Every diagnosis, every treatment had demanded a justification. And that was fine; that was as it should be in a learning situation. But the fact that she was now regarded as a complete professional by those who only months ago would have graded her performance gave her a keen sense of freedom. She was just a few months shy of her thirtieth birthday, and she had been working toward this one goal for half her life.

Ivy's desire to become a doctor had arisen out of the devastation at her parents' death when she was fifteen years old, on a night that was burned into her memory for all time. Dreams of her mother and father slipping through her fingers used to wake her screaming in the night, and it would take Auntie Babe ages to settle her down again while Jaz sat watching, wide-eyed, from the bed next to hers. She had eventually outgrown the nightmares, but the memories that remained, permanently embedded in her mind, had influenced the shape of the years that followed.

It was a memory that was more than half a lifetime old and she kept expecting its sharp edges to blur. It had faded somewhat over the years, but it simply wasn't the sort of night that was ever forgotten.

She had been a typical teenager when the evening began, thinking of little beyond her own desires. By the time Alison "Babe" Merrick, her father's sister, had arrived to take her home with her, she had matured considerably.

The memory always began on the mountain pass on a cold dark winter night; it never varied. She and her parents were driving to Ellensburg, a college town in eastern Washington, for a visit with her aunt and uncle. When Ivy wasn't complaining about it, she was sulking in the back seat of the car.

She didn't understand why she couldn't have stayed with Jaz and Uncle Mack and Auntie Babe. She'd called them to request permission and they had said sure, but Mom said no. It was so unfair. She'd had a horrendous crush on Tony Olmstead forever and finally he had taken notice of her too. He was a *senior*—so much more mature than the few sophomore boys who usually called her up. And just the other day he'd stopped by her locker to ask if she wanted to go shoot some pool with him Friday night. Shoot pool—so much cooler than the movies.

Mom and Dad thought she was too young to date, but since she was in high school now, where she maintained a highly respectable grade point average, they occasionally let her go despite their reservations. Not that boys by the droves were exactly beating down her door, begging her to go out with them the way they did with Jasmine. Most of the ones she knew were half a head shorter than she was. But Tony Olmstead wasn't. And naturally when he had asked, she'd accepted, certain she'd be able to convince her parents of the importance of this invitation. But the instant she'd brought it up at dinner, Mom had gone and pulled the rug out from under her, and the next day she'd had to turn around and tell Tony she couldn't go after all. She had taken care to explain why, but still he would probably never ask her out again.

She'd forgotten all about this stupid trip to Ellensburg, probably because she'd been hoping against hope that it would somehow miraculously be cancelled. Even before Tony's invitation, she hadn't looked forward to it. If they'd been on their way to attend a get-together of the Pennington/

Merrick clan it wouldn't have been so awful—not worth giving up a date with Tony, of course, but at least she could have looked forward to the prospect of a little fun. She always had a good time with most of the cousins on her dad's side, especially Jaz, Sherry and Terry, and Davis and Sam, the five to whom she was closest in age.

But this was Mom's family they were on their way to see, and she hardly knew them at all. Worse, when she was thrown together with *these* cousins, they usually just sat around and stared at each other. She thought they were dumb; they thought *she* was dumb; she could never think of a thing to say and they, apparently, suffered from the same problem. Talk about uncomfortable. It was bound to be a very long, very boring weekend.

It was dark outside the window, and once they left the lighted ski resorts and chalets on the pass, there was nothing, but *nothing*, to look at. Her mom and dad were conversing and singing along with the radio. Occasionally they tried to include her in the conversation or get her to sing with them, but she studiously ignored them. The temperature was frigid outside, but warm and stuffy in the car, and between the heat and the unrelieved boredom, Ivy began to nod off. Her chin, bouncing against her chest, kept awakening her with a start, and with a irritated mutter, she finally slid down until she was as prone on the back seat as her long legs would allow. Almost immediately, she fell fast asleep.

It was the relaxation of her body, the doctors afterwards said, that most likely saved her life.

The night just seemed to explode around her suddenly. She didn't understand what was happening; it wasn't until later that she learned of the patch of black ice and the semi that had jackknifed up ahead, causing a massive pile-up. At the time all she comprehended was that one minute she was fast asleep and the next she was being thrown violently forward against the back of the front seat, agony erupting in her left arm. The quiet murmur of her parents' conversation, which had helped lull her to sleep, had been replaced by the deafening cacophony of metal rending metal, the screech of locked brakes on wet pavement, and blaring horns. Her mother's abruptly silenced scream echoed in the confines of the car's interior. Hurt and confused, Ivy dragged herself up onto the back seat again.

Time passed in a blur. She knew that her father was badly hurt and the knowledge terrified her more than the pain throbbing in her arm. His breath rattled ominously in his caved-in chest and he kept drifting in and out of consciousness.

A shrill voice kept repeating, "I'm sorry, Daddy; I'm sorry Daddy," until her mother firmly ordered her to stop apologizing. *Your father,* she said in her I-mean-business tone of voice, *knows the difference between teen-age sulks and a serious difference of opinion, so you just hush.* Until that moment, Ivy hadn't even realized the shrill voice was her own.

She felt as if her world was tilting out of control, her only relief the knowledge that her mother seemed to be okay. She'd smashed her head with vicious force against the rearview mirror, but she was coherent as she twisted around to ask if Ivy was all right, to reassure her that she and Ivy's father loved her, and then to turn away to try to help her husband.

All was confusion in the darkness beyond their windows—footsteps pounded up and down the drenched pavement, people shouted, and flashlights stabbed the darkness. Up ahead, someone's horn was stuck and it blared with nerve-shattering irritation for the longest time before it abruptly stopped. A pervasive cold had seeped into the car's interior long before the emergency vehicles finally arrived to transport them to a small hospital nearby.

A medicinal scent that was at once comforting and disturbing permeated the institutional green walls of the hospital where they were taken. There were so many people involved in the highway accident that privacy was necessarily forsaken as doctors and nurses labored over the injured in the middle of the starkly lit emergency room, behind curtained cubicles, and in the surrounding corridors. They sorted out the most seriously injured and worked on them first.

Ivy lay on a gurney waiting for someone to set her broken arm. She clutched her mother's hand and both of them watched in strained silence while two stretchers away a doctor and a nurse labored with swift efficiency over her father. Her mother stroked her hair with her free hand and occasionally whispered a word of reassurance. Her touch kept Ivy anchored in a world where everything else had abruptly come untethered. Ivy prayed for her father and clung to her mother, believing—*hoping*—that everything would eventually be all right. It had to be. It would be . . . as long as she had her mother's hand to hold on to.

She could only stare in dumb horror when her mother suddenly collapsed.

It was the doctors that night and the way they worked so diligently that afterward stood out in her memory. Ultimately, they hadn't been able to save her parents: not her mother, when the hematoma swelling beneath her skull suddenly exploded in her brain, and not her father either, who had simply sustained too many internal injuries. But even in the midst of her grief, her confusion and the nagging sense of guilt she carried for a long time to come, she remembered their dedication. And in the aftermath of her parents' death, an ambition was born.

Jaz perched on a wooden stool and watched as Terry carefully removed the old fabric from Ivy's chair. "Why don't you just rip it off?" she asked.

He glanced up at her. "I want to use the old stuff as a pattern for the new fabric." He indicated with a jut of his chin the package on the counter before returning his attention to his work.

"Is this it?" She peeked beneath the paper wrappings. "Ooh, it's pretty, isn't it?"

"Uh huh."

"It'll be perfect with her new couch." Jaz covered it up again and sat silently for several minutes. Studying her fingernails, she chipped away a fleck of polish and then, out of the blue but with suspicious intensity, asked, "Terry, do you think I'm as smart as Ivy?"

His hands went still and he slowly raised his head to study her face. Her features were flawless as always, but masked just now, concealing her thoughts. "Sure," he said.

She wouldn't meet his eyes. Studiously stripping the polish from her nail, she persisted, "Smart enough to be a doctor like her?"

"Yeah, I imagine. If you wanted to be."

"Yeah, that's the problem, isn't it?" She sighed. "Ivy's known exactly what she wanted to be since we were kids. I still don't have a clue."

"Ivy had the knowledge thrust on her in a pretty brutal way, Jaz."

"I know." The eyes she finally raised to meet his were stricken. "And I'm not trying to diminish all the hard work she's put into becoming a doctor. It's just . . . I envy her sense of purpose so much."

She shrugged. "I'm jealous, if you want to know the truth, because sometimes I feel kind of lost. I know perfectly well I'm not really as smart as she is and I'm certainly nowhere close to having a great marriage like Sherry's, and . . . oh, hell, I don't even know what it is I do want." She did, of course. She just couldn't bring herself to say it out loud.

Terry also knew but pretended ignorance. "Whatever it is," he assured her gently, "you'll find it sooner or later. You *are* smart, Jaz. But more than that, you're probably the sweetest natured of us all."

Her smile took his breath away. "Thanks for not saying 'you're beautiful'," she said fervently. "You wouldn't believe how many people make me feel guilty because I lucked out in the gene pool, as if it's the height of selfishness to wish for anything more. You're one of the few people I know who's ever allowed me my moments of insecurity." A corner of her mouth remained tilted up as she studied him. "I really love you, Terry."

His heart sped up its beat even though he knew that what she actually meant was "I love you like a brother, Terry."

Sweet Jesus.

He'd been in love with her for what seemed like forever and much as he might wish otherwise, he was powerless to change the way he felt. It swamped him with guilt, as though the emotions he couldn't control somehow sullied her. And ever since the day they'd helped Ivy move—as if the constant warning his conscience sounded out wasn't enough—he'd had the echoes of Davis's voice to contend with as well. It chanted in his head at odd moments, sing-songing a nasty little refrain about cousins who produced drooling idiots.

But he'd long ago learned to dissemble. So he flashed her one of his carefree grins, replied, "I love ya, too, kid,'' and turned his attention back to the job he was doing on Ivy's chair.

Ivy loved the practice of medicine beyond all else, but some days were indisputably rougher than others. Such was the case the night they brought in Bess Polsen.

She'd been working double shifts for the past five days, and it was beginning to catch up with her. She'd volunteered for the extra duty when one of the ER staff doctors had had a family emergency, so she certainly had no one to blame but herself. And in truth, up until this evening she hadn't minded the extra work at all.

But tonight the emergency room was a madhouse. That, undoubtedly, was related to the full moon—they always seemed to get a surplus of cases at that time of the month. She'd heard through the hospital grapevine that the maternity ward was also doing a landslide business.

It was after midnight and her second shift had officially ended by the time she'd finished stitching up the high school student who'd been beaten by a gang of youths outside a fieldhouse at a Parks Department sponsored dance. Anticipating the cool shower she would take when she got home, she stopped by the waiting room to reassure the boy's parents and the group of teenagers who had brought the boy in and had been anxiously awaiting news of his condition. Then she headed for the staff lounge.

She had stripped off her soiled scrubs and was changing into street clothes when she heard her name being paged over the loudspeaker. They wanted her stat, so with a regretful look at the pumps on her feet, she kicked her comfortable Birkenstocks into the locker, grabbed a lab coat, slammed the locker shut and headed for the door, stuffing her arms into her sleeves and pinning her name tag over her breast.

Angie, one of her favorite triage nurses, met her halfway down the corridor. "I'm sorry, Ivy," she said as she turned to retrace her steps, trotting to keep pace with Ivy's ground-eating stride. "I know you're off duty, but the paramedics are bringing in what sounds to be a real mess. Their ETA is about seventy seconds, and everyone else is tied up."

"Don't worry about it," Ivy replied. "What have we got?"

"Rape victim with some carving, but that's not the primary problem. Apparently she's in shock. BP is 80 over 40."

"Oh, boy." They reached the main body of the Emergency room. "What have the parameds established so far?"

Just then the doors swished open and the paramedics rushed through, navigating the gurney. The one in front caught Ivy's eye and grinned. He was a wiry black man with beautiful model-perfect cheekbones. "Hiya, Doc. We've got one unit of plasma goin' and round saline." He dug in his pocket and tossed a small prescription drug vial to her. "Found these on her night stand. There was a jumbo bottle of Maalox there, too. Don't know if it will help."

Ivy glanced down at the name of the prescription as she strode beside the fast moving gurney. "Thanks, Ted," she said, looking up at the paramedic with a smile as they arrived at an available cubicle. "I think you just saved us one helluva lot of diagnostic time." Her attention reverted to the patient. "What's her name?"

"Bess Polsen," he replied. Paramedics lent a hand in the ER whenever they were able, but Ted stopped at the cubicle door and saluted Ivy with one dark finger to his forehead as the patient was rolled inside. "Full moon out there tonight, Doc. Gotta roll."

"Thanks again, Ted. You're the best." Ivy yanked the curtain on its track and turned to her team. "Okay, let's get a complete blood count, hematocrit and cross-match, stat. Tell the lab we'll need at least 4 units of packed red blood cells." She washed her hands, slid on a pair of surgical gloves, and bent over the patient, gently probing her throat. The skin there was pale, cold, and moist, and her pulse rate was weak and rapid. "Bess," she said gently. "Can you hear me? You're gonna be okay, Bess. Hang in there—we're going to take real good care of you."

She looked up at Angie. "Get another unit of plasma to hold her over until the blood comes. This one's nearly gone." To a male nurse, she said, "We'll need baseline studies of urinalysis, serum electrolyte and creatinine measures. Ted, bless his heart, brought us her prescription for Tagamet, so it looks like we're dealing with a hemorrhaging peptic ulcer. Insert a large-bore nasogastric tube to empty the gastric contents. Let's see if we can't verify the source of hemorrhage."

Until the volume of blood was raised, treatment for the underlying condition had to be delayed, so they worked swiftly to restore the patient's blood pressure to normal. With practiced efficiency they worked as a team, transfusing, treating the wound on her chest, and searching out an indicator that would support Ivy's diagnosis of a bleeding ulcer. The entire time, they talked to the patient in gentle voices, assuring her she was doing well, that she was going to be just fine.

In between the more lifesaving procedures, Ivy combed through Bess's pubic hair in search of foreign hairs, collected evidence of sperm, made note of vaginal bruising and tears consistent with violence, and did a series of tests that would help support a claim of rape should her patient's case ever come to trial. Ordinarily, she would have waited for the patient to be conscious and able to answer questions before she proceeded with the rape kit, but she feared that with surgery imminent, the need to collect evidence might get lost in the shuffle. Without it, the police would have a difficult time making a case to present to the DA, and a man who otherwise might be put away for a while would be free to hurt another woman. She placed her collected specimens in tubes and baggies, which one of the nurses labeled and placed in the refrigerator until it could be analyzed.

She stepped out once to speak to the surgeon she'd had paged and they made arrangements for Bess to be transferred to the OR as soon as she was stabilized. After a few moment's discussion, she returned to her patient. Bess's blood pressure was restored to almost normal levels and she was regaining consciousness when, a short while later, Ivy was called out again.

The last person she expected to see was her next door neighbor.

To say the feeling was mutual would be an understatement. Vincent froze when Ivy stepped out of the cubicle, his eyes flashing to the name tag over her breast. Oh, Christ, she was a *doctor?* Wonderful. When Keith said she could be a brain surgeon for all Vincent knew, he hadn't been that far off the mark.

Feeling like a prize ass, he consequently became very cool and professional. He flipped open his badge and identified himself.

Ivy's reaction was similar to his. He was a *cop?* She glanced down at the card he handed her. Detective

Vincent D'Ambruzzi, Seattle Police Department, Special Assault Unit, Investigations Bureau. She tried to imagine those cold black eyes showing compassion for a rape victim and failed dismally. Or maybe, she forced herself to admit with instinctive fairness, that was an unjust response to his previously displayed dislike of her.

"How may I help you, detective?" she inquired with a coolness that equalled his.

What *was* he doing here? Vincent wondered. He wasn't on call tonight, but a patrolman friend who had been on the scene had called to tell him about this latest victim. The patrolman had realized by the carving on her chest that it was highly probable she was the newest vic on a case Vincent had been working for the past three months.

A case that had generated too damn few clues.

The rapist he sought was meticulously careful and the two previous victims had not been good witnesses. Some women were amazingly succinct in recalling details of their attacks and at providing an accurate description of the attacker, but others became highly confused when it came to details such as eye color, size, and just about everything else. Often the man they picked out in a lineup had little to do with their original description. When they saw him, they recognized him, but they couldn't describe him with any degree of accuracy beforehand. Detectives often spent time in court explaining that to juries to prevent defense attorneys from making it sound as if their clients were being indiscriminately railroaded.

The two victims on this particular case had been in a weakened state and ultimately too traumatized to give much of a description at all.

So what was he doing here? Well, he wasn't following his normal procedure, that was for damn sure. Ordinarily he would have waited until the following day to question the current victim, but tonight he'd climbed out of bed and driven down here in hopes of interrogating her while the details were still fresh in her mind. Maybe she could tell him something that would give him a new direction to follow. God knew, he could use a little help getting this guy off the streets, and he wanted badly to do just that before another woman was hurt.

Instead of explaining some of this to I. Pennington, M.D., however, he said in a clipped voice, "I would like to speak to Bess Polsen. I understand she was brought in here." He was irritated with himself for wondering what the I. stood for.

"Detective," Ivy responded impatiently, reacting only in part to the tone of his voice, "I don't have time for this. Your questions will simply have to wait. I have a patient in there who is in hypovolemic shock and the instant we get her stabilized, she's headed for surgery. Now, if you'll excuse me?" She turned her back on him and disappeared into the cubicle.

Dammit! Vincent stepped in after her.

"Sir!" a nurse exclaimed. "You can't come in here!"

Ivy looked up from her patient, eyes darkening with anger.

"Can you at least tell me," Vincent snapped, "if you've run a rape kit?"

Ivy gave him a peremptory glare. "You will modulate your tone of voice while you're in here, D'Ambruzzi," she commanded, her own voice contrastingly controlled. She tilted her head meaningfully at the patient.

Vincent nodded.

"Then, in answer to your question: Yes, I have."

"Is there a heart carved . . . ?" he traced a spot on his own chest.

"Yes. At least, half of one." Bess moaned in agita-

tion, shifting in sudden restlessness and Ivy immediately bent over her. "It's okay, Bess," she said
softly. "You're going to be just fine. Try to lie very
still and don't get excited. We're transferring you
to surgery in a moment, where they're going to
take care of that ulcer of yours. Do you understand
me?" Bess nodded weakly. "Are you strong enough
to sign a consent form for the surgery?" Once
again Bess nodded and Ivy finally looked up at
Vincent as if surprised to find him still there.
"You'll have to leave now."

Vincent left. He stood in the hallway outside the
cubicle for a moment and then turned decisively
toward the nursing station.

An attractive nurse was charting and he waited
patiently until she had finished. Finally slapping
the metal cover closed on the folder and setting
it aside, she looked up at him, eyes alighting with
sudden interest. "May I help you?"

Vincent flashed his badge once again. "Dr. Pennington is working on a victim from one of my
cases," he said and gave her a smile of such charm
she blinked. It was a tool he rarely utilized, but he
wanted information, he wanted it now, and sometimes, with women, playing the game was the fastest
way to get it—an attitude that he knew would make
Keith and his wife Anna wince. "The doctor's busy
right now," he continued confidentially, "but I
need to talk to her as soon as possible. Could you
tell me when her shift ends?"

"Oh, Dr. Pennington was supposed to be off at
midnight, detective," the nurse supplied with an
eager smile. "I imagine she'll be free to talk to you
as soon as she finishes with her current patient."

"I don't want to miss her. If I wait in the waiting
room will I see her as she leaves?"

"Probably not. She'll most likely change in the
staff room and leave by the door back there. It's

closer to the doctor's parking lot." Propping her forearms on the counter that separated them, the nurse crossed her hands, leaned nearer, and smiled. "But I'd be happy to page her or leave a message that you're waiting if you'd like."

Vincent smiled again. "That won't be necessary, but thank you," he replied. "Perhaps you could point me in the direction of the doctor's lounge?"

For the first time her certainty faltered. "I'm afraid I can't do that, sir."

"Okay, no problem." With a final smile, he turned away.

Minutes later, out of view of the nurse, he stopped an orderly and once again flashed his badge. They talked for a few moments and then Vincent turned and strode purposefully down the hallway in the direction the man had indicated.

Chapter 3

Ivy was drooping with fatigue by the time she pushed open the heavy door nearest the doctor's parking lot. She tried to summon a little energy by reminding herself that things could be a whole lot worse—she hadn't lost anyone tonight. It didn't help her weariness, but what did help a little was the cooling, early morning breeze that dried her heat-dampened body and knowing that, starting now, she had two whole days off. She might just spend them entirely in bed, catching up on her sleep.

"Dr. Pennington?"

Clutching her car keys like a weapon, Ivy whirled toward the man stepping out of the shadows, assuming a combative stance as she faced him squarely. Her tiredness was swept away beneath an adrenaline rush, and the thundering of her heart lessened only slightly when she recognized her neighbor.

"God, D'Ambruzzi," she said in a carefully neutral voice as she resumed a normal posture and casually stuffed her hands in the pockets of her skirt to disguise their trembling. "You scared ten years off my life." Ordinarily, she tended to like most people. This guy, however, was truly beginning to get on her nerves.

"Sorry," he said. "Are you a Creedence Clearwater fan, doctor?"

"What?" The inquiry took her by surprise, and she shook her head in confusion. Of all the questions he might have asked, this was certainly not one she'd anticipated. "Creedence Clearwater Revival, the band, y'mean? Yeah, sure, I guess you could call me a fan. I like their music."

"Remember 'Bad Moon Rising'?" He walked up to her, singing a few bars in a pleasant baritone. "I can't seem to get that song out of my mind. Every time there's been a full moon these past three months, it's burrowed into my brain like a tick on a hound and I can't shake it loose."

Ivy made a concerted effort to understand what he was talking about, but she was tired, his words seemed senseless, and she failed miserably. Rubbing at her temples, she studied his face, wishing she didn't find it so attractive. Where was his rigid, sour look when she needed it? "I'm sorry, detective, but I'm afraid you've lost me. Do you have a point?"

"My point, Doctor, is that there's a rapist at large whom I would very much like to put behind bars. This man is angry, he's vicious, and he strikes once a month, during the full moon." He stared at the lunar orb in question for a moment and then returned his attention to her. "I used to like it when the moon was full, especially in the fall when they're big and low in the sky, y'know? But it's reached the point where I dread its arrival each month because I know that somewhere in the city another young woman is going to fall prey to this very violent individual. And you can trust me when I say she's going to be left scarred, Doctor. Mentally, physically, and probably for life."

"That's awful," Ivy said, "but what's it got to do with . . . ?" *Truly assinine question, Pennington.* "Oh . . . of course. Bess Polsen."

"Yeah. Bess Polsen." Vincent pushed his hair off his forehead with a frustrated swipe of his long fingers. He gazed out into the distance for a moment. Then he shifted his attention back to her with an intensity that riveted her in place. "Listen," he said in a flat, take-it-or-leave-it tone of voice, "I'm sorry for barging into the middle of your work tonight. I don't usually operate that way, but this case has me so frustrated I'm goin' in circles. I guess I wasn't thinking straight."

His tone was almost belligerent and as apologies went, Ivy had heard more gracious.

Still.

She would bet big bucks that apologies weren't something he offered up easily or often and if he'd sort of limped that one out, at least he had made the attempt. In return, she'd give credit where credit was due. "Okay."

He blinked. "Yeah? Okay?" That was easier than he'd expected.

She nodded.

"So, you'll work with me on this?"

"To the extent that I can," Ivy replied. "I can give you my findings from the examination. You understand, of course, that Bess Polsen is now out of my care and most of the specimens I collected for the rape kit this morning have already been sent to the lab for analysis."

He had a great many questions for her and she answered them, standing out in the cool, moonlit parking lot, as concisely and thoroughly as she could. Finally, he flipped his notebook shut and slid it into an inside breast pocket of his summerweight sport jacket. "Thanks," he said. "I appreciate your cooperation. Now if you'll give me a ride to my car, I'll see you safely home."

"Oh, no, really," Ivy demurred. "That's not necessary."

"I think it is."

She could tell he wasn't going to budge on the issue, so she gave in with reasonable grace. At this point, she would agree to just about anything if it meant getting off her feet and out of her pantyhose. She led him to her car and unlocked her door. Climbing in, she leaned over to unlock the passenger door.

As soon as he climbed in, he turned to face her. "You know, your hospital could stand to institute a policy to escort its female employees safely to their cars when they work a shift that ends after dark," he said. "I can't tell you how many rapes occur or originate in parking lots, and in recent years hospital lots have been especially popular."

Ivy shifted uncomfortably. "Uh, well, actually," she admitted with reluctance, "they already have one. I, um, was in such a hurry to go home, I didn't take time to grab one of the men to accompany me to my car." Easily interpreting the patent disapproval in his expression, she snapped, "Don't start, D'Ambruzzi, all right? It's been a long day. So where are you parked, anyway?"

Ivy hustled into the apartment house foyer, hoping to beat D'Ambruzzi to the elevator. Giving him that ride to his parking spot had been a bad, bad idea.

The sexual tension had begun to build in her car before they'd even left the parking lot. She wouldn't have thought it possible for so much chemistry to accumulate in so few city blocks, but it had crackled between them like trapped atmospheric phenomenon on the short ride to his car. It had been enough to make her know she didn't want to be stuck in an elevator with him as well. Not when she couldn't guarantee with the remotest degree of certainty where it might lead.

She didn't understand it—it shouldn't lead anywhere. The man had been so obnoxiously outspoken in his opinion of her that, by rights, she shouldn't feel the least bit attracted to him.

She shouldn't.

But what she should feel and what she in actuality did feel didn't necessarily equate. The reality was it felt as if he had high-powered magnets planted under his skin and she had steel filings under hers. Against her will, against all reason, she was drawn to him.

Oh, Lord, this didn't make any sense at all. She didn't even like him—did she? So why?

You like his body.

Well, *sure,* but a nice body alone had never been enough for her in the past. In previous relationships she had tended to get to know the person first, to become friends before the sexual element was added.

The elevator doors were beginning to close and Ivy was on the verge of congratulating herself for escaping a potentially volatile situation when the outer door banged open and D'Ambruzzi charged through. "Hold the door," he commanded and to Ivy's chagrin, her hand shot out to obey the authority in his voice.

Damn.

Vincent charged into the elevator and collapsed against the wall opposite her. The doors closed and immediately the limited space began to fill with the same tension that had seemed to consume all the available air in her car. He didn't say a word; he simply stared at her. Ivy had halfway hoped that all this tension was one-sided, originating and ending with her. But one quick glance at his dark eyes dispelled that notion. He was interested, all right. Those eyes were all over her, and his breathing was slightly accelerated. Maybe it had been a mistake for her to hightail it away from him so quickly after they'd parked their cars. Maybe it had triggered some ancient male-female response, some ancestral ritual of woman runs, man pursues. Ivy didn't know how else to explain this sensation of primal emotion set loose. She stayed very still, staring at the floor numbers above the door. Man, this was a slow elevator.

She was careful not look at him again, but then she really didn't have to—in her mind's eye she could picture him very clearly. He dressed as if he were two different men, which wasn't too surprising, really, considering he acted half the time as if he had a split personality. From the waist up, he was all buttoned down: starched white shirt, neatly knotted tie, nicely cut jacket. She wondered if it had anything to do with that portion of his body being closer to his brain. Because, from the waist down he seemed to be more in touch with the animal vitality he was currently exuding. He wore soft, snug jeans and Nikes.

They had reached their floor and the door was beginning to open when Vincent pushed away from the wall and approached her. Ivy's head whipped in his direction so quickly a strand of shiny hair, which had been working its way out of the neat French braid she wore to work, slid free and fell across her cheek. Several strands stuck to the corner of her mouth.

Vincent reached past her to punch the lock on

the Door Open button. "What's your first name?" he demanded in a low voice as one long finger reached out to hook the bright strands away from her mouth.

She had to lick her lips to restore a little moisture to them. "Ivy."

With his thumb, Vincent smoothed the hair he held taut over his index finger. "Well, Ivy Pennington, M.D.," he said and took another step closer. "Since you seem to be in a forgiving frame of mind tonight, how 'bout accepting my apology for the rotten things I said about you and your friends . . ."

Ivy could feel her heart pounding as she stared up at him. Dammit, D'Ambruzzi, she thought with a touch of exasperated desperation, don't go getting nice on me *now.* "Those were my *cousins,"* she interjected flatly.

Vincent winced. ". . . about you and your cousins, then. It was probably uncalled for."

Probably. What did that mean? Oh, who cares, who cares, accept his apology and get *out* of here! God, you could cut the tension with a knife and she'd never in her life felt so lacking in sense.

But still . . .

"Probably?" Extricating her hair from his grip, she stepped back, her chin rising pugnaciously. "You accuse me of having an incestuous orgy, but you think it was *probably* uncalled for?" She was grateful for her anger. It went a long way toward re-establishing some of her habitual control. "I'm sorry, D'Ambruzzi, but that's just too weak. You're going to have to do much better than that."

Vincent's head reared back as if she'd spit in his eye. He'd been wound up tighter than a cheap clock ever since he'd climbed into her car. Her flat refusal to accept his genuinely offered, if clumsily stated, apology sparked a knee jerk defensiveness of his own. He planted his hands on the wall above her head and glared down at her. "Just what the hell d'you *expect* a person to think, when you greet any stranger who knocks on your door with a bowl full of rubbers?"

"They were a *joke!* My cousins' idea of a funny housewarming present! But you didn't even bother to ask, did you? Oh, no, not Detective Righteous!" Her eyes glinted fiercely green behind narrowed lashes. "Without knowing the first thing about me, you just leaped to some preposterous conclusion that I . . . that we . . ." She exhaled impatiently. "Oh, let's just forget it, all right? I am not in the mood for this." She pushed past him with more force than manners. "I'm tired and I'm going to bed. G'night!"

She was furious and frustrated and didn't look back. Further resentment burned bitterly in the back of her throat when she observed the way her hand shook as she tried to apply her key to the deadbolt.

Lord above, and here she'd thought she'd tangled with some journeymen jerks in the past. Compared to Vincent D'Ambruzzi they'd been nothing but a bunch of apprentice pikers. Never, *never* had she met anyone who could rattle her cage with such quick thoroughness. And, oh, God, if she didn't get out of these pantyhose pretty soon, she was going to scream!

A hand, large, dark, and warm, suddenly covered hers where she was fumbling with the lock. It guided the key into the hole and turned it. Refusing to look at him, Ivy turned the knob and opened the door with her free hand, trying unsuccessfully to extricate the one he held.

Without touching her anywhere except that captured hand, he stood very close, almost curving himself around her back. The tendril that had escaped her braid clung to the stubble on his jaw as he lowered his chin to align his mouth with her ear.

"I was entirely out of line when I made those remarks, wasn't I?" he whispered. As if she'd been wielding a sledgehammer instead of words, her honest indignation had hit him squarely between the eyes. "I'm sorry." Releasing her hand slowly, he gave in to the need to touch her. Trailing one long finger over the back of her hand, he brushed it up her bare arm to her shoulder. His head turned until his parted lips touched her ear. Slowly he inhaled and his eyes drifted shut as he absorbed into his system the scent of shampoo, woman, and a faint, underlying medicinal aroma of antiseptic soap. "I am truly sorry, Ivy," he breathed. "I wish I could take it back."

"Oh, God." Why did he have to display a flare of sensitivity now? Without her anger, she was defenseless against all these feelings crowding in on her. Her heart was pounding, her skin felt hot, and she wanted him to touch her all over the way his eyes had in the elevator. The force of the need clamoring inside her demanding satisfaction made her shudder. "I have to go in now," she whispered in a desperate, last-ditch effort to put distance between them.

The tip of his tongue touched the backside of her ear. "Let me come in with you."

She shook her head and turned to face him, a very big mistake as it turned out. With her rational mind, she'd meant to deny his request. But he hadn't put any space between them and she brushed up against him as she revolved, sweeping hip, thigh, shoulder and breast across muscular corresponding body parts. Once she was fully around, their mouths were only inches apart and his eyes . . . God, his eyes. For once in her life,

her fine intellect didn't stand a chance against the
urging of her senses. She knew she should send
him away. She could do that. She could. But if she
did, she'd never know what it was like to be made
love to by this man. And she very badly wanted to
know.

She tilted her chin slightly, offering her mouth.

Vincent made a sound deep in his throat and
lowered his head. One hand came up to thread
through the thickness of her French braid; he
splayed the fingers of his free hand lightly against
the small of her back. With a vague intention of
keeping it gentle and light, he brushed his open
mouth against hers. Then he brushed it once again
and licked lightly at the gap between her lips. And
all hell broke loose.

Too many emotions had been building between
them to be easily diffused by soft, friendly kisses.
Ivy plastered herself against his hard length, her
arms wrapping around his neck, her fingers plunging into thick, soft hair to grip his head and force
him closer.

Vincent didn't need to be coerced. His arms were
already tightening, his fingers twisting in her hair
and gripping supple skin through the thin cotton
of her loose tanktop. The rough pressure of his
mouth drove her head back, grinding the knuckles
of his cupping hand against the doorjam. Heart
slamming against his ribcage, breath choppy, a raw
sound rumbled in the back of his throat as he
maneuvered them into her apartment and
slammed the door shut. He crowded her up against
the closed portal, pressing into her. His body
rubbed against hers with a determined pressure
that suggested an attempt to be absorbed into hers.
And still it wasn't enough. It wasn't nearly enough.

Abruptly ripping his mouth free, he leaned back
sharply from the waist and stared into her green

eyes. "Jesus," he breathed. "What are you doing to me?"

If she'd had the strength, Ivy might have laughed. What was *she* doing to *him?* He had that a little backwards, didn't he? The only thing holding her upright at this moment was the press of his lower body pinning hers to the door. Having no ready reply, she didn't even attempt to address his question with words. Instead, she reached behind her neck to slip off the clasp securing her braid and furrowed her fingers through her hair to separate the plaited strands. Shaking the loosened hair back, she gripped his tie and pulled on it to bring his mouth back to hers.

"Ah, God." She'd get no argument from him. His kiss was hot and rough, barely in control. Then he shoved himself away, shrugging out of his jacket. Grabbing her hand, he pulled her down the hallway.

The layout of her apartment was exactly like his, except in reverse, and he made a beeline for the bedroom. It was bathed in moonlight, but except for the rumpled queen-sized bed and the controversial bowl of condoms on the night stand next to it he noticed nothing of its furnishings. He tossed his holstered gun next to the bowl, pushed her onto the mattress and followed her down, sprawling over her body. Plunging his hands into silky strands of unbound hair, he tugged on it with unconscious roughness in a bid to angle her mouth up for his immediate consumption.

Ivy pulled his shirttail from the waistband of his jeans, then slid her hands around to the front of his shirt to wrestle his necktie loose. She was ruled by a desire to feel the skin she'd only looked at before. Wedging her hands between their bodies, she set to work on his buttons.

Without breaking contact, still kissing her hotly,

Vincent pushed up on his hands to allow her room to unfasten his shirt. In moments, she had it pushed off his shoulders to the middle of his back where it stretched tautly from elbow to elbow between the arms he still had locked and firmly planted on the mattress.

Before Ivy had an opportunity to do more than run her hands from his shoulders to the soft cloud of hair on his chest, Vincent was pushing away to sit back on his heels astride her. While he fumbled with the buttons on his cuffs, she grasped the hem of her tank-top and peeled it over her head, then unclasped her bra and unbuttoned the waistband on her skirt. He sank his mouth into the soft skin just beneath the angle of her jaw and Ivy moaned. Digging her fingers into the hard muscles of his shoulders, she arched her throat.

It was sweltering in the room and skin stuck to skin as he kissed his way down her throat, her shoulders, her chest. Circling her upper arms with long brown fingers, Vincent pressed them into the mattress over her head and pushed back slightly to look at her.

Lying on her back with her arms curled over her head, he thought she was the sexiest sight he'd ever seen. The moonlight leached only a little of the warmth from her red hair and her skin was flushed and glowing, so fair against the darkness of his hands. Her breasts were round and full, aureoles the same rosy color as the freckles dusting her chest.

He was consumed by a sudden desire to see all of her at once. Rolling off her, he reached out to release her zipper. He removed her skirt and peeled her pantyhose down her legs. Staring at her, he said hoarsely, "You've got the prettiest legs I've ever seen." Then he reached for the minuscule panties.

The compliment warmed her, but it was the seriousness of his intent expression that most arrested Ivy's attention. "D'Ambruzzi," she inquired with sudden curiosity as she raised her hips to facilitate the removal of her undies, "don't you ever smile?" It had just occurred to her that she'd never seen him do so.

He looked up at her. "Call me Vincent," he said.

"Vincent," she repeated obediently. She waited a beat but he didn't say anything further. "So, do you? Ever smile, I mean."

He tossed aside the scrap of peacock-blue satin and returned his attention to the bright triangle of downy curls their removal had revealed. Once in his sights, he found it difficult to look away. Finally, he raised his eyes to her face and a slow smile spread across his face. His teeth, Ivy noticed, gleemed with incredible whiteness against the swarthiness of his skin. "Oh, yeah," he replied, grinning. "When I see something as fine as this, I do."

He watched her for a moment and then a deep laugh of amazement rumbled out of his chest. "A blush!" Lying on his side beside her, he propped his head in one hand and reached out to press the fingers of his free hand into her chest. "I don't believe it—a genuine, honest-to-God blush." He snaked an arm under her waist and jerked her flush against his body. "You are some kind of woman, Ivy Pennington."

Always vaguely embarrassed to be caught blushing like a schoolgirl, she whispered gruffly, "You plannin' on talkin' all night, D'Ambruzzi?"

Vincent's smile widened. "No, ma'am." His amusement faded, however, when she curled her arms around his neck and hugged him hard enough to flatten her breasts against his chest. She rubbed his calf through the material of his jeans with the high-arched sole of one foot. God. If he weren't so damn hot to have her, he'd be more than a little leery about the sexual power she seemed to wield so effortlessly. He couldn't recall one other woman, not even LaDonna at her best, who'd ever had the ability to render him so excited his brain refused to function beyond the prospect of getting himself buried so deeply inside her that she wouldn't know where he ended and she began.

His hands stole down to cup her bottom and rub her in slow, rocking motions against the erection straining behind the fly of his jeans. Ivy's eyes closed and her head tipped back, soft gasps escaping her throat. Ducking his head, Vincent's mouth attached with barely controlled suction to the offered column while one of his fingers slid into her from behind.

Ivy gasped and hooked her bent leg up over his hip. Momentarily mindless, she moved against him with frantic need. Then she tried to pull back.

"Please," she whispered. "Take off your pants. Now. Please, Vincent? I want to see you—want to feel you."

Together they wrestled his jeans and jockeys down to his knees and then Vincent took over, bicycling his legs to kick them free. He was reaching to blindly plunge his hand into the bowl of condoms when her fingers wrapped around his erection and squeezed.

"Ahh, Jesus!" Condoms scattered as his back arched off the bed. "Don't." Gripping her hand, he peeled her fingers away. "God, Ivy, don't, or it's gonna all be over before it even begins."

She was reluctant to release him, but she did as he requested. She couldn't drag her eyes away from the sight of him jutting straight up from a dense tangle of jet hair. He was so long, so thick and dark; never in her life had she wanted anything more than she wanted this man inside her right now. Fingers trembling, she picked up one of the dropped condoms and handed it to him. "Hurry."

He put it on and looked up to see her kneeling at his side watching his every move. Reaching out to grasp her left arm and thigh, he tugged her over him, positioning her to kneel astride his lap. His fingers digging into her hips, he pressed them down until the blunt head of his erection slipped past slick folds to become impaled just inside her.

An aggressive inclination to slam her down on him until he was all the way home nearly overwhelmed him, but he was watching her face as his hands tightened and his hips came off the bed to do just that. Her eyes were closed and her head tossed back, pleasure transforming her expression at the slow invasion of her body. But although she didn't utter a word of protest when his handling suddenly turned rough, he noticed the sudden wince, felt the abrupt tension in her thighs, saw her catch her lower lip between her teeth. He stilled guiltily. "God, you're so tight."

Ivy's eyes opened and she looked down at him, grimacing ruefully. "I'm sorry," she whispered. "It's been such a long time." She braced her hands on the sheets next to his head and bent forward to change the angle of penetration.

"You don't have anything to apologize for," he said hoarsely. It had been a long time for him as well. Too long, maybe. "It was me—I was too rough." His fingers on her hips tightened convulsively and he sucked in a sharp breath as she pushed against him and slowly sank down. Suddenly, he was buried to the hilt in a humid, slippery vise. "Oh, Jesus, Ivy." His hands splayed over her buttocks to hold her in place.

He would have liked to remain perfectly still to savor the feeling for a moment, but already his pelvis had involuntarily instigated a minute rocking motion beneath her. He slid his hands up her long, supple back; then they slipped around front to cup her breasts. Ah, God, that was nice. They filled his large palms, weighty and soft, and they looked so damn fine, so contrastingly fair against the darkness of his fingers. He looked up into her heavy-lidded eyes and ordered hoarsely, "Ride me."

She made a sound of arousal deep in her throat and began to move. Leaning forward on her hands, she raised and lowered her hips. Wanting it to last, she moved with exquisite langor, feeling him stretch into her and retreat, invade her and retreat. She braced her hands on his chest and rotated her hips, slowly. So slowly. His hands followed her when she sat up, pulling at her nipples, kneading the lush weight of her in his palms.

Within moments, she found it impossible to maintain the pace. Too many sensations were bombarding her from too many different directions. Wiping her damp bangs off her forehead with her forearm, she looked down at him and panted "Vincent, it feels so good . . ." His hands left her breasts and gripped her bottom, directing her movements. Her voice spiraled several octaves higher, and deep inside sensations erupted with explosive violence, causing her body to jerk and shudder upon him. He watched her full lower lip go slack, saw the flush climb from her breasts to her forehead, felt the tight, slick, inner muscles clamp and contract around him and he lost control. Fingers biting into the resilient flesh of her butt, he held her hips hard against him while he drove into her. Sex words and words of prayer poured from his mouth. But it was her name that he roared as he came.

Ivy straightened her legs and slumped down upon Vincent's chest, not caring that they were both sticky and drenched with sweat. She didn't care that her apartment had been closed up all day in the middle of a heat wave and it was therefore too hot to snuggle. She wrapped her arms around his neck and shuddered with small, orgasmic afterquakes. Pressing a kiss into his wet throat, she tightened her grip. She felt so content. Never, *never* had anyone made love to her quite like that, and as soon as she caught her breath she was going to tell him so.

But she fell asleep first.

Vincent stood by the side of the bed and looked down at her while he pulled on his shirt. He wanted to crawl back in beside her and stay; he had to get the hell away from there.

Feeling satiated as a well-stroked cat, he thought if she had just stayed awake to talk to him, he might've been able to place a little trust in this strange feeling of completeness that saturated him to the marrow. She had a unique way of communicating that for some reason seemed to still all his reservations.

But her acerbic tongue was quiet and misgivings had begun to creep in just moments after he'd felt her weight settle over his body with that heaviness peculiar to deep sleep. Slowly, his hands had quit stroking her and rapidly he'd been consumed with doubt. It hadn't taken long before he'd begun to question the wisdom of what he'd just done.

He wasn't an impulsive man and the few times he had been he'd generally lived to regret it. Was this, too, going to turn out to be another huge mistake? It hadn't felt like one until she'd fallen asleep, giving his sharp-edged doubts a chance to assume full rein. But then, where women were concerned he wasn't exactly imbued with confidence in his own judgement.

It would probably be best if he left. No, not probably—it *was* best Hell, odds were he was making far too much of this anyway. The only reason she seemed special was because it had been over three years since he'd been with a woman. Most likely, any woman would have done.

Yeah? questioned a skeptical voice that for some odd reason sounded exactly like Keith. *You've been offered other opportunities before,* it whispered in his brain. *So why is it she's the only one who's managed to tempt you out of that celibacy you're so damn proud of?*

I've never had a tall redhead before, his well-honed defenses immediately retorted. I *couldn't pass up the opportunity to find out what it's like.*

Uh huh.

Dammit, what is this? She was a prime lay, okay? But now it's over, so get off my back!

Fine and dandy, son. No skin off my teeth.

He had to hunt through a pile of her discarded clothes on the floor to find his tie and one shoe. Jesus, for a doctor she sure was sloppy. Locating the Nike, he pulled it on and tied the laces, then searched further for his tie. It was lying on a satin and lace slip and he snatched it up and draped it around his neck. Then he simply stood there, staring down at her.

So what are you waiting for, son? You gotta run, remember? Better shake a leg.

But he leaned down and smoothed her hair off her cheek instead. A slight smile curved Ivy's mouth and she murmured in her sleep, leaning into his touch like a kitten being stroked. Vincent snatched his hand back as if it'd been scorched; then, exerting care not to touch her again, he reached out to cover her with the sheet. With one last look, he straightened, turned, and left the room.

After he'd shut her apartment door behind him,

with no way of letting himself back in, he was struck by second thoughts. Maybe . . . ?

No. Stacking it up against his romantic history, he shook his head and turned away from her door. Walking away wasn't merely the smart thing to do—it was the only possible move he could make.

Chapter 4

"You slept with him? Ivy, are you *nuts?*"

"Probably." Ivy winced at Jaz's incredulous expression. She and her big mouth. Ivy hadn't intended to say a word about last night's encounter when Jaz and Sherry had intercomed from downstairs demanding to be buzzed up. But Vincent's perpetual five o'clock shadow had left raw patches around her mouth and on her throat, and the first words out of Sherry's mouth as she'd breezed through the door had been, "Who's your new cosmetologist, Ive, Susie Sandblaster?" and the truth had just sort of tumbled out. She supposed, given Jaz's initial reaction, it was probably pointless trying to explain that she hadn't even felt the abrasiveness of his beard at the time.

"Ivy, how could you go to bed with that man . . . ?"

"Are you kidding, Jasmine," Sherry interrupted her. "Didn't you get a look at him the day he showed up here in his little red shorts? You could scrub your clothes on the man's stomach. I mean, what an absolute honey." She fanned herself with enthusiastic theatrics. "I bet he's got a big one."

"Sherry, for cripes sake! He accused her—accused *all* of us—of having group sex!"

"He apologized for that," Ivy said, but no one was listening to her.

"Oh, for heaven's sake, Jaz," Sherry was saying. "Where's your sense of humor? You know what I think? I think you're just the teensiest bit jealous because Ivy got a little. How long's it been since anyone's climbed into *your* undies?"

"Too long," Jaz snapped. "I admit it, okay? We aren't all lucky enough to have a fairy tale marriage like yours."

"Some fairy tale," Sherry retorted. "The princess bride in all those do-hicky fables isn't usually a size fourteen." She smacked her ample hips disparagingly.

"So you're full-figured. Big deal. At least you've got a groom who's a prince!"

Sherry surveyed her cousin critically. "I don't get you at all, Jaz; I really don't. I love Ben dearly, but if I were single and drop dead beautiful like you, I'd be out with a different hunk every night of the week."

"Huh. Shows how long it's been since *you've* been out there dating. It's a meat market. Just ask Ivy."

"Oh, am I to be included in this conversation after all?" Ivy looked up from the tray she was assembling for tea. "I thought maybe the two of you were just gonna post my score once you'd hashed it out between you. Whataya think? Am I conducting my romantic life with any semblance of common sense at all?"

"Now, now." Sherry grinned at her unrepentantly. "Ooh, is that Market tea?" She reached for a cup. "I knew you were good for something."

Blowing across the surface, she took a sip and inquired hopefully, "Got any treatsies to go with it?"

"No. I've been working a double shift all week and haven't had too many opportunities to hit Safeway."

"Just as well, I suppose." Sherry shrugged. "They go straight to my thighs, anyway. So, come on, tell us everything. Was sex with him as good as I imagine? How the hell did it come about, anyway? *Does* he have a big one?"

"Yes. I'm not quite sure, myself. Yes."

"Ivy! Don't be obtuse, girl. I want details!"

"Sherry, for pity's sake," Jaz protested. "It's bad enough she let him talk her into bed after all the rotten things he said to her—"

"Dammit, Jaz, he apologized for that, okay?" Ivy interrupted testily. "And he didn't *talk* me into anything. If you wanna know the truth, I've never been so hot for anyone in my life. If I feel foolish for anything, it's that I never even bothered to find out his sexual history and I'm not usually that careless."

"Good God, Ivy." Now Jaz's expression was truly concerned. "Tell me he at least wore one of those condoms we gave you."

"I said foolish, toots, not suicidal." Ivy gave her cousin a level look, which Jasmine knew from experience meant Ivy had been pushed as far as she was going to allow. Then she smiled. "Look," she said reasonably. "If I made a mistake by sleeping with Vincent, then it was *my* mistake to make. There's absolutely no reason for you to lose any sleep over it. And I want the two of you to do me a favor. Don't go spreading tales of this all over the family, okay?"

Ivy understood that Jaz's objections were only made out of concern for her, but the truth was last night hadn't felt like a mistake and she didn't feel like being placed in a position where she was forced to defend her actions. On the contrary, it had felt incredibly right—amazingly so, considering the manner in which they had met. She looked forward with eager anticipation to getting to know Vincent D'Ambruzzi much, much better.

It wasn't until Jaz and Sherry had left and the evening had worn on with no word from Vincent that she was forced to reassess the situation.

When she had awakened early this afternoon to find him gone, she'd assumed he'd had to go to work. After all, cops worked notoriously odd hours, didn't they? Not, she supposed, that two o'clock on a Friday afternoon could be classified as such. The point was: it would have been nice if he'd left a note or something, but the fact that he had not hadn't caused her undue worry since she'd fully expected to hear from him later in the day.

She would have been hard pressed to describe last night with any degree of accuracy and had dodged Sherry's attempt to badger her for details. How did one put that sort of explosiveness into words? That it had been short on foreplay and actually sort of slam/bam/thank you ma'am? That hardly did it justice. Besides, it had left her with a distinct impression of future potential. No man had ever made love to her quite like he had, and all that emotion had to account for something, didn't it? By the time she went to bed Friday night without having heard so much as a peep out of him, however, she was no longer sure of anything. He hadn't made any promises, of course; yet still she felt unaccountably hurt by his silence.

By the time she went back to work on Sunday morning, she merely felt used. Worse, she felt gullible. It appeared Jaz was the better judge of character after all. What Ivy had thought to be the most stupendous lovemaking of her life—and perhaps the start of something special—to Vincent apparently had been nothing more than a momentary itch that, once scratched, had left him indifferent and ready to move on. They'd had sex one time; because he'd probed some untouched emotion deep inside of her, she'd thought she instinctively knew him, thought she grasped the essence of the inner man.

Obviously that was a crock.

For the truth was she didn't have the first idea what made Vincent D'Ambruzzi tick.

In the cold morning light following his tangle in the sheets with Ivy Pennington, Vincent concluded the real mistake last night had been in forgetting his own rule of survival. The feelings that had welled up when he was with her endangered all his protective barriers. Luckily, standing outside her apartment in the early hours, he had gotten his determination firmly in hand once again, and if he'd tossed and turned for the rest of the night, well, that had nothing to do with his decision to sever all future association with her.

Any residual messy emotion had been firmly tucked away and it was back to business as usual by the time he got to work Friday morning. He was the first to arrive and the rare opportunity for a little elbow room in which to work was too good to pass up. He pulled out a file and spread out while he had the chance.

The Special Assault unit was housed in a small, dank room in the Public Safety building in downtown Seattle. The floor was perpetually dirty, the lighting dim, and the desks of two squads of detectives and their sergeant were crowded into an area approximately fifteen by fifteen feet. The city had provided one typewriter; all the others sitting on the jammed together desks had been brought from home by the personnel who used them. Their interview room was the size of a closet.

Already the din of ongoing construction down on the street was nearly deafening and the one small fan that whirred from side to side did little to alleviate the stifling heat. Vincent hung his jacket on the back of his chair, loosened his tie, and rolled up his sleeves.

As his fellow workers filed in and set to work, the noise level increased proportionately. One finger stuck in his free ear to block out the growing racket, D'Ambruzzi concluded a telephone conversation and hung up. Keith Graham was settling into the workspace facing his, observing Vincent's loose-limbed drape over the desk. Cocking an eyebrow, he grinned. "Son, if I didn't know better, I'd swear you got laid last night."

Dave Trevecky settled his bulk into the desk next to Keith's. He bit off a huge chunk of the donut in his hand and licked the oozing jelly off his fingers. "I don't know why everybody keeps makin' such a big deal outta D'Ambruzzi's celibacy," he said, throwing a napkin on a cleared space of desk and carefully placing his cardboard cup of coffee on it. "Us married guys have been practicin' it for years."

"Speak for yourself, big fella," Keith retorted. "This married guy gets his on a regular basis. The trick is in knowing how to keep the ladies satisfied."

Suse McGill hung up her phone, made a quick notation and looked up. "I agree with Dave." She gave Trevecky a sly smile. "I make it a point only to date married men—they're always *sooo* grateful."

Trevecky leered and invited her to meet him for a drink after work, knowing perfectly well, as they all did, that she was currently conducting a hot and heavy romance with a single patrolman from the South precinct.

"It's Friday, people," Sergeant Berry called out. "Who's gonna make the spunk run?"

"I'll do it," Vincent volunteered. "I've got to go over to the hospital anyway to interview a new vic. My full mooner got another one early this morning."

He had a ten o'clock lineup scheduled and spent an hour at the jail walking the aisles, selecting inmates who shared similar characteristics with the suspect. He offered likely prospects two candy bars and two cigarettes each to participate in the upcoming lineup. Taking the volunteers back to the station where they'd be held until needed, he let them eat their candy and have a smoke and then left them in the care of a guard. He returned to the office and spent the remaining time before his victim was due making calls and studying a rap sheet he'd run on a possible suspect. His caseload was such that there rarely seemed to be enough hours in the day to give each individual case the attention it deserved.

When his victim arrived, he ushered her to the auditorium. Unlike what she'd been led to expect by nearly every portrayal ever seen on television or in the movies, the SPD didn't use a room with two-way mirrors for its lineup situations, and the open auditorium made her feel jumpy and exposed.

"Don't be nervous," Vincent urged her in a gentle voice as he helped her into a seat in the darkened theater. "They can't see you."

Moments later several men walked onto the glaringly lighted stage. They filed in single file and arrayed themselves under cards with large, black numbers. An authoritarian voice from the darkness said, "Face front."

"I want you to take your time," Vincent instructed the victim softly. "Tell me when you want them to turn."

She had them turn left, turn right, and face front again. "I think it's number six," she whispered. "But . . . could I hear him speak?"

"Sure. What do you want him to say?"

She told him and he consulted with the officer conducting the lineup. "Number six," the officer said. "Step forward."

Six stepped forward and Vincent felt a small rush. This was their number one suspect.

"Say: Make a peep and I'll kill ya, bitch."

Number six repeated what he was told, using his most non-threatening voice. Even so, Vincent's victim reached over to compulsively grasp his wrist.

"Say it again with meaning, six!"

The suspect repeated it.

"Oh, God," she whispered. Her nails bit into Vincent's skin "Have him say: 'Whatsa matter, baby, y'frigid?"

The order was passed along the chain of command and number six duly repeated it.

"That's him," she whispered.

"You're positive?"

"Yes, absolutely. That's the man. As long as I live, I will never forget his voice."

"Okay, good," Vincent assured her.

Back at his desk, Vincent began the paperwork shuffle that would formally charge the suspect. He filled in the charge order and faxed it to the district attorney's office. The prisoner would then be entitled to a trial within sixty days. It was a right that a good percentage of the time was waived, as defense lawyers often urged postponement in order to build a stronger case. That didn't concern Vincent. Once he sent off the fax, he could file this case away and move on to the next one.

He arrived at the hospital shortly before one

o'clock and was ushered into Bess Polsen's room with a severely stated warning not to upset her. Given the reason that had landed her there and his need to ask disturbing questions, he only hoped he could comply.

He was sympathetic and she was cooperative, but she couldn't add a great deal to what was already known. Vincent dealt with the hardest part first, that of taking her through the attack of the previous night. He asked her to repeat as exactly as possible everything the rapist had done and said, and her own responses.

Then he went about extracting a description. Her attacker was a Caucasian male, approximately 5'11" tall, but his face had been covered by a dark, woolen ski mask the entire time. She hadn't noticed any identifying scars or tattoos. His voice had been threatening, but she couldn't describe its tonality. Just sort of average, she said. What she'd noticed most was his knife and she described that with a wealth of detail. Unfortunately, it sounded to Vincent like an ordinary hunting knife without fancy, identifying characteristics.

"What about his eyes, Bess?"

Responding without thought, she replied, "Angry. Full of hate . . . blue."

"Good. Light blue, dark blue?"

"Pale blue," she said thoughtfully. "Kind of washed out. And his eyelashes were real light and sparse. They made him look almost as if he didn't have any lashes at all." She looked surprised, as if wondering where that detail had come from.

"You're doing very well," Vincent commended her. "How about his skin? Was it olive complexioned like mine?"

She looked at his dark skin and shook her head. "No. Much lighter. It wasn't skim-milk white, but it didn't tan easily either."

Vincent looked up from his notebook. "Why do you say that?"

"I don't know." She looked startled. "Except I kept my eyes on the hand with the knife," she explained. A sudden shudder wracked her body. "He . . . he kept touching me with the blade and I was so afraid he was going to . . ." she broke off and Vincent told her to take several deep breaths and take her time. Finally, she said, "His hand—well, his wrist, really—he was wearing surgical gloves. It was . . . the skin was sort of reddish and flakey, as if it were getting ready to peel. Dishpan hands, my mom used to call 'em."

She had observed more than either of them had originally thought. "How large was his hand? Were the fingers pudgy, narrow? Long, short?" Vincent held up his own hand, long fingers spread. "Did it look anything like mine?"

"It wasn't nearly so big." She looked at his hand, and then admitted she wasn't positive of the exact structure but did her best to describe its general size and shape anyway.

He tried to coax further details from her subconscious for a while longer, then informed her of the social services available to help her cope with her attack. He urged her to contact them and took his leave. He took the elevator to the Sexual Assault Center where he collected the week's semen samples. Then he headed back downtown.

Hung up at work with a last minute phone call, he was tired and not in the mood to cook for himself by the time he cleared his desk for the weekend. He stopped on the way home at a Chinese restaurant for a take-out order of mu shu pork and hot and sour soup. Letting himself into his apartment a short while later, he planned to eat his dinner, maybe watch a little TV or read for awhile, and then go to bed and catch up on his sleep.

Unlike the majority of police work, the Special Assault unit worked regular hours: eight to four, Monday through Friday. It was a rare day when he got off precisely at four o'clock, but the hours weren't nearly as crazy as they had been on patrol or vice. The detectives in his unit took turns being on call evenings and weekends, but with two squads in the unit to rotate the duty it was unusual to be called out more than once every few months or so. It was simply a fluke that in the past month he'd been out on three late night calls. He'd only actually been called out twice, once on a night when he'd been on call himself and another when he'd filled in for someone else. Last night didn't really count, since it had been his option to leave home in hopes of obtaining information from Bess Polsen. But, count or not, two of those late nights had been this week and he was bushed.

Still, he didn't fall asleep as early as he'd planned. Much to his irritation, he was edgily aware that Ivy was on the other side of the wall. Flashes of her, of the two of them together in the early morning hours, kept streaking across his mind.

Dammit! Vincent's fists clenched as he restlessly paced the apartment. *You don't even know whether she's at home. Chances are she's working.*

Yeah, but what if she's not?

Doesn't matter. You've had your fun, but it's over now. Get her the hell off your mind.

It took him a long, long time to fall asleep.

Vincent wasn't the only one thinking about Ivy. Several miles away, a man was racking his brain trying to think of something nice he could do for her.

The Doc deserved something for all she'd done. He was a man accustomed to sticking with tenacious faithfulness to his original impressions of a woman, but he found himself making justifications for her height, her hair color, even her air of authority. Hell, hadn't she put that friggin' cop in his place and hadn't that been a joy to see? Besides, she was a healer—a white angel in a profession to be admired. But most importantly, she'd neutralized the corrosive anger that little Bess's conking out had threatened to explode back into existence only moments after he'd finally managed to assuage it. For that, if nothing else, he owed her. He owed her big time.

Attempting to function normally was so damn difficult when all that rage was clawing away at his gut like a crazed beast on a rampage. When he was in its grip, it pulled at him, distracted him, made him jumpy and almost unbearably sensitive to everything around him. It was an ungovernable monster living inside him part of each month, making its presence increasingly felt. It was a voice, harping coldly, demanding immediate action on his part.

That presence was the source of his power, his greatest strength. It was also his own worst enemy.

He'd learned from hard experience that it couldn't be pacified just any old time of the month. The predator within granted him omnipotence, but not without a price. It made him wait until the moon was full to engage his enemy.

The way the moon had been full when *she* had engaged *him*.

Small, dark, and so meek in appearance you'd swear butter wouldn't melt in her mouth, it was she who had taught him well that facades were a sham. Deceptive exteriors might try to hide the fact that deep down they *all* wanted it, but he was privy to their basest, innermost cravings.

He'd seen the way her face had invariably changed in the moonlight. It had been rapacious as a jackel's as she'd spewed her vile vocabulary over him, as she'd made him do things to her, to her friends. He hadn't been very old, but he'd been old enough to sustain an erection and the one time he'd thought to protest, she'd slapped his face and said that was plenty old enough. Oh, how she'd laughed and humiliated and pointed her finger at him. And all the while the merciless glare of the full moon had shone through the glass roof and walls of the greenhouse like a spotlight, turning night into day . . .

But he didn't want to think about that. The monster within was in hibernation now, its voice finally stilled, and he wanted to keep it that way for as long as possible. The Doc, that's who he wanted to think about. She had comforted him and taken away the rage, just like Aunt Flo used to do.

And he had to come up with something real nice, something he could do for her in return, to express his appreciation.

"Bingo." Vincent hung up the phone and met Keith's questioning gaze across their connecting desks. He grinned and tapped his forefinger against the piece of paper he'd been scribbling on. "That was the lab at Swedish—they just gave me some supporting evidence on my Dehalla case."

"The date rape?"

"Yeah. She invited him in for coffee at the conclusion of their date last night, said he forced himself on her and refused to take no for an answer. She insisted it was rape. He wouldn't even claim to consensual sex—he flat out stated there was no intercourse of any kind between them, and there weren't any outward signs of violence to support her allegation.'' He tapped his scratch paper again and smiled grimly. ''But the lab found evidence of sperm. Considering the patrolmen were at her door within ten minutes of when both parties agreed they had parted and a friend took her to the hospital to be examined the minute patrol finished up, it looks like our boy was lying through his teeth.''

He stretched in satisfaction. It was Tuesday afternoon and he was feeling pretty damn good. It wasn't only the uncommonly rapid conclusion to a case—that was simply the icing on the cake. Most of his gratification stemmed from knowing he had his body back under control and his mind back on track.

It had been a great deal more work than he'd originally expected. He'd had to pump more iron and run more miles this weekend to keep his thoughts occupied, but he'd finally put all extraneous images out of his mind. Everything was getting back to normal.

It was close to quitting time and half the squad around him was indulging in some extremely black humor. Listening to them as he made arrangements to have the date rapist picked up, Vincent laughed out loud several times at the commentary flying back and forth. Now and then he threw in an occasional sick comment of his own.

To an outsider, they'd probably come across sounding callous and uncaring, perhaps even cruel. Well, fortunately for them, at the moment there weren't any outsiders around to overhear. And grisly jokes—the sicker the better—were actually an extremely effective release valve, one they all used with regularity.

Next to homicide, rape was considered the most

heinous crime that could be perpetrated on a person, and according to half the victims he'd ever interviewed, it was debatable which was worse. Sexual assault victims commonly felt the rapist's actions managed to kill or severely maim something inside them anyway when he savaged their basic right to control their own lives.

Sex crimes tended to offend just about everyone's sensibilities and working in Special Assaults, being exposed on a daily basis to the results and having to deal with the victims' trauma, the unit couldn't help but be affected by the emotional laceration that ensued. So they blew off steam in the best way they knew how. They were all adults: they knew better than to make inappropriate remarks in the presence of anyone who'd be hurt or offended by them. But in a group comprised solely of their peers, they were able to cut loose a little.

"Vince!"

Grinning, he looked up at the sound of his name, aware that around him the jokes were petering out. Speaking of outsiders, apparently . . .

He turned his head, saw Ivy Pennington standing across the room beside the detective who had called his name, and felt as though he'd just been kicked in the chest by a mule.

Chapter 5

When she first saw the flowers, Ivy's mood soared magically from the gloomy discouragement that had kick-started her day. They were awaiting her at the hospital when she returned to work on Sunday, and instinctively, her initial reaction was that they must have been sent by Vincent.

"Dr. Pennington!" an excited nurse called her over to the nurse's station the minute she appeared on the floor. "Look! These came for you yesterday. Aren't they gorgeous?"

The floral bouquet was obviously professionally done, but unlike most of the arrangements Ivy saw delivered to the hospital, this one wasn't all concealed within a protective bubble of waxed paper tucked into a snugly supporting cardboard box. It sat on the counter in all its unwrapped splendor, an expensive arrangement of exotics, roses, baby's-breath and greenery.

"For me?" Ivy smiled in delight as she leaned over to inhale the heady, spicy scents. Her fingers searched through the blooms for a card. "Who unwrapped it?"

"No one. This was the way it arrived at our desk." The nurse shrugged. "Of course, knowing some of the eager-beaver candy stripers around here, there's no telling who mighta gotten their helpful little paws on it before it got as far as my station. Don't tell me there's no card."

"No, here it is. It was just buried." Ivy extracted the small white florist's envelope and ripped it open, smiling in anticipation.

Her smile faltered as she studied the card. Her eyebrows furrowed in puzzlement. These weren't from Vincent. Given the timing, his intensity, she had been so sure . . . Oh, dammit, she should have known better. Hopes that she'd believed entirely squashed this morning collapsed anew. She read the card again. "Are you sure these are for me?"

The nurse turned startled eyes her way. "The little striper who delivered it said flowers for Dr. Pennington. What does the envelope say?"

Ivy picked it up and turned it over. "I. Pennington M.D." She shrugged and smiled. "I guess they're mine, all right. It's just . . . they're not from the person I thought they'd be from."

The nurse snorted. "Well, poor you," she retorted. "So many admirers, so little time."

Ivy laughed. "Yeah, what can I say? It's nice to be loved." She slipped the card back into the envelope and slid it into the pocket of her scrubs. "Mind if I leave 'em here until quitting time?"

"You kidding? I'd love it." The nurse winked. "I think I'll just spread it around that they're mine."

Ivy took out the card and re-read it whenever she had a free moment that day. *Thanks for patching her up*, it said. *It would have ruined everything if she'd died, but now she can remember me.* It was signed "C." At least she thought that was what the signature was supposed to be. Instead of curving up, the bottom of the letter angled inward in a diagonal slash from the fullest part of the curve, making it the most stylized C she'd ever seen. But what else could it possibly be? And why did the sight of it tug at something in her memory? It was almost as if she'd seen that exact marking before. Wracking her brain, she couldn't remember a single instance to support the feeling, but something about it made her feel vaguely unsettled all the same.

It was probably ridiculous to invest it with so much mystery—five'd get you ten it was someone's initial. But whose? Some husband of a recent patient? Then why hadn't he simply signed his entire name, and what did he mean by *now she can remember me?* It was a puzzle that drove her nuts all day long.

She took the card and arrangement home with her. When her doorbell rang a little after seven, she was sitting at the table in the tiny dining area, turning the card end for end in her hand, still trying to determine exactly what it was about it that caused a sinking feeling of uneasiness in the pit of her stomach every time she read it. Thankful for a distraction to take her mind off what was probably just one of those unanswerable little quandaries that life sometimes handed out, she tossed it on the table and went to answer the door.

"Terry!"

"Hiya, kid." He leaned against her doorframe, smiling lazily. "Some little old lady downstairs held the door open for me—so much for security, huh?"

"Must be those Boy Scout eyes of yours." She opened the door wide in welcome. "Come on in."

"Why don't you come on down to the van with me instead," he countered. "I have something for you."

"What? My chair? You finished it?" She whirled away, grabbed her key off the kitchen counter and rejoined him. "Ooh, I can hardly wait to see it. How'd it turn out?"

"Pretty damn fine, if I do say so myself." He gave her a lopsided smile and stepped back to allow her through the doorway. "I probably could have wrestled it up here all by my lonesome, but I figured why bother when I've got such a big, strong girl-cousin to do it for me."

Ivy flexed her muscles for his admiration while they waited for the elevator.

He wouldn't let her remove the sheet shrouding it until they had it transferred to her apartment. Every time she tried to sneak a peek in the elevator, he slapped her hands down. After wrestling it through the door and setting it in place, he made her close her eyes. "Ta da!" he finally trumpeted, whisking the sheet away with a flick of his wrist. "Okay. You can look now."

She opened her eyes and stared, unable to believe what she was seeing. Her old, raggedy chair looked as if it had just come off a showroom floor. She had expected an improvement, but this . . . !

"It's beautiful!" Delight shone from the face she turned to her cousin. "Oh, my God, Terry, it's absolutely *beautiful!*" She walked around the newly reupholstered chair, stooping frequently to examine every seam. Looking up at him, she confessed, "I never *dreamed* you could do something this wonderful with it. Why, it's so professional—it doesn't look like the same chair at all." She stood back to admire the grouping it made with her new couch and shook her head. "Wow. This is incredible. It makes the whole living room look positively uptown."

"Does that mean you're gonna start dusting this

place once in a while?'' Terry ran a finger along the top of her stereo, leaving a streak.

"I guess I'll have to."

"No, really, Ive, it looks real nice in here. Usually we have to wade through your stuff, but tonight I can actually see the floor.''

She jabbed him with her elbow. "Thank you for pointing that out, Terry. I'll have you know I've turned over a brand new leaf." She looked around in satisfaction. "As you can see, I cleaned my little fingers to the bone yesterday. And who knows, maybe tonight I *will* dust, just to make the transformation complete."

"And flowers, too." He whistled and walked over to admire the lush arrangement she had placed on the bookshelf. "Casablanca lillies, roses—you really *are* becoming an uptown chick." He leaned down to smell them and then looked at her over his shoulder. "You buy these yourself or have you finally gone out and snagged yourself a rich boyfriend?"

"Someone sent them to me at the hospital, but I don't have the foggiest idea who it was." She explained about the flowers' arrival and her inexplicable uneasiness every time she read the message that accompanied it, then went to fetch the card from the kitchen. Returning to the living room, she handed it to him and hung over the back of his chair while he studied it. "Whataya think? Is that a 'C' or isn't it?"

"I doubt it. Look, here's a 'C' in patching"— his fingernail underscored the letter—". . . and another here in can. Neither of 'em look like this. You know what this reminds me of?"

"Dopey's ear?"

He craned his head over his shoulder to stare up at her. "Say what?"

"You know, *Dopey*." She walked around his chair

and perched on the edge of the davenport facing him. "One of the dwarfs in Snow White? That's what it reminds me of. All it needs is a billiard ball head to attach it to." She intercepted his look and admitted, "Okay, so it's been a few years since I've seen *Snow White* and maybe his ear wasn't shaped like this at all. It just sorta popped into my mind. But I guess that's not what you were gonna say it reminded *you* of, huh."

"Well, no," he replied. He scratched his cheek with the stiff edge of the card and grinned. "I can honestly say that never once entered my mind. What it reminds me of is making valentines."

"Oh, well, sure. That was gonna be my second guess." She gave his ankle a swift kick with her bare foot.

"Remember when you were a kid how you'd fold a piece of red construction paper in half and then draw half a heart on it? Or if you were as cool as I was, you'd skip the tracing part and just cut it out freestyle. In either case, when you opened it up you'd have a perfect Valentine with both sides exactly the same."

"Let me see that again." She reached for the card and studied it. "It does look like half a heart; I see what you mean." Looking back up at him, she smiled in admiration. "How on earth do you remember these things? I haven't even thought of making valentines in about a billion years."

"I'm a kid at heart, I guess. Besides, I made one last Valentine's Day for the girl I was seeing at the time. Grabbed her right where she lived, too."

"I've seen some of your dates, Terry. A stick of bubble gum would probably grab 'em right where they live." Abruptly, Ivy quit laughing. All the color drained from her face and she sank back into the cushions of the sofa. "Oh, my God," she whispered and tossed the card on the coffee table as if she'd suddenly discovered it to be covered with a highly toxic substance.

Terry leaned forward in concern. "You all right?"

"Oh, God, Terry, that's it," she said, looking at her cousin with dawning horror. "That's what's been bothering me about that signature." Without divulging Bess Polsen's name, she explained the salient points of the case she'd worked on in the early hours of Friday morning. "D'Ambruzzi said that part of this particular rapist's MO is to carve a heart on the chest of each of his victims. In my patient's case he carved only half a heart, but I think we can assume that had more to do with her going into shock than with a sudden desire to change his style."

Terry retrieved the card from the table and read it again, holding it carefully by the edges. He quoted, " 'It would have ruined everything if she'd died, but now she can remember me.' " Setting the card back down on the table, he met his cousin's eyes, his own somber. "It ties in, doesn't it?"

Ivy nodded weakly.

"Get a baggie from the kitchen," Terry directed her. "It's too bad you and I have already handled it so much. We've probably obliterated any other prints by now, but who knows what sort of technological wonders the police can perform these days." When she just sat there staring at him, he said patiently, "Ivy, you do understand you have to take this to D'Ambruzzi, don't you?"

"No!" If anything, she grew paler. "I can't." She didn't give herself time to think it through; her response was purely instinctual.

"Why can't you?" Terry queried her softly. "Because you and D'Ambruzzi are sleeping together?"

Ivy's jaw sagged in shock. "How did . . . who . . . ?" Sudden color flooded her face. "*Sherry!*

She told you! Damn her eyes, I asked her not to go blabbin' it to the entire family."

"She didn't tell the entire family, Ive," Terry said placatingly. "I doubt she's even told Ben. She stopped by to see me yesterday afternoon and I could tell she was all excited about something, so I wormed it out of her. You know Sherry: she loves a romance and she's never been able to hold out on me when I'm really determined to learn her secrets."

That was true. Sherry and Terry were fraternal twins who shared an especially close bond. But of the two, Terry had always been the stronger-willed, able to manipulate his sibling whenever the mood struck him. Usually it amused Ivy to watch him work his wiles on his sister, but, dammit, why had Sherry had to go and cave in with *her* business? It was supposed to have been confidential.

"Hey," Terry said and gave her a nudge. "Relax, Ive. This is ol' Father Pennington you're dealin' with here. You know your secrets will never pass my lips."

Ivy relaxed. That was also true. Terry wasn't a gossip, and unlike a lot of her other family members, you never even had to specifically request that he honor a given confidence. He just naturally kept his own counsel. Then she tensed up at his next words.

"But the fact remains," he said, "that whether you're sleepin' with D'Ambruzzi or not, he's the cop in charge of this case and you're going to have to inform him of this newest development." He looked at her in puzzlement. "I would've thought your personal relationship with him would make that easier, not harder."

"It probably would," she told him stiffly. "If we had a personal relationship. As it is, sex with me once was apparently all he wanted. I haven't seen or heard from him since.''

"Oh, shit, babe. I'm sorry."

She met his eyes and hers were filled with all the hurt and turbulence of the past few days. "I feel so used, Terry," she admitted in a low voice. "He turned me inside out . . . and then he just walked away without a word." She laughed shortly. "Just to show you what a chump I am, I even thought the flowers were from him until I read the card."

"Hey, if there's a chump in this scenario it's not you. And I hate like hell to be the one to break this to you, but you're still gonna have to take him the card and tell him about the flowers." When he saw the resistance on her face, he said, "Think, Ivy. You're one of the smartest women I know, but you're not using your head right now."

"Why?" Ivy inquired testily. "Because I desire not to put myself in D'Ambruzzi's path again?"

"No," he replied quietly. "Because you haven't once asked yourself how this rapist knows you were the doctor who kept his victim from dying."

Terry was right, of course. She'd been thinking with her pride instead of her intellect. How *had* the rapist known that? The only sure way was if he'd been at the hospital that night. Had he made an inquiry at the desk? Passed himself off as a relative, maybe? It was highly unlikely he had ever actually seen her, for the work lanes weren't situated in plain view of the waiting room, and non-personnel wasn't allowed to just freely roam the trauma center corridors. But how then had he known she was a female? Though as for that, she supposed, the gender of the attending physician might not have been a relevant factor in his decision to send flowers.

In any event, she couldn't dispute that this might be a break in Bess Polsen's case.

Ivy had assured her cousin that she would contact Detective D'Ambruzzi the next day, and despite her mixed feelings about him she had fully intended to do just that. What she hadn't counted on was the gunshot wound that came in minutes before her shift was supposed to end on Monday. It turned out to be touch and go, a royal mess that had her up to her elbows in severed arteries and splintered bone, and by the time she and her team finally got the patient stabilized enough to rush to surgery, and she had showered, changed, and driven to the precinct, it was to discover the Special Assault Unit didn't work evenings and had already closed for the day. So much for a cop's notoriously odd working hours.

On Tuesday she made it a point to get there in time.

She paused outside the door to Vincent's unit, finding it necessary to take several deep breaths before she could force herself to go in. It was at that point she quit trying to fool herself into believing she wasn't nervous about facing him again.

Face it girl, she told herself bracingly. *Being rejected is never exactly easy on the ego, but you can rise above it. You're an intelligent, reasonably attractive woman, and if he can't see what he's passed up, then screw him.* Unfortunate choice of words. Wincing, she amended it: *That's his loss.*

On another deep breath, she entered the squadroom.

She spotted Vincent almost immediately across the small, incredibly jammed room. He had a phone receiver tucked between his ear and one hunched shoulder, the mouthpiece tucked beneath his chin while he laughed at something one of the other detectives was saying. As she watched, he sobered, brought the phone up to his mouth, spoke briefly, listened, spoke again, and then broke the connection, placing the receiver in the cradle. He made a low-voiced comment that caused those around him to grin. Ivy approached a nearby officer.

At least she had the advantage of being prepared. Vincent, when the detective at her side called out his name, was manifestly caught off guard to look up and see her there, and it took him several seconds to replace the stunned expression on his face with a professional mask. Even then his eyes were wary as he watched her approach, and Ivy felt a little thrill of vindictive satisfaction. Undoubtedly this was an immature and unworthy reaction on her part, but damned if she was going to waste time feeling guilty about it. The last few days had been pretty bleak because of this man and if she experienced a split second of gratification for his wariness . . . well, she felt she was entitled. Besides, just what did he think she was going to do— denounce him with all the theatrical flair of a hapless heroine in some third-rate melodrama? The rampaging butterflies in her stomach began to settle.

Vincent stood at her approach. "Dr. Pennington," he said neutrally, aware of the curious looks of some of his coworkers and most especially of Keith's head suddenly snapping up. "Doctor?" Keith said at the same time that Vincent inquired, "Is there something I can do for you?"

Oh, the temptation of a truly snide reply. One corner of Ivy's mouth curled up slightly, but before she could formulate a way to tell him about the flowers and card, Suse McGill suddenly snapped her fingers.

"That's why you look so familiar," she exclaimed, rising to her feet and smiling at Ivy. She extended her hand and introduced herself. "I knew I'd seen you somewhere before, but I couldn't place you in your street clothes. You're one of the trauma docs over at the Center, aren't you?"

Vincent watched Ivy as she conversed with McGill for several moments and wondered what the hell she was doing here. Catching himself in the midst of mentally undressing her, he angrily blinked her clothes back on and turned away. Son of a bitch. Just when he was getting his shit together, she had to show up again.

Keith caught his eye and gave him an admonishing look. "You've been holdin' out on me, son," he said in an undertone. "We're gonna have to have us a little chat about that come morning." Then he pushed back from his desk and rose to leave for the day—but not before coming around to Vincent's side for a quick survey of Ivy's legs. With a low whistle and an appreciative smile, he turned on his heel and strode from the room.

When Ivy turned back to Vincent after her conversation with the pretty blonde detective, she was surprised to see the crowded room clearing out. She glanced back at Suse, saw her retrieving her purse from a desk drawer, and snuck a peek at her watch, only to discover it was after four. Damn. She should have gotten here earlier. Her plan had been to talk to Vincent in a room full of police officers, not all alone. Thank God at least three other detectives were still working at their desks.

Vincent pulled up a chair for her. "Have a seat."

Settling herself, she crossed her legs, flipped open the flap to her leather clutch bag, and extracted the florist card in its plastic baggie. She slid it across the desk until it was directly in front of him. "This came with some flowers that were delivered to me at the hospital on Saturday. I think they may have been sent by the man who attacked Bess Polsen."

Vincent's eyes snapped up from their involuntary perusal of her legs to gaze at her face and then drop to the card in front of him on the desk. He studied it silently for several moments and then looked back up at her, much quicker to pick up the implications, she noticed, than she had been. "The signature?" he said. "Half a heart like the one he carved on her chest?"

"Yes."

Vincent's dark eyes narrowed, pinning her in place. "You received flowers from a rapist on Saturday, but you're just now bringing it to my attention?"

Ivy's teeth tightened, but she managed a non-confrontational tone of voice when she replied. "I didn't return to work until Sunday and it took me until Sunday night to figure out who had sent them to me." She would choke on her own tongue before she'd admit to D'Ambruzzi that for one brief moment she'd actually thought he had sent them. Expelling a breath, she met his eyes coolly. "I did come in yesterday immediately after my shift ended, but of course by then your department was locked up tight."

He wasn't sure how she did it, given her perfectly polite tone of voice, but she somehow managed to make him feel personally responsible for the department's hours. "Were the flowers professionally arranged?"

"Yes. But I don't have any idea who the florist was."

"What about the box they came in?"

"There wasn't one. None of the usual tissue around the blossoms, either. It was unwrapped by the time it reached the nurse's station in the ER, but nobody seems to know if that was the way it originally arrived at the hospital or if someone along the line unboxed it.''

Vincent whispered a curse. ''Was there an envelope?''

Ivy leaned forward to flip over the baggie and he saw the envelope lined up behind the card. He bent forward to read it, but beyond her name printed in neat block letters across the front, it was free of print or logos. When Ivy turned her head to gauge Vincent's reaction to the blank envelope, she discovered her face to be much too close to his and eased back in her chair. ''No florist's name,'' she pointed out helpfully.

''Well, maybe we'll luck out and pick up some prints.'' Not that the rapist had displayed that kind of carelessness up to this point, but perhaps . . .

''Uh . . . I'm afraid that might be a little difficult under the circumstances,'' she said softly. His eyes snapped up to lock with hers, penetrating and abruptly accusatory, and she shifted uncomfortably. ''Terry and I handled it quite a bit,'' she admitted. Then she forced herself to sit quietly, refusing to let herself be intimidated by him.

''It wasn't deliberate,'' she explained reasonably. ''I received the thing first thing Sunday morning and although something about the card bothered me from the outset, I couldn't pin down exactly what it was. I must have taken it out to study a dozen times that day, trying to figure it out. Then, when Terry came over Sunday night, I had him look at it. I'd thought at first that maybe the signature was C, and I wanted his opinion.'' One of her shoulders inched up in a tiny shrug. ''It was he, actually, who finally figured out what it was supposed to be, but by that time we'd passed it back and forth several times.'' She looked at Vincent hopefully. ''Terry said maybe you guys possessed some sort of advanced technology that would make that not matter?"

"No," Vincent said flatly, "we don't. And who the hell is this Terry character, anyway?" Oh, shit, that came out sounding way too belligerent, as if he cared personally. "Uh, I may need to interview him."

"Terry Pennington," Ivy said. "One of my cousins."

"Oh." Vincent rolled his shoulders. Then he tapped a long finger against the plastic sandwich bag containing the card. "Well, we'll run this through the lab all the same and see what we get."

"Good." Ivy pushed back her chair. "Well, if that's all . . ."

"Not so fast, Doctor. I've got a few more questions for you."

"But I've told you everything I know—"

"I'm taking off now, Vince," interrupted a detective who'd been working at a desk in the front part of the office. "You wanna lock up here when you're through?"

Vincent looked around and saw that he and Ivy would be the last to leave. "Yeah, sure, John," he replied. "I'll take care of it. See y'in the morning."

He watched him walk away and then turned back to Ivy, aware of a sudden unwelcome shift in the atmosphere. How could this familiar, dirty, furniture-crowded room suddenly feel so intimate? He'd been alone in it on a hundred different occasions with other women—victims or witnesses of varying degrees of attractiveness—and he'd never felt anything other than businesslike with any of them. But now, left alone with this particular tall redheaded physician and her spectacular legs, his professionalism was fading fast, to be replaced with a distinctly unprofessional craving to . . .

He yanked his tie loose at his throat. "You were saying?"

"I've told you everything I know." Ivy sat cautiously still. God, how did he do that? It was exactly like the other night in her car and the elevator. The minute that other man had left, Vincent began exuding pheromones like a musky aftershave, and her body chemistry responded with a vengeance. Well, that would *not* do. She tensed all over, cursing the give away thinness of her skin as she felt scalding color surge to her cheeks.

"Tell me how the hospital works," he suggested huskily and then cleared his throat. "Explain how this guy knew you were the doctor in Bess Polsen's case."

She told him everything she knew, which admittedly wasn't much, and in the process she was very careful to act with the same professionalism she would display if she were dealing with a patient. She made eye contact, she was articulate, she was aloof. She managed to get through it in one piece and the minute he finished questioning her, she rose to her feet. "If that's all?" She didn't offer her hand.

He rose also. "Do you need a ride home?"

"No."

Let it go, Vincent told himself. Just *once* since you've met this woman, be smart and let it go. But he couldn't. He reached for her arm. "Then I'll walk you to your car."

Ivy didn't attempt a subtle removal of her arm from his grasp; she jerked it free. "I don't need to be walked to my car."

"Ivy . . ."

"I'd appreciate it if you didn't call me that." Her chin shot up, green eyes darkened by hostility. He'd lost the right to address her with any familiarity. "I'm Dr. Pennington to you."

Vincent's head reared back as if she'd slapped him. He reacted instinctively, temper flaring as he crowded in close to her. "Yeah?" he snarled, remembering her all too well naked, willing, and responsive. "And are you Dr. Pennington to *all* the men you've fuc—"

She did slap him then, fast and hard, with enough force to turn his head. "You lousy . . ." She couldn't think of an obscenity mean enough and for a few seconds simply stood there, chest heaving as she fought for breath. "I thought it was *special,* damn you! I thought *you* were special. But you were just another user looking to get laid, weren't you?" Her laughter was hard and bitter. "Well, of course you were. The minute you got what you wanted, you disappeared."

She hated herself for the tears that rose to her eyes and angrily dashed them away with a knuckle. Taking a deep breath, she faced him with her chin raised. "I may not have understood the rules going in, but no one can accuse me of not being a quick study. Obviously this is just some twisted game to you, one at which I admit you're very accomplished. Well, you can leave me out of it from now on. You burned me once, D'Ambruzzi. Don't think you'll ever get the chance to burn me again."

She about-faced smartly and strode with long-legged fury from the room.

Vincent stood as if frozen, watching the way her hair swung against her shoulders and blazed under the overhead lights just before she disappeared from view. He groped blindly behind him until his hand fumbled across the back of a chair. Slowly he pulled it forward and lowered himself onto it.

Lifting his hand to touch his cheek and jaw where she had struck him, he pressed his fingers against slightly welted skin. It stung with the pulsating rush of blood to the surface. He felt like a cheap economy car that had just been broadsided out of the blue.

I thought it was special. I thought you were special.

He hadn't thought of her at all.

He hadn't concerned himself with how she might feel to wake up alone Friday morning with all communication between them abruptly severed. He'd been too damn busy devising ways to protect his own battered emotions. Too preoccupied with denying the effect their lovemaking had on him to spare a thought to how it may have affected her. Well, he guessed he knew now, though, didn't he? Yes indeed, he certainly knew now, and he wasn't going to forget that look in her eyes anytime soon.

Automatically, Vincent turned to his desk and began gathering his notes. Moments later, however, he found himself simply sitting there staring at them without the slightest comprehension of what he'd just read.

Why did he keep making the same damn mistakes with her? He'd thought he was being so clever, thought he'd covered his ass so well. The decision had been made to forget her because for one brief hour she'd managed to get much too close, and that smacked of a danger he wouldn't countenance. No one was allowed to crawl under Vincent D'Ambruzzi's skin. No one.

Vincent laughed hollowly as he found a folder for his notes. What *was* it about her that made him so delusional? He'd always refused to blind himself to reality, even if the truth weren't pretty, weren't welcome. For years that had been a source of pride with him. But he'd sure as hell let reality skirt him by this time.

As he cleaned up his desk, turned out the lights and locked up, Vincent tried to reassemble his defenses. In an attempt to dispel a feeling of guilt, he recited all the reasons that had always stood him in good stead for avoiding involvement in the past. He cataloged the wrongs done to him by LaDonna; he reminded himself that this was a graceless age they lived in, where social diseases tended to flourish better than most relationships. Knowing that he truly had burnt all his bridges this time should simply make it that much easier to force her image out of his mind for good.

Except it didn't. Somehow Ivy Pennington had managed to crack the wall he'd built around his emotions. He was no longer content in his solitude and what once had been a solace now merely felt lonely.

Well, too bad. He was a grown man, not some callow youth, and what was done was done; there was no sense dwelling on it. But as he headed for home he decided that if he could only do one thing to atone for the way he'd mishandled this entire sorry situation with Dr. Ivy Pennington, it would be to track down the rapist who knew her name.

Chapter 6

His name was Tyler Griffus. He was thirty years old, the sole proprietor of his own business, and considered by many to be an attractive, desirable man. By any standards he was judged a productive citizen, and on all but one night of each month he actually did lead a relatively normal life. Now the first faint rumblings of the predator within were making themselves felt. The voice in his head had begun its chanted litany of demands.

God, he hated it. Oh, not the acts of violence that the voice extorted him to commit—in fact he reveled in the feeling of absolute power he experienced during those brief moments of commission and in the rush of quietude that followed. But the incessant demands echoing in the chambers of his mind were something else again.

What was the goddamn point? It wasn't as if he could do a blasted thing to address all that rage fomenting inside of him. So wouldn't you think that it would just shut up and leave him alone?

But, no. It snarled and snapped ... and then allowed him only one night out of the month to appease its fury—one lousy night to unleash all the accumulated, pent-up rage. He was granted a single moment of bursting glory and release.

The rest was all a load of horseshit he could happily do without.

It was too soon to appease the internal phantoms, and so as was usual of late, he sought distraction in thoughts of the Doc. She had become his talisman, a source of comfort amid the irritating demands of the distracting voice that nagged, nagged, nagged for his attention.

He'd wanted to send her something more original than flowers. Hell, he dealt in flowers all day, every day; it was scarcely an imaginative gift. Naturally, he had personally hand-picked every blossom and assembled the arrangement with a lavish hand, but even so ...

With his customary caution, he had waited until his two employees had left for the day before he'd begun to assemble the bouquet. Once it had been arranged to his satisfaction, he'd donned a pair of thin surgical gloves from the box he kept in a locked drawer in his office and wrote out the card and envelope. Then he'd carefully wiped off the vase. His prints were a matter of record from a time when he was younger and foolish ... but he was worlds wiser now. Wise enough not to provide any freebies for that pushy detective he'd seen at the hospital.

He'd wondered often in the days that followed if the Doc had liked his offering. Had she even realized who sent it? He'd really wanted to stick around that day to personally watch her receive them and thus gauge her reaction, but caution was his middle name these days. Staying out of jail— an institution he never cared to re-inhabit—was the direct product of keeping a low profile, of not leaving anything to chance. So instead he had prominently displayed the card, watched the reception desk in the hospital lobby until it was especially busy and then slid the arrangement onto the high counter. He'd pocketed the paper towels that had kept his hands from touching the vase and melted out the door.

But a method so indirect distinctly lacked the satisfaction gained from the hands-on approach, and he had just reached a decision. He was going to abandon his customary caution. The demon within was growing stronger, its voice louder and more peremptory by the hour. He was heartily sick of listening to its clamoring demands before the one night of the month when he could effectively satisfy its needs. The Doc seemed to counteract the effects of his predator, but it had been too damn long since he'd seen her and her power was diminishing, growing ever weaker.

He needed to know more about her. Much more. He needed some sort of personal contact. If gathering information on her meant spending some time at the hospital, and that meant exposing himself, then so be it. It was a calculated gamble. Hell, when all was said and done he was a smart man—He would simply have to find a way to minimize the risks.

Because the Doc was the antidote. And he was determined to get the maximum dosage.

They blew through the entrance door, a boisterous group of off-duty doctors and nurses all loudly laughing and talking at once. Ivy, buried in their midst, directed them to a group of tables in the corner and continued alone across the room, threading agilely between vintage mahogany cocktail tables and leather upholstered chairs.

"Hi, Uncle Mack," she called in quiet greeting. Placing her purse on the bar, she slid onto a bar stool.

Her uncle, who'd failed to notice her when he'd glanced up at the noisy group's entrance, abandoned mid-sentence the conversation he'd been having with one of the patrons down the bar. Hastily excusing himself, pleasure suffusing his expression, he trotted down the length of the bar. "Ivy! How's my favorite M.D.?" He stretched up to lean across the expanse of mahogany dividing them. "Give us a smooch, then, sweetheart. It's been a while."

She met him halfway, giving him an affectionate smack and a hug made awkward by the width of the bar that separated them. Pulling back, she grinned and scrubbed at his lower lip with her thumb to remove the trace of lipstick her kiss had transferred. "Oops! Better get rid of this before Auntie Babe sees it and thinks you're playing fast and loose with her affections." She looked expectantly toward the door that led to the small kitchen. "Is she around? I've missed you both."

Mack chucked her under the chin. "Whatsa matter, sweetheart, nobody feedin' you at three o'clock in the morning anymore?"

"No!" Reminded of all the times she'd dragged herself home to her garage apartment in the early morning hours only to be intercepted by her aunt or uncle, insistently urging her into their warm kitchen for a bit of sustenance before she hit the sack, Ivy laughed wistfully. "And, boy, do I miss it. If I want a meal now, I have to make it myself—and you know I don't cook nearly as well as Auntie Babe."

"Not many do, sweetheart," he agreed, prideful

on his wife's behalf. "Not many do." Then he beamed at his niece, a smile that brimmed with delight. "Oh, she's gonna be so tickled to see you. She oughta be here any minute." He jerked his head toward the high-decible hilarity issuing from three tables in the corner. "Who're your noisy friends, hon?"

"Second shift Trauma Unit—my co-workers." Sinking back onto the leather-padded barstool, she blew out a weary exhalation. "Fix me a bourbon and water, please? You'd better get a waitress over there as quick as you can, too. We had a particularly rough day in ER—there was a massive pile up on I-90 and, Uncle Mack, we lost too many of 'em."

Mack hailed one of his waitresses as she came out of the back hallway that led to the restrooms and pool room. "Sandy!" His chin jutted toward the group in the corner. "Got us a bunch of burnt-out M.D.'s lookin' for a little TLC and a lotta prompt service. Take care of 'em for me, will you, hon?"

"Sure thing, Mack." With a brisk stride, she set out for the tables in the corner and Mack reached for a highball glass, quickly and efficiently building Ivy's drink. He tossed a paper coaster on the bar and placed her drink on it. "Here you go, sweetheart." Seeing her hand reach for her wallet, he gruffly ordered her to "put that away." Then he studied her drawn features with concern while unnecessarily wiping down the spotless bar in front of her. "When's the last time you ate?"

"Lunch," Ivy replied absently and took an appreciative gulp of her bourbon. The liquor burned a path down her throat and exploded warmly in her stomach. "Oh, that's good." Another burst of loud laughter came from the corner and she looked up at her uncle with a hint of apology for the rowdy intrusion into his normally mannerly establishment. "More than anything, we just needed to get out of the trauma unit and blow off a little steam," she explained. "So I suggested coming here." She didn't realize a ghost of the last few traumatic hours lingered yet to haunt her gaze.

Voices of the emergency room personnel, her own among them, still echoed in her mind the way they had sounded a short while ago, calling plans back and forth with an uncharacteristic lack of discretion. Concern for their professional image for once had not been uppermost in their minds.

They'd been at the end of their shift, covered in blood, sick over the patients they'd been unable to save and jumpy with unspent adrenaline. Possible solutions for ridding themselves of a lingering sense of powerlessness had been voiced from the furthermost work lanes clear up to the nurse's station near reception. Ivy's suggestion had been greeted with enthusiasm when she'd mentioned the nightly singing at her uncle's bar. Music was something that sounded wonderfully far removed from sudden, unhelpable death.

Marginally subdued once they had a destination in mind, the voices had then relayed address and directions and everyone had hurried to finish their charting and head for the showers, turning the temporarily quiet emergency room over to the new shift.

"Here." Mack's gruff-toned voice interrupted her thoughts and Ivy looked up from contemplating the bottom of her drink to find him pushing a tray containing several baskets of pretzels across the bar. "Take these to your friends, sweetheart, to tide them over. And if they don't mind potluck, I'm sure Babe can whip up something hot and filling when she gets here."

"Oh, really, Uncle Mack, you don't have to go to all this extra trouble for us."

"Yes I do, hon." Attempting to disguise his basic generosity beneath a characteristic gruffness, he justified brusquely, "The last thing I need is a bunch of fallin' down drunk doctors leaving my bar tonight. Somebody'd be bound to sue my pants off." He reached for Sandy's order pad as soon as she reached the bar, sparing only a scowling glance for his niece. "Now get outta my way so I can make your friends their drinks."

Ivy had known him too long to be fooled by his brusque facade. "I love you, Uncle Mack." She placed her drink on the tray he'd prepared and picked it up. Holding it with an expertise gained working this very bar during her college vacations, she leaned across the bar to press a kiss on Mack's balding pate. "You're the best. Thank you."

"Get outta here," he snarled, but Ivy knew the pink tinging his face stemmed from pleasure, not temper.

For sheer stress relief, she reflected as she balanced her tray and threaded between tables and chairs, five minutes of her uncle's company had more impact on her frazzled nerves than five strong drinks. Mack and Babe were special to her beyond words, their generosity without discernable limit.

She had discovered exactly how generous they were on her twenty-first birthday. She'd known for years they were unique—not just anyone would unquestioningly accept responsibility for an orphaned adolescent with the unfailing warmth and fairness they'd displayed. From the moment they had brought her home to live with them, her aunt and uncle had treated her as a part of their family. Never had they displayed what would be a quite natural favoritism to Jaz, their own flesh-and-blood daughter, and the more Ivy had been exposed to other family relationships over the years the more she had come to appreciate that particular parenting skill. Then, on her twenty-first birthday, she had met with the lawyer who'd handled her parents' estate.

That was when she'd learned the true extent of her aunt and uncle's generosity. They had housed, clothed and fed her for six years. They'd handled all the details of her parents' modest estate. And consistently over the years, they had flatly refused to be recompensed in any manner for anything they'd done.

Ivy's parents had made specific arrangements in their will to ensure that Mack and Babe would become Ivy's guardians should anything happen to them. Knowing, however, the inflated expense of raising a child, they'd scheduled a monthly allowance to be paid the Merricks by the estate to help alleviate the additional financial burden on their budget. As the lawyer had turned her inheritance over to her, he'd disclosed that Uncle Mack, with Babe's full endorsement, had bluntly apprised him to plow that allowance back into the estate. Ivy was going to be a doctor, Mack had proudly informed him. She would need all the financial assistance she could get to realize her goals.

What touched Ivy most deeply was knowing that they'd never told a soul what they had forfeited. There had been times when money had been tight, so refusing compensation had required a degree of sacrifice on her aunt and uncle's part. It would have been natural for them at least to have mentioned it to one of the other relatives, if only as an option they'd had but hadn't wanted to use. Yet not a whisper had ever reached Ivy's ears—and given the gossipy nature of her family she knew she would've heard had they mentioned it even in passing. If the lawyer hadn't told her, she never would have learned of their selflessness . . . and in her eyes, that was perhaps the ultimate measure of their generosity.

Ivy rejoined the ER staff. The pretzels Mack had sent over and the drinks Sandy delivered moments later were greeted with a rousing cheer. Conversation was loud and rowdy and she tried to throw herself into the festivities surrounding her, determined to put this afternoon's failure behind her.

One of the mortalities today had been hers. It was difficult under the best of circumstances to lose a patient, but auto-related fatalities were the hardest. They invariably brought back memories of her parents' deaths and she took her inability to save each and every accident victim directly to heart.

Partying was not the way she usually came to terms with her inability to save a patient, however, and as hard as she tried to adopt an attitude, she simply couldn't shake a growing depression. She found more genuine relief talking with her aunt in the kitchen while Babe threw together a stroganoff and heated some bread.

"It all helps, of course," Ivy told her, waving her glass. "The drinks, the jokes . . . being with other people who've shared the same experience." Watching the cloud of steam that billowed and curled around her aunt's shoulders as she dumped noodles into a colander, Ivy asked, "Auntie Babe, are you sure there isn't something I can be doing to help?"

"Just keep me company, honey. That's all the help I need." Babe glanced at her niece over her shoulder and asked, "But?" Seeing Ivy's blank look, she elaborated. "I hear a 'but' in there somewhere, Ivy Jayne. It all helps . . . but?"

"But . . . I don't know. It's just not my usual way of coping, I suppose. Everyone seems to have their own way of dealing with the strain. Some drink, some get belligerent and pick fights, some indulge in hot, raunchy sex with the first warm body they encounter.''

"I vote for that one," Babe interjected.

Ivy grinned. "Yeah, that'd be my first choice, too. The only problem is you've gotta have someone to indulge it with." An image of Vincent's face, dark and intense in the moment of his orgasm, flashed across her mind, making her smile fade. Forcefully shoving the memory down, she said, "The point is everyone has something that works best for them, and I guess partying just isn't it for me."

Babe checked her sauce and then glanced over her shoulder at her niece again. The dejection she saw on Ivy's face as she sat studying the melting ice cubes in her glass pulled at Babe's emotions. "So what does work best for you?" she inquired softly.

Ivy looked up. "Oh, I don't know . . . you, Uncle Mack. Family, I guess. In a lot of ways, with my co-workers, I still feel like the new kid on the block. I can't seem to get past the feeling I should be projecting this macho-woman front with them." She shrugged. "With you guys, I can just be myself . . . warts and all." Fearing that sounded too self-pitying, she rattled the ice cubes in her empty glass and attempted to change the subject. "I'd better switch to club soda now. I have to work in the morning."

Babe wasn't about to let her get away with the conversational shift. She knew Ivy too well—if someone didn't stop her, she would worry her failure to save a patient into next Tuesday, and she'd do it all by herself, not wanting to impose her problems on anyone. "So this macho-woman business is what's expected of you by your co-workers?"

"Probably not," Ivy admitted. "It's more what I expect of myself."

"But why, Ivy? Aren't these people your friends?"

"We're friendly, sure ... but friends? I don't really have any friends, Auntie Babe. Not anymore, not outside the family. With all the craziness of the past few years, I've lost contact with most of my old friends, and I simply haven't taken the time to make new ones." She shrugged. "My old pysch professor would probably say I overcompensate by trying to be the world's best M.D." That made her laugh. "Psychology never was my favorite rotation," she admitted, but then her good humor fled.

"Oh, hell," she said with abrupt unhappy impatience. "Forget I even brought it up, okay? You'd think I was the only doctor to ever lose a patient." Her mouth twisted in disgust as she jerked her chin in the direction of the bar. "Every one of those people out there lost someone today, too, and here I am whining as if my failures are more painful than theirs could ever be. I knew perfectly well what I was getting into when I chose trauma care over a nice, cushy private practice ... so I sure don't have any business kicking about it now."

"Now, that is enough," Babe said with sudden sternness. Wiping her hands on a towel, she slung it over her shoulder and crossed the room to stand in front of Ivy. She reached out and swept an errant tendril of bright hair away from her niece's troubled face. "Why are you always so hard on yourself, child?" she demanded. "Yes, you most likely could have saved yourself a passel of heartache if you'd gone into private practice and, yes, you voluntarily opted for trauma care instead. But where does it say that you're never entitled to feel depressed when you lose a life? It must hurt like the devil to feel one slipping through your fingers, knowing there's nothing you can do to prevent it."

"It does," Ivy whispered.

"I can only imagine." Babe's hands transferred to Ivy's shoulders and she gave her niece a little shake. "But you've got to cut yourself some slack, honey. Aren't you the same woman who told me the lives of half the patients you see are hanging by a thread by the time they get to you? You've gotta learn to do the best you can and then let go. You can't save 'em all, Ivy Jayne. I know you'd like to, but you can't. And I'll be damned if I'm gonna let you brood yourself into an early grave over how you should have done this or might have done that . . ."

"But maybe I *could* have—"

Babe pulled her into her arms. "Oh, honey," she sighed. "What am I going to do with you?" Then she resolutely marshalled her arguments. Stroking Ivy's silky hair from crown to nape, she stated with no-nonsense crispness, "In your heart, Ivy Jayne Pennington, you know perfectly well you did everything humanly possible to save that poor young woman's life. So please don't do this to yourself." She leaned back to see into her niece's eyes. "Go out there and share a few drinks and a few laughs with your co-workers, Ivy. You have the time to make friends now—so get started. It'll be a lot more productive than beating yourself black and blue over something that's too late to change."

Ivy forced a smile. "You're right," she agreed. "I think I probably just needed a hug," she confessed.

"And a hot meal," Babe interjected, stepping back and once again smoothing Ivy's hair away from her face as she smiled down at her. "You'll feel better after you've eaten."

Somewhat to Ivy's surprise, she did. And if Babe's meal didn't revive her one hundred percent, it cheered her up to the extent that she could enjoy her colleagues' pleasure in the spectacle that nightly transformed her aunt and uncle's sedate leather and mahogany lounge into a musical carnival.

Much to the ER crew's uninhibited delight, the regulars began singing just moments after the dishes from Babe's meal had been swept from their tables. In no time at all, her co-workers had thrown themselves wholeheartedly into the spirit of Mack 'N Babe's. They sang along with every tune they knew and zestfully applauded and cheered the performances of those they didn't. Ivy found it impossible to remain unaffected when she was surrounded by such enthusiasm.

For as long as Ivy could remember there had been singing at her aunt and uncle's bar. Legend had it, in fact, that it was the a cappella harmonies which had kept the lounge from closing down in nearly the same breath that it had opened for business.

According to the family rumor mill, Mack and Babe had had a difficult time getting the bar off the ground. Established in Pioneer Square well before the early 70's renovation that had made it a desirable location, they'd struggled from month to month to stay afloat. Babe's brothers and their wives had come as often as they could to lend their support, and as was usual whenever the Penningtons got together, they'd invariably ended up harmonizing. That had caught the interest of the few clients who weren't related to them, and they had begun coming back for more, bringing their friends. Soon the friends were also returning and telling other friends. And so it went, until the bar was suddenly an established business with a cappella singing a nightly feature.

The lounge sported a miniscule stage at the

north end of the mahogany bar, and every night there was an open mike that all were welcome to use. There was never a shortage of those who enjoyed performing on a stage; others chose instead to share their favorite tunes from wherever they sat. Between the two, the lounge was rarely quiet.

The entire bar was engaged in a bluesy rendition of "Summertime" when suddenly masculine hands thumped down on Ivy's shoulders. Strong fingers curled against her collarbones and thumbs skillfully massaged the tense muscles at the base of her skull. Caught off guard, she squawked dissonately, cutting herself off mid-note as her head snapped back to see who had her in his grip. Hanging over her was the inverted face of her cousin Terry, grinning down at her. "Hey babe," he said. Beyond his shoulder she could see Jaz, Davis and Sam.

"Hi!" Pushing her chair back from the table, she rose to greet them. "What are you guys doing down here on a Wednesday night?"

"Mom called," Jaz replied. "Said you'd lost a patient today and could use a little family support, so here we are." She reached out to give her taller cousin a hug. "I'm sorry, Ive. It musta been tough."

Swift tears rose in Ivy's eyes and she smiled tremulously as she gave each of her cousins a quick squeeze, a kiss and a whispered "thanks." It was exactly this kind of solidarity that made her relatives so special. There were times when the lack of privacy in her family was enough to set her teeth on edge, but just when she thought she'd had it up to her eyebrows with everyone knowing her business and happily spreading it to all the other family members, she'd get hit between the eyes with a day like this one. There they would be for her, without hesitation or reservation. Made it kind of difficult to complain.

"I couldn't get a hold of Sherry and Ben," Jaz said and grinned with familial maliciousness. "And ain't she gonna just chew nails when she finds out she missed out on something?"

Ivy laughed. "C'mon over and let me introduce you to some of the folks I work with," she invited.

"Well, I hope to spit, sister," Jaz retorted inelegantly, regarding her cousin with mock haughtiness. "You weren't laboring under the illusion that I came here strictly for your benefit, I trust."

"No, I'd pretty much figured out it was the rumor I'd shown up with men that had you hotfooting it on down here," Ivy replied wryly.

"Yeah, she heard you were here with some *real* doctors," Davis contributed.

The familiarity of trading of insults with her cousins did what nothing else had been able to accomplish. It washed away the final vestige of Ivy's depression, and it was with a much lighter heart that she introduced her cousins to the ER staff at the three tables in the corner.

Jaz's flawless beauty made its usual impression on Ivy's male colleagues and if the women present were a little less than thrilled to see her show up, they perked right up at the sight of the three unencumbered men Ivy had in tow. Chairs were scooted over to make room for the new arrivals.

Her relatives had a knack for fitting into any group they found themselves in, which was a fortunate ability as it didn't take the bar regulars any time at all to recognize the Pennington kids as they were commonly known (even though Jaz was a Merrick and none of them were exactly kids anymore). They'd barely had a chance to absorb the introductions before demands that they get up on stage and perform picked up supporters throughout the lounge. Obligingly, they excused themselves to Ivy's co-workers and climbed up on the minute stage.

Putting their heads together for a ten-second consultation, the five of them launched into a vintage madrigal, segued into a medley of Fifties hits that had the entire bar joining in, and complying to several shouted demands, finished up to thunderous applause with *Zombie Jamboree.*

Flushed and exhilarated, Ivy climbed down from the stage, collapsed into her seat and reached for her club soda, marvelling how easily she forgot between times exactly how much fun singing could be. One of the nurses was passing around an empty pretzel basket, collecting donations for the dinner, and Ivy pressed the cold glass to her hot forehead as she fished her contribution out of her wallet with her free hand. To her astonishment, she was besieged from all sides with compliments for her performance on stage. She'd been singing with her cousins all her life, and it had never struck her as being anything particularly special. Yet suddenly here were nurses and even other doctors—people she worked with daily—all asking her questions and regarding her with something close to awe. It was enormously ego-boosting.

She gazed around the bar. An attractive man who appeared to be her age stood at the edge of the tables. He was watching her and when their eyes met he gave her a barely perceptible salute with his glass. Before Ivy had a chance to even begin to preen, however, his gaze had already slid past her to Jaz and there it skidded to a halt. The expression on his face went from mildly admiring to downright moonstruck.

Well . . . shit. Ivy sighed in resignation. Talk about

typical; ever since the year she and Jaz had gone through puberty together this sort of thing had been happening to her. Guys always thought she was pretty cute . . . right up until the moment they laid eyes on her cousin. Then she generally ceased to exist. Not that she blamed them, really. Ivy knew she was reasonably attractive, but Jasmine was drop dead gorgeous. Not to mention small enough to make a man feel protective and strong. Well, maybe the height thing was sour grapes, but it got a little old to always be standing in the shrimp's tiny little shadow.

Ivy was so accustomed to being overlooked by males when she was in Jaz's company that she immediately dismissed the man from her mind. She didn't notice that his gaze promptly returned to her the instant her attention shifted away from him. He smiled to himself in satisfaction.

"Ivy?" Jessie Chapman, the nurse who'd been passing the collection basket came up to her. "Come with me while I give your uncle this money."

"Sure."

Mack flatly refused to accept it. "You didn't ask to be fed," he said with gruff impatience. "I offered."

"But Mr. Merrick," Jessie protested, "it must have set you back some to provide that wonderful meal for all of us."

"You're Ivy's friends," Mack countered stubbornly and then stated categorically, "I ain't taking your money."

Jessie, Ivy noted with a trace of amusement, must have a few brusque relatives of her own, for she refused to be dismissed. "It's not exactly a fortune we're offering here, sir. Let us at least pay for the supplies and Mrs. Merrick's time and effort. That meal was spectacular and it spared us from having to eat cafeteria fare. You can't know what a treat that is.''

"Oh, well, that Babe," Mack said proudly. "She's some cook, isn't she?"

"Yes, sir she is," Jessie replied sincerely and Ivy leaned down to pluck the roll of money from the nurse's hand. She tucked it into Mack's shirt pocket and gave it a pat.

"You take this, Uncle Mack. You're a businessman—use it to buy more supplies for when my friends drop by again. Or buy Auntie Babe something pretty." She gave him a cocky grin. "Or if that ole urge to blow your profits gets too much for you, pour my buddies some drinks from your unwatered stock."

"Why, you little brat. You ain't so big I can't still tan your hide for you, Ivy Jayne." He wrapped his arm around her, gave her an admonishing bear hug and shook his head. "Watered stock, my Aunt Agnes."

A short while later Ivy tracked her aunt down to the kitchen. "I'm taking off, Auntie Babe," she said.

"Oh, honey." Babe straightened from unloading the industrial-sized dishwasher of glasses and ashtrays, swiping the moisture off her forehead with her forearm. "You're leaving already?"

"Yeah, I've got work in the morning. Thanks for dinner—it was great."

"Your friends gave us much too much money for it, Ivy."

"No they didn't," Ivy disagreed. "They simply paid what it would have cost to eat in the cafeteria, and your food leaves theirs in the dust." She tossed her purse on the counter and helped her aunt rack the glasses. "To tell the truth, Auntie Babe, I was kinda proud of them. They really are nice people, aren't they?"

"They're trying to make me a rich woman," Babe agreed dryly. "I can't help but like 'em."

"Yeah, me too. I'm going to take your advice and make time to get to know them better."

"Good. And how about a boyfriend? No one special, you said?"

"No." Ivy shook her head, and then added honestly. "Well, there was this one guy, but that's over."

"Tell me about him," Babe demanded, her curiosity piqued by the myriad expressions chasing across her niece's face. "What was he like?"

"Oh God, Auntie Babe, all twisted steel and sex appeal." A little shocked by what had popped out of her mouth, she attempted to backpeddle. "No, actually that's not it at all. Vincent is . . . different. Different from any man I've ever met. For about five minutes he made me forget I'm supposed to be smart and made me feel like the sexiest woman on earth instead." She sighed. "But I think maybe he's got a lot of personal history I don't know anything about. Anyhow, it's over." She picked up her purse. "Well listen, I'll give you a call next week and we'll set up a time for you and Uncle Mack to come over for dinner."

"I'd like that, honey. I'm dying to see the chair Terry recovered for you. Jaz tells me it's something."

"Oh, wait 'til you see it, Auntie Babe. He did such a beautiful job it's hard to believe it's the same chair." She blew a kiss to her aunt and left.

Pioneer Square, where Mack 'N Babe's was located, wasn't the safest place in Seattle for a woman to be alone at night. There were always street people congregating in Occidental Park or shuffling unsteadily from one tavern to the next. Sometimes it was even necessary to step over a recumbent form sleeping it off on the streets. Sam and Davis walked Ivy out to where she'd parked her car in a nearby pay lot and remained there talking for a short time after she'd driven away.

They would have been pleased to know that in doing so, they unwittingly prevented Tyler Griffus, who had trailed Ivy from a discreet distance, from following her home.

Chapter 7

The holding cell had been painted pink expressly for its calming influence. Vincent left his prisoner there and went in search of Suse McGill. He found her working at her desk.

"Hey, McGill."

When she looked up at him warily, he barely even winced. It was an expression he was growing increasingly familiar with, the one with which most of his fellow officers greeted him these days.

So he'd been a little hard to get along with lately. Big deal. His co-workers' sudden wariness in his presence generated only the remotest sense of regret for his recent behavior. Hell, they weren't always sweetness and light themselves.

More than anything, lately, he seemed to feel just plain tired. He hadn't allowed his lethargy to affect his caseload, of course. But today he wanted a solid confession from the prisoner cooling his heels in the holding cell, and he was afraid obtaining one would simply require more energy than he could summon.

Which was why he needed McGill's help. When it came to extracting incriminating statements that would hold up in court, she was one of the best.

"What can I do for you, Vincent?" she asked. Suse's inquiry was surprisingly cordial considering she, like practically everyone else in Special Assaults, had felt the sharp sting of D'Ambruzzi's temper.

But then, Suse thought perhaps she understood his recent outbursts. Without coming out and actually saying so, Keith had managed to intimate that Vincent's uncharacteristic surliness had something to do with the statuesque redheaded doc who'd dropped by last week. That wouldn't surprise Suse in the least. What was truly amazing, in her opinion, was that D'Ambruzzi hadn't chafed beneath the restrictions of his self-imposed celibacy long before this.

"I need a favor, Suse." Vincent worked overtime to inject a bit of vitality into his voice and to maintain a pleasant tone as he outlined his needs.

Once upon a time it had amused Vincent to watch the tough-guy cops on television and in the movies browbeating their suspects into giving a confession. When it came to interrogation—particularly the interrogation of sex offenders—intimidation rarely proved to be the effective tool that Hollywood insisted on depicting.

In most real-life situations, the trick was relating to the suspect and getting them to warm up to the interrogating officer in return. Suse McGill was particularly good at this. She had a knack for building up a suspect's self-image to the point where he was comfortable enough to handle a confession, and her primary tool was an adept ability to minimize his crime. By making it sound as if it could have been a lot worse than it actually had been, she allowed him to garner the strength necessary to confess.

She was young, pretty, soft-spoken and non-aggressive . . . not at all what most sex offenders expected. They found her immediately less threatening than most of the male detectives and thus warmed up to her more quickly. Also, she harbored a very real desire to know what made them tick, and the genuineness of her interest was readily apparent.

All Special Assaults personnel had at one time or another undergone the same orientation training—they all knew that most sex offenders had been sexually abused themselves at some point in their lives. Many of the detectives, however—Vincent among them—had worked the unit too long to feel much empathy for a rapist's ancient pain. He, for one, had dealt too often with its ultimate result, had seen too many victims whose lives had been destroyed by it.

He handed Suse his report and a sheaf of notes and she read them as they walked to the pink room. Stopping outside the holding cell, she finished reading and then looked up at Vincent. "Has he been read his rights?"

"Yes. He understands them and waives the lawyer. Lay it all out for him, Suse, and see what you can do." He hesitated a moment, jingling the change in his jeans pocket as he looked down at her. Then with a touch of awkwardness he said, "I appreciate this."

She patted his arm. "No problem." She looked in on the prisoner and when she turned back to Vincent, she was shaking her head. "I can never get over how pathetic and shrunken they look in interrogation. My God, Vince, they must simply *grow* with the power while they're committing their crimes, because right now he looks like my six-year-old niece could whip his ass—with one of her little arms tied behind her back."

Vincent took her into the pink room and introduced her to the suspect. "Dan, this is Det. McGill. She's going to help you make a statement." He took a seat behind the man and settled in. Suse had agreed to let him observe as long as he didn't distract the suspect or make him nervous to the point where it interfered with her interrogation.

She kept the rapist's attention focused on her by speaking to him softly, asking him to clarify a point from the report here, confirm a detail there. She continued until he forgot anyone else was with them in the room.

At one point, she looked up from the papers in front of her. "You had a knife, is that right?"

Dan shrugged.

"That's not so bad," she said softly. She appeared to be speaking to herself. "It could have been worse—it could have been a gun." She shuffled through the papers again, finally set them down on the table in front of her and tapped her fingertips against the top page, looking up at the suspect.

"All right, Dan, let me see if I have this straight," she said calmly. "You went to the victim's house at approximately 11:45 p.m. to deliver a pizza, and she came to the door dressed in a robe. That's a pretty suggestive thing to do. Then, instead of having the money ready, what does she do? She goes to the bedroom to get it. I mean, she wants you there—you *know* she wants you there. So you follow her to the bedroom and one thing leads to another." Suse's voice was warm and it began to pick up speed. "You start touching her, start kissing her . . . and she wants you. She wants you—doesn't she? Doesn't she? Now really, Dan, now really, you had a knife, right? Isn't that right, you had a knife?

It could have been worse, you could have had a gun. Did you hold a gun to her throat—did you, Dan, did you?"

"No, I didn't hold a gun to her throat."

"What was it?" Suse demanded. "It was a knife—it was *just* a knife, wasn't it?"

He nodded.

"You didn't *use* the knife, did you, Dan? You just laid it down after you showed it to her, right? I mean, did you use it, Dan?"

"No, I didn't use it."

"Okay, you threatened her with a knife, but you didn't kill her. You could have killed her!" She thought about it for a second and then gave him an approving nod. "You didn't kill her. Listen, I talk to hundreds of rapists every day. Some of 'em kill their victims. *You* didn't kill her. For God's sake, you were nice to her—didn't you help her get dressed? Hey, you're not so bad. You pay your taxes—you've got a wife. I know what you feel, Dan. You've got pressures, trying to do your job . . . working all day. You deliver pizzas at night for a few extra bucks and whataya got? Ya got this woman who's vulnerable, sad, lonely. Why else would she call you in the middle of the night and make you wait to grab her while she gets the money? Why else would she?"

Vincent could see the suspect visibly gaining a little strength while Suse talked. Soon, she had him agreeing with each point that needed to be covered to gain a conviction in court.

They had their confession. Every detective in the unit had his or her own method for extracting one, but basically this was the way they were obtained. Surprisingly, except for the moments when the crime was actually being committed, most rapists didn't feel good about what they did. There were exceptions, of course, but most needed to be made to feel that their crime wasn't as heinous as others the detectives had seen..

Vincent thought if the victims ever heard the way their attackers were pumped up by detectives who deliberately made it sound as though the women had been asking for what they'd got, they'd probably feel raped all over again. But the method was necessary. Browbeating didn't work, and in the long run a signed confession did work in the victims' favor, for it often saved them the humiliation of a trial. Or if the case did come to trial, then the confession was more likely to guarantee a conviction and hopefully a longer sentence. So, yeah, it was necessary. And he'd extracted them himself in a similar manner. Today, however, Vincent was tired to the bone and fed up to eyebrows. And he really didn't have the stomach for this.

The desk sergeant put down the phone and turned to Ivy. "I'm sorry, ma'am," he said. "They've all gone home for the day."

"Damn!" Ivy's palm slapped the counter and she was whirling on her heel and striding out the door before the sergeant had a chance to tell her he could page the on-call officer.

Now what? She fumed as she hit the street and stared at the heat waves shimmering above the pavement. She breathed shallowly to avoid pulling the exhaust-laden air too deeply into her lungs. Was she supposed to wait until morning? Lord, she'd be a wreck by then.

She had known the Special Assault Unit's hours, of course. She'd even feared it would be too late by the time she got to the precinct. Still, she had hoped against hope that D'Ambruzzi or someone in his unit would still be working late. If only she had left the trauma unit the moment she'd received the note . . .

Well, it was no use pursuing that line of thought. What else could she have done—she certainly wasn't capable of ignoring that poor child's agony. No one else had been available except a newly assigned, extremely nervous intern, and the little boy had needed immediate treatment; he'd had to be stabilized before she could turn him over to the burn unit. Then his parents had needed considerable calming. Besides, she still might have made it before they closed if she hadn't run into such heavy downtown traffic.

Wiping perspiration off her brow as she climbed steep streets through muggy late afternoon heat to the parking lot where she'd left her car, she reflected that attaching blame or thinking "if only" was a pointless endeavor. It didn't change the fact that she had simply been too late to catch anyone still in the unit.

But what was she supposed to do now?

Vincent was trying to summon the energy to start dinner when his doorbell rang. Ordinarily he liked to cook and tended to think of it more as an enjoyable hobby than as a chore, but this past week he'd been so damn tired it was all he could do to draw his next breath.

At the sound of the bell, he yawned and considered ignoring it. All he wanted was to stay right where he was on the couch, where he'd flopped the moment he'd entered his apartment. It was probably just some kid selling magazines subscriptions anyway, so why expend unnecessary energy? They did occasionally manage to bypass the security door by slipping in behind another resident. The bell rang again, however, and expelling a weary breath he dragged himself to his feet.

He didn't seem to be anyone's friend these days, but the very last person he expected to see when he opened the door was Ivy Pennington.

Without preliminaries she thrust a baggie-protected envelope at him. "He knows who I am." She had been pacing her apartment for the past hour, scared out of her mind, and had by now lost the last vestige of her composure.

Vincent didn't question the renewed vitality that suddenly roared along his nerve endings. He glanced down at the envelope and immediately recognized the block printing from the last card she'd brought him. "Oh, shit. Another one. You receive more flowers, too?"

"No. Just the note."

Wrapping his long fingers around her arm, he pulled her into his apartment and slammed the door behind them. He half led, half towed her into the living room where he pushed her gently down on the couch. Studying her drawn features with concern, he inquired, "Are you all right?"

She hopped back up to her feet, regarding him incredulously. "No, I'm not all right!" She paced his living room and flapped one slender hand at the baggie he held. "Read it! That rapist, that man who's—how did you characterize him? Vicious and violent?—He *knows* who I am, D'Ambruzzi!"

Vincent went into his kitchen and rummaged through the junk drawer in search of a pair of tweezers. Ivy followed, crowding into the tiny area with him, nervously picking items up off the counter and then immediately discarding them. The third time she thumped one of his belongings down, he glanced up from his search. She was in the process of poking through his utensils and as he watched, she pulled out the wire whip, dragging several other gadgets along with it. She made an abortive attempt to keep them from spilling, but they scattered noisily across the counter. He inquired dryly, "You want something to drink, Doctor?"

Ivy picked up the utensils and stuffed them back into the pottery container. When all except the wire whip were returned, Vincent's voice belatedly seemed to penetrate. She looked at him blankly. "What?"

"You want a drink?"

"Oh, yes. Please." She plowed her fingers through her hair. "God—I'm a wreck."

He turned to the small cupboard where he kept his liquor. Ivy was standing directly in front of it, rhythmically slapping the wire whip into her palm as she stared into space. Knowing he'd probably have to speak several times before he gained her attention, he simply grabbed her by the hips and moved her aside. Then he squatted in front of the cupboard and surveyed the contents. "I've got vodka, bourbon, and about half an inch of rum. Or there might be a beer in the fridge." He looked up at her. "What'll ya have?"

He had to repeat himself. "Bourbon," she finally responded. She slapped the wisk twice more into her cupped palm before she recalled her manners. "Please," she added quietly.

"Bourbon it is." Vincent pulled out the bottle and stood. "Check the fridge for me and see if there's a beer." He found a glass and splashed in a healthy measure of whiskey. "You want it straight?" No reply. "Doctor? You want it straight?"

"Add a splash of water. Please." Ivy slammed the refrigerator door and turned to hand him the beer. She dropped an ice cube she had collected from the freezer into the glass he passed to her, stirred it with her finger, and then tossed back a sizable swallow. She shuddered, giving him an appreciative nod when he caught her eye. "Thanks. I needed that."

Vincent popped the top off his beer, flipped it into the sink, and picked up the baggie and tweezers. "Come on," he said. "Let's go to the living room. We might as well be comfortable, and this kitchen's too small for that."

As with the last time he'd tried to settle her on his couch, she was up and prowling before the cushions had had a chance to settle beneath her weight. Vincent tried to ignore her restless movements but it was difficult to concentrate with her rattling around his living room, picking his possessions up only to immediately discard them in favor of the next item to catch her eye.

Using the tweezers to extract the envelope from the plastic sandwich bag, he set it on top of a newspaper he'd spread out on the coffee table. The envelope's flap wasn't tucked in and he used a ballpoint pen to flip it open and hold it while he reached in with the tweezers to pull out the enclosed note. It was a single sheet of generic white dime-store stationary, folded in thirds. He set it down on top of the envelope, clamped the tweezers down on what would be the top corner when it was opened, and shook it out. The entire message consisted of one line, hand printed in block lettering in the middle of the page, and the now-familiar signature of half a heart. It was short and to the point, stating simply: *I like the way you sing*.

Vincent replaced it in the envelope and slid it back into the baggie. He looked up and located Ivy out on the small balcony. She was staring into space, clutching her drink to her chest with one hand and restlessly tapping the slender fingers of her free hand on the railing. "What does he mean by this?" he called to her. She was apparently tuned in to some inner dialogue, for she didn't answer. "Ivy?"

Still no answer.

"Ivy!" he barked. She jumped and turned swiftly in his direction, as if surprised to find someone else there. "Get in here and sit down," he ordered with clipped authority. "I need your attention and I'm tired of having to repeat myself to get it."

Somewhat to his surprise given what he knew of her nature, she meekly complied. Once she was perched next to him on the couch he inquired yet again, "What does he mean when he says he likes the way you sing?"

Ivy blinked several times, staring hard at him in order to focus. Good God, she had to get control of herself. She had managed to submerge her feelings mere moments after she'd received the note this afternoon only by sternly reminding herself that her young burn victim deserved the best care possible. And she'd kept those feelings submerged, more or less, until she'd gotten home.

But then she'd come unhinged. She couldn't seem to concentrate on anything for more than a second at a time; her thoughts were scattered. Spoken words beat disjointedly at her consciousness like kamikaze moths flapping at a light source before they eventually sorted themselves into coherent sequence, and only then after they'd been repeated several times. Fear seemed to have rendered her deaf.

"Ivy," Vincent was saying once again with strained patience, "what does his note mean when he says he likes the way you sing?"

She carefully watched the movement of his full mouth as if she had to lipread to comprehend. Then abruptly, for the first time since she'd rung his doorbell, she actually saw him.

He was wearing Levis and a white shirt with the

sleeves rolled up and the top two buttons unbuttoned. Apparently all he'd bothered to remove on his arrival home was his jacket and his shoes and socks; the former was draped over the back of the couch, the latter kicked under the coffee table. He was still wearing a leather holster of surprising compactness clipped to his belt and his shirt was wilted by the heat. As she stared at the businesslike butt of his gun, her unraveled nerves finally began to reknit themselves into something resembling normalcy.

A man with a gun was surely more dangerous than a man with a knife. And this particular man with a gun lived right next door.

"A group of us from the hospital went to Mack 'N Babe's last night after our shift ended," she told him, and Vincent was gratified to see her eyes finally lose that unfocused terror. Her voice regained a vestige of its usual crisp authority. "That's my aunt and uncle's bar," she clarified, and then added, "They raised me from the time my parents died."

Now, why had she told him that? She was surprised at herself. More surprising yet was that Vincent actually became sidetracked by her comment instead of—as she would have expected—brushing it aside as immaterial.

"How old were you when your folks died?"

"Fifteen. So, anyway—" she continued, trying to side step the interruption and get back to the subject at hand. But he wasn't ready to let it drop.

"How did they die?"

"In a car wreck. I was in it, too, except I was asleep on the back seat."

"Oh, man, that's brutal. And you were only fifteen? I was in the Navy when my mom died," he told her. "So I must have been twenty-one, maybe twenty-two. And I was almost thirty when my dad had his heart attack. That made me a little better equipped to cope with a loss of that magnitude than a kid would be, but it was still hard to accept." He rapidly assessed what he knew of her and then guessed shrewdly, "That's what made you want to become a doctor, right?"

"Yes." She was conscious that her jaw had gone slack as she stared at him and she closed her mouth with a snap. A personal conversation? Between her and D'Ambruzzi? It occurred to her suddenly that while they had been as intimate as two people could possibly be, they had never once shared personal information about themselves.

"What were your aunt and uncle like as surrogate parents?"

"Oh, the best." Ivy smiled for the first time in hours. "The absolute best." Knotted stomach muscles began to relax as she shared some of the things Mack and Babe had done for her. And then she told him about their bar.

"So that's where he heard you sing? Last night in the bar?"

"It had to have been." She looked down at his bare foot braced on the cushion next to her thigh. His skin, she noticed, appeared particularly dark in contrast to the pale thigh emerging from the hem of her shorts. "But don't ask me how he knew to find me there," she said, "Because I don't have a clue." She stared off for a moment. "Unless . . ."

When she didn't say anything else, Vincent prompted gently, "Unless?"

She looked up. "Unless he heard us making plans in the ER," she said slowly. She told him what a madhouse it had been, explaining how the staff had called their suggestions up and down the work lanes, everyone contributing an idea. "We aren't usually so unprofessional, but it had been a hell of a day. Patients were piling up like cordwood, coming in faster than we could keep up with, and too many were cases that we didn't have a prayer of saving." Her head dipped into her hands.

Vincent looked at her downbent head. He would like to have seen her expression but a wing of glossy red hair had swung forward to block it. "Were one of those yours?" Her head snapped up but she refused to look at him. He persisted anyway. "A case that couldn't be saved?"

"Yeah." She tucked her hair behind her ear and darted a sideways glance at him. Then she looked back at her hands in her lap. "A young woman who was six months pregnant. She wasn't wearing her seatbelt."

"Ah, Jesus, that's rough." He watched her profile. "How do you deal with it?"

The little breath of laughter that escaped her was not filled with amusement. "Poorly." One corner of her mouth curled up. "Very poorly. Auntie Babe says I need to learn that I can't save them all."

Her stomach suddenly growled with loud insistence and she pressed the heel of her hand against it, hoping to muffle the sound. Vincent was on his feet in an instant, extending a hand to her. "C'mon." He hauled her to her feet and led her to the kitchen. "Stand here; it's out of the way— or I can grab you a chair."

"No, this is fine. Why? What are you gonna do?"

"Make us dinner."

"Oh, no, please." She was embarrassed, certain her noisy stomach had forced the invitation. "Really," she insisted. "That's not necessary."

Head in the refrigerator, Vincent looked at her over his shoulder. "The hell it's not," he disagreed flatly. "I'm hungry and so are you."

"Hey," she said, edging away, "maybe I'd better

just leave. Okay? You just get on with whatever it was you planned for this evening."

"Ivy, pull up a goddamn chair and sit down!" he barked impatiently without even looking up from his perusal of the refrigerator. It wasn't a request.

Ivy didn't respond well to snapped orders. She opened her mouth to tell him so in no uncertain terms, then she closed it again. The truth was, she felt safe here and the last thing she wanted to do was go home and be alone. Plus—and she would eat a slug before she'd admit this out loud—in all honesty she really didn't care to put him to the test by arguing with that tone. Not tonight.

She pulled up a dining room chair to the kitchen doorway and sat down.

He assembled ingredients and banged pans; serious gourmet pans, she noticed, not beat-up old hand-me-downs like the ones she owned. He finished chopping garlic and onion and used the blade of his knife to scrape them from the butcher block into the pan. Adding a splash of olive oil, he sauteed them over the burner, shaking the pan and deftly flipping the ingredients. He glanced at her over his shoulder. "Was the note delivered to you at the hospital in the same way that the flowers were?"

"Yes." She couldn't take her eyes off his hands and the pan. "Where did you learn to cook like that?"

He grinned and touched his forefinger to his thumb, cocking his hand in the only ethnic gesture she'd ever seen him use. "D'Ambruzzi's Fine Italiano Cuisine." He kissed his joined fingertips. *"Bellissima."*

"Really? A family restaurant? Where?"

"Gentry, Iowa." He shot her another glance and then rolled his shoulders dismissively. "I don't expect you've ever heard of it. It's a dot on the map—a very small dot.''

"Iowa, huh? So, how'd you get clear out here?"

"I was stationed in Bremerton when I was in the Navy. I liked the area; I didn't like Gentry.'' He shrugged again, reached for the package of linguini and dumped it into a pan of boiling water. "You wanna set the table?'' He shot her a glance. "If you'd like to eat out on the balcony where it's cooler, there's a card table under my bed. Plates and glasses are in that cupboard.'' He indicated which one with a nod of his head. "Knives and forks are in the drawer below.'' He added clam nectar to the pan and went to the refrigerator to pull out the makings for a green salad.

She went to his bedroom to fetch the card table. She looked around and noted how neat he was: a place for everything, everything in its place. Even his bed was made up . . . and not just with the covers thrown up the way hers usually was. His was made with a military precision you could bounce a coin on.

She quickly averted her gaze. The last thing she needed to do was speculate on the action that bed had seen. It was a small miracle of sorts that she felt as comfortable in his company this evening as she did. Undoubtedly that was due to the fact that for once there hadn't been one iota of sexual tension between them.

She planned to keep it that way. He and his gun might make her feel safer than anyone she'd ever known, but she'd already run afoul of those hit-and-run hormones of his and she wouldn't willingly trust her affections to him again. Not ever.

Over dinner, Vincent said, "The good news is, the rapist apparently doesn't know where you live. Otherwise he wouldn't still be sending his messages through the hospital.'' He waved a fly away from the bowl of linguini. ''Hand me that plate; we'd better cover this up.'' Once that was done, he returned his attention to her. ''Do you work a regular shift?''

''Yeah, more or less. Most weeks I work eight to four, Sunday through Thursday. They schedule me to work every fourth weekend and then I have Mondays and Tuesdays off.'' Ivy held out her plate. ''May I have just a bite more of that?'' She licked at a dot of clam sauce in the corner of her mouth. ''It's wonderful.''

''Thanks.'' He slapped another helping on the plate she held out. ''If you work the day shift, why were you at the hospital the night they brought in Bess Polsen?''

His groin stirred as he remembered the night in question, but he forcibly pushed the memories out of his mind. For the first time since they'd met, they were easy in each other's company. He was actually in her presence without going out of his mind wanting to jump her bones, and he wasn't about to let a wayward surge of testosterone take over now and blow the little bit of progress he'd managed to make.

If he'd learned nothing else this past week, he had learned to at least quit fooling himself. He could tell himself she didn't interest him until he was blue in the face, but the moment he'd opened his door and seen her standing there, he'd been forced to admit that he was still so interested he could taste it.

Not that such an admission was likely to do him much good. He'd already made a mess of things and in truth he was tired of feeling he had to apologize for his actions. But he could at least cop to a little honesty. If it did nothing else, it might spare him and everyone around him from another week like this past one.

"I was filling in for another doctor that week," Ivy was replying. "Working a double shift. My regular one back to back with the four-to-midnight rotation."

He studied her face for a moment. "We'll have to work on the assumption that he knows your schedule by now."

Ivy pushed her plate away with an abrupt movement. "I hate this," she said in a low, intense voice. "God, I hate it. I have never in my life been afraid of anything." She waved a qualifying hand. "Oh, I've been afraid I'd blow Grand Rounds or that I'd make an incorrect diagnosis. But I've never known what it's like to be physically frightened. Now along comes this guy . . ."

She bit her lip and looked away. "He terrifies me," she admitted in a low voice to the balcony railing. She looked back at Vincent. "That son of a bitch terrifies me, and I hate it!"

Vincent wasn't happy about it either. This particular rapist had always stuck to a strict pattern during the commisson of his crimes. Now, all of a sudden, he was changing that pattern. It felt almost as if the man regarded Ivy as his personal mascot, and if that were the case Vincent was at something of a loss, for he had never dealt with a similar situation.

Generally, non-homicidal rape cases could be counted on to be fairly straightforward. They didn't involve all the extraneous bullshit that was beginning to crop up in this one. And Vincent especially didn't care for the fact that Ivy appeared to be caught in the middle of some psychotic reasoning process that he couldn't even begin to fathom.

But she needed reassurance, not more pressure. Besides, he would work it out one step at a time— just like he always did. Sooner or later something was bound to break. One of the most difficult things about this case had always been the lack of evidence the rapist left behind. Exerting extreme care seemed to be as much the man's trademark as the signature heart he carved in his victims' chests. But if he was suddenly hanging around the trauma center in an attempt to garner information on Ivy, then his customary caution was slipping. All Vincent had to do was find a way to make use of that.

He reached across the table to touch his fingertips to the back of her clenched fist. "Sometimes fear can be a useful emotion," he told her. "It keeps you careful." He watched her in the gathering dusk as she stood and began collecting the soiled dishes. "He doesn't know where you live, Ivy. Concentrate on that. Actually, the only thing he does know about you is your work schedule and the location of your aunt and uncle's bar."

She seemed to be ignoring him, avoiding eye contact as she industriously stacked the dishes, and he felt like grabbing her hands and stilling them until he had her complete attention. But he remained seated; his hands continued to lie motionless on his thighs. "While we're on the subject of your relatives," he said, "probably the first thing you should do is apprise them of the situation and ask them to keep a particular eye out for anyone who appears to be showing an interest in you."

That finally got her attention, but not exactly in the manner he had anticipated. She frowned at him, her hands going still. "No," she said flatly, shaking her head. "No. I don't want Uncle Mack or Auntie Babe to know anything about this. It'll only worry them."

"That can't be helped," he argued. "And given everything you've told me about them, they sound like strong people. They can take this." She was clearly unconvinced and her continued resistance made him impatient. "Listen," he said. "The more people who are aware you've attracted this deviate's attention, the safer you'll be. I've got a caseload like you wouldn't believe, so I'm unable to devote my full energies to this."

He might not have spoken at all for all the attention she paid him. He shifted irritably in his chair. "Dammit, Ivy, don't get stubborn about this! You need to enlist the assistance of everyone you can think of. If your friends and family are aware of the situation, they'll help you by keeping their eyes peeled. Now, I plan to contact hospital security and I'm going to talk to the nurses, orderlies and doctors in your unit. But you'd better resign yourself to the fact that I'm also gonna talk to your aunt and uncle. You've only got one choice here: you can prepare them first or let me approach 'em cold—it's up to you. I believe that they'll be a lot less shocked if you prepare them first."

She slammed the plates back down on the table and stared at him stonily. "Damn you," she said in a low, furious voice. "This is *my* life we're talking about! Not yours, not some faceless, bad-luck victim's—mine! But then, I don't know why this should surprise me. You've never given a moment's thought to *my* wishes anyway, have you?"

Without giving him a chance to respond she turned on her heel and stormed into the apartment.

Chapter 8

He caught up with her just as she was about to let herself out the front door and pressed his hand against the door to prevent her from opening it. "You came to me for help," he said.

"And now I'm leaving," Ivy muttered to the door panel. She hadn't turned around when his hand had suddenly reached over her shoulder to hold the door closed and she didn't turn now.

"To do what?" he inquired with deceptive mildness. "Try and handle it yourself?"

She shrugged. "Maybe." But already she was beginning to feel foolish, knowing full well she was acting as petulantly as a spoiled child who'd been denied her way. Unfortunately, she also had a sneaking suspicion that if he dared point that out, she'd end up defending her position to the death.

"Dammit, Ivy!" Vincent wasn't interested in scoring points off her. It was all he could do just to keep his temper from exploding. She had a way of blowing into his life and then storming out of it until he didn't know which way was up. He grasped her shoulders and turned her around to face him. "Is that it, then? You come to me for help, but the minute you hear something you don't like, you're just gonna walk out, no discussion? Well, hell, go ahead then." His hands dropped from her shoulders and he stepped back in disgust. "That seems to be your usual reaction when you're mad at me anyway."

Her head snapped up, transferring her gaze from his chin to his narrowed black eyes. "*My* reaction? Dear God, D'Ambruzzi, that is truly rich, coming from you!"

"Oh, you wanna talk about that night now, Ivy?" His hands slammed onto the door panels on either side of her face and he leaned on them heavily, looming over her. "You think you can bear to stick around long enough to hear the reasons I disappeared after we made love?"

He took them both by surprise with his willingness to bring that potentially explosive subject out in the open. He'd thought he could let it pass, thought he could let her go, but he discovered a need to fight it out and clear the air. He was tired of feeling guilty and he would not allow her to punish him for that one action forever. "That *is* what this all comes down to, isn't it? You're not willing to trust me personally—or professionally— because I slept with you and then walked away."

"That has *nothing* to do with this," she denied emphatically. She looked him straight in the eye, but she wondered: Did it? *Was* she refusing to take his professional advice because he'd hurt her on a personal level? She didn't believe so, but all she knew for certain was that she in no way wanted to discuss this now.

"Bullshit," he flatly contradicted her.

"It doesn't!" She stared at his closed, controlled

expression. "I've simply decided I'm going to handle the situation myself."

"Yeah? And how do you plan to do that, Pennington? You tell me how you're gonna handle the attentions of a rapist when you were so freaked out by one little note from him you could barely function. Jesus, lady, you had the attention span of a two-year-old when you arrived here tonight. I had to repeat everything I said three times before you heard me." He looked at the stubborn set of her mouth and then dove straight to the heart of the matter. "And whether you handle it or I handle it, your aunt and uncle still need to be questioned."

"No!"

"Yes," he contended flatly, and the fact that he spoke through clenched teeth did not render his tone of voice any less final. He meant business and to underscore the fact, he stiff-armed himself away from the door, turned his back on her and walked back into the living room, leaving her to stay or go as she pleased.

Ivy was too furious to leave. With every intention of seeing this situation settled in a manner that she deemed suitable, she stormed after him. Catching up with him by the couch, she grabbed his arm and yanked with all her might to make him turn back to her. "Who do you think you are?" she demanded with outraged hoarseness.

Vincent jerked his arm out of her grasp and just as furious as she, bent his head until their noses were an inch apart. "I'll tell you who I am, lady. I'm the detective in charge of this case! You wanna punish me on a personal level, then do it. But don't you go tellin' me how to do my job. You'd never stand for it if I tried to tell you how to be a doctor, and I'll be damned if I'll stand here and listen to you instructing me on how to be a cop

when you don't know the first goddam thing about
it!''

Ivy's anger collapsed and so did she, onto the
nearest handy surface, which happened to be the
couch. ''Oh, shit,'' she said, plowing her fingers
into her hair and raking it off her face. ''Shit, shit,
shit.'' She looked up at him. ''You're right,'' she
admitted wearily. ''Not about punishing you,'' she
hastily qualified with a silent curse for her ubiquitous blush, ''but about telling you how to do your
job. I did do that and I shouldn't have. I'm sorry.''

Surprised by her sudden capitulation and recog-
nizing the exhaustion that etched faint lines in
her forehead, Vincent's anger also drained. He sat
down next to her. ''Why does the thought of your
aunt and uncle knowing upset you so much?''

Her fingers tightened their grip in her hair. ''I
don't want them worrying themselves sick. They've
done so much for me and I just can't bear the
thought of burdening them with the knowledge of
this, of this . . . *sickness*, when there's nothing they
can do.''

''Hell,'' he said. ''Parents—guardians—worry.
But don't you think you're underestimating their
resiliency a little?''

''No,'' she categorically stated. Then, less certainly, ''Well, maybe.'' Her hands dropped into
her lap and she sighed. ''Oh, God, I don't know.''
Hooking her heel on the couch cushion, she
wrapped her long arms around her shin and then
turned her head to look at him, her cheek resting
against her updrawn kneecap. ''You're probably
right. They're very strong people, Mack and Babe.
And I suppose they'd simply be that much more
upset if they discovered I was trying to shield
them.'' Her smile was a small, ironic tilt of her lips.
''And naturally, it *would* get back to them. You can't
imagine how few secrets there are in my family.''

She buried her face against her leg. "I don't know what I was thinking of," she muttered.

She sounded so defeated that Vincent's hand involuntarily reached out and stroked slowly down her shiny fall of hair from the crown of her head to the blunt-cut ends. "Are you all right?"

"Yeah, sure," came her muffled reply. As if realizing the lack of conviction in her tone, her voice summoned a little strength. "I'm just tired."

She rolled her head back to look at him again, conscious of his hand resting warm on her back. She experienced a surprisingly strong desire for the type of terms between them that would allow her to ask to be held. He was so solid and she needed just for a moment to feel safe. He had the ability to make her feel that way, she knew. It was against all reason, but he did. Except for that one episode of explosive sex and tonight's surprisingly relaxed dinner, however, their relationship could generally be classified as more adversarial than friendly. "I don't want to be alone tonight, Vincent," she said instead. "Would it be okay if I called my cousin Jaz from here and maybe stayed until she arrives? I know it's getting late and you said the rapist doesn't know where I live, but . . ."

"Why don't you just stay here instead," he interrupted. "You can have my bed; I'll sleep on the couch."

"Oh, I couldn't do that."

"Sure you can. As you said, it's getting late. There's no sense in rousting your cousin out at this hour."

It was true that Jaz was probably already in bed; she tended to retire early on the evenings she didn't go out. But to stay here? That was sort of asking for trouble, wasn't it? She opened her mouth to politely refuse and instead heard herself say, "Then let me take the couch."

He let out the breath he hadn't even realized he'd been holding. "No." He held up a hand to forestall her protest. "And before we get into a big argument about that, too, just remember that according to what you yourself have told me of your schedule you don't have to work tomorrow; am I right?"

"No . . . I mean yes: you're right. Friday's one of my days off. But what has that got to do with—"

"Because I do. And it'll be a hell of a lot easier getting ready in the morning if I don't have to tiptoe around worrying about waking you up. Take the bed."

"Are you sure?"

"Yes."

"Okay, then. Thanks." As she rose to her feet, the mess on the balcony caught her eye. "At least let me clean up the dinner dishes."

Vincent stood also. "I'll do it," he said. "You go grab your toothbrush or whatever it is you're gonna need."

She was back before he'd had time to do more than clear the card table, wipe it down and put it away under his bed. She insisted on helping him load the dishwasher and clean the counters. When they were finished, she stood in awkward silence for a moment, smoothing the dishtowel with unnecessary care over the drying rack. "Well." She looked up at him finally. "I guess I'll go to bed. Goodnight, Vincent."

"Goodnight, Ivy."

She walked into the bedroom and closed the door.

It was late morning when Ivy awoke and at first she was confused about where she was. She brushed her hair from her eyes and gazed in bewilderment around the unfamiliar room, blinking to dispel the tenacious cobwebs of slumber that clouded her mind. It wasn't until she had absorbed various impressions of the ordered neatness surrounding her that the cobwebs parted and memory of yesterday's events returned. The instant she realized whose room she was in she remembered everything.

The note.

Her fear.

Vincent's dinner and her temper tantrum over the way he'd insisted on informing Uncle Mack and Auntie Babe of her situation.

Agreeing to stay the night in his apartment, and her last conscious memory: falling into bed and hugging his pillow to her; breathing in the comforting male muskiness that clung to it.

Then nothing. Just a tumbling, headlong free fall into a dark and dreamless state.

She was accustomed by her work to awakening fully alert; to be so out of it this morning meant she must have slept like the dead last night. She threw back the covers and padded on bare feet into the bathroom. She used the facilities there, splashed cold water on her face and brushed her teeth. Finally feeling a return of her customary energy, she returned to the bedroom.

She pulled on her shorts and shirt over the teddy she'd slept ·in and then simply stood there a moment digging her bare toes into the carpet while she tried to decide what to do next. Vincent's rumpled bed caught her eye and she made it up, taking care to emulate the militarily squared corners she'd noticed yesterday.

There was a note taped to the front door, fluttering at eye level. She discovered it when she was preparing to let herself out a short while later. It read, in barely legible penmanship: *Plan to interview your aunt and uncle at their bar this afternoon. If you want to be there, meet me around three.* He'd signed it with a hastily scratched "V."

It was closer to four by the time he got there. Ivy was sitting at the bar talking to Mack and Babe when he arrived and all three turned anxiously when the door opened. They were silent as they watched him pause momentarily just inside the door to let his eyes adjust to the dim interior. Scents of the afternoon thunderstorm blew in with him, a mixture of clean rain and hammered dust.

As he crossed the room, a flash of lightning briefly illuminated the rainwashed window and dulled the glow of neon on the beer signs that hung there. Vincent had almost reached the trio by the time accompanying thunder cracked in its wake. Mack came out from behind the bar to greet him.

"Mr. Merrick?" Vincent sized him up while he offered his hand. "I'm Detective Vincent D'Ambruzzi. Has Ivy had a chance to tell you why I'm here?"

Babe went on full alert as soon as he identified himself, her concern over this sudden madness in Ivy's life temporarily overshadowed by speculation. Ivy hadn't mentioned the policeman's first name when she'd been explaining everything else. A funny thing, that.

She'd told them she was working with a Detective D'Ambruzzi and that he was her neighbor, but she'd neglected to cite his first name as Vincent. Remembering a certain conversation with her niece in this very bar just the other night, Babe pulled her attention away from the policeman long enough to consider Ivy thoughtfully. Her niece's giveaway blush and the way she avoided eye contact confirmed Babe's suspicions and she turned back to the detective with increased curiosity.

Her interest was reciprocated. Vincent was curious about the Merricks after listening to Ivy talk about them. Her Aunt Babe stood to offer a firm handshake. She was a tall, big-boned woman with greying brown hair and Ivy's intelligent green eyes. They seemed to peer right into his soul as if in search of some vital truth.

Mack Merrick was an inch or two shorter than his wife and niece. He was a solidly built man with a wide barrel chest and short, muscular legs. His grey hair grew in a neatly trimmed fringe around a tanned, age-spotted pate and his eyes were large and brown beneath bristling grey eyebrows. Vincent had already discovered in his brief conversation with the man that Mack was blunt in speech. Both he and his wife exuded a natural warmth, however, and a concern for their niece's plight that they couldn't quite disguise.

They settled at the bar. Vincent and the two women took a seat on the padded stools, while Mack assumed the position in which he felt most at home: behind the bar. Without asking, he pulled a draft, tossed a coaster on the bar and set the foaming glass in front of Vincent. For a moment nobody spoke and the only sound to break the stillness was the steady drum of rain beating against the tinted windows.

Vincent took a sip of his beer and set the glass down on the paper coaster in front of him. He swiveled his seat sideways in an attempt to face his audience.

The older couple's faces showed signs of strain and Vincent addressed his first remarks to them.

"I won't tell you not to worry, because I know that's asking the impossible," he said, turning his head side to side to meet their eyes directly. "And

I won't BS you. This situation is serious and I want you to treat it as such. I realize you're probably wishing to God your niece wasn't involved in this, but through no fault of her own she is and we can't change that. But I'd also like you to know it's not as bad as it could be.''

"A rapist is sending her flowers and love letters," Mack said gruffly. "How much worse could it get?''

Vincent didn't attempt to sugar-coat it. "He could know where she lives," he replied flatly. "He could have knowledge of her telephone number." He took a sip of his beer and then sat holding it, rolling the glass between his palms. He turned slightly to meet Mack's gaze head on.

"Disturbing as all this is, Mr. Merrick, there is a bright side. As of this moment the man only knows two things for certain: where she works and the location of your bar. We're assuming from the note she received yesterday that he was here some time on Wednesday night when Ivy came in with her colleagues; there's simply no other reasonable explanation." He turned back to face Ivy, looking at her closely for the first time since he'd walked into the bar. A strand of hair, which had escaped the rest of the glossy mass swinging straight to her collarbones, kept snagging his attention. It bisected her cheek, gossamer as a cobweb, and stuck to the corner of her mouth. He tried to ignore it, but in the end it proved to be too much for him and he found himself reaching out almost against his will to brush it away. "Did you explain to your aunt and uncle your suspicions as to how he learned you were coming here?" he inquired.

"Yes."

He addressed the Merricks again. "The most helpful thing you can do for Ivy is to undertake a surveillance in her behalf.''

"You got it," Mack said with grim determination

and when Vincent turned to Babe he saw her nodding her agreement.

"Did either of you notice anyone paying undue attention to her Wednesday night?"

"No." Babe shook her head regretfully. "We talked about this before you arrived and we can't think of anyone. There were several new people here that night, but except for some of Ivy's group I can't picture a face to save my soul."

"If it helps," Vincent supplied, "the man we're looking for is believed to be a blue-eyed blond, five feet eleven or so, of average build."

Mack scoured his mind for even the vaguest image to fit the description but finally shrugged. "Sorry." His expression plainly stated his self-disgust.

"Don't go beating up on yourself over this, Mr. Merrick," Vincent advised. "You had no particular reason to be on the alert that night. Now that you know, just keep an eye peeled. I have a feeling that, forewarned, you won't miss a trick."

Ivy impulsively reached for his hand and gave it a squeeze. This was turning out to be much less awkward than she had anticipated and she was particularly grateful for Vincent's gentle handling of her relatives' feelings. When he turned in surprise at her touch and met her eyes, she tried to silently convey that message.

He rubbed his thumb over her knuckles but when her uncle suddenly slapped a basket of pretzels on the bar in front of him he started and dropped her hand guiltily.

"Call me Mack," Merrick advised. "Hearing you call me Mr. Merrick makes me want to look over my shoulder for my father—and the old man's been dead for nearly a decade now."

"And I'm Babe," Ivy's aunt insisted. She had been observing the small interactions between the detective and her niece with interest. Like a good many bar owners, she was a people watcher by nature. And from what she'd observed here today she'd lay odds that their attraction for each other had by no means run its course, despite what Ivy had said to the contrary the other night.

"It occurs to me," Babe continued thoughtfully, "that the man must have come in after the bar was already pretty full. I spent most of my time that night in the kitchen, but I'm sure Mack would have noticed if he'd arrived when the place was still half empty."

Mack nodded. "That's true," he confirmed. "Babe and me like to watch folks when we've got the time. Particularly folks we don't ordinarily see; we compare little histories we've invented for them. Also, I can state with ninety-nine percent certainty that he didn't sit at the bar or I would have noticed him for sure. That leaves the two waitress stations and they were manned by . . . let's see . . . Babe, who was on that night?"

"Sandy was," Ivy supplied. "She had our tables."

Mack snapped his fingers. "Yeah, that's right. And Judy had the other." He leaned his forearms on the bar. "One of the girls is bound to remember a lone male. Sandy's due in at six, Detective, if you wanna stick around to talk to her. Judy has tonight off, I'm afraid, but I can either give you her number or question her myself." His face was alight with the prospect of doing something concrete. "Also, there are any number of regulars we could talk to. One of them might have noticed something."

Vincent felt a small tug of excitement, which he sternly tried to squash. He knew better than to get his hopes up, but this was the first opportunity this case had ever generated to obtain a potential description . . . something more concrete than the nebulous blond and blue, five feet eleven. He swiveled his stool around to face the man behind the bar. "What're the chances of some of the same patrons that were here Wednesday dropping by tonight?"

"With this weather . . . ?" Mack shrugged. "Hard to say. Our clientele's pretty loyal, though, and we don't call 'em regulars for nothing. I imagine a good portion of them are likely to show up."

"Do you have an office or any other room where I could interview them privately?" He moved aside his glass and the basket of snacks and leaned further toward the older man.

"Tonight?" Ivy touched his sleeve. When he turned his head, it was to see her regarding him with an expression of guilt. "Vincent," she said, "you're off duty now. We don't expect you to give up your free evening."

Glancing over his shoulder at her aunt and then back at her uncle, he could see they didn't agree at all. Clearly, if their expressions were any indication, they wouldn't object if he sacrificed every free moment he had—not if it meant removing this threat from their niece's life. They held their silence, however, and allowed Ivy the right to try to talk him out of it without their interference. He had to admire their restraint. "It's all right, Ivy," he said. "I don't mind."

"But we can't just rob you of your Friday night. I'd feel awful."

"Don't," he advised. "I didn't have anything planned and I'm not doing this strictly for you, anyway. I've been working this case for three months now and it's like chasing a damn shadow. This is the closest I've come to an opportunity to put a face to the man I'm seeking." He looked from her to Mack to Babe. "It has to be handled as discreetly as possible, though. For all we know, the guy may still stop by periodically hoping to see

Ivy. If that's true, and he hears the police have been brought in, it could unhinge him entirely . . . and above all else we want to avoid that. We don't want to precipitate any action that might ultimately be harmful to her.''

As soon as he had ascertained there was a room he could use, he pushed back from the bar. ''I'd better go grab some dinner while I have the chance,'' he said. ''I'll be back in about an hour.''

''Now don't be silly,'' Babe said and rose from her stool. ''You relax, young man—unwind a little.'' She turned to her husband. ''Mack, fix him a drink. I'll whip us up something to eat; it'll only take a few minutes.'' She strode away.

Standing by his stool watching her walk away, Vincent opened his mouth to protest, but Ivy nudged him in the ribs with her elbow. ''Save your breath,'' she advised, looking up at him with a lopsided smile. ''Nobody argues with Auntie Babe and wins—not, at least, once she's made up her mind to feed them. And trust me, Vincent, it's an argument you won't mind losing anyhow. Just look at Uncle Mack's waistline. She cooks even better than you do.''

Mack laughed and slapped his comfortably expanded stomach. ''That's the God's truth, detective; Babe's the best damn cook in town. So what can I fix you to drink?''

Vincent glanced toward the windows and saw that the rain was still sluicing in sheets down the panes. Turning back, he gave in, wondering at himself all the while. It wasn't like him to not maintain his professional distance.

Then again, there hadn't been one iota of normalcy in his life since the moment he'd first clapped eyes on a particular long-legged, red-headed M.D. He accepted a drink and discussed with Mack until dinner was ready the chances of the Mariners making the World Series. They ate at one of the tables in the lounge and while the women cleared the dishes, Mack showed him to the small crowded office in back.

Working easily together, they rearranged several cases of liquor to free a little room around the desk, pulled up a chair in front of it, and laid out a tablet and pen on its top.

"Is there a back door somewhere in the bar?" Vincent asked as he straightened from loading the last case. He slapped his dusty hands against the seat of his pants.

"Christ Almighty, boy, what do you think we just finished blocking?" Mack tilted his head toward the wall of cases. "The entire time we were moving them, I was prayin' to God the fire department don't show up tonight."

"Oh, hell, I thought that was a closet." Vincent looked around at the confined space. "I guess I'll move them over to that corner," he finally said. He looked at Ivy's uncle. "I don't want to alarm you when chances that the rapist will show his face here tonight are practically nil," he said. "But on the night we believe he first spotted Ivy, I spent some time talking to her at the hospital. Now, I can't be sure he even saw her that night, and chances are he never saw me. But to be on the safe side, I'd just as soon leave by this door when I've finished here tonight."

Mack studied him thoughtfully. "You're a mighty cautious son of a bitch, aren't you?"

"Yeah, I suppose I am." Vincent returned Mack's look, meeting his eyes squarely. "Most likely I'm being a lot more cautious than's necessary. But I'd sure hate to see Ivy get hurt because I overlooked something simple."

"Can't argue with that," Mack agreed and bent

his back into helping Vincent move the cases once again.

"What's out there anyway?" Vincent grunted as he hefted two cases at once. "Alleyway?"

"Yeah." Mack unloaded the case he was transferring and stopped to pull a clean handkerchief from his back pocket. Mopping his brow, he said, "There's a couple of parking spaces just outside the door. You might as well move your car back here and have Ivy move hers, too. I'll move ours to the lot down the street to make room." He hefted the last case. As soon as he'd settled it in its new spot, he grabbed a windbreaker off a hook on the back of the office door, rummaged up a key, and opened the door into the alley. Vincent went out into the lounge to collect Ivy's keys. Meeting Mack in the rain-drenched parking lot moments later, he tossed him the keys to her car and they transferred both vehicles to the alley.

Several of the regulars began to trickle in soon after that. One had been present Wednesday night, and Vincent took him back into the office. It was a short interview, as the man had left before the bar had begun to really fill up and he was sure there hadn't been an unfamiliar young blond man present while he was still there. ("I been comin' to this bar for nigh on twenty years, son, and I know who's familiar and who ain't. 'Cept for the Pennington kids' group, there weren't nobody new while I was here.") Vincent ushered him out and discovered that the cocktail waitress named Sandy had arrived for work. He summoned her into the office.

Sandy remembered two lone men in her section that night, but one was dark and had been there several times before. The other man had worn a baseball cap, which he'd never removed.

"He might have been a blond, Detective," she

said uncertainly, "but I couldn't swear to it. For a Wednesday, it was unusually busy and I didn't pay attention."

"Had you ever seen him before?"

"No, sir. He was like a lot of the new ones, though. Watched everyone and didn't sing much himself. He hasn't been back."

"Do you remember what time he left?"

Sandy consulted a mental memory bank. "Early, I think. Let's see . . . he nursed a vodka and tonic and must have left around . . . oh, ten, I'd say. Yeah, I'm pretty sure it was ten, because the Garrisons took his table and they usually get here around that time."

"Okay, Sandy, thanks." Vincent walked her out, silently berating himself for his unrealistic expectations. How had he let himself hope for an easy identification? He knew better than that. Hell, he'd be lucky if the waitress who was off tonight had anything more to contribute.

He leaned against the wall in the shadowy hallway that led to the rest rooms, pool room and office and watched Ivy for a moment. She had taken over for Sandy and was threading between tables with a tray of drinks balanced on her palm. He watched her reach a table in the corner and deftly serve the four people there. Laughing at something one of them said, she bent forward to collect a dirty ashtray and replaced it with a clean one. Watching the faded denim of her jeans stretch tautly over her bottom, Vincent had a sudden flash of her in his bed early this morning.

He'd slipped into his room to collect his clothes for the day, fully intending to be quickly in and out. But the sight of her had stopped him cold just inside the doorway.

She'd been curled on her side, the blankets kicked down and only the sheet twisted around her. Her head had rested on a corner of his pillow; the rest she'd had hugged in her arms and her hair had spilled across her face, hiding her features. The pillow had covered her front, the sheet most of her back. But one bent leg had been exposed from mid-calf clear up to the high-cut, silky little one-piece thing she'd been wearing. The lace that edged it had faithfully cupped her hip and a small visible portion of her rounded white butt.

He'd stood there staring at that long sleek leg and experienced such a hot swell of resentment he'd hardly known what to do with himself. Unable to tear his eyes away, he'd called himself ten kinds of fool. Dammit, hadn't he settled this once and for all last night when he'd finally stopped trying to convince himself he wasn't attracted to her?

Apparently simply admitting he was sexually attracted, no matter how unwillingly, did not equate with actually accepting it.

He'd had no other choice this morning but to acknowledge the extent of his inability to control his reaction to her. At the same time, however, he'd fiercely resented his own weakness and the effortless power she seemed to wield over him. The strength of wanting that had swept over him as he'd stood there staring at her and his helplessness to prevent or control it had generated a hostility that had been transferred directly to her.

As he watched her now he knew he had to come to terms with the way he felt, and he either had to fish or cut bait, as the farmers back in Iowa had been fond of saying. He didn't *want* to want her, that was a given. But he did anyway.

So, was he going to fight for what he wanted— and quit resenting her for causing him to covet it—or was he going to back out of her life entirely . . . even if that meant finding himself somewhere else to live? He sure as hell couldn't go on the way he'd been. Until he made some sort of a decision, all he could do, as he had done this morning, was back out of range and remove himself from the sight of her.

He interviewed several more regulars throughout the night and by the time he'd finished with the last one he was discouraged and frustrated. The final result reminded him of one of those old vaudville good-news/bad-news routines. The good news was: one or two people remembered seeing a man Wednesday night who fit his admittedly ambiguous description. The bad news? Those who remembered such a man couldn't seem to agree when it came to the details that might enable him to put together a composite drawing.

He had managed to extract a commitment from them to come down to the station some time during next week to look through the mug-shot books, but God alone knew how successful that would turn out to be. At the moment he wasn't exactly bristling with optimism, but you never could tell; perhaps once he'd had the weekend to unwind, his outlook would improve.

He wasn't holding his breath, however. The longer he sat alone in this crowded, utilitarian office, listening to the sounds of lighthearted camaraderie that filtered through the walls, the more irritable and alienated he began to feel.

He was so damn tired of being left out of everything. Which was kind of a ridiculous attitude, considering this little Pioneer Square bar hardly compared to the entire town of Gentry, Iowa, where he'd grown up in the only ethnic family in a farming community of close-knit, fourth generation Swedes. His presence had been tolerated only until he'd hit puberty. That was when the local farmers had suddenly begun fearing for their pretty blonde daughters' virtue in the company of that dark-skinned, foreign looking D'Ambruzzi boy. The isolation he felt here tonight had nothing to do with that one-horse-town kind of mentality. It was entirely different . . . and yet somehow managed to feel the same.

No, that was crazy. *He* had been the one to decide he was staying away from the bar and all its attendant festivities tonight. Reminding himself of that, however, seemed to have little impact on the growing blackness of his mood.

Get a grip, D'Ambruzzi. Vincent tried very hard to short-circuit his moodiness with a stern lecture. He reminded himself that self-pity was pretty damn unattractive—marginally understandable in a teenager, perhaps, but hardly suited to a man in his mid-thirties.

But dammit, on the other hand, it was Friday night, his work was done, and he didn't feel like packing it up and going home to his empty apartment. *She* was out there in the other room, probably living it up without a care in the world, while he was stuck back here all by himself, listening to everything from a distance, excluded from the fun.

As usual.

Besides, who ever said mood swings were supposed to be rational? Emotions were what they damn well were . . . and, like it or not, he was in a bad mood.

So sue him.

Chapter 9

Contrary to Vincent's black-tempered suspicions, Ivy wasn't having the time of her life. She was, however, fairly content to be where she was. For minutes at a time, surrounded by the family members who had shown up tonight and other regulars whom she had known for years, she was able to forget the dangerous new twist her life had taken. She felt safe here, and safer yet knowing Vincent was just down the hall in the office.

She kept expecting him to join them in the bar when he finished questioning the regulars. A patron she knew Vincent had been interviewing returned to the bar, but watch as she might, no one got up to replace him. Still Vincent didn't appear. She allowed an additional twenty minutes to go by before she finally pushed back from the table and rose to check on him. Surely he wouldn't have gone without even saying good-bye, would he?

Striding briskly down the hallway, she had to

admit she didn't have the first idea what Vincent D'Ambruzzi might do.

When the door to the women's restroom suddenly opened and Sherry stepped out into the hall, Ivy had to pull up sharply to avoid a collision. The next several seconds involved them in a silent, satiric ballet. Intricate footwork was executed in an attempt to dodge out of each other's way before their eyes suddenly met and they burst into laughter.

"Now that was an interesting little piece of slapstick," Sherry said as she stepped back and grinned at her cousin. "And speaking of the witless, has Terry introduced you to his latest little boopsie yet?" She shook her head in disgust. "I wish to God my brother would just once ask out a normal woman."

"Define normal," Ivy challenged.

"Someone who doesn't squeal 'Hoop-wow, thanks for the refill' when he blows in her ear," her cousin promptly responded.

Ivy couldn't help her spontaneous laughter. "Sherry MacDonald, shame on you." Then, thinking she probably shouldn't encourage her, she added lamely, "How rude." She tried to make her tone of voice remonstrative but knew she was just blowing smoke.

Sherry knew it too. She shrugged. "Am I wrong?" She raised a brow. "Forget she's every bit as airheaded as his usual parade of bimbettes—I've almost grown accustomed to that. But this time he's probably flirting with a jail sentence as well. If this one's legal I'll eat my shirt."

"Well, prepare to chow down," Ivy said, "because I happen to know she's over twenty-one." She gazed at her cousin with suspect guilelessness. "I was sitting right there when Sandy carded her."

"Swell." Sherry laughed and shook her head. "I

don't get it, Ive, I really don't. He's so intelligent himself, you'd think he'd at least want someone who could carry on a conversation once the sex was over." Then she shrugged her brother's taste in women aside and her expression sobered as she wrapped a plump arm around Ivy's waist to give her a squeeze. "So, how're you holding up? Auntie Babe told Mom, who told me what's been going on."

Ivy admitted to being spooked by the notes she'd received. "But I'm hanging in there. Vincent—" she tipped her chin in the general direction of the office "—gave up his Friday night to interview some of the M & B regulars who were here Wednesday. He's hoping to get a description of the guy who sent it to me."

"Oh, yeah?" Sherry glanced speculatively at the closed door. "He still in there?"

"I don't know," Ivy replied. "I was just going to check."

"Ooh goody." Sherry's arm at Ivy's waist guided her down the hallway. "What are we waitin' for? I gotta get another look at this guy to see if he's as hot as I remember."

When they burst into the office, it was to find Vincent tilted back on his chair, feet on the desk, staring moodily at the ceiling. He had removed his jacket and loosened his tie and Sherry stared in fascination at the gun clipped to his belt as she said, "Why are you sitting here all by yourself? Come on out and join us in the bar."

"We've been expecting you," Ivy added. She was pleased to see he hadn't left, but wary of the expression in the dark eyes he turned their way. She approached him cautiously. "Is something wrong, Vincent?"

He swung his feet off the desk, letting the front legs of his wooden chair thump against the linoleum floor as he straightened. Tempted to unload his vituperative temper onto her, he barely managed to restrain himself. Reminding himself grimly that it wasn't her fault he was feeling misused and knowing he had let the silence stretch out too long, he finally replied shortly, "No. I'm just feeling sorry for myself." Before they could ask why, he turned assessing eyes on Sherry. "Who are you?"

She flashed him a smile and replied cheerily, "Ivy's favorite cousin."

"I'd forgotten you haven't actually met," Ivy said and performed the introduction.

"Charmed, I'm sure." Sherry smiled widely, her ebullient mood unaffected by Vincent's curt nod of acknowledgement. "Now that that's out of the way, c'mon out and join us."

Torn between a desire to cling to his bad temper and the draw of her sincere friendliness, for a moment Vincent didn't say anything at all. Then he acknowledged he was acting like a jerk. He turned to Ivy's cousin and declined her invitation with genuine regret, telling her the same thing he'd told her uncle.

"Oh." Sherry looked crestfallen. "Well, sure, that makes sense, I suppose. But I can't say I'm not disappointed. I was hoping to get to know you." She watched the brooding expression that crossed his face as his attention wandered from her to focus on Ivy. Then as if her words had belatedly registered, he glanced back at her and a small smile curved his full mouth.

"Another time maybe." He shrugged a shoulder. "Thanks for the invitation, though," he added. "I appreciate it."

He rose to his feet and began shuffling his papers together. "There's nothing more I can do here, so I guess I might as well take off."

"I'll go with you," Ivy said. When his head jerked

up from the contemplation of his notes to stare at her, she added in sudden confusion, "I . . . that is—perhaps you have other plans." Oh, God, he'd probably made a date with some other poor woman he planned to have sex with and leave. "Forget it. I can get one of my cousins to see me home."

"No," he immediately vetoed that option. "I'll follow you in my car. I would have suggested it myself but, uh, are you sure you don't want to stay awhile? It's Friday night. Just because I'm afraid to show my face out there doesn't mean you have to pack it in so early." Ivy shook her head and they left by the back door.

Out in the bar after Ivy and Vincent left, Sherry said to her brother, "That's one relationship I sure as hell don't understand. I know they've slept together and it's obvious there's still something hot and heavy going on, but whatever it is, neither of them seems to trust it. He radiates this moody-broody sexuality whenever he looks at her, and Ivy doesn't act like herself at all." She swirled the ice in her drink and shook her head. "You should have heard them tripping all over themselves to provide the other with an excuse for not having to leave together."

Terry made a noncommittal noise and Sherry studied him with sudden suspicion. "*You* don't happen to know what's goin' on, do you?" she asked. "If you do, Terry, you'd better spit it out. After all, it's your fault she won't tell me anything anymore."

"How do you figure that?"

"You made me break her confidence."

Her reasoning made him smile, but unlike his sister he knew how to keep his mouth shut . . . regardless of who put on the pressure. "She hasn't said anything to me, either, Sher, but I wouldn't sweat it. Either they'll work it out or they won't." Next to him, his date giggled shrilly at something that was said across the table and he shifted so she was subtly blocked by his shoulder. He leaned toward his twin. "Sea of Love" was started by one person, soon joined in by everyone, and he had to raise his voice slightly. "Speaking of recently strange behavior," he said with studied casualness, "What's the story with Jaz these days?"

Men, Jaz could have told him had the question been directed to her instead of Sherry. Wasn't it always? Or to be more precise, the deficiency of one special man in her life.

She'd never harbored a burning desire for a career the way Ivy had, and upon occasion she'd regretted that lack . . . but never for long. As Terry had pointed out, Ivy had had to watch her parents die for that ambition to be born and Jaz remembered the nightmares, which for years had plagued her cousin, far too well to ever begrudge Ivy her hard-earned success. No, for the most part, she was perfectly content with her position at the bank. Besides, you had to desire a calling of that nature to an almost obsessive degree to be willing to sacrifice as many years as Ivy had to get where she was now. Jaz knew that she didn't have that kind of singleminded drive.

She envied Ivy her sense of direction, but the person who really stirred her deepest, most covetous emotions was Sherry.

What *she* had was what Jaz most wanted out of life. Just one nice, ordinary man to love her simply for herself the way Ben so clearly loved Sherry.

It drove her crazy that Sherry never seemed to realize just how lucky she was. Not that her cousin didn't love Ben to distraction—she did. But at the same time, she harbored this ludicrous assumption that Jaz's life must be so much more exciting than her own. She had a blind spot when it came to Jaz's looks and to the fact that she didn't have to wage the same war against weight that Sherry constantly struggled with.

Jaz's own emotions were mixed when it came to her physical attractiveness. Part of her honestly believed the only thing it had ever accomplished was to scare off all the decent, normal men. She seemed to intimidate the nice guys, while attracting more than her share of the shallow pretty boys. She got more attention than she needed from men who didn't desire *her* so much as they desired the acquisition of a decorative prize.

Yet at the same time, she couldn't deny that she did everything in her power to stave off the ultimate deterioration of her beauty. She exercised, she dieted, she took care of her skin; and still she was feeling the pinch of desperation as she approached her thirtieth birthday. Not only was her biological clock ticking louder and louder, her looks were not going to last forever and deep inside she feared if she didn't find someone to call her own before they faded, she never would.

Her mood these days flucuated like a yo-yo, but for the most part she tended to be an optimist and at the moment her spirits were on a definite upswing. For yesterday a man had approached her desk at the bank seeking information about investments, and to her pleasure had stayed to talk to her once their business was concluded. He was attractive, single, and owned his own flower shop. And best of all, he had appeared to see beyond the perfection of her face to the person underneath.

She was crossing her fingers for her dinner date tomorrow night with Tyler Griffus. She hoped it would be the beginning of something special.

* * *

The rain had stopped by the time Vincent and Ivy arrived back at the apartment house. Without speaking, he met her at her car and escorted her to the building, deftly steering her around the puddles that dotted the parking lot.

By the time the elevator doors closed behind them they still hadn't exchanged a word, and the silence wasn't a comfortable one. He stood much too close and stared at her much too intently to allow for relaxation. Was it really necessary to leave only an inch of air space separating them when there was an entire, if not overly-large elevator to house only two people. That damn sexuality of his was once again in overdrive, but from the look on his face it appeared that it was against his will. He wanted her, that was clear. But he wasn't happy about it.

And with a blast of insight, she suddenly realized that it probably hadn't been game-playing after all that had made him walk away without a word after they'd made love. As she stared into his smoldering black eyes, she also took note of the heavy black brows gathered in displeasure over his nose. In a flash of revelation, she thought incredulously, "You were scared. Oh, God, I'll be damned. Big, tough Vincent D'Ambruzzi was *scared*."

That was not a possibility she'd ever considered. Okay, perhaps she hadn't considered anything from his point of view, she'd been too busy slapping Band-Aids on her own wounds. Yet it seemed to make sense. She had long suspected some sort of failed relationship in his past, a history that, at the very least, contributed to his ridiculous suspiciousness. Not once, however, had she directly connected it with his treatment of her.

Not that it excused him, of course, but it was kind of . . .

No! Oh, no no no no no. The elevator door slid open at their floor and Ivy pushed Vincent aside and headed purposefully down the hall, furious with herself. *Are you out of your pointy little head?* she demanded in silent outrage. *That must be the oldest trap in the world. Don't you dare go romanticizing his actions—not when they hurt so damn much!*

Slow to divorce himself from the perpetual battle that seemed to rage between his brain and his hormones whenever he was in her company, Vincent caught up with her at her door. He watched as she fished her key out of her purse, waited while she inserted it in the lock and opened it. She stepped inside her apartment, turned to look at him with large, wary eyes, and with a murmured goodnight started to close the door.

Vincent pushed himself upright from his lounge against the wall. What was this? He didn't like being asked to follow her home only to get dumped on her doorstep. Reaching out, he wrapped his long fingers around her upper arm to stay her. "Wait a minute!" he demanded. "That's it then? Just slam the door in my face—no conversation?"

"Yes," she agreed flatly. It wasn't conversation he wanted in any case, and she needed time to think.

"At the bar . . . Why did you offer to leave with me?"

She shrugged.

This was a first. She *never* shied away from giving him an earful. Not once had he known her to back away from a confrontation as she was doing now, and her apparent indifference left him feeling hampered and unsettled. "What happened to Ivy Pennington, stellar communicator?" he demanded in a voice loaded with enough sarcasm to guarantee she'd come out swinging.

She declined to rise to the bait. "She took the night off."

He ground his teeth in frustration. "Dammit, why won't you talk to me? What are you so afraid of?"

Ivy met his eyes incredulously and her laughter was edged with bitterness. "Oh, God, Vincent, where do I start?" *Do I begin with the fact that even though you've hurt me once and I've sworn never to give you the opportunity to do it again, I'm seriously contemplating excuses for your past behavior?*

No. She sure as hell wasn't going to tell him that.

Instead, she turned the tables. "I could ask you the same thing, couldn't I? What are *you* so afraid of?"

His hand tightened briefly on her arm, but suddenly his face was wiped free of all expression. "I don't know what you're talking about," he denied stiffly.

It was more or less what she'd expected, but that didn't stop her from feeling angry and disappointed. "No, of course you don't." She peeled his fingers off her arm and looked him in the eye. "So why don't we just leave it at that?"

That's exactly what they should do, he told himself. Yet he couldn't seem to prevent himself from demanding, "No, dammit, let's not. I want to know what you mean by that."

She could hardly say, "Did you disappear without a word the night you spent with me because it got to you?" Instead, she said, "I'm talking about your hit-and-run sexual habits, Vincent. How many women have you suckered into bed, only to disappear as soon as you got what you wanted?" Then she held her breath, suddenly doubting the veracity of her so-called revelation. What if he said "dozens, baby, so what's it to ya?"

Bracing herself for the worst, she was caught unprepared when instead of replying verbally, his long arm whipped out and wrapped around her waist, jerking her to him. His free hand tunneled beneath the hair at her nape and he held her head in an iron grip as his mouth slammed down on hers.

It was a kiss filled with anger, lust, frustration. All demanding suction and wet, carnal probing, it was hot enough to raise blisters on the surface of her veins.

It devastated her. She'd almost convinced herself he couldn't have been nearly as good as she'd remembered, but this ravishment of her mouth and senses shattered that theory beyond recall. Helpless to do anything else, Ivy kissed him back, her fingers curled around his jacket lapels to anchor herself.

Too soon, he ripped his mouth away and pushed her back, holding her at arm's length. "None," he said hoarsely and gave her a slight shake. "Okay? Are you happy? Until you, I'd been *celibate* for three years."

For just a second she didn't connect his words with the question she'd put to him. Then her mouth dropped open.

Seeing her raw disbelief made him edgy and furious with himself. Jesus, how had he allowed himself to get sucked into this? She'd given him the chance to drop it, but, no, his ego hadn't been able to face that hint of contempt in her voice and he'd just had to push, hadn't he?

Disgusted with himself, he released her and plowed his fingers through his hair. Then, gripping the tension-tightened, knotted muscles in his neck, he turned his back on her.

Ivy stared at his bowed head, the brown hand kneading his neck, the stretch of jacket across tensed muscles, and whispered, "Why?"

His hand stilled and he turned his head to look at her. "Why was I celibate?" he clarified coolly. "Why you? Why didn't I stay?"

"*Yes!*"

He dropped his hand to his side, turned to face her fully and sighed. Looking up and down the dimly illuminated hallway he said wryly, "Do you think I could come in?"

"What? Oh!" She had forgotten where they were: out in the hallway where he'd yanked her out of her doorway to kiss her. She could feel her cheeks heat and hastily stepped back and gestured him in. Vincent closed the door behind him and followed her to her kitchen, where she turned to look at him. "Do you want some coffee?" she asked.

What he really wanted was to be anywhere but here. He wasn't ready for this. He knew he owed her an explanation, but, Jesus, he didn't want to go into LaDonna or his refusal to get into another relationship. He hated displaying his private life. Why couldn't they just screw their brains out, ignore the past, explore whatever this thing was between them until it burned itself out? Why did women always want to talk while men preferred action? "Yeah," he finally said. "Coffee'd be fine."

She made a pot and they took their cups into the living room. Seated on the couch facing him, one foot tucked up beneath her, Ivy took a sip and studied his closed expression over the rim of her cup. A faint, ironic smile tipped up one corner of her mouth and she shook her head. "My God, Vincent. You look as if you'd rather be having root canal surgery without anesthesia."

He grunted.

Her good humor deserted her. "Listen," she

said impatiently, "you're the one who was so hot for a conversation. If you've got nothing to say, let's just say good night."

"I thought instead of shuttin' the damn door in my face you at least might have asked me what I found out tonight."

"Oh!" She blushed. "You're right." Ivy set her cup down on the table and leaned toward him. "What did you find out?"

"Nothing, really." Nothing concrete, anyhow.

She stared at him in exasperation. "Then I guess it would've been a mighty short conversation, wouldn't it? Hardly worth your getting so bent out of shape."

"Dammit, Ivy, that's not the point!" Vincent leaned forward, disposed of his cup, and then rubbed his hands roughly over his face. Turning his head to look at her, he said in a more moderate tone, "Look, this isn't easy for me, okay?"

She nodded.

"First of all, I'd like to get something off my chest. I'm sorry for the way I disappeared without a word after we made love." His expression lost its disgruntled expression as he reached out to brush a strand of hair away from her cheek. "I've been wanting to tell you that for a long time now, honest to God, but the opportunity never seemed to present itself."

"It hurt, Vincent. I felt used."

"Yeah, I discovered that when you laid into me at the precinct last week, but you gotta believe . . ." He looked away, rubbing the side of his neck. After a moment, he looked back, sighed, and said, "Look, I really don't have an excuse. I didn't deliberately set out to hurt you, but I guess the truth is I was thinking of myself, period. I didn't consider how you would be affected by my actions. That night, Ivy . . . it was good. It was very good. And not just because it had been a long time.''

"But?''

"But, dammit, it was almost too good, and maybe you're right—maybe I was afraid. Afraid it'd lead to something . . . I don't know . . . monogamous. Afraid you'd expect things from me I don't think I'm equipped to give. I've learned the hard way that relationships and me just aren't compatible. So I took a walk to avoid getting into one with you.''

Ivy studied his rigid expression. "You've been through a particularly rough relationship, I take it.''

His bark of laughter was harsh and humorless. "Yeah, you might say that,'' he agreed flatly, spearing her with bitter eyes. "I was married for four years to a slut who spread her legs at the drop of a hat.'' He watched her eyes widen and just in case she might have missed his meaning, clarified, "Not just for me, Ivy—for any guy who had the wherewithal to get it up.''

It explained so much, yet at the same time she was shocked, both by the knowledge he had been married—something she'd never considered—and by the image his words painted of his ex-wife. "Oh, Vincent, I'm sorry,'' she said, impulsively reaching for his hand. Squeezing it, she added, "Truly. I don't know what to say to you. I'm . . . surprised.''

Humiliation tended to make him nasty and he jerked his hand free. "I don't need your commiseration,'' he snarled. Swell . . . she was offering him pity. *Just* the emotion he wanted to evoke. "And exactly what do you find so damn surprising? That any woman would ever marry me in the first place?''

"No,'' she retorted with gentle truthfulness, meeting his enraged stare head-on. "That any woman would have the strength to mess around on the side after she'd been made love to by you."

"Trust me," he assured her cynically, "When it came to sleeping around, The Bitch was inexhaustible." His tone didn't encourage further condolences. Nevertheless, her words went like a healing balm straight to a wound on his ego that had festered unchecked for the past three years.

The way he'd uttered the rude appellation as if it were his ex-wife's given name captured Ivy's attention and she asked with unthinking curiosity, "Why do you call her that—'The Bitch?'" Then she immediately grimaced and flapped her hand dismissively. "Sorry. Incredibly stupid question."

Vincent actually smiled. "As a matter of fact, I'm not the one who bestowed the title on her—that was courtesy of Anna Graham. She and her husband Keith are friends of mine, and Anna disliked LaDonna on sight. Unlike me," he said without rancor, "Anna recognized The Bitch for what she was the moment they met. In any case, although I never heard about it until after we broke up, that's how Anna invariably referred to LaDonna whenever she discussed her with Keith." He shrugged indifferently. "It's apt."

"So," Ivy questioned hesitantly, "are you still in love with her, Vincent?" Was that the reason he was so gun shy about a relationship?

"Hell, no!" He was seriously offended. "I just finished telling you she slept with every guy in town—what d'ya take me for, Ivy, some wimp-willed idiot?"

"Sor-ree." She'd thought it a reasonable enough question—God knew, even when circumstances were at their worst it wasn't always possible to turn off emotions. "Why do men always get so macho whenever they're asked about their feelings?"

"Probably because women are always asking assinine questions!"

She took exception to his reply. "It's not assinine! I'm just trying to figure out where I stand in all this."

"Where you . . . ?" He sat up straight. "What's it got to do with you?"

"The insulting way you've treated me from the moment we met hasn't been a result of your past history?" He just stared at her as if he couldn't believe her herculean ego and she added with some confusion, "I'm sorry, I guess I don't understand why you've told me all this. When you said I was the first woman you'd slept with, I thought perhaps you meant . . ."

"Don't flatter yourself, sister," he interrupted with insulting speed and an arrogance of tone she found offensive. "I didn't say you were the first since LaDonna, just the first in a long while." He wasn't about to discuss with her the way LaDonna's faithlessness had left him with a shattered sense of masculinity or the brief, intense period he'd spent trying to restore it between the thighs of a parade of faceless women. Neither was he going to stroke Ivy's ego by letting her know that no other woman had ever managed to get to him the way she did.

"Well, excuse me." It hurt that he'd gone out of his way to slap down her illusion. His experience with his ex-wife explained much, but as genuinely sorry as she was for what must have been a very painful situation, his attitude was rapidly cooling her sympathy. "Just what do you want from me, Vincent?"

He didn't know, dammit. Why did she have to pin him down? Frustrated and defensive, he told her the only thing he was absolutely certain of. "Your body."

"My body," she repeated, feeling as if he'd just

smacked her to her knees. Folding her arms over her chest she regarded his closed expression and said in a tight little voice, "Let me see if I have this straight. What you seem to be saying is that you'd like me to service you when you're horny and disappear when you're not. You don't want to get to know the real me, and you don't want a monogamous relationship . . . so I guess my services needn't be exclusive. Is that fairly succinct?"

"No, dammit, it's not!" He rammed his fingers through his hair. "Jesus, Ivy, does this have to be decided right this minute?"

"Oh, you don't like the timing either?" She would not cry—she *would not*. "Gee, I think it's awfully swell, myself. I mean, yesterday I got a love letter from a rapist and today I've got a hormonal cop who wants me to be his personal whore."

"Goddammit!" he bellowed. "That's not what I want." He nearly ripped the hair from his head in frustration. Taking a deep breath, he harshly expelled it; then in a more moderate tone he admitted, "I don't *know* what I want, okay?"

"Then perhaps I should tell you what I'm willing to give." She stared down at her clenched hands in her lap. "I'm not your slutty ex-wife, Vincent, and I'll be damned if you're going to make me pay for her sins. If all you want from me is sex, then stay out of my life." She looked up at him. "I can't take this any more—this habit you have of being all hot one minute then cold the next." Watching expressions cross his face where seconds ago there were none, she saw that he was probably every bit as mixed up as she was. "I want you, Vincent," she confessed gently in light of the frustration and confusion he displayed. "But not so much that I'm ready to be your plaything." Liar, liar, liar. But she'd be damned if she'd let him know exactly how vulnerable she was with him.

She stood and eyed him coldly until he, too, rose to his feet. Leading him to the door, she opened it, pushed him gently out into the hall and said, "When you have a clearer idea of what you want from me, let me know."

Then she firmly closed the door in his face.

Chapter 10

Tyler Griffus picked up Jaz Merrick's personal address book. *Ivy*. The name echoed throughout his mind and warmth spread from his chest out to his extremities. He'd learned her first name that night in the bar.

He flipped to the "P's," then swore softly when her name wasn't there. He was backtracking to check the "I's" when Jaz's voice floated out from the kitchen.

"Did you say something?" she asked, poking her head around the corner.

He surreptitiously closed the book and turned so his body blocked it from Jaz's view. "No. Well, not in any way that counts." He shrugged and flashed his teeth with a self-deprecating humor he knew the women loved. "I was just talking to myself."

She smiled. "Dangerous habit, that." Her head withdrew. "Coffee'll be ready in a minute."

"Take your time." Tyler flipped open the floral,

cloth-covered book again. Maybe he was going to have to rethink this entire stratagem. His original plan had been simply to gain access to the Doc through the comely Ms. Merrick's address book. Date Jasmine, help himself to the information, disappear. What could be simpler?

Now, however . . .

Oh, the possibilities that presented themselves. He could actually meet Ivy Pennington. If he played his cards right, he could stand face to face with her, talk to her.

Placate his demon in the aura of her understanding.

Of course it would mean forcing himself to initiate some means of intimacy with Jaz Merrick, but then she was beautiful and he had been known to do that before. Not often, perhaps, but hell, it wasn't as if his little monthly forays made him a degenerate or anything. He knew how to conduct himself.

It really was unfortunate, however, that she wasn't just the tiniest bit meeker. He much preferred women with less self-confidence.

Using his teeth to peel away a minute strip of skin next to his fingernail, he plucked it off the tip of his tongue with delicate fingertips and thought of the next full moon. It was only a few days away. Perhaps . . . ?

For just a moment, he toyed with the idea of donning his disguise and forcing his way back in here to show Jaz his real power. Now that would be a kick, an absolute study in contrasts as it were. Simply contemplating the possibilities started a familiar constriction in his loins.

But . . . no. Regretfully, he decided it probably wouldn't do. Even he could see that Ivy might not feel too kindly disposed toward the man who harmed her cousin. He just knew that deep down

she understood the compulsions that drove him—
he felt it in his gut. Her empathy soothed him,
enabled him to function normally while in the grip
of the predator's rage. Still, there was such a thing
as family loyalty.

It was the closeness he'd sensed between the two
women that night in the bar which had driven him
to follow Jaz home ... once he'd gotten past the
disappointment of being denied the opportunity
to follow Ivy. He'd watched them together that
night. As he'd floated from location to location in
the lounge, ever careful to blend in and never
stay in one spot long enough to catch anyone's
attention, he'd also absorbed random bits of overheard conversations concerning all the Pennington cousins.

Once he'd discovered where Jaz lived, it had
been child's play to find out where she worked as
well, and from there to arrange a meeting. He had
planned to keep it simple. Meet her, gain access
to her apartment, get the Doc's pertinent statistics,
and vanish.

Well, the strategy was about to undergo a slight
shift. The ultra cautious portion of his persona,
that guardian of admonishment that had kept him
one step ahead of the brainless law all these years,
rang warning bells, issued demands that he reconsider, argued there was danger in getting too close.

He ignored it all. Those arguments didn't stand
a snowball's chance in hell against the need in him
that clamored so insistently. He couldn't *get* close
enough to that calming influence.

The moment Vincent stepped into the trauma
unit, he could tell he'd have his work cut out for
him. He'd long ago stopped expecting easy solutions; still, it struck him that he'd managed to

underestimate yet another situation—in this case, the controlled pandemonium that comprised an emergency room. It was something he should have remembered more clearly from his days on patrol.

Stepping out of the flow of foot traffic swirling around him, he leaned against a wall to observe. In under ten minutes he'd watched more drama than most moviegoers saw in an evening.

He observed personnel run out in response to a car that slammed to a halt, horn blaring, outside the ER door. They had the passenger extricated from the car, on a stretcher, and down one of the hallways in record time. The nearly hysterical driver was directed to the reception desk, where harried nurses tried to elicit information for their forms even as she pleaded with them for a reassuring word over the ultimate fate of her rider. She had to compete with family members of other patients, all of whom were agitating for the nurses' attention with demands for information or quicker service for their loved ones.

Paramedics, navigating a gurney, barreled through the same door moments later. They were immediately joined by a medical team, which took one look at the blood-covered man on the cart and began treatment with organized speed even as the patient was being wheeled down a corridor.

Doctors and nurses came and went in the area where he stood; taking it all in, Vincent thought it wasn't difficult to comprehend how one man, determined to blend in, could easily be overlooked.

But just as he'd forgotten what a madhouse the ER could be, he'd also forgotten how abruptly it could clear out. Suddenly, all the waiting patients had been escorted back to examining rooms, the drunk had been wrestled onto a gurney, strapped down and wheeled away, and the crowd around the reception desk had diminished. Even the frantic driver was seated in the waiting room, filling out forms. Vincent pushed away from the wall and approached the desk to inquire for the person in charge.

For the next several hours he talked to trauma room personnel, catching them on the fly between emergencies. He spoke to doctors, to nurses, to aides, orderlies and administrators. The purpose of his interviews was twofold: he was seeking to garner whatever information he could and he wanted the hospital to be aware of the potential danger to one of their staff so they would be on the alert.

He saw Ivy only once, from a distance. She was covered from the top of her head to the tip of her toes in wrinkled green; if not for her leggy stride as she trotted alongside a swiftly maneuvered gurney, he probably wouldn't have recognized her. Watching her until she disappeared around a corner, he lost the train of his questioning for a moment.

He'd said it before: he had to quit fooling around and decide what he wanted from her. Well, actually, he had—several times. Trouble was, no matter how firm were the decisions he made when he was by himself, he invariably forgot them the minute he was alone with her. He always ended up acting defensive, hostile and horny instead.

For hours last night when he should have been sleeping, he'd torn his bed apart tossing and turning. It didn't take much perception to realize his restlessness stemmed from thinking of all she'd said . . . and his behavior every time he saw her. She had every right to expect more than he was offering—a great deal more. Hell, if he wasn't willing to get involved, there were probably plenty of guys out there who would be.

He hated how deeply the thought of that ate at

him; he simply could not afford to have her matter that much. Hell, it was no big surprise how badly he wanted to get her back in bed—his dormant sex drive had resurrected itself with a vengeance from practically the first moment he'd laid eyes on her and he hadn't exactly been shy about confronting her with it at every opportunity. What had shocked him was the rage he'd felt when she'd made that crack last night about her services not necessarily being exclusive.

He damn well did want exclusive rights; the thought of another man having her the way he had filled him with murderous impulses. But, Christ, every time he thought in terms of a relationship he broke out in a cold sweat.

He'd had a relationship, and just that *word* had the power to conjure up visions of the afternoon he'd arrived home early from work with the intention of surprising LaDonna. He'd surprised her all right—surprised her in bed with Ray Lenderbaum.

It was so hard to believe now that until that moment he hadn't suspected a thing. But he'd been trusting then . . . something he was unlikely ever to be again. Even when he'd seen her flirting at parties he hadn't been jealous. Flirting was harmless and jerk that he was, he'd been proud that other men found her attractive. Perhaps he had even been just the tiniest bit smug to know that he would be the one to take her home and make love to her.

That was always good for a laugh. Him and any other willing stud.

But he hadn't learned about that until later. Walking into their bedroom that afternoon, he'd been caught unprepared and in that one instant everything he'd previously held to be true had turned upside down and inside out.

He'd never understood why he had pulled his

gun and held it to Ray's head and not LaDonna's. Maybe it had been easier to deal with the ramifications of his betrayal. Up until that moment he'd believed that Lenderbaum was, if not a friend, precisely, at least a friendly acquaintance.

Of course, neither had it occurred to him that his wife might ever be unfaithful to him. What a Midwest hayseed he must have seemed. The depth of his naivete was truly astounding.

The exact words said in that room remained a blur. He remembered viewing everything through a red mist of anguish and rage and recalled loud pleas, hysteria. Only one thing stood out clearly— LaDonna defiantly screaming, after he'd holstered his gun and told her she wasn't worth going to jail for, that she was glad she'd aborted his baby, glad! He'd very nearly killed her then after all, but awareness of just how calculated her words were to wound had stopped him.

Without a word he'd turned and walked away. Some time later, without a clue as to how he'd arrived there, he'd found himself at Keith and Anna's house. Hard on the heels of a painfully enlightening conversation with them he had headed straight for the nearest lawyer.

For weeks afterward he had striven to prove— to himself and to everyone who had been aware of LaDonna's whoring long before he had—that she hadn't managed to emasculate him. Over and over again he made love to innumerable faceless women, finding joyless release and precious little satisfaction. Then one morning he'd awakened in the bed of yet another strange female and realized he didn't even know this one's name. Disgusted with himself, he came to the realization that he didn't need to prove anything to anyone. He'd been celibate from that day on . . . right up until the night he'd seduced Ivy Pennington.

Now he had to decide whether resurrected lust was a good enough reason to risk getting involved again.

Ivy left little Jaime Newman resting in a nurse's care and stepped out into the hall. She slumped back against the wall and closed her eyes. What a day.

Vincent was somewhere in the building, his presence felt if as yet unseen. She could really use a little respite from that man, but by all accounts he'd been busier than a hooker at convention time around here today. She'd lost track of the number of people who'd approached her throughout the course of her shift, some shocked, some curious and all eager to offer sympathy over her plight. She knew they meant well, but rehashing again and again how it felt to be the unwilling recipient of a rapist's attention was not her idea of a good time. She was beginning to feel the strain.

The real kicker was little Jaime's case. It was shaping up to be one of those no-win situations, like too many others she had seen. God but she was sick of it.

At first she had believed the mother's story that the four-and-a-half-year-old little boy was an uncoordinated child who had tumbled down the basement stairs during a split second of inattentiveness when her back was turned. The woman had been jumpy with nerves but patently worried about her child. Of the father, Ivy had caught only the merest glimpse when the parents were informed that due to a lack of space only one of them would be allowed back in the examining room with their son. The impression she'd received was of a silent, angry man, but she'd seen enough parental reaction to a child's injury to know better than to jump to conclusions. Too often concern came across that way.

When the X-rays had come back from radiology, however, her stomach had sunk to her toes. The moment her nurse clipped it to the light Ivy had noticed the two old breaks. She'd silently indicated the mended bones to Ellen and their eyes had met with sick comprehension. "Call CPS," she'd instructed in a low voice.

Ellen turned immediately to do her bidding, but Ivy had reached out a detaining hand and said, "Wait." She'd turned to Jaime's mother. "Mrs. Newman, I'm going to have to ask you to join your husband in the waiting room while we put on Jaime's cast. We need the room to prepare."

The instant the curtain had swished closed behind the woman, she'd turned back to Ellen. "After you reach Child Protective Services," she instructed in a soft voice, ". . . call down to Records. See if Jaime's ever been admitted before. If they find anything, anything at all, have them send it to us STAT." With gentle care, she and the remaining nurse set Jaime's broken arm. As they'd worked on him they'd questioned the child carefully. It was his innocently given responses that had ultimately driven her out into the corridor. She needed a moment to regroup.

"Ivy?" Her eyes snapped open and there, standing close, was Vincent. She wasn't even surprised to see him. Her eyes tracked his as he studied her face with concern. "Are you all right?" he finally asked.

"No." She indicated the curtain with a jut of her chin. "I've got an abused child in there," she said in a low voice.

"Oh, shit."

"Yeah. My sentiments exactly." Ivy pushed away from the wall and walked a short way down the corridor to be absolutely certain her voice wouldn't be heard in the cubicle. She whirled to face Vincent, who had trailed her. "He's not even five years old yet, Vincent, and this is the third time he's had the same arm broken. The *third time.* God, I hate these cases. CPS is on the way and I'll tell you, chances are good they'll remove Jaime from his parents' custody. From everything he told us, there's very little doubt that his father's the abuser."

"So, that's good, right?" Vincent studied her defeated expression and then nodded in comprehension. "Except it means that the kid's gonna be taken away from everything familiar and get hooked into the foster system."

"Yeah," Ivy sighed. "And we both know what a crapshoot that can be."

"He might be one of the lucky ones, Ivy. There are some good homes out there."

"I know there are," she agreed. "But if he lands in the wrong one, it's just the first step down a long road to becoming the criminal of tomorrow."

He couldn't disagree; that was the way it worked. His division dealt with the child molesters of the world and every one he'd ever talked to had been molested himself as a child. It was hard to dredge up any sympathy for the adult offender, but in truth, if society as a whole took better care of its children, the escalating, much-lamented crime rate would drop dramatically a generation down the road.

He didn't have an easy answer for her, and he didn't attempt to offer one. Listening to Ivy and seeing her discouragement, however, helped him come to the decision he'd been worrying off and on since he'd left her last night. Taking a deep breath, he expelled it and said, "Listen, I can't offer you a solution, but I've got just the thing to take your mind off it."

"Oh, yeah?" She tilted her head slightly and gave him a weary smile. "And what might that be?"

"Why don't you come to Anna and Keith's annual backyard barbecue with me on Saturday." As soon as the invitation left his mouth, he wondered if he were crazy.

"Oh, Vincent, that sounds wonderful," she said, and then added with genuine regret, ". . . but I have to work this Saturday."

He didn't hear the regret, only the refusal. "No problem," he said stiffly. "It was only a suggestion." He started to turn away.

"No, wait." She reached out and grabbed his arm to keep him from leaving, but dropped her hand to her side immediately when she felt his muscles contract beneath her touch. Such a prickly man. "Let me call you tonight. If I work this right, I can probably switch days with someone . . . or at least arrange to get off early."

With a maddening lack of expression, he said coolly, "Don't go to any trouble on my account. It was just a thought."

His unrelenting rigidity frayed her already over-burdened nerves. "Dammit, Vincent," she snapped, "would you just, for one minute, quit acting like such a goddam *stiff*? I said I'd like to go and I *said* I'll try to get the time off. Why do you have to be so impossible all the time!" She whirled on her heel and stormed back to the cubicle. Just before she entered it she looked back down the hall and saw that he was still standing where she'd left him, staring after her. "I'll call you tonight," she reiterated.

*   *   *

The doctor whose shift she'd been covering the night Bess Polsen was brought in agreed to take over her rotation, and she found herself riding alongside a silent Vincent Saturday afternoon. From the moment he'd arrived at her door to pick her up, he'd been uncommunicative.

Capturing her blowing hair in one fist, she propped her elbow in the open car window and watched the scenery pass by. She was unwilling to force a conversation he clearly did not desire, but the strained silence between them made her wonder what kind of day this was going to be. Why had he bothered to ask her out if he didn't even want to talk to her?

Then at the next light, he abruptly turned and looked her over. "You look nice," he said softly.

"Thanks," she replied and smiled a little ironically, remembering their conversation when she'd called to let him know she'd found a replacement for her shift and could therefore accept his invitation. "What shall I wear?" she'd asked before they'd hung up.

"Huh?"

"You know, clothes? What do the women usually wear to these shindigs? Pants, sundresses, shorts? My bikini, perhaps?"

"Hell, Ivy, how should I know?" he'd asked, sounding faintly exasperated. "Wear anything."

Easy for him to say. He knew everyone who was going to be there; she wasn't going to know a soul. She wasn't particularly shy when it came to meeting new people, but she did want to at least be suitably attired. Another woman would have understood instantly; he, clearly, didn't have a clue.

She glanced down now at her olive-drab pleated shorts and the little black halter top tucked into them and then looked back up at him. "This'll do, then?"

"Yeah, it'll do very well. Especially this." He took one hand off the wheel long enough to reach over and tweak the angle of material where it notched between her breasts. Careful not to let his skin touch hers, he rubbed the fabric briefly between his thumb and forefinger. "Nice."

She could feel herself blush clear up to the roots of her hair and was grateful he'd returned his attention to the road. Trust him to zero in on the one feature that had made her hesitant to don this top in the first place.

Actually, she thought defensively, it was really quite demure. Really. For the most part. Constructed of opaque black cotton, it had wide, sundress straps and a fitted bodice that cut straight across the top of her breasts where they began to curve out from her chest. No bursting cleavage, no plunging neckline. It wasn't at all revealing . . . except for a small, boned V of material notched out between her breasts. And even with that, one could only catch a glimpse of a white rounded curve here, a pale curve there . . . from certain angles. She wasn't trying to entice him. The garment was sexy only in the subtlest sense.

She quit worrying about it when Vincent finally began to talk to her. The remainder of the ride passed pleasantly.

It was a revelation watching Vincent with his friends and acquaintances that afternoon. Ivy had never had an occasion to see him when he was this relaxed, had never seen him smile or laugh so much. She spent a good part of the day standing beneath the casual drape of his arm in one room or another in the Graham's house or out in their backyard. He introduced her to everyone in sight and diligently saw to it that she was included in the conversations.

At one point, Suse McGill dragged her away to

meet her date, and at another she found herself
alone with Anna Graham in the temporarily
deserted kitchen. She sliced tomatoes and pickles
for a condiment tray while Anna bustled around
the room taking salads out of the refrigerator,
readying plates and cutlery for dinner. Sounds of
masculine laughter and the smell of grilled meat
wafted through the open kitchen door.

Anna added napkins to the large tray she was
preparing. Checking its contents against a mental
list, she paused to smile at Ivy. "I'm so glad you
could come today," she said. She reached for the
salt and pepper containers and set them atop the
paper plates.

"So am I," Ivy responded, smiling in return.
There was something about Anna that was comfortable—she felt as if they had been friends for a long
time instead of acquaintances of only hours. "It's
certainly been interesting," she added and then
acknowledged with a wry smile, "I've never seen
so many guns at a party before."

Anna laughed. "Yeah, that's cops for you. I used
to try to mix Keith's colleagues with mine at these
get-togethers, but I gave it up after a while. Cops
can be a little cliquish and between their attitude
and their hardware, they tended to intimidate my
friends." She glanced up at Ivy. "You seem to be
holding your own, though."

"Oh, I've had a rough moment here or there,
but it hasn't had anything to do with attitudes or
hardwear." She grimaced wryly. "I've gained a
whole new appreciation of what it must feel like
to be a sideshow freak."

"Oh, God." Anna laughed. "Has it been too
awful? Those clowns aren't exactly long on tact."
She shrugged slightly. "You probably know you're

the first date Vincent's brought to a cop function since he divorced The Bitch. And of course, everyone knows he's been celibate for years, so they can't help but be fascinated by you.''

Ivy's jaw sagged. "They *know* about that?"

"Sure." When Ivy stared at her incredulously, Anna elaborated, "Keith said you'd been down to the unit—you must have seen how packed together those desks are." She shrugged good-naturedly. "There tend to be damn few secrets in a squad room."

"Good gravy," Ivy said faintly. Then: "Sounds just like my family."

"In a way, that's exactly what they are. Anyway—" She waved aside the subject and got back to what she had been saying before—". . . I'm glad he brought you today, Ivy. I've been hearing about you from Keith, so it's nice to finally meet you. But more than that, it's been like having the old Vince back again. He's always been a favorite of mine, but these past few years his personality has undergone a change. And not for the better."

Ivy nodded in complete understanding. "I've had several encounters with his temper myself." She reached for the head of lettuce and began breaking off leaves to add to the condiment plate.

"Oh, no; that's not what I meant at all." Anna shook her head in denial. "I haven't seen him lose his temper in years," she divulged with a wistfulness that Ivy, who had been on the receiving end of his anger more than once, found oddly misplaced. Anna must have read the puzzlement in her expression, for she tried to make her understand. "Don't you see, that's just the problem. Ever since that woman messed up his life, he's been so . . . controlled."

Placing hamburger buns into a roasting pan, she

slid them into the oven and then straightened to face Ivy. "Vincent's always been a little on the reserved side anyway, but never to the point where he was completely able to subdue that Italian heritage of his. When he was happy he'd roar with laughter; when he was angry he'd yell like an injured bull and get it out of his system. And tease . . . ?" She smiled in remembrance. "God, he was such a tease." Then, her humor fading, she went on, "But for the past three years he's been like . . . oh, I don't know—like the walking wounded. He's closed himself off and allowed nothing to ruffle his composure. Watching him with you, though, is like—"

Ivy never got to find out what it was like, for their conversation was interrupted by the entrance of several policemen's wives, who had trouped in from the back yard to offer their assistance getting dinner on the table. The women set up a buffet on the dining room table and just moments after they had finished arranging dishes, Keith carried in a platter heaped high with barbecued hamburgers. Everyone crowded around the table to load up their plates.

Sitting jammed together hip to hip at the crowded picnic table outside, Ivy gave only half her attention to the conversations around her as she thought of the things Anna had revealed about Vincent. She was very conscious of the warm press of his hard thigh against hers. Was she being too stringent insisting there could be no sex between them? Maybe . . .

"Are you really a doctor?"

It took a moment to gather her thoughts when she realized she was being addressed. Focusing her attention on the young patrolman's wife seated across from her, she mentally flicked sweat from her brow with her fingertips. Whew. Dangerous thinking, that. "Yes," she replied. "I'm an emergency room doctor over at the trauma unit."

"Wow," the young woman breathed, staring across the table at Ivy in wide-eyed awe. "That's something. I don't do anything," she confessed shyly. "Well, I take care of the house and the baby, of course, but . . ."

"If you ask me," Ivy interrupted her gently, "I'd say being a mom is probably the most important job of all. Vincent and I were discussing that very thing just the other day—weren't we, Vincent?"

"Yeah." He smiled across the table at the young woman. "Ivy had to treat a little boy who was abused by his father and it really got to her. One of the reasons I invited her here today was to help take her mind off it."

"What parents do is so vital," Ivy added insistently. "Why, you have the power to mold a person's life. Is your baby a boy or a girl?"

"A girl. Hilary. She's thirteen months old." The young woman's smile was filled with pride and love. "Would you like to see her picture?"

"Yes. Very much," Ivy said with an easy smile.

After dinner, Vincent lounged in the grass with the other men. He was propped on one arm, long legs stretched out in front of him and crossed at the ankles. Sipping infrequently from the beer bottle in his hand, he threw in an occasional comment just to prove he was attuned to the various conversations flowing around him. Mostly, though, he watched Ivy, who was still seated at the picnic table with several women.

She was so different from LaDonna. He knew it was unfair to make comparisons, but he couldn't help himself. Physically, of course, they were nothing alike. LaDonna had been a little under average height and almost as dark as he. Appearance always uppermost in her mind, her hair and fingernails had seemed to be her paramount concern and had featured prominently in many of their private conversations. She'd had a penchant for bright colors and blatantly sexy clothes. Never, with her, had it been necessary to give himself eyestrain the way he'd damn near done today attempting to get more than a stingy glimpse of the full, pale curves inside that infuriating little top of Ivy's.

The differences, however, went a whole lot deeper than the physical. Vincent tried to imagine his ex-wife sitting with the women or putting herself out to make a shy young mother feel that raising her child was every bit as important as any doctor's career. He snorted. Not bloody likely. LaDonna had usually ignored the women. She could always be found where the men were, which in all probability should have been his first clue.

The women rejoined the men as the sun sank behind the Olympics. Vincent shelved all thoughts of LaDonna. The hell with it. He was rid of her, he felt good; why analyze it? The evening was still and warm, the conversation good, the beer cold. A white glow from the full moon bathed the Grahams' backyard. Who could ask for anything more?

It was never wise to get too complacent, a nagging voice whispered inside his head.

When the phone rang inside the house, chills of premonition didn't shiver down his spine. A distant corner of his mind registered the slap of the wooden screen door when Anna ran into the house to answer it and again when she returned to the yard. Most of his attention, however, was focused on the argument he was having with Keith and Ivy over rock and roll versus classical music. He smiled up at Anna when she bent over him, picking up the hand she touched to his shoulder and holding it in his own while he finished driving his point home. The instant he paused for a breath, she squeezed his fingers.

"Sorry to interrupt the interview, Rolling Stone," she said with more than a little irony, "but there's a phone call for you."

Chapter 11

"Son of a bitch." Vincent gently replaced the receiver in its cradle and turned away from the telephone stand. He plowed both hands through his hair to rake it off his forehead. "Son of a *bitch!*"

Okay, so it came as no real surprise. But when he'd left Keith's number with the desk sergeant and the detective on call in his own unit, requesting a call should his full-mooner hit tonight, he had really hoped he wouldn't get one.

Shit.

The irony was he'd known perfectly well at the time that the hope was a futile one. His guy hadn't missed a month yet, so he'd sure as hell had no reasonable expectation of getting a break during this month's full moon. On the contrary, Vincent had fully expected to have his evening interrupted, but he'd become so involved in having a good time for a change that he'd actually managed to forget.

So the question was: what did he do now, stay

at the party—which was what he really wanted to do—or leave? There was nothing in his job description that demanded he see the victim tonight. He certainly didn't harbor any burning desire to go off to interrogate some poor woman who in all probability would be too traumatized to give him a coherent account anyway. He'd be perfectly justified in waiting until Monday . . . and ordinarily he would do just that.

The trouble was, this case was far from ordinary. It differed radically from damn near every other case he'd ever handled.

Statistically—and his experience seemed to bear it out—seven out of every ten women raped were assaulted by someone they knew, or with whom they'd had at least a passing acquaintance, but serial type rape by a total stranger was something else again.

That wasn't to say he hadn't handled cases where women were sexually battered by unknown men, for of course he had. Never, however, had he handled a case quite like this one, where the rapist was so utterly meticulous in the execution of his crime; neither had he dealt with a perpetrator of such ritualistic bent. Rapists didn't generally wear ski masks and he was accustomed to having *something* to work with, used to sorting through the various components until they finally coughed up at least a minimal clue that gave him a place to begin. But this guy . . .

Oh, hell. He had to go talk to the victim; he'd known he didn't actually have a choice in the matter from the moment Anna had informed him of the call. The department might not require it of him, but he required it of himself.

Vincent looked down at himself, at the red T-shirt, rubber flip-flops, and cutoff jeans, and swore softly under his breath. He'd have to go home and change first. The bottom curve of one of his Levi front pockets poked out from beneath a crooked hem, and unraveled strings straggled untidily down his thighs. As barbecue attire went, it was appropriate enough, but he could hardly show up at a victim's hospital bedside looking this way.

Ivy was silent on the ride back to the apartment house, her head averted as she stared moodily out the window. Vincent found himself darting frequent furtive glances at her profile.

"I'm sorry I had to drag you away like that," he finally said, and as the words left his mouth he was utterly sincere. She'd been having a good time and it was a shame he'd had to cut it short.

Trust wasn't exactly his long suit, however, and not for a minute had he even considered getting someone else to take her home. He'd seen her popularity with his co-workers—and not only with the women. The way Ryan Bell, for instance, had been eyeing her all evening long hadn't escaped his notice. The guy was big, blond, and notoriously successful with the ladies. No way in hell had Vincent been tempted to leave her behind.

Surprised by his apology, Ivy turned her head to look at him. "I didn't mind leaving," she assured him. "But, Vincent . . . ?" She swiveled in her seat until she faced him fully. "The reason we left has something to do with the rapist who's been sending me stuff, doesn't it?"

It was his turn to be caught by surprise and he had to backpeddle mentally. He'd just sort of assumed it was dissatisfaction at being rushed home early that had had her brooding. Instead, she'd been nursing suspicions about his reasons for cutting their evening short, suspicions he sensed she would be just as happy to hear him deny.

He hesitated, seriously tempted for a moment to lie. His natural honesty was an entrenched characteristic, however, and it took him just a bit too long to think up a plausible lie to reassure her.

Before he could limp something out, Ivy said with an impatient frown, "Look, you don't have to coddle me, okay? You said something came up at work that couldn't be put off, but I'm not a total idiot, Vincent." Stabbing a finger to indicate the night sky beyond the windshield, she announced flatly, "There's a full moon out tonight. He's raped another one, hasn't he?"

"Yes." He shot a glance at her face and seeing the sick expression there, wished he were a better liar. Well, it was too late now. "I'm going to change my clothes as soon as I drop you off and then I've gotta go to the hospital to see if the victim can tell me anything."

"Dear God," she whispered. "Where'd they take this one?"

"Swedish." It wasn't much, but at least he could give her that. Her hospital wasn't going to be involved this time.

"And it's just like it was with Bess Polsen, the heart on her chest, everything?"

"Yeah." Pulling up at a light, he turned his head and looked over at her. "Only this time he had enough time to carve the whole thing. That's how they knew to contact me."

Even in the dimness of the car he could see the goosebumps that cropped up on her thighs. But she didn't say anything further. Instead, she stared at him a moment, bit her lip and then turned away to stare out the side window once again. Vincent's fingers tightened on the steering wheel.

* * *

What on earth was she getting herself into?

Ivy wandered restlessly throughout her apartment without bothering to turn on the lights; the moon shining through the slatted blinds provided sufficient illumination to keep her from stumbling over the furniture. She paced from living room, to kitchen, to bathroom, to bedroom, and then she reversed the circuit, too keyed up to stay anywhere for any length of time.

Jumpy and agitated, she didn't know quite what to do with herself. It was too late to call any of her relatives; yet it was too early to go to bed. The images that raced through her brain made the idea of sleep laughable anyway.

Her thoughts bounced back and forth between Vincent and the rapist. How had it come to this? How the *hell* had it come to this?

She'd made herself a promise that she'd keep Vincent at arm's length. A simple enough vow to make when he was nowhere near; but the moment he was . . . Lord, what a joke it became then.

She shouldn't be seeing him at all. With an attitude like his, there was just too much potential for heartbreak—and it was *her* heart that was going to get broken. Yet all he had to do was crook one of those long brown fingers and she knocked herself out to accommodate him. Like a bad rash, he was under her skin, an itch she couldn't seem to stop herself from scratching. Just look at tonight.

She'd been saying all the correct things as they'd stood outside her door—thanks for the evening; I had a wonderful time. All sincere enough, but her mind had been only partially on her words; the rest had been preoccupied with disturbing thoughts of the rapist. Right up until the moment

Vincent had kissed her goodnight. *Then* her mind
had shut down entirely.

So, all right, perhaps offering him her hand had
been a mistake. She knew they were miles beyond
that, but it had just sort of poked itself out there
to be shaken. He'd looked at it, smiled crookedly
as he'd shook it firmly, and then reached for her
other hand as well and pressed them both back
against the door panel on either side of her head.
"Ah, Ivy," he'd whispered, crowding in on her.
"When you do stuff like that, it just drives me crazy.
All I can think is gimme more." His voice all soft
and raspy, he'd crooned, "Gimme, gimme,
gimme."

And Lord had she! All hormones and no brains,
that was she. He'd leaned into her, a full body
press, and without so much as a whimper of protest,
she'd opened her mouth to his and kissed him back
for all she was worth. No thoughts had cluttered her
mind; she'd been aware only of his taste, his scent,
the feel of his body, especially of those bare thighs,
so hard and warm against hers.

She'd wrapped her arms around his neck and
arched her back, pressing her breast into his hand.
Left up to her, in fact, they probably would have
ended up screwing their brains out right there in
the hallway where any fourth floor resident could
have seen them. It was *he* who'd suddenly recalled
he had places to go, people to see.

He'd broken their kiss reluctantly, his knees
bending under him until his cheek, rubbing down-
ward across the exposed skin of her throat and
chest, had rested against her breast. His breath
had blasted hot through the fabric of her top. "I'm
sorry," he'd panted hoarsely, "I'm sorry. I have to
go." He'd squeezed her breast and bit down gently
on her protruding nipple through the material. "I
don't want to, Ivy, but I've got to." And his hand

had slid out from beneath her top, his legs had straightened. He kissed her again then, fast and hard; said, "I'll call you," and before she could catch her breath, he had disappeared into his own apartment.

She alternately cursed him and herself as she prowled from room to room; yet deep inside she knew she was fighting a losing battle. She might as well stop and simply admit it, because even if she couldn't define precisely what it was about him that got to her, got to her he did. No two ways about it: he had her well and truly hooked.

She sighed in discouragement. In all probability, her heart was going to end up in pieces by the time he got through with her. Yet she was rapidly losing the strength to continue fighting both Vincent's blandishments and her own traitorous needs. And if that weren't enough to scare the socks off any woman who'd ever valued her independence, throw in one attentive rapist.

She wasn't exactly proud of the sense of relief she'd experienced upon hearing the victim had been sent to another hospital's ER. The best she could cop to was that at least she'd had the grace to first feel horror for the poor woman, and in truth she'd felt sickened to her very soul—it was every woman's worst nightmare. Overlying it all, however, was a purely selfish desire to remain uninvolved. She'd been thoroughly unnerved by the rapist's attentions of late and was ashamed of how sincerely she hoped he'd redirect them toward whomever was treating tonight's victim. Call her selfish, but there it was.

She didn't begin to comprehend a nature so morally twisted it enabled a man to do something so vicious. He was an animal, pure and simple. Not satisfied to merely commit the most horrendously intimate violation possible, he had to carve his victims up as well in order that they'd forever bear a physical reminder of what had been done to them. What sort of mind could devise such a thing?

Ivy's wanderings brought her back to her bedroom for about the fourth go-around and this time she noticed the discarded clothes she was wading through. She was getting better at this housekeeping business, but to date she'd concentrated on keeping up the living room, bathroom and kitchen—areas guests were most likely to see. The bedroom still had a tendency to look like Beirut on a bad day. Desperate for something to clear her mind of all these negative thoughts, she set about straightening it up.

It was actually quite soothing, puttering in the moonlit room, sorting clean discarded clothes from soiled, hanging up the former and throwing the latter in a basket to be washed. When she could once again see the carpet, she pulled up the covers on her bed, fetched a glass of wine from the kitchen and sipped it as she dusted. Unconsciously beginning to hum to herself, she spent several moments contentedly arranging the tangle of shoes in her closet into neat pairs. By the time she'd finished with the vacuum cleaner and put it away, she had unwound enough to feel drowsy.

Feeling virtuous out of all proportion to what had been accomplished, she carried her empty wine glass to the kitchen, stowed it in the dishwasher and wiped down the counters. In the bathroom she stored everything in its proper place, and she even went so far as to stop herself from leaving her clothes where she'd kicked them off when she changed into her short satin nightie. She crossed to the window, twirled the wand that closed the slats on the blinds and slid into bed, feeling downright tranquil.

She was just drifting off, nearly asleep, when the

telephone rang. She jerked upright, heart pounding, visited by that universal fear that accompanies late night phone calls. Less an articulated thought than an instinctive dread that something awful had happened to a member of her family, Ivy was alternately convinced, in the few seconds it took her to fumble for the receiver, that Uncle Mack had suffered a heart attack, Jaz had been involved in an auto accident, Terry or Sherry had . . . "H'lo?" she gulped.

"Dr. Pennington?" The voice was male, muted, and it took her a second to realize he was whispering. Oh, God, why was he whispering? Was the news so dreadful he feared to use a normal tone? Was this the professional intonation of a morgue attendant?

It took both hands to grip the receiver to her ear. "Yes, this is she." Please, oh please, let everyone be alive. They could deal with anything else, one day at a time, if need be . . . if only everyone were still alive.

"I had to call you, Doc," the voice whispered triumphantly, "because I knew you'd understand. Nobody else does, but you do. I've felt your empathy from the first time I saw you and I just wanted to let you know I'm finally at peace."

"What?" A sudden draining sensation, comprised in equal parts of relief and anger, made her flop weakly back onto her pillow, the receiver still clutched to her ear. She'd just been scared out of several years growth by a *crank call?* A spurt of energy brought her back up to a seated position. "Do you have any idea what time it is?" she demanded furiously. "Do you? My God, you scared me half to death, calling at this hour. Who *is* this, anyway?" she demanded—then suddenly she knew.

She knew . . . and the knowledge made her break out in a cold sweat.

"I'm sorry," he whispered. "It wasn't my intention to frighten you; I merely wanted to share my news with you, because I knew you'd appreciate its importance." He hesitated only briefly before adding, "And *you* may call me Hart."

The line went dead on the heels of a small, self-satisfied chuckle. Ivy huddled in the middle of the mattress with her knees hugged to her breast, left to wonder how she was supposed to apply rational thought to this latest installment of horror.

Just how the *hell* was she supposed to do that?

Tyler Griffus was a little disappointed in the Doc's response as he hung up the phone, but decided that on the whole he was satisfied. She was merely upset because he'd called so late. When she had a chance to get over her nerves, she'd appreciate knowing he'd attained a tranquil state.

What mattered to him mattered to the Doc—he felt it in his bones.

Perhaps he ought to call back at a more reasonable hour, if only to hear her voice, to feel that connection. It was a thought definitely worth further consideration, but he'd have to be cautious; it wouldn't do to call too often. He couldn't afford to leave a trail for the cops to trace. It never once occurred to him how diametrically opposed those two schools of thoughts were.

A fist pounded on the door and Ivy nearly jumped out of her skin. "Ivy!" Vincent's voice was a roar. "Open up!" He pounded again, even louder. "It's me. Open up."

She was up and across the room, pulling the door open before the last word was entirely out of his mouth. Across the hall, one apartment down, a door was yanked open and a man with an irate expression poked his head out into the hallway to glare at them. As he opened his mouth to give them hell, Ivy grabbed Vincent's lapels and pulled him into the apartment, pushing the door closed behind them.

He grasped her upper arms and held her away from him, straining to study her features there in the entry where the moonlight didn't reach. "Are you all right?" he demanded. "I got home as fast as I could." When she nodded uncertainly, he set her loose and crossed the living room to a window overlooking the street. Prying apart two slats in the mini-blind, he peered out.

Ivy stared at his hunched back. There was that word again: *home.* He'd said it before, when she'd had him paged at the hospital. *"What?"* he'd demanded incredulously when she'd poured out the details of the phone call. There had followed a brief string of creatively arranged obscenities, then: "Sit tight; I'm coming home: Leave the lights off and stay away from the windows and door until I get there, y'hear?"

Vincent dropped the slats and turned back to her. "It's probably okay; I don't see anyone," he said and then exhaled noisily, ramming his fingers through his hair. Bracing himself for a possible argument, he looked at her standing across the room and commanded firmly, "Grab some stuff, whatever you think you'll need. You're spending the night at my place."

Ivy was not the least bit inclined to argue. With a clipped nod, she turned on her heel and silently left the room. In her bedroom, she gathered underwear and clothing for the next day and then turned and stared thoughtfully at the bowl of condoms. *Home,* he'd said. Twice. He'd insisted under pressure that all he wanted from her was her body.

Now his actions and unguarded words seemed to convey something else entirely.

Or was she rationalizing? Oh, hell, even if she were, who cared? She was tired of fighting the urges he inspired, and tonight in particular she could really use a little physical contact to make her feel whole again. She grabbed up a handful of condoms and stuffed them into the pocket of her small overnight case.

She rejoined Vincent in the living room. He reached out to relieve her of the small case, and with his free hand lightly riding the small of her back, ushered her from the apartment.

Vincent watched Ivy with increasing bafflement as she sat quietly on his couch a short while later. He'd broken every traffic law in the book in his race to get home to her. And the entire way, he'd expected to be met at the door with a bombardment of voluble indignation or fear, by acerbic demands to know how the rapist could have learned her unlisted phone number. At the very least he'd expected to see a replay of the restless inattentiveness she'd displayed that day she'd received the note commending her singing.

Instead, she hadn't said so much as one word since he'd arrived on her doorstep. No tears, no rage, no response at all that might give him a clue how to proceed. It was very unIvy-like, and it was beginning to unnerve him.

He looked at her sitting there, abnormally still in her thin floral wrap kimono, bare feet stacked slightly pigeon-toed one atop the other, head bent to stare blindly at the tensely clasped hands in her lap. She appeared numb, and Vincent didn't know if he should simply put her to bed and deal with it in the morning, or force it all out in the open the way you'd lacerate a festering sore. God only knew what was going on in her mind. Then he noted the tightly drawn skin along her cheekbones and jaw and abruptly made his decision. The hell with it; what she probably needed more than anything was a good night's rest. He could revert to being a cop in the morning—tonight he'd just be her friend.

He extended a hand to her and with uncharacteristic docility, Ivy allowed herself to be pulled to her feet and led down the hall to Vincent's bedroom.

Releasing her hand, he dumped her overnight case, which he'd snagged on the way out of the living room, onto the dresser top, and crossed the room to turn down the bed. He plumped up a pillow and turned back to her. The sight that greeted him made him freeze in his tracks.

She had dropped her kimono to the floor and stood at the dresser rummaging through her overnight case. The only thing protecting her modesty was a brief satin nightie of emerald green. Unable to look away, he swallowed dryly.

Brief seemed to be the operative word. There was six feet of woman standing with her back to him across the room, wearing a scrap of satin that most likely had been fashioned with an average-sized woman in mind. Cut from narrow straps to a low V in the back, it skimmed her rounded bottom and ended not far from the top of her thighs, exposing a great deal of pale skin and those long, glorious legs. She turned around and he saw that it was also cut in a low V in front. There was probably only two dollars worth of material in the entire garment.

Gratified by the way his eyes stayed glued to her body as she walked across the room toward him, Ivy decided he shouldn't be too difficult to seduce. Good; because she really needed him tonight.

Ever since the moment she'd pulled herself together enough to call Vincent at the hospital, she'd struggled with the oddest sensation of shrinking. The phone call had generated an inner need to draw into herself, to make herself as small and still as possible . . . as if doing so would somehow make her a lesser target. It was a disquieting sensation to find herself feeling less than whole. She felt as though a part of her identity had gotten lost tonight and she desperately needed the forgetfulness of lovemaking to restore it. Or to at least restore . . . something. Something that the phone call had robbed from her.

Vincent was so engrossed in the subtle body movements beneath that outrageous excuse for a nightgown that he was caught unprepared when she suddenly launched herself at him.

He staggered beneath her weight and they fell over backward, landing in a tangled heap upon the mattress. Gone was the unnatural inertia which had held Ivy in its grip. Clasping Vincent's stubble-roughened cheeks between her hands, she kissed him with frantic need: his mouth, his eyes, his throat. All wild motion, she wrestled him to his back and crawled on top of him, rubbing herself against his clothed body with unchecked urgency. Hands racing ahead to clear the way for her mouth, she kissed her way down his neck, nipping with her teeth, licking with her tongue. By the time she reached his collarbone, she'd already ripped two buttons from his shirt in her haste to uncover his chest.

Vincent wrapped his fists in her hair and twined his calves around hers in an attempt to subdue the worst of her frenzy. Utterly aroused by the bombardment of simultaneous sensations—the scent of aroused woman, the rub of exposed flesh and the slide of smooth satin against his chest, the bump and grind of hot, damp womanhood against the painful rigidity of his erection—he nevertheless experienced a stab of unease. There was a sense of desperation in the way she went about setting his body on fire that seemed oddly impersonal. That mouth of hers was driving him nuts, with its damp kisses, its huskily whispered litany of broken words that spoke of desire and neediness, and yet . . . it didn't seem to be directed at him specifically. Not once did she call him by name.

"Wait," he said hoarsely. Rolling her onto her back, he loomed over her, grasping her hands as they reached out for him, pinning them to the mattress. "Ivy, wait a minute."

"Nooo," she whimpered, arching beneath him in an attempt to get closer, closer. "Love me. Please?" She raised her head to press hot, open-mouthed kisses against his rough jaw. "Love me."

He wanted to. Ah how he wanted to, but he had to be one hundred percent certain . . . "What's my name?" he whispered fiercely.

"What?" She lowered her head back to the pillow and looked up at him with unfocused eyes. "What's your . . . ? It's . . . Vincent."

His ex-wife's betrayal had conditioned Vincent to be suspicious, and it seemed to him that Ivy's hesitation was damningly long. His reaction was to lose all desire, as if someone had suddenly dropped him off a pier into Puget Sound. "Jesus," he whispered in stunned disbelief, pushing himself up on stiffened forearms. Staring down at her, his black eyes glowed with accusation. "Anyone would have done," he charged her bitterly. "Wouldn't they, Ivy?" Releasing his grip on her wrists, he started to lever himself away from her.

Ivy blinked, not comprehending his abrupt mood shift. Where was he going? Did he plan to leave her—just like that? No! She needed him, she needed the forgetfulness she knew she'd find through his lovemaking.

It was the last straw. His question had barely penetrated her erotic haze and not connecting it with Vincent's history, she understood only that he was pulling away right when she needed him most. Rage, which up until that moment had been sublimated by sick terror and a need to hang on to her crumbling composure, suddenly exploded in a hot, blinding rush. Unthinkingly, she struck out at him with both hands.

"Damn you, Vincent!" she screamed, pummelling at his head, his shoulders, anything she could reach. *"Damn* you. You've been hounding me to sleep with you for *weeks,* but you're nothing but a miserable tease . . ." Consumed by a desire to annihilate him, she continued to strike out with blind fury.

Vincent dodged her blows as best he could, amazed at her strength as he fought to gain control of her flailing arms. Finally he got her by the forearms and forced them to the bed, lying on her full length to pin her down. Both of them were breathing in harsh, ragged pants by the time he pushed up enough to see her face, and the tiny bit of space that separated them fairly crackled with antagonistic sexual frustration. "If all you want is a little oblivion, lady, just say the word and I'll fuck you right through the mattress," he snarled furiously, giving her a shake. "But damned if I'm gonna do it before you even know who you've got inside you!"

"What?" She went still, blinking in shock. "That's not true!" she whispered hoarsely as it dawned on her what he was thinking. Bucking furiously in an attempt to dump him off her, her rage burned a few degrees hotter at the ease with which he rode out the attempt. "Dammit, D'Ambruzzi, that is not

true! When are you going to get it through your thick head that I am *not* your ex-wife? My God! Just for the record, I never pledged fidelity to you. But let me clue you in—if I had wanted just anyone, there are other men I could have called!''

His dark eyes burned with the betrayal he felt. ''Then why the hell didn't you even know my name?''

''I *did!*''

''Yeah, right, after you'd thought about it for five minutes.''

She bared her teeth, growling in frustration. ''Five minutes, my butt! That's a crock and you know it.'' Then with insulting slowness, as if communicating to someone a little less intelligent than the mentally impaired, she stared him straight in the eye and said, ''I . . . was . . . all . . . set . . . to . . . make love, you . . . cretinous jerk. It . . . took . . . me . . . a . . . few . . . seconds . . . to . . . change . . . gears. But read my lips, D'Ambruzzi,'' she commanded, resuming a normal speed and pronouncing each word with exaggerated precision. ''I knew *exactly* whom I was trying to seduce.''

Then, abruptly, it all became too much and her face crumpled. Her passion had been effectively squelched and she was simply too weary to sustain her anger. That left her with no reserves to hold off the terror she'd been trying so desperately to keep at arm's length. She started to shake. ''Oh God, oh God, Vincent,'' she sobbed. ''I'm so scared. Please don't be mad at me—all I wanted was a little forgetfulness for awhile and I knew your lovemaking would give it to me. Okay? That's all I wanted. I knew it was you.'' She was aware of him rolling them over and his arms, warm and strong, tightening around her. She raised her cheek up off his chest to stare at him. ''Why is this happening to me? God, it's like he's trying to build me a personality to satisfy some specifications only he understands. What's gonna happen when he finds out it doesn't fit?'' Tears streamed down her face.

"Shh, shh," Vincent crooned, brushing damp strands of hair off her cheeks and mopping at her tears with his fingertips. "Don't cry, Ivy. Shh, now, don't cry.'' Guilty about his suspicions and rattled by her abrupt loss of composure, he pressed her head back onto his chest and held her protectively. Stroking her back with one hand, he kissed the crown of her head. "Nothing's going to happen, because we're not going to let it get that far. It's going to be all right, Ivy," he promised her. "I'm gonna find that bastard and see to it he can't hurt you. It's going to be all right."

But long after she'd fallen into an exhausted slumber in his arms, Vincent lay awake wondering just how in hell he was going to keep that promise.

Chapter 12

Ivy awoke to find herself draped over Vincent D'Ambruzzi's chest. Shaking her hair from her eyes, she removed her long leg from its warm position between his thighs and pushed up on her palms to look down at him. A tender smile tugged up one corner of her mouth at the sight that greeted her.

Poor baby. For a guy who only wanted her for her body, he sure had the oddest ways of showing it.

He'd been fully dressed when she'd attacked him last night or early this morning or whenever it had been. For the most part he still was. He'd removed his gun—it was in its holster up in the corner of the mattress—and had wrestled his way out of one arm of his wrecked shirt. But the arm wrapped around her even in sleep was still fully clothed, and most of the shirt itself had ended up wadded beneath his back. He'd managed to toe off his shoes but was still wearing his socks, and although the waistband of his slacks had been opened to provide him a measure of ease, the slacks themselves had not been removed. Altogether, it couldn't have made for a very comfortable night.

For a man who professed to want only one thing, he sure went that extra mile for her. Grinning, she eased away from him, almost laughing aloud when he mumbled her name in protest, his arm tightening around her momentarily before going slack. She was almost certain he was harboring more emotions for her than he was willing to admit.

Oh God, he'd better be. She was about to stake her pride on the belief. Grabbing her toothbrush from her case, she walked down the hall to the bathroom, closing the door softly behind her. She snapped on the overhead light and turned to the sink.

Ivy leaned into the mirror as she brushed her teeth, peering at the intricate pattern Vincent's chest hair had left imprinted on her cheek. Spitting toothpaste foam into the sink, she rinsed, wrapped her hair in a towel to hold it off her face and borrowed his Ivory. She was in need of a little damage control and it was the only thing available.

Moments later, as she raised her dripping face to the mirror to assess the results, she experienced her first second thought. Perhaps she should take a minute to reconsider what she was about to do. After all, she'd tried seducing him last night and look where that had gotten her. Maybe she should . . .

No.

She wanted this; she did. She was aware there was a lot they needed to discuss, but it didn't have to be the very first item on their agenda. A better time surely would be after he'd made love to her. Yes, afterward, when she was relaxed by Vincent's brand of loving, she'd be better able to handle this hellacious mess with the rapist. And if he ultimately broke her heart . . . well, that was simply a chance she'd have to take. *Someone* had to make the first move.

Something was tugging at Vincent's awareness, urging him to wake up, but he didn't want to. Not, at any rate, before this dream of Ivy making love to him had run its course. No one in their right mind would choose consciousness over that, not when consciousness meant an empty bed in an empty apartment. Not when instead of being the recipient of the granddaddy of all wet dreams, it meant he'd once again find himself merely a solitary man with a solitary morning hard-on. No thanks—that was a cold dose of reality he was in no burning hurry to face.

There'd been too damn many such awakenings lately. And if they'd never possessed the power to bother him before he'd met the good doctor Pennington, they'd sure as hell gained power since.

Unfortunately, it didn't matter how hard he fought it—his mind was nevertheless struggling to surface from the murky depths of sleep. He strove to hang on to his dream state, and ironically, by focusing his concentration on that goal, he reached full consciousness before it dawned on him that this was no phantom lover arousing his body to a fever pitch.

He knew the feel of that skin and that satin; he'd felt it before.

"God," he mumbled hoarsely, opening his eyes. Now he remembered: it had been last night. She'd been frantic to make love last night but a jealous mistrust of her motives had made him refuse to cooperate. He recalled having made some crude accusation, recalled her fury and how she'd fallen apart . . .

Her voice, husky and warm, drove the fuzzy recollections from his mind. "Mornin', Vincent."

He raised his head and looked down the length of his body. He was naked; when the hell had that happened? Last night he hadn't managed more than a halfhearted attempt to undress himself. That had been his own damn fault, of course—if he had been willing to release her for a couple of minutes he might have done the job right. In any event, Ivy was now lying between his bare, sprawled thighs, pressing kisses into his equally bare stomach. And when she tilted her head back to give him a soft smile, he realized that what he'd thought to be a dream was, in fact, reality. She actually had slipped out of the straps of her nightie in order to nestle his erection between her breasts. "Ivy?" he whispered uncertainly. This wasn't happening; it had to be a continuation of his dream . . . and any second now he was going to wake up for real.

But nobody's dreams were this good. "Mmm," she acknowledged, giving him a lazy smile, and then dropped her head to press more kisses into hard abdominal muscle. He felt himself squeezed deeper into her cleavage as her body shifted fractionally.

"Jesus!" He shoved up on his elbows, staring wild-eyed at the back of her bent head. Her hair had parted at her nape, revealing the slender line of her neck where it curved into her shoulders. He could feel the sweep of her hair against his stomach, see the dimples in her shoulders, and had to clench his teeth against the groan building in his throat.

Eyes tracking down the long curve of her back and longer expanse of her legs, he observed that except for the emerald green satin still bunched around her hips, she was all bare, firm, creamy freckled skin. He was aware of her mouth, soft and sweet, stringing kisses across his stomach, of her forearms and hands warm against the skin of his thighs and abdomen. Most of all, he was aware of her breasts. Pushed together by arms held clamped to her side, they generated a heat that drove him to the point of insanity.

His fingers curled into the sheets. He wanted to reach out and stroke his hands down her back; he wanted to bury them in her hair and guide her mouth down to where the head of his erection strained between her breasts. Instead, he heard his voice with hoarse interrogation demand, "Who taught you that?"

It was an unforgivable question and he knew it . . . but he couldn't seem to prevent himself from asking it. The thought of her doing this to another man had crept into his mind and expanded like a malignancy until it blocked out everything else.

Ivy went very still for an instant. Then her lips left his flesh, her hands slid from his body to the mattress on either side of his hips, and she slowly raised her head to stare up the length of his chest at his face. "Don't do this again, Vincent," she said very quietly. "No one taught me anything, okay? I'm an inventive woman; why can't you just accept the fact that there's no valid reason for your paranoid jealousy."

She pushed up onto her hands and knees, rocking back in one fluid motion to sit on her heels between his sprawled thighs. Glancing from his erection to his face, she was once again struck by the duality of his nature. It seemed his mind was forever at odds with his body. He was gazing at her with a lack of expression that was nearly puritanical in its sternness, yet it was a look belied by the tousled sexiness of his rumpled hair and morning-shadowed jaw, discredited by his erection. *That* seemed to say: I don't believe half the things that come out of my mouth. Convince me I'm wrong; it's not as if I *want* to be suspicious all the time.

One corner of her mouth quirked wryly. "I couldn't help but notice this as I was undressing you," she said, gently trailing her fingertips over him in an attempt to tease him out of his jealousy. "It seemed such a shame to let it go to waste."

She waited for a response, any response, hoping that for once he would not be so damned intense. Please, her mind whispered, just once can't you simply accept the lighthearted out I've provided you? Please, Vincent. Let's move on.

The odds of receiving a positive reaction, she figured, ran about neck and neck with the possibility that his response would be negative. The one thing she didn't expect was that she'd fail to elicit any reaction at all. In the end, that was what she got—nothing. Vincent simply stared at her with unreadable eyes.

Raking her fingers through her hair, she knelt upright in the middle of the bed, returning his look. Unselfconscious in her semi-nudity, she had no awareness of the lift of her breast when she raised her arm or the silky way her hair feathered through her fingers to drift back into the thick curtain that swayed against her collarbone.

But Vincent was aware. It tore him in a hundred different directions, because more than anything he wanted to reach out and accept what she was offering him. Yet something stopped him from doing just that. Feelings of possessiveness and suspicion consumed him, were new to him, and he couldn't seem to get them under control. Rife with raging confusion, full of conflict, and unwilling to expose his vulnerability, he simply lay there and gazed up at her impassively.

Ivy sighed in defeat and reached for the straps of her nightgown. "I give up," she said heavily, pulling them into place. Climbing over his leg, she moved to the side of the bed where she sat with her back to him for a moment, wondering how on earth they were going to work together now. She had a million questions about the rapist and what had happened last night. She should have pursued those instead of this ridiculous seduction attempt, because she sure as hell didn't know how to talk to him now with this tension so thick between them.

She glanced at him over her shoulder. "I'm going to use your shower," she said with stilted formality and rose to her feet. "I'll be quick . . . and then I'll get out of here." Wishing he'd say something—anything—that might prevent her from going, she walked from the room without a backward glance.

Vincent remained where he was, waiting for his panic to subside. It had began clawing at his gut the moment he'd heard her admit defeat. When after several minutes he realized it wasn't going to abate, he lunged up off the bed.

As he let himself into the bathroom, he didn't have a single idea about what he was going to say. All he knew was that he couldn't let her leave like this—not and still live with himself. He picked her discarded nightgown up off the floor and stood pulling it distractedly through his fist while he tried to marshall his thoughts. Then he turned, caught a glimpse of his reflection in the mirror and the dilemma was momentarily sidetracked.

Good God Almighty. Now there was a face to inspire trust. Unaware he was duplicating Ivy's earlier actions, he leaned closer to the mirror. Hell, it was a miracle she hadn't run screaming from his apartment the moment she'd awakened; he'd *arrested* men who looked more respectable than he did. Glancing at Ivy's outline through the shower door, he decided a little judicious grooming was in order—well worth the extra few minutes it was going to take if it'd just provide him with better odds of having her listen to him.

He looped the strap of her nightie over the hook on the back of the door and reached for his razor and toothbrush.

Ivy wasn't a woman to whom tears ordinarily came easily. As she stood beneath the pounding spray, however, she found herself crying for the second time in twelve hours. It seemed to her she'd bawled more since she'd met Vincent D'Ambruzzi than she had in the past year total.

Dabbing her tongue at the corner of her mouth to catch the steady flow of saline that rolled down to her lips, she silently damned Vincent, his ancestry, his infuriating hot-and-cold sexuality, and the helpless attraction that still made her desire a relationship with him. And damn his bitch of an ex-wife, too. If anyone was the villain in this scenario, it was her. The way that woman had destroyed Vincent's ability to trust was nothing short of criminal.

Staring through teary eyes at the white formica wall opposite her, Ivy was slow to associate the snick of the shower door opening with the object of her thoughts. She turned her head in its direction. Vincent stood framed naked in the opening.

Immediately, she turned her back on him and stuck her face under the spray, furiously embarrassed to have been caught crying. She was aware of him stepping into the enclosure behind her and pulling the door closed.

The stall had not been built with two tall adults in mind and Vincent was forced to crowd against

Ivy's back. That was okay with him; he wanted an excuse to touch her anyway. "I'm sorry," he said. He tried to kiss the contour of her neck but she scrunched her shoulder to her ear, giving him the option of either backing off or having his jaw crushed. He backed off. "I'm sorry, Ivy," he repeated, rubbing his jaw against her temple instead. "I am. Please . . . I don't want you to leave."

When she failed to respond it didn't exactly astound him. He hadn't overlooked the tears pooling on her lower lids and rolling down her cheeks; the sight had twisted his gut with regret.

She'd cried last night, too, and sure, it had shook him. He knew her well enough to understand she wasn't a woman who easily lost control. But those tears he'd mainly attributed to an overload of shock and anger . . . the shock of being called at an unlisted number by a known rapist and anger at him for his suspicious nature. *These* tears he knew to have been caused solely by him.

He reached for the soap and sudsed up his hands. He worked the lather into her shoulders and neck, utilizing strong fingers and thumbs to knead the tense muscles he discovered there. "I don't know why I say half the things I say to you," he admitted in a low voice to her averted profile. "You said there was no valid reason for my jealousy and I recognize the truth of that. But emotionally . . . ?" Ivy felt his shrug against her back.

He kneaded her neck in silence for a few moments. Then he laughed, briefly, nearly silently, and with no genuine humor. "I've never behaved like this with anyone else," he admitted. "And I swear to God I don't understand it myself . . . so how am I supposed to explain it to you? There's just something about you that gets to me and makes me crazy-jealous. I can't stand the thought of other men seeing you like this, making love to you."

She bristled under his hands and he said, "Do you know that practically since the first moment I laid eyes on you I've had this running fantasy where I handcuff you to my headboard and violate you six ways from Sunday? I mean, this after three years of celibacy when I wasn't even particularly *interested* in sex."

"I can't take much more of your mood swings," Ivy stated flatly. She swiped surreptitiously at the tears on her cheeks, briefly glanced at him over her shoulder, and then turned her face back to the wall. "One day you make love to me but the next I'm ignored," she said bitterly. "Then you pursue me with everything you've got, but when I give you what you want—or God forbid, dare to initiate something myself—either I don't know who I'm with or I'm a slut."

Vincent winced. "I know," he acknowledged and slid his large, soapy hands up and down her arms. "I've been acting crazy and irrational—"

"You don't trust me—that's what it boils down to. How are we supposed to go forward if there's no trust?"

"It's not you, Ivy," he tried to assure her. Then with painful honesty, he confessed, "I—I . . . I'm not sure I know how to trust anymore. I think somewhere along the way I lost the ability."

"You mean you let that bitch wife of yours steal it from you!"

His hands tightened on her shoulders; he had to consciously will them to relax. "Yeah, I guess I did. But I'll get it back," he promised, turning her around to face him in the narrow confines of the shower stall. He watched the shower spray sluice the bubbles from her shoulders before he raised his gaze to her eyes.

"Keith once said that LaDonna really messed with my mind, and I guess he was more right than

I cared to admit at the time. But I promise you I'll work at not taking it out on you anymore." He slicked her wet hair back and took her head in his hands, pressed kisses into her eyelids, the shadowed hollows beneath her cheekbones, her temples. Raising his head, he looked into her eyes, which were leaf-green now with her emotions, and said, "I don't want you to leave, Ivy. Please. We can work this out. Say you'll stay and I'll do whatever it takes to make this up to you."

He kissed her then, and Ivy knew she was going to grant him everything he asked. There was a corner of her mind that wished to hang onto her grudge—if only to feel she had more willpower than to allow herself to be manipulated by her sexual urges like some teenaged girl in the throes of her first crush. But the truth was, his mouth was hot, his tongue was knowledgeable, and she *wanted* to be convinced.

Lifting her arms, she reached to clasp his cheeks between her hands, a little shudder of appreciation shivering along her nerve endings at the smooth feel of the freshly shaved skin beneath her fingers.

Vincent made a sound deep in his throat and whirled her a half turn, pressing her up against the slick, warm wall. Water from the showerhead hit their sides, and Vincent freed a hand to fumble for the controls, shutting it off.

Ivy felt the muscles of his cheeks lengthen beneath her fingers as his mouth widened over hers; she tasted the deeper reach of his tongue. Her head was driven back against the enclosure wall, and she inhaled sharply as his hand returned to insinuate between their bodies, splaying possessively over her breast. They both began to breathe in a harsh, choppy rhythm that was magnified by the acoustics of the shower enclosure.

Vincent ripped his mouth free and stood, chest

heaving, staring at her langorous eyes, her swollen lips. "Oh, God," he whispered reverently and bent his knees to kiss his way down her throat. Breathing heavily, mouth open against her damp, fragrant skin, he murmured, "Sweet, sweet Jesus. What you do to me." His tongue bathed the hollow at the base of her throat, his teeth scraped over her collarbone.

He liked the fact that she wasn't much shorter than he. It meant he didn't get a crick in his neck when he kissed her; meant too that they fit together better than he had with any other woman.

It meant he didn't have to squat so low to bury his face in her cleavage.

Pressing his long, brown fingers against the sides of her breasts to surround his lean cheeks with their warm, creamy fullness, he rubbed against them like a cat. Ivy made a sound deep in her throat at the rubbery stroke of smooth skin on smooth skin and kneaded her hands over his shoulders and down his back as far as she could reach. Her head tipped back and her fingers anchored themselves in the hard muscles halfway down his back when he suddenly decided to involve his tongue.

Vincent released his hold on the outer curves of her breasts and came up for air. Licking his way up one full slope, he opened his mouth around a straining ruby nipple. As his tongue curled and lips pursed to suck on the distended morsel, he reached for its unattended mate and in the process cracked his elbow viciously against the enclosure wall. Mouth going slack, he fell back against the wall behind him and clutched his funny bone until the flashes of exquisite agony stopped zinging along his nerve endings.

Ivy's eyelids slowly opened and she blinked at him in lethargic confusion. "Vincent?" she murmured. "What . . . ? Why'd you . . . ?"

Suddenly her eyes cleared, only to immediately narrow. "Damn you, Vincent D'Ambruzzi, don't tell me you've changed your mind again!"

He grinned at her indignation and straightened away from the wall, bringing him back chest to breast with her again. "I haven't changed anything," he said, catching her bottom lip between his teeth. He tugged at it teasingly and then set it loose. "Let's get the hell out of here," he murmured wryly, "before I end up crippling myself."

Barely allowing her to pause long enough to wrap her sopping hair in a towel, he aimed a few desultory swipes at the moisture beading both her backside and his chest and then tossed his towel aside. One large hand shackling her wrist, he pulled her with ill-concealed impatience down the hallway. Kicking the door closed behind them, he hustled them across the room to the bed, where the force of his dive landed them mid-mattress in a tangle of arms and legs.

"This is more like it," he stated in a low rough voice as he pushed up on his hands to loom over her. He looked her up and down thoroughly before he met her eyes. Bending to brush his mouth over the full curve of her bottom lip, he said with hoarse ferocity, "God, you're so pretty."

Ivy blushed; she felt unaccustomedly shy and uncertain how to respond. There was something about the intensity of his compliment that had a paralyzing effect on her vocal cords.

Vincent didn't appear to expect a response. He lowered himself on top of her, kissing her with a power that drove her head into the mattress. Thumbs locking on her temples, his long fingers tunneled behind her neck, knocking her towel loose as he tipped her head back to give him deeper access to her mouth.

Ivy's fingers were digging into the warm muscles

of his back by the time he lifted his mouth. She was highly aware of his body, hot, damp and naked upon hers. God, he was so hard all over, shoulders, arms, chest, stomach and legs all blanketing her in muscular heat and scent. She loved what he was doing to her, the way he made her feel . . . physically, at least. Emotionally . . . ? Well, emotionally, she was very much afraid she was falling in love with him.

It probably wasn't wise; it certainly wasn't in her own best interests, but there was a very genuine likelihood that she was tumbling headlong all the same. Being reminded of all that potential heartbreak caused her to stiffen up defensively for a moment, as if by denying herself physically she could somehow guarantee her future safekeeping.

Then Vincent slid down to kiss her breasts. She arched beneath the double-barrelled sensation of seeing his lean brown cheeks flex and feeling the resultant tug as he sucked her nipple into his mouth . . . and decided she'd worry about the state of her heart tomorrow.

Tangling her fingers in his hair, she held him to her. Her breath caught in her throat and she closed her eyes; but a moment later the steady assault on her senses prompted a restlessness that had her watching him once again. She ran her hands down his neck, across his shoulders, scratching her nails down his back. Vincent shuddered and his mouth went lax around her nipple as his eyes snapped up to look at her.

"Oh, God, *yes,*" he groaned, his eyelids weighted by pleasure. "Touch me, Ivy. I want to feel your hands all over me." He rubbed his cheek against her breast. "God, you're incredible. You taste so good . . . feel so good."

He slid off her and rolled to his side. She turned to face him. Propping herself up on an elbow, she trailed her hand over his chest, weaving her fingers through the cloud of jet hair. She tugged on it, combed her fingers through it, then burrowed beneath it to worry the flat copper disk of his nipple.

His breath hissed through his teeth and he jerked. But he remained very still, allowing her the freedom to toy with him. He kept the hand not trapped beneath his head firmly at his side as she leaned forward to nip at his neck and brush her breasts teasingly against his chest.

Ivy pulled back until their bodies no longer touched . . . except for her hand, which moved everywhere—palpating the muscles of his shoulders, grazing down his side, bumping over the ridges in his stomach and cresting the rise of his hip to reach around and grip a hard, rounded cheek. She insinuated her knee between his legs and rubbed it up and down his inner thigh, coming close to but never quite touching that which he most wanted touched.

"God." His fingers were clenched into hard fists and sweat sheened his body and face as he leveled hot, black eyes on her. "You really like dancing on the rim, don'tcha?"

Her smile was that of a smug cat toying with a spider. "Um hmm."

"You know what the only problem with that is, Ivy?"

"No, what?" Her knee grazed the hard shaft straining between them.

He sucked in a ragged breath and his voice was unnaturally rough when he said, "Two can play this game," and before she knew what was happening, he had her flat on her back, both her hands pinned above her head by one of his.

Ivy grinned up at him. "I was counting on it," she whispered. She wiggled her hands experimentally to see if she could free them, but his grip held her. "Is this part of that handcuff fantasy you mentioned?"

Vincent's teeth flashed white against his swarthy skin. "Something along those lines," he agreed and lowered his head to kiss her. Raising it again, he said, "You're quite the little tease. But my mama always taught me it's much more blessed to give than to receive. Let's see if she was right."

And then it was his hand that trifled with her responses. He fondled her breasts, but ignored her nipples. He stroked his fingers up her thighs, brushed them over the downy triangle of tangled red curls, but didn't deepen the caress, even when her thighs spread and her hips raised pleadingly. Ivy began to pant, small needy whimpers sounding in her throat. She arched and twisted in an attempt to follow his tormenting fingers.

And then she begged. "Oh, God, Vincent, please. I don't want to play this game anymore—touch me! Please, Vincent, touch me."

He groaned and released her wrists. Rolling on top of her, he kissed her—a wet, frantic, edge-of-control kiss, and his hand moved between their bodies to delve into damp, red curls, finally touching her the way she craved to be touched, his fingers slipping up and down slick, welcoming folds. He nudged her thighs wider with his knees, lowered his hips and then, the head of his erection prodding her threshold . . . remembered he didn't have a condom on . . . or any in the apartment, for that matter.

The obscenity he roared snapped Ivy's eyes open. "What, what? Don't *stop*, Vincent!"

"No condoms," he panted. "Oh, shit! Why did

I tease us both this way . . . Ivy, I don't have any condoms!'' His hips pressed forward. "I'll pull out, I swear I'll pull out—''

"No, wait." She pressed against his shoulders. When he continued muttering, she cupped his jaw in her hand and forced him to look at her. "Vincent, it's okay, I brought some. My big seduction last night, remember? They're in my case.''

He was off the bed and across the room in a flash. Ivy squeezed her thighs together in an agony of impatience and stared at his long, brown back. She listened to him rummage through her case, hearing the small tearing of the package and his whispered swear words as he fumbled it on.

"Purple?" he snarled in disgust. "Ivy, I've got a big purple—''

"Oh, God, Vincent," she wailed, "who cares? Quit bragging and get over here!''

"Yes ma'am." And then he was back, sliding on top of her, pushing up on his forearms to look down into her flushed face. "But if you know what's good for you," he said with a sweet, crooked smile, "you won't cast your eyes on my studly *luuv*-tool. It looks like someone took a hammer to it." He shook his head then, not sure whether to be ego-whipped or amused. This wasn't exactly the way he would have planned this little scenario. "Damn, I'm suave," he muttered.

She laughed. She hadn't expected this. The intensity, the almost unbearable arousal, yes . . . but not this endearing self-deprecating humor. Wrapping her arms around his neck, she responded without thinking, "Love-tool? Oh, Vincent, I love you.''

She could have bitten her tongue in two. If she scared him off now, she'd open up a vein—she swore she would. But he only groaned her name and kissed her, the way he'd been kissing her before the condom crisis had interrupted them. His hand returned to its nest between her legs and then he was entering her.

He was big and hard, but so gentle, easing into her in stages, giving her time to acclimate to the intrusion before pressing forward a little bit further. He inhaled sharply through clenched teeth when he suddenly sank all the way in. "How could I have forgotten how tight you are?" he wondered hoarsely. He looked down at her. "You okay?"

She tilted her hips slightly, which had him sucking for breath again. "Oh, yes," she murmured. "I feel great."

"Oh, God, I'll vouch for that," he agreed fervently. His hips pulled back and thrust gently forward, pulled back and thrust, long, smooth strokes that robbed Ivy of breath. He slid his hand out from between their bodies and scooped his arms under her to cup her bottom in both big hands, fingers gripping, pulling her sharply into each thrust.

"Oh my God, Vincent." Ivy wrapped her arms around his neck, her legs around his waist, and moved with him. "Oh my God."

She wanted it to last forever; she was striving frantically for that final completion. Already nerves deep in her body were winding tighter and tighter, screaming for release. Head dropping back, neck arching, she dug her fingernails into the hard muscles of his shoulders. Little gasps caught in her throat as she moved her legs higher and felt him bump against that coil of neediness. Then he had retreated. "Vincent!" And he was back again. Then gone. Then back. "Oh, please . . ." she whispered mindlessly.

And like an overwound clock, she suddenly erupted in a series of ever-harder, farther-reaching explosions. Crying out harshly, she froze, arms tightening in a stranglehold on his neck, legs clamping down to hold him deep as she jerked with each successive spasm, his name a long, attenuated wail that wrenched her throat.

"Oh, man." Hearing her, feeling her squeezing him like a wet satin fist, sent Vincent over the edge. Toes digging into the mattress, he slammed into her. One of his hands slid free of its grip on her buttocks to splay over her throat, his thumb digging into one angle of her jaw, his fingers into the other. He kissed her feverishly, groaning into her mouth as with a final thrust he came in a wild torrent. When the last scalding pulsation was complete, Vincent suddenly collapsed, sending the breath in Ivy's lungs whooshing into his mouth.

"Sorry." He pushed up a little to give her room to breathe.

"No, don't move." She tugged him back down. "I like bearing your weight."

"Oh, God, you're somethin', Ivy." He pressed his mouth to her cheeks, her forehead, to the hollow behind her ear and in a path down the side of her neck. He shivered beneath the fingernails she scratched along his back and buttocks. "You are something so special."

It was the aftermath she'd missed out on by falling asleep the last time they'd made love and she discovered to her great delight, that Vincent was a post-coital cuddler. Long after the orgasm had faded, he seemed perfectly content to prop himself over her, combing his fingers through her damp hair, trailing them over her features and down her neck. He pressed more kisses into her shoulders, her face, her throat, anywhere he could reach. His tenderness went a long way toward softening the inevitable shock.

Which was when he looked into her eyes, sighed and said regretfully, "Much as I hate to bring this up, Ivy . . . we've gotta talk about that phone call you received last night."

Chapter 13

With an involuntary grimace of distaste, Ivy went very still. Then she nodded, echoed his sigh, and let her arms drop leadenly to the mattress. "Yeah, I suppose we do."

It shouldn't have taken her by surprise; after all, she'd known from the moment she'd awakened that it was a subject requiring discussion. And in truth, there was a large part of her that genuinely needed to talk about it.

Yet somehow it still managed to catch her off guard. It probably had more to do with her lack of readiness to let reality intrude than with anything else.

Vincent slid off her, but when she rolled toward the edge of the mattress in preparation to rising, he snaked out a hand to tumble her back. Wrapping his arms around her waist, he pulled her flush against his body and without relinquishing his grip rolled onto his back, so she ended up draped atop him. Spitting her tangled hair from her mouth,

Ivy braced her forearms on his chest and pushed up in order to look down at his face.

"I didn't mean you had to race away right this second," he said softly. "How 'bout a kiss before we get down to business?"

She was only too happy to oblige and after a mere moment of giving it her best effort felt some telling results pulsating against her stomach. Vincent groaned and his hands, which had been stroking up and down her back, suddenly gripped her head and moved it away.

"Maybe that wasn't such a hot idea," he panted and dumped her onto the mattress. This time it was he who rolled over and climbed to his feet. Turning to look down at her, he said, "Why don't you, uh, put some clothes on. I'll make us breakfast."

When Ivy joined him in the kitchen a short while later, she was dressed in an ancient pair of jeans and a copper tank top, her hair neatly French-braided away from her face. She stopped in the doorway to watch Vincent, who hadn't bothered to do more than pull on the same disreputable pair of cutoffs he'd worn to yesterday's barbecue. As he deftly managed two fry-pans at once, she found herself marvelling. God help her. She knew she was in big trouble if she found such mundane actions so enthralling. "Want me to set the table?" she asked.

"Yeah." He smiled at her over one bare brown shoulder. "And pour the juice. Or there's milk, if you'd rather have that. Or—" his chin jutted at the pot on the stove "—I've got coffee made."

"Juice is fine with me." She gathered the necessary implements from cupboard and drawer and arranged two place settings at his small table. She had fetched the orange juice and salt and pepper shakers and was folding napkins next to their plates when he brought over a platter heaped with sauteed mushrooms, scrambled eggs and pan-fried potatoes. They seated themselves, tacitly deferring conversation until they'd finished eating.

"I'll get the coffee," Vincent said and pushed back from the table. "Finished? Hand me your plate." He carried the small stack of dishes back to the kitchen. "I think maybe you oughta move in with me," he called out casually and reappeared in the doorway a moment later holding the coffee pot. In his other hand two mugs dangled by their handles from a crooked finger.

Ivy, still seated at the table, gawked at him in silent stupefaction and Vincent rolled his shoulders uneasily. Okay, so maybe that had come out sounding a little offhand, and he hadn't actually expected her to leap at his offer, but neither had he anticipated sending her into shock. "Say something," he ordered gruffly, thumping the pot and mugs on the table. He straddled the chair across from her. "No, on second thought, hear me out first—"

"Move in with you?" she croaked.

"It makes sense, Ivy, if you think about it." He talked rapidly to forestall an outright refusal. "You'd be safer here. We can get call forwarding for your phone and redirect all your calls here without having to change the number. No one would ever know they weren't going to your place." Her expression had yet to change and Vincent rammed his fingers through his hair. "Listen," he urged, "It bothers me that this guy somehow got ahold of your unlisted number. I don't like it. Hell, if he can do that, then chances are he also has your address now. At least if you're livin' here and he goes so far as to show up on your doorstep, you won't be there." That came out a little confused, but he hoped she got the drift.

"So you want me to move in with you so I'll be safe," she clarified flatly.

He almost said yes; the temptation was so strong. It would be an easy way out, a way to protect himself against saying anything that might be construed as a commitment . . . a way to salvage his pride if she laughed in his face and told him to forget it. But he looked into her eyes, observed the way she was holding herself with unnatural rigidness, and knew in his gut that if he did that he'd lose the last bit of credibility he still had with her.

She'd sacrificed her own pride more times than he'd deserved by swearing she'd never allow him close enough again to hurt her and then turning around and making a liar out of herself by letting him back into her life. And he'd rewarded her, more often than not, by making her cry. The least he owed her now was the truth.

"That's part of it," he admitted. He poured a cup of coffee and slid it across the table to her. "An important part, but you know damn well that's not all there is to it."

He hesitated, aware of Ivy clutching her coffee cup in both hands, watching him with big solemn eyes. He felt stymied by his need to convince her to move in without letting her know how important it was to him. He owed her the truth, yes. But not if the price was putting himself in a position where his heart was going to get stomped on again. Taking a deep breath, he finally said, "I want to wake up to you in my bed. To be able to reach out and touch you whenever I want. I want to know more about you—what your favorite foods are, your favorite color, if you're a dog person or a cat person."

Still she didn't respond, and he struggled—none too successfully—with frustration. "Dammit, Ivy," he admitted gruffly, "I think about you all the time, whether you're here or not. I've tried not to, but I do. I guess what I'm saying is that I want a—'' he nearly choked ''—monogamous relationship with you, okay?'' When she blinked but remained silent he blew. ''Say something, dammit! Are you gonna move the hell in with me or aren't you?''

Ivy raised the coffee cup to her lips to give herself a second to think. He was so volatile. He'd started out attempting to persuade and ended up practically yelling at her.

And yet . . .

He'd progressed from ''I want your body'' to ''monogamous relationship.'' If he'd looked a bit as if he were trying to swallow a golf ball getting the phrase out, well . . . he was trying.

Acknowledging in her heart her own fiercely held desires and remembering Anna's remark yesterday about the abnormal control Vincent had imposed on his emotions since his divorce, she decided to try viewing his mercurial temperament with her the same way that Anna did—as an improvement over never allowing his composure to be ruffled at all. And in all honesty, she did prefer his temper to the few times she'd watched that wall descend between them, the one that masked his expression or made it go blank. A temper was something she could fight, whereas his control sometimes seemed impenetrable.

Taking a sip of her coffee, she lowered the cup, looked him in the eye, and replied to his belligerent inquiry. ''Yes. I am.''

He'd already marshalled his arguments and had his mouth open to present them before it kicked in that she'd agreed. ''Yeah?'' His smile was slow, pleased, and impossibly beautiful to Ivy.

''Yeah.'' Returning his smile, she reached across the table and touched her fingertips to his lean cheek, moved when he immediately wrapped his fingers around hers and leaned into her touch. "God only knows how it'll work out, though, Vincent. I've never lived with anyone before and you're so damn tidy. I'm not all that neat myself—"

"Yeah, I've noticed that." His grin grew wider.

"—although I'm getting better. The biggest problem, though, is what my family's going to have to say about it. After that very public accusation you made the day I moved in, there's no predicting—"

Vincent shifted uneasily on his chair. Moving her hand away from his face, he carried it to the tabletop and folded it in both of his. He ran his brown thumb back and forth over the pale fingertips sticking out of his grip, his eyes tracking the movement as if it were the most fascinating sight in the world. "Um . . . about that, Ivy—we've gotta talk."

"About my family?" She eyed his down-bent head suspiciously. "Is this something I don't want to hear?"

"Probably." He looked up at her. "I'd, uh, rather you didn't tell them about us just yet."

"You'd rather . . . ?" Offended, she sat very erect. "And why, pray tell, is that?" She tried to tug her hand free, but he tightened his clasp.

"Don't, Ivy—don't pull away from me." Without releasing his grip, he freed a hand and reached out to curl his fingers under her chin, lightly rubbing his thumb back and forth over her lower lip. "And don't look at me like you think I've got some hidden agenda, either, because it just ain't so. We never got a chance to talk last night about that call you received, but unlisted numbers aren't that easy to obtain." Seeing he had her full attention, he released her chin and continued, "Now, this Hart guy may work for the telephone company, in which case he'd possibly have access. But it could also be that he knows someone who knows you. Our primary objective is to keep you safe, and having it widely known that you're living with a cop is not the way to go about it."

"My relatives don't associate with rapists!"

"I'm sure you're right and I'm probably creating problems where none exist. But it's not as if you can tell a sexual deviate just by looking at one either, Ivy; their appearance is as normal as yours or mine and so is their usual social behavior. Maybe he's a friend of a friend or a friend of a relative, or maybe he has nothing whatsoever to do with any of the people you know. Look, just give me a couple of weeks to exhaust my normal methods; that's all I'm asking. We'll get call forwarding for your phone and I'll have a trace placed on any incoming calls. If we're lucky, we'll track him down that way." She was regarding him round-eyed and he asked gently, "You wanna tell me about the call you got last night? What'd his voice sound like?"

She repeated, more coherently than she had before, what she'd told him upon tracking him down at the hospital the previous evening. "He was whispering, Vincent. I don't know if I'd even recognize the voice if I heard him speak in normal tones. You know, my family's not stupid," she said out of the blue, suddenly reverting back to their previous topic. "They're going to figure something's up if I'm never home when they drop by."

Her persistence made him smile, albeit a bit wryly. "The security door downstairs works through the phone," he reminded her. "That's gonna be forwarded along with your regular phone calls. All you have to do is buzz them up and meet them in your own apartment."

"Oh, God, Vincent, it's all so complicated. Maybe we're rushing into this without giving it enough thought."

"Where are you gonna feel safest, Ive? Living here with me or alone next door?"

"Well ... here. But we'll be paying two rents, and I won't be able to use my beautiful new furniture, and I won't even have any *food* to offer my relatives when they drop by." Elbow firmly planted on the table top, she wrapped her free hand around her braid and pulled hard, regarding Vincent through troubled eyes. "I told Auntie Babe I'd invite her and Uncle Mack over for dinner and I never got around to it. Now what am I gonna do?"

"Ivy, it's not going to be forever. Invite your aunt and uncle over, fix 'em a meal and then come home when they leave. It's not as if I don't want to get to know your family—I just need a little breathing space to see if I can get a bead on this character first. Right now he's like distant thunder: a threat, but one that's still on the horizon. I want to keep him from getting close enough to burst his madness right over your head ... can you understand that?"

"Yes." She tugged her hand free and pushed back from the table. Circling it, she mimed for him to push his chair back also and, when he did, swung a long leg over his thighs to perch astride his lap. Meeting his dark eyes, she said seriously, "But you have to understand something too ... playing games with the truth this way makes me feel like a liar. Can't I at least tell Auntie Babe and Uncle Mack? They'll keep it to themselves if I ask them to."

He thought about what he knew of Ivy's aunt and uncle and finally nodded. "Okay," he agreed. "Invite them here for dinner sometime this week and we'll tell them then. They're reasonable folk; I imagine they'll understand the need for discretion."

"Thank you, Vincent." She smiled, looped her

arms over his bare shoulders, and kissed him. Pulling back, she eyed him with a hint of cockiness and said, "Maybe this living together business is going to work out after all."

The look he returned was stern. "As long as you don't expect to get your own way every time."

"Hey, I'm a reasonable woman. And I'm always willing to compromise." She wiggled her bottom experimentally and grinned when his eyelids drooped lazily and his long fingers wrapped around her hips to encourage a continuation of the rocking motion she'd instigated. "As long as you are."

He inhaled deeply through his nose, lifting up slightly in his seat to maintain contact. "Compromise is good," he agreed hoarsely.

Telling her aunt and uncle turned out to be less awkward than Ivy had feared it might be. She met them in her apartment Tuesday night and after giving Babe sufficient time to rave over Terry's upholstery job, she took them next door where together she and Vincent explained Ivy's new living arrangements and the phone call that had precipitated it. Her aunt and uncle were both horrified over the newest development, but while Mack also appeared a little flabbergasted by Ivy's decision to move in with a man he'd thought to be a near-stranger to his niece, Babe seemed not at all surprised.

Vincent had fixed them a sumptuous meal and the only awkward moment of the evening occurred when Uncle Mack said out of the blue, with his usual brusque directness, "This living together bullshit is all very well as a stopgap measure, I suppose. I understand when you say Ivy will be safer here." He drilled Vincent with his sharp brown eyes. "But it's still just a rationalization . . . unless she's sleeping on your couch." By the dull red staining Vincent's cheeks, he thought it safe to assume that particular scenario unlikely. "I'd better be hearin' some wedding plans from the two of you before the year has passed."

Poor Vincent—Ivy could tell he didn't know what to say. He sat very stiffly, meeting her uncle's look with a blank mask of composure. She imagined, however, that given how difficult it had been for him to admit to wanting even a simple relationship, he was probably hearing the steel-toned echoes of a trap door being sprung closed about now. Coming to his rescue, she kissed her uncle's bald spot as she passed with the coffee pot behind his chair, leaned to refill his coffee cup, and said lightly, "You goin' home tonight to clean and oil your old shotgun, Uncle Mack?"

He scowled at her over his shoulder. "You think it's funny, Missy, but I might do just that."

"Leave the children alone, dear," Babe said serenely, holding her cup up to Ivy for a warm-up. "They're old enough to know what they're doing . . . and I'm sure they'll come to a decision in their own time."

"Damn well better be the right one," was all Mack had time to mutter before his wife adroitly changed the subject.

"Well, that went pretty well, I think," Ivy said later and wisely kept her amusement to herself as she watched Vincent slam through his dresser drawers. She expected at any moment to hear that her relatives had better keep their noses out of his love life.

Vincent whirled on her with a thunderous expression. His shirt hung open and he wrestled blindly with his cuff buttons as he stared at her in disbelief from across the room. "Oh, it went just swell," he snapped sarcastically. "Your uncle hates my damn guts!"

That's what was bothering him? Ivy regarded him with surprise. Why, that wasn't what she'd thought he was brooding about at all—that was actually kind of sweet. With a straight face, she countered, "But he *did* agree not to mention our living arrangements to anyone, and that's the important thing, right?"

"Dammit, Ivy, he doesn't exactly have a poker face—I think he's contemplating castration!"

"Well, you *are* fornicating with his favorite niece." Then, seeing how sincerely disturbed he was by what he perceived to be her uncle's poor opinion of him, she stopped teasing and crossed the room. Stopping in front of him, she pulled his dangling cuffs over his clenched fists and tossed his shirt aside. She reached out to knead competent hands over his smooth shoulders, using her thumbs to massage the tight muscles on either side of his neck as she assured him softly, "He doesn't hate your guts, Vincent—Uncle Mack's from a different generation, that's all. He missed out on the sexual revolution, so some of his ideas about propriety tend to be a bit more old-fashioned than yours or mine." She gave him a crooked smile. "But look on the bright side. He *was* raised in an era that decreed boys will be boys. In his day it was considered the female's responsibility to draw the line sexually; so if he's disappointed with anyone, it's bound to be me, not you."

Vincent studied her expression through narrowed eyes, not thrilled with that scenario either. He knew how important Ivy's aunt and uncle were to her. "And that doesn't bother you?"

"It'd be nice if I could please everyone, wouldn't

it? Too bad I haven't found a way to do that." She shrugged. "Of course I hate to disappoint Uncle Mack; I love him dearly. But I figure I've ultimately got to do what *I* can live with . . . and I have to decide for myself first what that is before I can start worrying about what other people prefer me to do." One side of her mouth tilted up in a self-deprecating smile. "So, I suppose I'll just continue to bumble along, making my own choices."

"Jesus, you've got character." He wrapped his arms around her waist and hugged her. "And for what it's worth, Ivy, this is one choice I'm real glad you made." Flattening his palms against the back of her waist, he slid them slowly up and down the curves of her butt. "I still wish he liked me better, but at least your aunt seems to think I'm okay— what the hell *is* this?" His fondling halted when his fingers bumped for the third time over a pencil-shaped protuberance in her hip pocket. He fished it out.

"Uh, nothing, really," she muttered, blushing painfully. "Here, give me that." She tried to snatch it away.

He held her off, studying first her expression and then the stainless steel tube in his hand. "A scalpel?" He thumbed off the cap, verified the identity of the surgical instrument in his hand, and then looked back at her. "Planning on doing a little midnight surgery?"

"Oh, poop. This is embarrassing." She tried to pull away, wanting nothing so much as to avoid having him learn how far she'd diverged from her principles when she'd stuck that scalpel in her pocket. He wasn't likely to believe she had much character then.

But Vincent's arm tightened around her and he gazed at her impassively, his intention clear. She was not strolling away without an explanation.

Exasperated, she snarled, "I've been packing it around ever since *he* called, okay?" and then nearly winced at the petulant overtones in her voice. Lord, she sounded like a bad-tempered thirteen-year-old. She was embarrassed and ashamed, emotions which occasionally made her react that way.

"Jesus," Vincent breathed. He couldn't believe he'd missed the signs of just how terrified the possibilities, which the rapist's fixation had opened up to her, had made her. Bending to retrieve the cap, he restored it to the scalpel and handed it back to her. He watched as she sulkily repocketed it, all the while pointedly avoiding his eyes. With a sigh, he pulled her over to the bed where he sat them both down. She stared off across the room.

"You've been packing this around in your hip pocket since Sunday morning?" Her face reddened again, but she refused to answer. Vincent brushed his fingers over the hot, soft·skin along her jawline, exerting gentle pressure on her chin until she looked at him. "Have you?"

"Yes," she replied grudgingly.

"For protection?"

She shrugged.

Vincent smoothed his fingers down her throat. "Listen, with luck it'll never come to a need for that, but if it's personal security you desire . . ." He hesitated and then offered, "I could always teach you to use a gun."

"Oh, God, no." Her exhalation was audible as she turned to face him fully for the first time since he'd extracted the scalpel from her pocket. "Just carrying the damn scalpel around poses enough of a moral dilemma."

"Why should protecting yourself be a dilemma?"

She met his eyes. "I took an oath to do my damndest to *preserve* life, Vincent, and it meant— it means—something to me. You know what the main obligation of the Hippocratic oath is? First do no harm." She shook her head. "My God, it's bad enough that I can't seem to put this damn scalpel back in my bag where it belongs. The need to hang onto it has me all tied up in knots, because let's face it, I'm carrying it for the express purpose of harming a man. Yet at the same time, neither am I about to be caught defenseless the way Bess Polsen was. But the idea of a gun. . ." Once again she shook her head. "If push comes to shove, I *might* be able to use the scalpel. I'd hate to put money on it, but I might. And maybe, just maybe, I could somehow justify it to myself afterwards. But somehow I don't think I could ever bring myself to point a gun at a man. And if I *did* actually use one, I'm not sure I could find a way to learn to live with that decision." She peered up at him. "I'm not making a whole lot of sense, am I?"

"Not a lot." He stroked her hair for several silent moments before pressing her head against his bare shoulder. As far as he was concerned, if push came to shove, she had a perfect right to defend herself. He didn't see it as a moral quandary. But then, he was looking at her situation from an entirely different perspective—his own. Trying to see it from hers, he rubbed his jaw against the top of her head and finally said, "But I guess what you're saying is that you're feelin' pretty torn between your dedication to saving lives and maybe having to save your own at the expense of someone else's."

"Yes, exactly." Ivy discovered a particularly soft patch of skin between his shoulder and collarbone and pressed her cheek against it. She sighed. "And it's sure got me spinning my wheels."

Ivy was privately amazed by the ease with which she adjusted to living with Vincent. It was true she'd lusted after him from practically the moment they'd first laid eyes on each other, and of course she already had more than a sneaking suspicion she was falling in love with him.

Okay, had fallen.

What she hadn't envisioned was how much she was going to *like* him.

For the most part he was remarkably easy to live with, and that came as a true surprise. She'd conjured up only the haziest of images, but what she'd been able to picture was the two of them either fighting bitterly or making love with a passion hot enough to scorch the sheets. She hadn't foreseen anything in between. So far, however, they hadn't fought once.

Not that it had been that long, of course—only a week. All the same, she'd certainly never pictured Vincent urging her to sit on the couch with her feet in his lap so he could massage them with his strong hands when he noticed how tired she was after having been on them all day long in the ER.

She'd never imagined him talking so freely to her on so many different subjects or making her laugh so hard she couldn't breathe as they prepared dinner or straightened his apartment. In truth, she never would have credited him with having much of a sense of humor at all. Anna Graham had tried to tell her that day in her kitchen what a tease Vincent could be, but Ivy had only half believed it, for she'd rarely seen that side of him for herself.

She was seeing it now.

It wasn't all roses, of course. He withdrew into himself at odd moments, shutting her out with a deliberateness that was hurtful. He never mentioned the word love and his failure to do so apparently didn't cause him any hardship. She, on the other hand, found it necessary to bite her tongue to keep from expressing the emotion every time he touched her. And he never used endearments, not even the occasional meaningless ones uttered in the throes of passion.

But what passion. She'd never known sex such as this truly existed. Insatiable, inventive, uninhibited, Vincent had already put a considerable dent in the vase of condoms they'd transferred to his apartment. He'd made love to her in locations and in ways she'd never imagined . . . and until this past week she would have sworn she'd at least *heard* it all. For a man whom she'd at one time suspected of being repressed and puritanical, he'd proved to have a sexual wild streak that wouldn't quit.

On balance, she believed she would probably be almost ludicrously content if not for the ever-present knowledge of being some rapist's pet that darkened the edges of her life.

The way the man who called himself Hart had attached himself to her life kept her constantly off balance. Ordinarily a time like this in her life should have been unconditionally exciting, filled as it was with so many possibilities. She had a job she loved, family she loved, and—facing it truthfully—a man she loved.

Unfortunately, there was nothing ordinary about their circumstances. Hell, chances were she wouldn't have been invited to move in with Vincent in the first place if it hadn't been for the threat of this unbalanced man. And if somehow he still *had* asked her to live with him, they certainly wouldn't have had so many restrictions to contend with.

Vincent's insistence on keeping their living arrangements a secret had not changed. In addition, it had been decreed by him that she always answered the phone; he always answered the door. She never went to her car unaccompanied. In the mornings, she and Vincent left together. When she arrived at work, there were usually several people arriving at the same time with whom she could walk into the hospital; if there weren't, he'd given her strict instructions to remain in her car, with the doors locked, until someone showed up. At night she found a strapping male to walk her out, and she never failed to use the cellular phone Vincent had installed in her car to let him know her arrival time home; he was always there to meet her in the parking lot.

Schedules and secrecy. What kind of way was that to build a relationship?

They seemed to be cautiously building one, nonetheless, despite every impediment put in their way. Yet at the same time, at *all* times, there was a level of her consciousness that refused to let her relax entirely. It constantly held its breath waiting for Hart to make his next move.

Which he hadn't done, not so far. She had yet to receive another call from him . . . but that didn't prevent her from tensing every time the phone rang. She had come to dread the sound of its ring.

Neither did his silence convince her to put the scalpel back in her medical bag where it belonged. On edge all the time on one level or another, she continued to pack it in a pocket, continued to stubbornly close her ears to the reprimands of her conscience.

Vincent had gained access to a call tracer and it was all set to go. But now that Ivy half wished the pervert would call and get it over with, he didn't. This waiting for him to make his next move only served to inject an incredible amount of tension and uncertainty into her daily life. Ivy feared something was going to give.

She could only pray it wouldn't be her nerves.

Chapter 14

Vincent uttered a silent obscenity when he opened his front door and saw who was standing there. Good God, did her entire family have some sort of radar where she was concerned?

"Hi," Terry Pennington said. "Have you seen Ivy around today?"

He didn't bother to identify himself; but then it wasn't really necessary since Vincent already knew who he was anyway. Just a few days ago Ivy had sat with her legs draped over his thighs, her photo albums spread open across both their laps as she'd proudly identified each person in every snapshot for him.

For one brief moment, Vincent considered descending into sarcasm and asking if he looked like an answering service, or simply saying no and sending her damn cousin on his way. But he really was a lousy liar . . . and besides, he could hear Ivy stirring from the couch in the other room. He knew she could hear them and didn't particularly care to deal with her wrath. Unenthusiastic but resigned, Vincent stepped back and opened the door wider. "Come on in."

Having recognized Terry's voice, Ivy was already on her feet by the time the two men walked into the living room. For just a second, she let her gaze stray past her cousin to Vincent, taking in the ridge of clenched muscle along his jawline. Clearly he was not happy about her cousin tracking her down here. Not exactly pleased herself with the aggressive way he was staring at Terry or the long finger he idly smoothed over the butt of his gun, which stuck out of its holster at the small of his back where he'd clipped it when the doorbell rang, she tried to keep one eye on him as she turned her attention back to Terry. She gave him a slight smile. "So how'd you get past the security door this time?"

"Hey, it wasn't as if I needed to do anything tricky," he retorted a little defensively as he crossed the room to give her a quick peck on the lips, an action which for no good reason made Vincent feel even more hostile. "The security in this place sucks." He gazed around the living room, absorbing in one comprehensive glance, the casual amalgam of odds and ends that scattered the area. Several of those items he identified as belonging to Ivy, and he looked back at her, one eyebrow elevated. "So what's the deal, babe? You living here now?"

Vincent's jaw muscles were really working overtime now, Ivy noted, but what was she supposed to do? If he thought she was going to start lying at this stage of her life, he could think again. A blush stealing across her cheeks, she nodded. "Yep."

Immediately, Vincent ordered in a tone that was

unnecessarily peremptory, "Don't go making that common knowledge, Pennington."

"Oh, Terry would never . . ." Ivy began, only to be cut off by her cousin.

He whirled on Vincent. Painfully cognizant of the other man's hostility from the instant he'd been admitted to his apartment, Terry put his own interpretation on it. "You saying my cousin's not good enough to live with you publicly, D'Ambruzzi?" he demanded furiously, taking a threatening step toward Ivy's lover. "You son of a bitch. I should have broke your damn neck when you slept with her the first time and then just waltzed out on her like she was some two dollar . . ."

"Y'want a shot at me, you're gonna have to take a number!" Vincent interrupted with a roar as his frustration reached the boiling point. Dammit, he'd known it! He'd known goddam good and well that the moment her cousin found out she was living with him, he'd try to take her away from him. Shit! He just couldn't win with the males of her family, and he was tired of facing off with them like some scruffy Tom cat forced to defend what was his. "Take your best shot, Pennington—I'll be more than happy to oblige you. But you'd better get in line—it forms behind Mack Merrick!"

Terry's expression went blank with surprise. Then he actually took the time to study Vincent and decided maybe he'd sort of jumped the gun. The guy looked more beleaguered than smug. Reassured, he broke into a grin. "Oh, man, I would have loved to've been a fly on the wall when Uncle Mack heard about this."

"Yeah, you probably would've gotten a real charge out of it," Vincent agreed sourly. "He hates my guts."

"Oh, Vincent, we've been over this before, and he does not," Ivy snapped. "As for you," she said, turning to her cousin in irritation, "you can just apologize right now. Vincent is not ashamed of me, and I think I resent the implication that there might be a reason he should be." Succinctly, she itemized the reasons for keeping their relationship quiet. To his credit, Terry promptly turned to Vincent when she had finished.

"Sorry, D'Ambruzzi."

Vincent shrugged ungraciously.

He turned back to his cousin. "Sorry, Ive. I guess if any woman is unlikely to put up with a guy who fails to see what a prize he's got in her, it's you."

Still a little miffed at all the testosterone-powered aggression the two men had been displaying, Ivy demanded testily, "What are you doing here, anyway?"

He smiled lopsidedly. "You don't believe I'd just drop by to see one of my favorite cousins?"

Ivy regarded him unblinkingly.

"Okay, okay." He rolled his shoulders uneasily, hesitated a moment, and then blurted. "Do you know what the story is on Jaz's new boyfriend? How come no one's met him yet?"

Tyler Griffus was beginning to think he was never going to meet the Doc. Damn it anyway. He couldn't very well come right out and suggest it, and for some reason Jaz was being obtuse when it came to an introduction to her family. Deliberately so? He seriously considered the possibility for the first time.

It was true she had acted a bit cool the last couple of times he'd seen her. He'd been playing hard to get sexually since he'd first began cultivating her acquaintance. Deliberately he had strung her along, and now he couldn't help but wonder if that was what was bothering her.

And yet it didn't quite add up. She'd never expressed a particularly pressing interest in a sexual relationship with him either. Her apparent indifference hadn't registered before, primarily because it had suited his purposes just fine. Hell, the last thing he'd needed was the headache of trying to satisfy some strong-willed woman. Not exactly his cup of tea.

Now, however, he was starting to feel the pinch of anxiety. What if he'd somehow transmitted his own disinterest to her? What if she dumped him as a result?

The very thought threatened to expand anxiety into full-blown panic. Jesus. She couldn't do that; he wouldn't allow it.

Not before he got to meet the Doc.

"I don't see that there's any big mystery," Ivy replied to Terry, puzzled by his agitation. "When's the last time *you* rushed one of your rocket scientists over to meet me, or took one home to meet your folks?"

"That's different!"

"Hey, maybe she's living with the guy, or he's living with her," Vincent interjected hopefully. He liked the sound of that. It might take the heat off him; hell, at the very least Mack's attention would be divided. Cheered by the idea, he reached out to hook an arm across Ivy's chest, pulling her to stand in front of him.

"Yeah, you wish." Ivy tilted her head back and gave him a lopsided smile over her shoulder before she turned back to Terry. "Different in what way, Slick?" She could hardly wait to hear this; some woman really ought to take the time, someday, to maintain a record of all the rationales men were forever limping forward in order to keep the old double standard alive and well.

"I don't know," Terry said testily, "just different, is all."

"Oh, well," Ivy retorted sarcastically, "who am I to argue with that cutting logic?"

"All right!" he snapped. "For instance, everyone's made their opinion of my choice in women painfully clear, so it makes sense to keep my girlfriends as far away from the family as I can. But Jaz has no need to do that. What's the matter with this clown that she has to hide him from everyone?"

"For heaven's sake, Terry." Ivy was perplexed by his intensity and the clumsiness of his arguments. Usually he could be counted on to debate rings around the rest of them. "Maybe," she suggested with slow thoughtfulness, "Jaz is only looking for a little time to herself. Perhaps she wants to get to know the guy a little better before she subjects him to the scrutiny of the Pennington/Merrick clan. This family can be a bit daunting to a newcomer."

"Tell me about it," Vincent muttered. He rubbed his hand up and down Ivy's upper arm as he examined her cousin over her shoulder. The man was tense, visibly perturbed, and Vincent instinctively recognized it for what it was. "How long you been in love with her?" he asked before he considered the wisdom of voicing the question aloud.

Ivy's shoulders jerked in shock against his chest and he immediately regretted not having given the matter some thought before he'd spoken . . . or better yet, wished he'd simply kept his mouth shut. Her head tipped back to stare at him incredulously. "Vincent, what a thing to say. Terry's not . . ."

The very stillness of her cousin's posture caught her eye and quelled the words in her throat. Slowly, she turned her head back to gaze at him directly.

"Oh, God," she breathed. "You are. Does Jaz have any idea?"

"No! Christ, no; are you crazy?" His face twisted violently for an instant before he got it back under control. "You think I'm gonna burden her with that? With a goddamn, incestuous—"

"Stop it!" Unable to bear the harsh self-loathing she saw reflected in his eyes, Ivy pulled away from Vincent and reached out to wrap her arms around Terry, hugging him fiercely. He stood stiffly in her embrace. "Just. . . stop it, Terry. Don't do this to yourself."

"That's what it is, Ive." He pulled his head back and stared at her, his expression rendered deliberately blank. "Remember what Davis said about cousins having drooling idiots for kids?" he said coolly. "And, hell, what's the old joke—incest is okay as long as you keep it in the family? Well, I'm not about to lay the burden of my feelings on her shoulders. Christ, all Jaz has ever wanted out of life is a decent husband and some kids." Terry regarded Ivy with hard eyes, but in the depths of them she saw vagrant glimmers of his torment.

"Oh, Terry," she whispered helplessly, aching for him.

Hoping to diffuse the tension filling the living room, Vincent impulsively offered, "If you want, I can run her boyfriend through the computer— just to make sure he's on the up and up."

Terry broke free of Ivy's embrace, stepping back as he scrubbed his fingers over his face. "I don't even know the bastard's last name," he muttered. Then his hands dropped to his side and he looked directly at Vincent. "But I could find out." He nodded, once, using the decision to clothe emotions that had been stripped naked in the middle of his cousin's living room. "Thanks, D'Ambruzzi; I'd appreciate that."

Shortly thereafter he left, leaving Vincent to watch Ivy's unhappiness as she tried to grapple with her new-found knowledge.

On edge, he deliberately left her to it. He was getting sucked into her affairs way too deep as it was. This wasn't what he'd had in mind when he'd asked her to move in with him. He'd just wanted a nice, easy, sexual connection. Monogamous, sure; but nothing too serious, nothing too deep. He wasn't supposed to care what her uncle thought about him. He wasn't supposed to become involved in her family's problems.

And he wasn't going to, dammit. He was going to track down the sonofabitch who was stalking her and see to it that he was put away for a good long time. And then he was moving her back into her own place, pronto.

He stole frequent glances at her, observing the way she slumped dejectedly in one corner of the couch, her knees partially drawn up and a throw pillow clutched to her stomach. She'd planted her heels in the cushion and her feet were flexed as she stared pensively at her bare toes. Well, she could just work out her feelings about her cousin's surprising hots for their mutual cousin on her own. It had nothing to do with him.

He swept the scattered sections of newspaper together and neatly folded and stacked them. He gathered the coffee cups and plates they'd been using earlier and carried them to the kitchen. When he came back, she was still sitting where he'd left her, still contemplating her feet with unhappy eyes. He tidied up a few more items . . . most of which belonged to her, he noted sourly. Unclipping his holster, he slid it onto the coffee table and found himself sitting down next to her. He picked up one of her bare feet and massaged the high arch with his thumb. "I probably should have kept my big mouth shut," he admitted in a low voice.

"No." Shaking her head she looked up at him. Immediately she scooted closer, draping her legs over his thighs and wrapping her arms around his middle. She held him tight, her head on his chest, as close as she could get without actually crawling onto his lap. Hell, that left him no choice, really, but to hold her in return. He wrapped his arms around her.

"Now that I know," she admitted, "I'm sort of surprised it never occurred to me before. It explains so much, Vincent. His airheaded girlfriends. The way he could look so lonely sometimes even with a woman fawning all over him." She sighed. "What a mess. And y'know what the real tragedy is?" She tilted her head back to look up at him.

"No, what?" He used gentle fingertips to brush back her hair.

"He'd probably be perfect for Jaz. He's steady and decent and very strong. He'd cherish her. Exactly the guy she's always wanted."

"But you don't think it'll ever happen."

"No." The slight smile she attempted was edged with sorrow. "I don't think it'll ever happen."

Ivy couldn't get it out of her mind. It was the first time she had come face to face with the realization that there did exist objectives in life that simply could not be achieved, regardless how diligently a person worked, no matter how exemplary his behavior. It contradicted everything she'd ever believed to be true. And never having personally endured a broken heart, it also came as something of a revelation . . . and not one she was a bit happier having realized.

It forced her to acknowledge her feelings for Vincent once and for all. Well, she supposed that deep down she'd known for a long time how she truly felt, but that hadn't prevented some fancy dancing around the knowledge. It was time to come right out and admit it.

She loved him. For good or for ill; her feelings weren't going to change so she quit trying to swallow the words every time he made love to her, and it was such a relief not to have to hold back any longer. The first time she said the words out loud, the night of Terry's visit, he went very still for a moment. He was deep inside her at the time and he froze, hips arched as his head reared back and he stared at her. Then he went into a frenzy, more out of control than she'd ever seen him, hands bruising, mouth voracious, hips pistoning like a jackhammer gone berserk. From his reaction, she was pretty sure he liked hearing it.

Yet he never said a word in return.

It hurt; she couldn't deny it. But at least they possessed the potential to work out their relationship. She held onto that, reminding herself every time he went nuts at her words and then withheld what she most needed to hear himself.

It was more than Terry had.

As was usual, Ivy answered the phone.

"Heyheyhey, bay-bee," Sherry said with her customary ebullience. "It's me 'n Jaz. Buzz us up."

She hung up the phone, hit the buzzer and went into a panic. Grabbing her keys, a six-pack of Pepsi from the fridge and a bag of pretzels from the cupboard, she whirled on Vincent and demanded, "Oh God, oh God, what am I supposed to say, how am I supposed to act? Usually Jaz is the first person I go to for advice in a situation like this. Now, *she's* the one I can't tell. God, I miss it so much, having someone to talk to."

Vincent struggled with a flash of guilt. She had tried to talk to him about it instead, but he'd done everything in his power to discourage her without coming right out and saying that he didn't want to be involved.

"You'll do fine," he assured her uncomfortably.

"Thanks a heap, D'Ambruzzi," she retorted flatly, suddenly fed up with attempting to find excuses for the inexplicable distance he'd been putting between them lately. "I can't tell you what a comfort that is." She slammed the door when she left and an instant later he heard her front door bounce off the wall next door.

Refusing to feel repentant, he cancelled call forwarding, rechanneling her calls back to her apartment. It was his day to be on call at work and he needed to be able to answer the phone if it rang. Then he paced.

There were snares out there and he felt as if one unwary step was going to find him snapped up and swinging by his heels. She kept telling him she loved him, and every damn time the words were uttered his need to hear them acted like a new rope binding him more closely to her.

Whatever concerned her seemed to concern him. He'd like to deny it but he couldn't. Hell, all that effort he'd put into avoiding the issue of her cousin's romantic troubles—and all it had accomplished was to tarnish the way Ivy regarded him. It hadn't done a damn thing to prevent his personal entanglement in the soap opera that was her family life, which had been his original intention. Despite his best efforts, *that* seemed to grow with every day that passed.

And what the hell had ever possessed him to promise Terry Pennington he'd run Jaz's new love interest through the computer at work? It had seemed like a good idea at the time, given all the emotional tension floating around that day, but when Terry had called last night with the guy's name Vincent had wanted to swear with frustration. Now he was going to have to remember to take time out of his schedule Monday morning to run a make on this clown. As if he didn't have enough to keep him busy.

Shit. It was beyond him how one long-legged, red-headed woman—even if she did come with a bunch of problematic relatives—could turn his life upside down with such ease. It used to be so orderly.

"It used to be boring, son," Keith informed him flatly. "Boring and stagnant."

"Ah, hell," Vincent said in disgust. "I should have known better than to think you'd under-stand."

"Oh, I understand perfectly. You're moon-faced in love and it's scaring the shit outta ya."

"Bull." Vincent stared out the open sliding door and then turned back to his friend. "It's a beautiful Saturday," he snapped pointedly. "Shouldn't you be home mowing your lawn or screwing your wife or something?"

"Nah, she kicked me out. She's havin' some sorta basket party—whatever the hell that is. I'm yours for the afternoon." Keith grinned maliciously, knowing it was the last thing Vince wanted to hear. "Got any beer?"

Vincent grabbed them each one and they took them out onto the tiny balcony. Indicating the call-tracing equipment with a wave of his bottle as they passed it on their way out, Keith dropped into a deck chair and inquired, "What have you heard from the deviant?"

"Nada," Vincent said and frustration bit deep in his tone. "Zip. Not a damn peep."

"Great. That's gotta be adding to the tension."

Vincent grunted his agreement.

Keith could see the subject was not lightening Vincent's mood, so he changed it. "Those women I rode up with in the elevator must be Ivy's cousins, huh?" When Vincent only shrugged, he added, "The little brunette's a major looker."

"I guess," Vincent replied, shrugging indifferently. He stared at the wall that connected his lanai to Ivy's. "I wonder what they're talking about over there."

"She left here pissed?" Keith snorted and raised the bottle to his lips. Lowering it after he took a swig, he surmised, "Five'll get you ten, son, that they're probably trashing your good name and your prowess in bed."

"My good name, maybe." For the first time since Keith's arrival Vincent smiled, and its cockiness probably would have earned him a smack if Ivy had been around to see it. "Ivy's real big on honesty, though," he added confidently. "So my rep in the sack is secure."

"Men are pigs," Jaz pronounced.

"Amen." Ivy was still angry with Vincent and readily agreed. She was tired of always being the one to make concessions in this relationship. Then she shot her cousin a puzzled glance. "But I thought you had yourself a hot new honey."

"Yeah, when're we gonna meet this guy, anyway?" Sherry demanded.

"Maybe never." Jaz shrugged one elegant shoulder. "I'm considering giving him his walking papers."

"No kidding?" Sherry sat up straighter, interested as always in the prospect of hearing a little dirt dished. "How come?"

"I don't know; I can't figure him out at all."

Ivy snorted. "Have you ever met a man you could?"

That made Jaz smile. "True. But even taking that into account . . ." She struggled to find the right words. "This guy's real different. The way he treated me at first, it was almost as if . . . well, I thought this might be the one. The Prince, y'know? I mean, those first couple dates he seemed almost too good to be true . . ." She shrugged. "Well, you know what they say about that."

"Yeah—it usually is."

"Yeah." She hesitated and then said, "Actually, he's extremely charming. Most of the time. But every now and then he gets so . . . God, I don't know—so intense."

"But that's what's so exciting," Sherry declared enthusiastically. "Like Ivy's broody Italian neighbor . . . all those caged hormones."

Ivy's vaginal muscles shocked her by contracting sharply at the mention of Vincent's caged hormones and the thought of what they could make him do.

"That's exactly the thing, though, Sher," Jaz protested, sitting up straight. "I mean, that is *it* in a nutshell. There's absolutely no chemistry with this guy—not a caged hormone in sight." She sighed. "Tyler was all romance at first and it fooled me. He was like this dream date: so attentive and complimentary . . . not like some of the Neanderthals I've dated whose idea of foreplay is saying, 'Hey, baby, you're lookin' real hot!' He brought me flowers; he took me to the symphony, for God's sake." She sighed. "Then, to top it off when he didn't even try to kiss me on our first couple of dates, I thought, 'This is too sweet; he's shy.' But,

I mean, he's *never* tried to kiss me, let alone sweet talk his way into bed. That's not shy, folks; that's disinterested. And for once I don't even blame myself for it. I really think this guy is just plain asexual."

"Could he be gay?" Ivy inquired. "Maybe he just hasn't made up his mind to come out of the closet."

Jaz was shaking her head. "I actually tried to tell myself that, because at least it would be some sort of an explanation. Not exactly an ego-boosting one, but on the other hand it wouldn't have anything to do with me per se—the situation would apply to any woman. But I don't think so, Ive. Oh, hell, I don't know. Maybe I *should* introduce him to you guys. Maybe one of you can figure him out; I sure as hell can't."

"But I thought you said you were going to dump him," Sherry said in confusion.

"Well, half the time that's what I think I should do." Jaz smiled crookedly. "But then I ask myself: and do *what* for an escort?"

Ivy laughed. Sherry continued to look confused for an instant but then her brow cleared and she laughed too. "Yeah, how many guys are there out there willing to shell out the bucks to take you to the symphony?"

Jaz shrugged self-deprecatingly. "I'm not sure if that makes me refreshingly honest or just very, very shallow."

Ivy was still laughing when the phone rang. Her nerves jumped in surprise but then steadied as she remembered that Vincent was on call today. He must have cancelled the call-forwarding in order to receive his own calls.

She rattled the icecubes in her glass as she rose to answer it. "I need a refill. One of you grab me the can of pop I left in the fridge while I get that, will you?"

Jaz jumped up to comply and Ivy crossed to the telephone stand. "Hello," she said cheerily.

The whispery voice that greeted her salutation was one she had by now given up expecting to hear. She was aware of Jaz crossing the room toward her, but before she reached her with the can of cola, Ivy's glass had slipped through nerveless fingers. It bounced on the floor, scattering ice cubes across the hardwood.

Tyler had nearly lost it when Jaz informed him she was going to the Doc's apartment with another cousin that afternoon. Not only had she not invited him, she'd added insult to injury by also refusing his invitation to go out later that evening. His rage had been such it had been all he could do not to hurt her and hurt her badly. At the very least, he had ached to dress her down in the manner she so richly deserved. Arrogant bitch.

But he was stronger than that. He'd retained his composure and it had been shortly thereafter that he'd come up with the brainstorm to call the Doc while Jasmine was there.

Oh God, it was the next best thing to perfect— he was too fucking brilliant for words! If he couldn't be there himself, why, then he'd simply call her when he knew for certain that there would be a conduit to the Doc's reactions in place. He needed that to keep the voice in his head pacified. At the very least he needed that.

And next time he wasn't going to make the mistake of calling Jasmine beforehand, either, to inquire whether she wanted to get together. He was simply showing up on her doorstep first thing tomorrow. He wished he could do it tonight, but she'd already told him she planned to make an early night of it and he'd been playing the game long enough to know you don't get information out of a woman who is pissed at you for disregarding her wishes.

All he had to do now was wait. Tyler's eyes burned with unhealthy fervor as he sat in his locked office staring at the unfinished paperwork on his desk. All he had to do was wait.

Sometimes, that was the hardest part.

Chapter 15

"If the day ever comes when I need elective surgery," Jaz joked as she stooped to pick Ivy's glass up off the floor, "remind me to choose a physician with a little more coordination than you." She dropped the recaptured ice cubes back into the glass and tilted her head back to grin up at Ivy.

The expression on her cousin's face froze the laughter in her throat. "What?" she whispered anxiously, rising slowly to her feet. "What is it?"

Palming the telephone's mouthpiece, Ivy reached out her free hand and hauled Jaz up. Her long fingers bit into her cousin's forearm as she leaned into her and breathed, "Get Vincent, Jaz. *Quick.* Tell him—" tipping her chin significantly toward the phone receiver "—it's Hart."

Sherry's loud demand of, "What the hell's going on here?" made Ivy start, unaware that her own stiffly held posture, emanating tension, had drawn her cousin over.

"For God's sake, keep your voice down!" she

instinctively lashed out in a harsh whisper and immediately turned back to Jaz, shoving her toward the door, "Go, Jasmine—*now!*"

Responding to her cousin's urgency, Jaz turned on her heel and ran from the apartment with Sherry close on her heels. Ivy turned her attention back to her caller.

Oh God, she had to pick up the conversational thread and her mind was a blank. What had he said? It seemed like an eon ago that she'd picked up the phone, but she knew only fifteen, maybe twenty seconds had passed. How had he greeted her salutation? *Think*, dammit! It had been something along the lines of: "I imagine you've been expecting my call" hadn't it? To which she'd automatically responded with a noncommital, "Um."

Now, cautiously, she inquired, "Is this Hart?" knowing already that it was. The mere act of asking, however, and of hearing the apparent calmness in her own voice, made her draw an easier breath. All right then; good. She didn't sound nearly as nervous as she felt. Her hand went instinctively to her back pocket to finger the scalpel. Perhaps the trick was to pretend that this was medical school and she was once again back on the psych ward. Never her favorite rotation in medicine, she had nevertheless managed to get through it with credible results.

As she would get through this.

"Yes," the voice whispered, "It is. Are you alone?"

Ivy debated for about five seconds. "No," she finally said. "I have company.

"What kind of company?"

She didn't pause to analyze her reply; she simply reacted instinctively, retorting with cool crispness, "That's really none of your concern. Is there something I can do for you?"

Her door opened and Vincent charged in on bare feet, grasping the call-tracer in one white-knuckled hand, trailing cords. He squatted down next to her and began fumbling with the wires. By rights, considering the fierce expression on his face, he should have been cursing at the top of his voice, but he didn't make a sound. Jaz, Sherry, and Keith Graham followed in his wake, but they all stopped well back and gave him plenty of room to work. Not a whisper was exchanged.

"Simply by being, you do something for me," her caller assured her. "You exist, Doc. Therefore I am."

Ivy's jaw sagged. "I *beg* your pardon?" Oh, shit. She really hadn't meant to say that, particularly not with that almost snotty tone of incredulousness . . . it had just sort of popped out. But, good God above, existentialism? *Just* what she needed to round out the day.

"It's as if we're one, Doc," he elaborated, apparently unfazed by her skepticism. "I can feel how attuned you are to the way I think. No one else understands, but you do—and knowing that helps quiet the voice."

"You hear a *voice?*" Ivy's voice cracked on the last word. Heat crawled up her throat onto her cheeks and her hand groped blindly for Vincent's shoulder, an action she didn't even realize until she felt the warmth of his skin beneath her gripping fingers.

Her words had caused his head to snap up and for an instant they were a frozen tableaux: Vincent crouched at her feet staring up at her, Ivy staring down at him, her fingers digging with unconscious strength into the muscle that joined his shoulder to his neck. Oh God, she was entirely out of her depth here.

"What does the voice tell you to do?" she forced

herself to inquire in a carefully neutral voice as she reluctantly released her grip on Vincent's shoulder and brought her hand to the receiver to help steady it. Vincent tore his eyes away; his head lowered and he reapplied himself to the call-tracer with a vengeance.

"It orders me to administer what they deserve," Hart retorted without emotion. "It demands that I ensure they remember me."

His lack of emotion got to her. "Who is 'they,' Hart?" she inquired in a non-empathetic tone. "The women you've hurt?"

"I didn't do a fucking thing they didn't ask for!" he snapped and for just an instant his voice rose above a whisper. Then, as quickly as it had arisen, his indignation seemed to evaporate. His voice sank back into the raspy tones she'd grown accustomed to hearing from him. "There's something about you that makes the voice not bother me so much," he informed her with renewed calmness.

"Let's see if I've got this straight," Ivy murmured with a careful lack of inflection. "You hear a voice that urges you to do the things you do. But by talking to me—"

"Or even just thinking of you—"

"—or even just thinking of me," she neutrally repeated his interruption, "you can silence the voice?"

"Maybe not silence it. But turn down the volume, yes."

"So . . . are you saying you don't desire to do what the voice exhorts you to do? Are you seeking help to stop?"

"Don't be ridiculous," he retorted with a cool disdain that flicked her on the raw. "I merely hate its incessant nagging. After all, Doc, it's not as if there's a damn thing I can do to address its demands before the moon is full anyway. So why the hell should I have to listen to them?''

She wanted to ask about that, to probe further into what it was about the full moon that set him off, but as if a silent alarm had gone off in his head, he suddenly said, ''Well, I gotta go.''

''No, Hart, wait! Tell me about—''

''Another time,'' he whispered. The line went dead.

''Damn it,'' she breathed fervently as she gently recradled the receiver.

''Son of a *bitch!''* Vincent roared. He tossed aside the one remaining unattached wire and surged to his feet. Grasping her shoulders, he studied her face intently, ''You okay?''

She nodded and dropped her head onto his shoulder, in need of his comfort. Vincent pulled her into his arms, holding her tight. He rubbed his jaw against her temple. ''I'm sorry, Ivy,'' he said with harsh self-recrimination. ''I'm sorry. I shouldn't have turned off the damn call-forwarding.''

''No,'' she exonerated him, ''it's not your fault. You had to have the line free in case they called you in to work, and it doesn't even bear contemplating how Hart might have responded if you'd been the one to answer the phone.'' Her arms tightened around his waist even as she was tilting her head back in order to see his face. ''Besides, don't you think it's just too coincidental for words, Vincent? What are the odds, do you suppose, of him calling me the one day I'm not in your apartment?'' It was almost as if her life were being observed through a peephole, a thought that was guaranteed to make her skin crawl.

''Ordinarily I'd say pretty slim.'' Vincent's rough-tipped fingers kept touching her face: following the line of a brow here, brushing a wisp of hair away there, stroking the smooth hollows beneath her cheekbones. "But it was a Saturday the other time he called too, wasn't it? Looks as if we just got caught up in a streak of bad luck."

A slight sound caught his attention and he tore his eyes away from Ivy for the first time since she'd recradled the telephone receiver. Glancing over her shoulder, he met her cousins' eyes with a jolt of surprise.

He had forgotten for a moment that anyone else was there. But Keith was in the hallway, nonchalantly studying the paint job on the walls, and the two women were standing not two yards away, staring at Ivy and him in open-mouthed amazement. Vincent exhaled quietly, disgusted in part with the situation—which seemed to be rapidly deserting his control—but mostly with himself. Son of a bitch. From the very beginning, Ivy had insisted it was impossible to keep her family in the dark regarding their relationship, but had he believed her? Oh no. He'd refused to give her words much credence at all. Hell, how hard could it be, after all, to keep one little secret?

Which just went to show you he didn't know jack when it came to this sort of thing, and she, apparently, had known precisely what she was talking about. First her aunt and uncle, then her cousin Terry, now this. And the way the cousin everyone seemed to think was such a beauty was regarding him made his back stiffen defensively. She looked at him as if he were something that needed scraping from the bottom of her shoe.

Feeling his sudden tension, Ivy realized it was just dawning on him that their cover had been blown. Well, he couldn't say she hadn't tried to warn him. She turned in his arms and faced Sherry and Jaz.

"Soooo—you guys are living together?" Sherry arched a brow at them, taking in Vincent's possessive hold on her cousin and Ivy's long-fingered hand resting lightly on his stomach as she stood facing them in the circle of his left arm.

Cheeks coloring, Ivy nodded.

"And you're actually living next door these days instead of here?"

"Yep."

Sherry looked fairly amused, but Jaz felt as if someone had just slugged her in the stomach. "So why the big mystery, Ive?" she demanded, struggling with a sensation of betrayal. "What the hell was the point of this whole charade here today? Meeting us in your apartment, bending over backward to make us believe that everything was status quo?"

She was all but reeling, such was the shock. There had been a lifetime of shared confidences between her and Ivy, a lifetime with damn few secrets between them. Now, suddenly, she was finding herself out in the cold. "God," she whispered, wounded to the quick but desperately determined that *he,* at least, with his cool, non-admiring eyes, not realize it. "I can't believe I sat here spilling out my guts to you about Tyler and you never said a word in return about . . ." Her chin tilted up as her hand flapped expressively between Ivy and Vincent. It felt suspiciously as if she were the butt of some obscure joke, but she'd be damned if she'd let it show.

"I've *wanted* to tell you, Jaz," Ivy replied. "It's just all been so damn . . . complicated." She sent Vincent a look that had him and Keith excusing themselves to return to his apartment.

"Five minutes, Ivy," he said, stopping in the doorway on his way out and by his tone it was not a request. She seemed to place more importance on providing an explanation to her cousins than on working with him to catch the deviant who'd just called her. It knotted his gut with jealousy and that infuriated him. He looked the three women over with a sternness of expression Ivy hadn't seen from him in quite a while before he turned back to her to add coolly, "We've got more important business to attend to this afternoon than your cousin's bruised feelings." Stepping out into the hallway, he closed the door softly behind him.

Jaz's feelings *were* bruised; they felt, in fact, as though they'd been stomped black and blue. The fact that he could tell so effortlessly only added insult to injury. She resented everything about him: his easy insight into her emotions, his damned sexuality ... the fact that he was apparently important in her cousin's life and she hadn't even known. "He's a real charmer, isn't he?" she snarled with impotent fury.

"He can be, Jaz," Ivy replied. "He's under a lot of pressure right now." She was feeling pretty pressured herself. Running her long fingers through her hair, she sighed. "Look, let's sit down and I'll do my best to explain everything, okay?"

It took a while, but ultimately she managed to placate her cousins. Sherry was a pushover, to absolutely no one's amazement, finding the situation romantic. Jaz was much tougher to conciliate. She clung stubbornly to her crushed feelings.

Finally Ivy lost patience. "Listen, Jasmine," she snapped, "I don't have a lot of time here, so let me make this as succinct as I possibly can." She took a deep breath and then said, "You probably know me better than anyone else in the world. We grew up in the same house, slept in the same bedroom. I thought that you, more than anyone, would know I'm no more accustomed to being the recipient of some madman's delusions than ... well, than you would be." She was puzzled by her cousin's attitude and more than a little hurt by it. With building anger she demanded, "Dammit, don't you even care what this guy is doing to me? I'm sorry if I'm not handling everything to your satisfaction, but I've told you why Vincent wanted our relationship kept quiet and why I went along with it. I wasn't thrilled about it either, Jaz, but Vincent is not, as you seem to be insinuating, trying to keep me from the family. Either accept that or don't, but get off your damn high horse and—"

"I'm sorry," Jasmine interrupted. "Oh, God, Ive, I don't know what's the matter with me." She rubbed at the little furrow digging a groove between her finely drawn eyebrows. "Of course I'm worried about the situation you're in. But . . . well, I guess I'm a little jealous, too." Dropping her hand to her side, she met her cousin's eyes head-on. "Oh hell, I'm crazy jealous, if you wanna know the truth. And more than a little concerned that he's going to take you away from me . . . from us." And that was the God's honest truth. She had never seen her cousin look at a man the way Ivy looked at Vincent D'Ambruzzi, and he clearly seemed to view Jaz as a selfish, good-for-nothing bitch. What if he demanded that Ivy choose between them? It wasn't as far-fetched as it might have seemed on any other day. She'd been aware of an awkwardness in Ivy's manner toward her several times already this afternoon.

Not realizing Jaz had picked up on the strain of discomfort Terry's confession had caused, Ivy's mouth dropped open. "My God, Jaz," she said in astonishment. "How could you possibly think that Vincent would ever, *could* ever . . ." She broke off, shaking her head. "You're like a sister to me. Nothing—no one on *earth*—will ever change that. And jealous of what for heaven's sake?"

"Are you kidding Nobody looks at me the way D'Ambruzzi looked at you. As if . . . as if . . . Oh shit, Ivy, you know I'm not good with words." Jaz turned to Sherry. "But you understand what I'm talkin' about, don't you, Sher?"

"Yeah. Like a wino with his last bottle of Mad Dog; like a junkyard dog guarding a tasty bone," Sherry contributed, mixing her metaphors with cheerful disregard. "It'd be clear to a blind woman that the man's crazy about you."

Ivy could have shared a whole shipload of private concerns regarding that assumption and probably would have if Jaz hadn't already been teetering so unsteadily on the rim of disliking Vincent. Ivy didn't want to risk pushing her over—at any rate, not before she had an opportunity to get to the bottom of her cousin's unexpected hostility.

It was beyond her, however, to stop herself from at least confiding that he'd never actually put his feelings into so many words and that he never used endearments. "I wish just once he'd call me baby," she said dreamily. "I've always had this secret hankering to be called baby." Then she caught herself and smiled in wry amusement. "Yeah, right. Like that's something a six-foot woman's ever gonna hear, huh?"

Vincent, who had just opened the front door to tell the women in no uncertain terms that their time was up, eased back out into the hall and soundlessly closed it behind him again. Turning until his back was against the wall, he slumped, head back, raising both hands to grind the heels of his hands into his eyes. He sucked in and blew out several deep breaths, attempting to deal with the defensiveness that bound his stomach into knots.

He didn't have time for this. There were more important matters to attend to—and damn it, he'd never made her any promises. He'd been extremely careful not to make any promises, careful never to use any words she could possibly misconstrue. He had nothing to feel guilty about, nothing at all.

Why, then, he wondered hollowly, didn't reminding himself of that do a damn thing to block out the self-contempt in her voice, or keep the echoes of it from eating away, like acid dripping on a stone, at a place in his gut?

Sherry, too, took serious umbrage with Ivy's statement. "You wanna tell me what your height has to do with anything? Does it make you somehow less worthy? And applying those same standards, Ivy, does that mean I'm too fat to be called by the endearment of my choice?"

"No, of course not," Ivy denied. "It's just that— I don't know, Sher—doesn't it seem sort of a simpy thing for a woman my size to yearn for?"

"Jesus, Ivy, if the feminists of the world could hear you now they'd break down and cry." Sherry sighed, unable to believe her ears. From a woman who was usually clearheaded in the extreme, this was simply too damn lame to entertain. "I doubt their problem would have anything to do with your stature, though. Once they got through weeping over your pitiful lack of self-respect, they'd probably have a collective heart attack over your choice of endearments. Last I heard of the Party rhetoric, 'baby' was considered derogatory and demeaning." She shrugged and said with a crooked smile, "I've always found it sorta sexy, myself."

"Sherry's right," Jaz interceded. "But aren't we getting away from the real subject here? Ivy, does D'Ambruzzi really believe someone in the family might actually *know* this pervert who's been calling you?"

"He thinks it's a possibility, Jaz. Or perhaps a friend of a friend does. That's why you've got to keep my relationship with him to yourselves. I know it's hard for you guys to keep a secret, but this is important. It bothers him that Hart got ahold of my unlisted number, because apparently they aren't that easy to obtain.''

Struck by a sudden possibility, Jaz whispered, ''My God, what he's saying is that it could be someone like Tyler! I *did* meet him about the time all this stuff started happening to you.'' She shivered but then immediately brightened. ''But that's hardly likely, is it? Not when I just spent the better part of the afternoon complaining about his lack of sex drive. This is, after all, a rapist we're talking about.''

Had Vincent opened the front door just five seconds sooner, he would have corrected that misconception in no uncertain terms. Rape was considered by experts less a crime of passion than one of violence. It was for that very reason that his unit had changed its name from Sex Crimes to Special Assault some years back, and why so many other so-called Sex Crime units across the nation were making similar changes. Despite the manner in which they were perpetrated, the crimes they dealt in daily actually had more to do with the exertion of power and brutality than they did with sex.

But he was a few seconds shy of hearing Jasmine's remarks, so it was a lecture he was not destined to present.

He reentered the apartment wearing his professional demeanor like a bulletproof vest. Unable to deal with the conflicting emotions trying to pull him in different directions, he shut them off entirely. He was coolly authoritative as he cautioned Ivy's cousins not to discuss her situation with anyone. When he then informed them it was time to go home, his impersonal aura of command guaranteed that neither woman even considered arguing with him.

The instant the elevator doors closed behind them, however, his professionalism evaporated like so much mist in the sun. He turned on Ivy and pinned her in place with a look of such heat and conflicting signals that she couldn't begin to interpret it. Before she could sort it out, he'd already snapped his long fingers around her wrist like a human handcuff, hauled her back to his apartment, and sat her down on the couch next to Keith.

Adrenaline, anger, and confusion all surged through Vincent's veins as he paced in front of her. Finally, he stalked over to the phone, punched in the call forwarding code and then, avoiding Ivy's eyes watching his every move, returned to sit on the other side of her on the couch. "Okay," he brusquely ordered. "Talk."

"He disguises his voice," Ivy told him. She was more than a little mystified by Vincent's conduct but willing to put off a discussion about it for the moment. "But he can't disguise his education. He used several college-level words, and listen to this . . ." She repeated Hart's existentialistic phrasing as succinctly as she could recall. "Have you ever heard such bullshit in your life? Sounds like Philosophy 101, doesn't it?"

"What was that business about a voice?" Keith asked. When she'd finished telling them, the two men exchanged glances.

"What," Ivy demanded, looking back and forth between them. *"What!?"*

"I don't like this," Vincent finally admitted.

"Neither do I," Keith concurred. "The man could truly be delusional . . . or it could be he's already setting up his defense."

Ivy couldn't believe he was actually serious, but there wasn't a bit of levity in his expression to suggest otherwise. "Oh, Keith, surely not," she protested when it sank in that he wasn't fooling.

"He strikes me as much too cold-blooded and smug to ever believe he could actually *be* caught."

"Cold-blooded and smug," Vincent repeated. "That about covers it, all right." For the first time since giving her that look by the elevator, his black eyes bored into hers and held. Emanating an anger Ivy didn't understand he informed her, "He may be hearing voices he hasn't even mentioned yet. And I don't mind telling you," he admitted in a rough voice, "that it scares the shit out of me to think he's focused on you as his one true savior." He moved closer to her on the couch, crowding her. "But I'll tell you something else," he said through his teeth when they sat nose to nose. "That sure as hell didn't stop him from knowing, right down to the friggin' *second*, when he had to hang up the phone in order to avoid being traced. So, if he's crazy, Doll Baby, he's crazy like a fox."

Vincent's unexpected use of that particular phraseology electrified both of them. Each went momentarily still. Ivy's eyes went wide; Vincent's narrowed. Dammit to hell, he hadn't meant to say that. It was a mistake . . . it had just slipped out . . . he hadn't meant to . . .

"Vince, maybe now would be a good time to take this up with Doc O'Gally," Keith suggested.

Vincent's gaze was pulled past Ivy to his friend seated on her other side when Ivy immediately turned to Keith and demanded to know who Doc O'Gally was. "The department shrink," Vincent replied before Keith could, thereby forcing her attention back to him. Then, easing out a breath, he edged back onto his own cushion. Once again the fact that they weren't alone had slipped his mind. This had to stop.

"Good idea," he said to Keith. Then, rising from the couch and extending a hand to Ivy to help her up, he commanded with curious formality, "Grab your purse, Doctor. We're going to go pay the psychiatrist a call. Maybe she's exactly what we need to give us some insight into what we're dealing with here."

"Being cautious, Detective, doesn't necessarily negate the genuineness of your rapist's delusional episodes," the department psychiatrist, Doctor Margaret O'Gally, informed him.

Not exactly the news Vincent had been hoping to hear. Somehow, a calculating deviant seemed to him more manageable than one whose actions were fueled by dementia.

"Most rapists have the ability to distort the truth," she continued. "They can hold a knife to their victim's throat and be totally convinced she's enjoying it." She tapped the pad containing the notes she'd taken during Vincent's narration. "But it seems to be more than that in this case. Going on the information you've provided me, it's likely your rapist has been through the system to an extent where he's learned to make caution work for him. By all appearances, before all the attention to Dr. Pennington began, he'd avoided taking chances of any kind." She turned to Ivy. "Something about you has clearly accessed a responsive chord in this man."

"I exist, therefore he is," Ivy said wearily. She was suddenly so tired, an exhaustion whose origins were not solely caused by these disturbing episodes with the rapist. Everyone seemed to want a piece of her these days and no one was happy with what she had to give. Her family was dissatisfied with her and God only knew what Vincent's sudden, inexplicable attitude signified. The ride to the precinct had been accomplished in a stony silence that she found baffling. Why was he so full of anger all of a sudden?

Dr. O'Gally looked at her askance and Ivy waved an apologetic hand. "I'm sorry," she said and explained the reference. "What do you suppose caused him to focus on me?"

"That's difficult to say without talking to him or at least seeing a case history," Dr. O'Gally replied. "There could be a number of reasons. You could remind him of someone who was once good to him. He could have a thing for tall redheads—"

"All his victims so far have been small and dark," Vincent interposed.

"Then perhaps he has a thing for female doctors, Detective. Or perhaps Dr. Pennington was simply in the wrong place at the wrong time and just happened to catch his attention. We could speculate about it all day long, I imagine, but without hard data to back it up speculation is all it would be." She paused a moment and then made determined eye contact first with Ivy and then with Vincent. It was his gaze that she held when she said, "The thing that needs to be stressed, I believe, is that his delusions appear to be genuine. They share too many characteristics of classic delusional behavior to be faked."

Vincent uttered a rude swear word and, surprisingly, Dr. O'Gally gave him a wry smile. "I know it may not always appear so, Detective D'Ambruzzi, but I am sympathetic to your frustration," she told him. "It's amazing the things we can sometimes do in psychiatry. But it's an inexact science at best, and there are too many other times when our hands are simply tied." She tapped her pencil eraser on the desk top. "I'm afraid that all I can tell you with any authority are the things you likely already know."

Vincent was nodding and Ivy glanced back and

forth between him and the doctor. "Such as . . . ?" she prompted.

"Such as," Vincent replied for the doctor, "the probability that Hart was sexually abused himself at some point in his life, most likely as a child or young adolescent. It's probable too that his abuser was small and dark—thus his predilection for choosing victims that match those general characteristics."

"Women are sexual abusers too?"

"More often than you'd care to imagine," Vincent confirmed in a cold, flat voice. Dr. O'Gally nodded in confirmation.

For some reason, the idea was even more repugnant to Ivy than the more commonly accepted one of men as sexual deviants. Her concept of women as nurturers, she supposed, was as firmly entrenched as the next person's.

"The only encouragement I can offer," Dr. O'Gally said, "is that Hart appears to be very admiring of you, Dr. Pennington. You're not at all like his usual victim, so it's unlikely he'll seek to harm you." She hesitated and then continued, "That's the pleasant news. The unpleasant news is that we have no way of knowing the frequency of his delusional episodes. I'd feel remiss if I didn't warn you that his grasp on reality may be growing more tenuous. This is yet another supposition, of course, nothing more. But the possibility does exist that you could unwittingly do something he'd construe as a betrayal. If such were the case, he could turn on you without warning."

"Swell. I can't tell you how it heartens me to hear that." Ivy's chair screeched against the linoleum floor as she abruptly shoved back from the desk and rose to her feet. Turning her shoulder to partially block the room's other two occupants from view, she gazed blindly out a grimy window that overlooked an equally unappealing alley and tried to collect her thoughts.

It seemed to be just one thing after the other these days. Her emotions were being hammered from so many directions at once that it was getting to the point where she hardly recognized up from down. Turning back, she said, "Thank you for your time, Dr. O'Gally." She walked back to the desk and offered her hand to the psychiatrist and then turned to Vincent. "Would you mind taking me home now, Vincent?" she inquired with polite formality. "I'm really rather tired."

And she was. So tired of this whole damn convoluted mess.

Chapter 16

Vincent's relationship with Ivy deteriorated rapidly in the days that followed, and the fault, he knew, was primarily his.

But not entirely.

Dammit, if she hadn't abruptly stopped arguing with him and started holding herself aloof instead; if she hadn't suddenly become so distant . . .

In every way except sexually she had withdrawn. That was one arena in which she never denied him. Even when extreme emotion caused him to make increasing demands, her physical participation was still enthusiastic. Out of bed she was perceptibly remote, and even in bed, she no longer told him she loved him. All of a sudden he was the proud possessor of the purely sexual relationship he'd thought all along he wanted—which should have been a relief.

It wasn't.

Instead, he found himself laboring to make her say the words again. He was a wild man in the sack, withholding his own pleasure until he had her screaming for release. He was generally damn near ready to scream himself by the time he finally let go. But it didn't matter what he did, or how hot he made her; the words he wanted to hear never passed her lips.

And if he proved to be a tiger between the sheets, he found himself turning into the worst sort of paranoid dual personality the moment he rolled out.

But, dammit, she had turned so scrupulously polite all of a sudden, and he couldn't stand it. What the hell had become of the woman who'd cheerfully challenged nearly every word he'd ever uttered? What was she up to?

And the darkest thought of all, forever lingering like a bottom feeder in the subterranean recesses of his mind: was there someone else?

No, that wasn't possible . . . was it? Hell, she came straight home from work; she never went out in the evenings without him. Just when would she have the time to play around? But what was he going to do if he was wrong about this? He gave up trying to fool himself: she was important to his mental well-being. And should the day ever come that she betrayed him . . .

It didn't bear contemplating. It would be a thousand times worse than LaDonna's treachery.

He found himself watching her like a suspect in a stakeout, the only result of which, it seemed to him, was seeing her retreat even further. Then, on Friday, he took it one step further.

And drove her away entirely.

What a week it had been. Ivy threw her purse on the coffee table, toed off her heels and flopped on the couch. Five minutes, she promised herself as she arched her throat to catch the breeze wafting through the sliding door; five minutes and then she'd get up, change into some comfortable clothes and get a jump on dinner. For the moment all she wanted was to savor the unexpected solitude—practically the first she'd been granted since this madness in her life had begun.

Under ordinary circumstances—or as ordinary as they got these days—she never arrived home from work before Vincent. Having a moment in which she didn't have to deal with his recently escalated suspiciousness was an indescribably restful change.

She didn't know how much more of this she was going to be able to take; she truly didn't. She loved him so much, and yet harbored such fury towards him.

His suspiciousness was destroying them. In books and in the movies jealous lovers always seemed kind of exciting. Well, in real life they were a horror show. Vincent's lack of trust was eroding the very fabric of their relationship.

How it hurt, that look in his eyes when she caught him watching her. She wasn't stupid; she knew what it signified. How could he love her (which she would swear he did, even if he'd never actually said the words) and still wonder if she was cheating on him?

She understood where his doubts came from, realized that they were fueled by a history of betrayal. But, honest to God, when it came right down to it, that excuse had worn thin. This was *her* he'd been regarding with those mistrustful eyes and by now he should certainly know her better than to think she would ever do to him what LaDonna had done.

In the most childish of retaliations, she'd started withholding her "I love you's," knowing it would drive him insane. So what if it was about as mature as packing up her marbles in the middle of a game just because it wasn't going her way? Her empathy had been growing weaker daily and had dissolved entirely around Wednesday. If that made her response to his appalling lack of faith a little on the infantile side, too damn bad. He should trust in her.

This was no way to live.

Which was one reason she hadn't hesitated when Jaz called her at work earlier and suggested getting together later that night at Mack 'N Babe's. An additional incentive had been Jaz's wry addendum that this would give Ivy the opportunity to meet Tyler, Jaz's new beau, while he still *was* her new beau. Her week hadn't been appreciably better than Ivy's, apparently. She'd sounded as if she, too, could use a little emotional support.

Vincent, without a doubt, was going to chew nails over the prospect, but that was tough. Jaz's call had also been in the nature of extending an olive branch, and Ivy was going.

As it turned out, Vincent did more than chew nails. He crossed the line.

The *instant* Jaz Merrick's usefulness was at an end, Tyler Griffus *swore* he was going to make her pay. Arrogant bitch. Who did she think she was dealing with?

She hadn't told him a thing, not a goddamn thing. He'd asked her how her day with her cousins had gone; she'd replied "not so blessed great," and then refused to elaborate.

He had to meet the Doc. It had assumed a critical importance in his life. The voice had ceased its whispering and was beginning to roar and she could control it; he knew she could. But how the hell was she supposed to do that if he couldn't even meet her?

So all right then, he thought, clutching his aching temples. He had to put his ire aside. He had to concentrate. He'd charmed the pants off of Jasmine Merrick once; he would simply do it again. He'd manipulate her into doing exactly what he wanted her to do and if she screwed it up this time, she'd rue the day she was born.

When Vincent had left for work that morning, his intentions had been the finest. He'd realized as soon as Ivy turned her head away from his goodbye kiss that something needed to be done if he wanted a relationship to come home to. Accordingly, on the drive into town he had more or less made up his mind to sit down with her that evening and not allow either of them to budge until they had hammered out a resolution to some of their problems.

What he hadn't factored in was being assigned to little Jeremy Dowdy. It was a case custom-made to destroy the best of intentions.

There was an entire bagful of tricks detectives often used to offset the pressures that were always present in their jobs. Every case invariably generated a ton of administrative paperwork; surprisingly enough there were actually moments when Vincent gave thanks for it. Periodically, he'd find himself gratefully immersing himself in paperwork in order to avoid being affected by the emotional aspects of his job. The stress in Special Assaults could be such at times that he'd deliberately have to put it aside and focus on what he needed to make his case. It was a ploy he particularly tended to utilize when it came to perpetual victims.

They were a stratum of society he had never

dreamed existed back in his academic days. Habitual criminals, sure. But perpetual victims? Come on.

Yet they existed.

In his division those were the women with a history of being abused their entire lives. The victimization generally started when they were children, often with a molestation by a family member or trusted friend or neighbor, and continued, for the most part, all the way up to their adulthood. By the time Vincent saw them, there often wasn't much he could do to help them, a fact that depressed the hell out of him.

He'd seen it more times then he cared to admit. This type of victim had no self-esteem, no defense mechanisms. She had no way of correcting the deviant things that had been done to her her entire life, no means to reverse the effects. And it often happened that as an adult she had already fallen into a pattern. One that led her to hook up with the worst possible man for her, someone almost guaranteed to continue sexually, physically or mentally abusing her.

These women got to him the worst. There were days when in order to keep from eating his gun over the sheer grimness of some of their lives, Vincent concentrated instead on the ever-present paperwork.

But even they were a picnic in the park compared to sexually abused kids. There wasn't a ploy in the world that could effectively divert the stress when it came to dealing with those cases.

Perhaps the worst part was that this abuse appeared to be a self-perpetuating problem. According to some of the most recent statistics to come across his desk, a pedophile was likely to molest three hundred victims in his lifetime. Three hundred. Now, if it were true that child molesters were generally molested themselves as children, then the numbers became staggering. For, in Vincent's estimation that meant society as a whole was busy breeding pedophiles. Part of his job was dealing with victims. Some of those victims were babies. It created a stress for which there simply were no tricks capable of decreasing the despair.

Jeremy Dowdy was eight and a half years old, cute as a button, and probably started on the road to a future of deviant behavior. Upon overhearing Jeremy make a sexual reference that was stunningly inappropriate for a child his age, an alert school counselor had taken him aside and gently persuaded him to open up to her. She'd discovered that for the past three years Jeremy had been molested on a regular basis by his uncle, his mother's brother. Long after Vincent had left the child's house that day, he was haunted by the look in the little boy's eyes.

And yet he couldn't help but wonder if ten years down the road he wasn't going to be sitting next to some other hollow-eyed child while he or she picked Jeremy out of a line up for doing to them the exact same thing that had been done to him.

Which was no real excuse for the way he'd behaved with Ivy when he got home, of course. But it had been an altogether shitty day and he was tense.

He couldn't believe he'd lost it over a few pieces of underwear and a lousy pair of pantyhose, though. Good God, it wasn't as if she hadn't had the stuff hanging from the shower stall nearly every damn day since she'd first moved in—it had never bothered him before. On the contrary, in some unacknowledged corner of his mind, it had actually given him sort of a covert thrill to feel them brushing unexpectedly across his face or snagging on his shoulders.

But he hadn't gotten a kick out of it after work that evening. He'd blown sky high when he'd stepped out of the shower and had to battle with several pieces of her lingerie. It wasn't until much, much later, when the dust had settled and he'd had several solitary hours in which to think, that he acknowledged that he had most likely already been seeking nearly any excuse to pick a fight with her.

"Son of a bitch!" he roared as he batted aside the pair of pantyhose that stuck like a particularly annoying cobweb to his five o'clock shadow. They'd already repeatedly brushed across his face before they'd made the grab for his stubble. He plucked a pair of satin floral panties off his shoulder and tossed them to the floor. With one irate swipe of his big hand, he knocked all the rest from their precarious perch atop the shower stall railing.

"Hey!"

He turned to see Ivy standing in the doorway, indignantly observing his actions. She swept into the room, muscled him aside and stooped down to pick up her fallen lingerie. Glaring up at him, she accused, "You got them all wet!"

"Tough," he snarled. "I'm tired of finding this shit all over the place."

"Just where do you suggest I dry them, Vincent, if not in here?"

"How 'bout out on the friggin' balcony? Give the whole neighborhood a thrill."

"Cute." She rose to her feet. Turning her back on him she began to carefully rearrange her under-wear back on the railing.

"Screw cute," Vincent snapped. Glaring at her back, he dabbed his towel irritably at the water still dappling his body, then wrapped it around his waist. "At least out there I wouldn't find myself being ambushed by the nasty little suckers every damn time I have to take a leak!"

Ivy uttered a little "tsk" of distaste and curled her lip at him. "Charming as usual, D'Ambruzzi."

"Yeah, well, screw that too. I'm sick of tripping over your crap every time I turn around."

She turned to face him. Tempted to inform him there was a simple solution for that, she instead took a deep, calming breath and slowly eased it out. She was trembling with the need to hit back, yet she knew that if she got started, something could conceivably be said that could never be taken back. Well, she hadn't quite come to the point where she was willing to risk that—not yet.

"I'll see you later," she instead said through clenched teeth. Forcing herself to relax her jaw, she added, "I had planned on asking you to come with me tonight, but considering the mood you're in, I don't think that's such a hot idea."

For the first time Vincent noticed she'd changed out of the leggings and T-shirt she'd been wearing when he'd arrived home from work. Disregarding her words with their implicit message that only his temper dictated she leave his company behind, his blood ran cold to observe the short, swingy little skirt, the suede pumps, the tank top—*his* tank top, by God; at least that's how he'd come to think of it . . . the one she'd worn that day to Keith's barbecue. She also sported a little more makeup than she generally wore. She hadn't mentioned a word about this during the tense fifteen minutes they'd called dinner this evening. Oh, God, it *was* happening, just as he'd known all along that sooner or later it would.

She was stepping out.

He'd been so steeped in suspicion waiting for the day to arrive when she would ultimately leave him that he had almost believed having the other shoe finally drop might actually come as something of a relief. He discovered now that it did not.

"Just where the hell do you think you're going?" he demanded, crowding close to her.

Ivy was not the least bit intimidated; she was much too furious. Her chin shot up, her eyes met his dead on, and she replied with tart succinctness, "Mack 'N Babe's."

"Not without me, you're not."

"I've already covered this ground, Vincent. I'm not going anywhere with you. Not tonight, not as long as you're acting like Neanderthal Man."

"Don't mess with me, Ivy," he said in a low, dangerous voice. "it's been a lousy day."

That tore it. "A lousy day?" she whispered. "A lousy *day?*" Her fury and her voice escalated a pace. "Well let me tell you something, D'Ambruzzi, for me it's been a lousy *week!* Read my lips, 'cause I'm only going to say this once. I am so damn sick of you and your stinking suspicions. Life with you lately has *not* been fun." Her chest heaved while she attempted to get her temper back under control. "Well, I want a little fun; I want some relaxation. And, dammit, I'm going to get it tonight . . . with my family. You are not welcome."

"Your *family?* Jesus, I'm sick of your damn family." His nose centimeters from hers, black eyes boring into green, he whispered, "And just what *is* your idea of fun, Ivy? Or should I ask whom?"

"Exactly what are you trying to say, Vincent?"

"You know precisely what I'm saying. Who are you gonna fuck tonight—for fun?"

Every last drop of color drained from Ivy's face. It hurt; oh, God, it hurt. She couldn't believe he'd actually come right out and said it, no matter how often this past week she'd read the suspicion in his eyes.

"You son of a bitch," she said in a hoarse whisper. "You goddamn, lousy, son of a . . ." Then her back straightened. "Get out." She cleared the lump from her throat and her voice emerged much more strongly. "Damn you, Vincent, *get out!*"

Much later he realized he should have done exactly that. That was the point at which he should have left, giving them both time to cool down. What he did instead was curl his lip and eye her insolently. "This is *my* apartment, Doll Baby, remember? I live here."

Ivy went stiff all over. She just stood there, staring at him for several heartbeats. "Fine," she whispered and pushed him aside so she could get to the door. "Fine. *I'll* leave then." She paused with her hand on the doorknob, wanting desperately to hurt him as much as he had hurt her. Staring dead ahead at the door, she accused hotly, "In your eyes, I've been nothing more than a slut for the better part of a week now." She looked at him over her shoulder. "Well, Vincent, I've had the name. Maybe tonight I'll play the game."

And in the next second she was gone, leaving him to stare at her swinging nightgown on the back of the bathroom door, while the reverberations of the slamming front door echoed throughout the apartment.

Chapter 17

Ivy wasn't entirely sober. She was aware of her cousins' concern, most likely brought on by the fact that this was not at all typical of her. Explaining the reasons behind her tipsiness, however, simply required more effort than she was in the mood to summon.

Under ordinary conditions she never drank more than two or three drinks in one sitting—not since third year med school when she'd discovered the hard way that it tended to affect her work long after the effects of the drinks themselves had worn off. It wasn't merely the possibility of a hangover that deterred her; she'd found her judgement wasn't as sharp, her hands weren't as steady. It wasn't, in short, intelligent.

Tonight she didn't care about intelligent. How could he have said that to her? Damn him, *how*? She purposefully sought something to help dull the pain, and bourbon was elected.

Tyler Griffus was also helping.

In her slightly inebriated state, Ivy found Jaz's boyfriend utterly charming. His lightly flirtatious attentiveness was a balm to the gaping wound Vincent's viciously worded lack of trust had slashed in her ego.

Leaning into Jaz, Ivy said under cover of the music, "Honey, I sure can see how you might have mistaken this guy for The Prince." She gave Jasmine a brilliant smile that was somewhat loose around the edges. "It really is a pity he doesn't do the Wild Thing, huh?" Then she straightened, planted her elbow on the table, her chin in her palm, and transferred her tipsy smile to Tyler, who was sitting across the table. "So, are you absolutely *certain* we've never met," she demanded, leaning forward and raising her voice to be heard over the lounge's rendition of "Stormy Weather." "There's somethin' awf'lly familler"—she laughed and corrected herself—"uh, *familiar*, about'cha . . . I know I've seen you *some*where before."

Tyler waited for the song to end and then leaned toward Ivy. "Have you ever bought flowers at a shop called "Florals by Ty" in Ravenna?" he asked.

"Nope."

"You live anywhere in the vicinity of the Roosevelt area?"

Ivy shook her head.

Knowing he had her hooked, feeling powerful, Tyler gave her his practiced, boyish, self-deprecatory smile and shrugged. "Then I guess I must simply have one of those faces."

Ivy giggled. "Guess so."

Jaz's chair screeched in protest across the floor as she abruptly pushed back from the table. She smiled at Tyler through gritted teeth. "Excuse us a second, won't you?" Grabbing Ivy by the arm, she yanked with a strength that caused her cousin, whose coordination was not up to its usual standards, to tip sideways out of her chair.

"Whoops." Ivy saved herself from tumbling to the floor by hastily planting a hand on the seat of the chair Jaz had just vacated. For some reason it struck her as hilariously funny and she giggled again as she straightened, scooping her hair from her eyes with her free hand. "Don't try this at home, kids," she advised, smiling around the table. "It took this trained professional years and *years* of practice to hone her razor sharp reflexive powers."

"Ivy!"

" 'Scuse me, won'tcha." She climbed to her feet and docilely ambled along in Jasmine's wake. Sherry hurriedly excused herself also and trailed after them.

The instant they were through the restroom door, Jaz shoved Ivy onto the vanity stool in front of the mirror. Lifting her feet, Ivy let the momentum spin her around, rotating a complete 360 degrees. When she finally rocked to a stop it was to find Jaz scowling down at her.

"What the *hell* is the matter with you?" she demanded. Sherry leaned against the wall, hands in her sweater pockets, watching them both.

Ivy blinked owlishly up at Jaz. "Huh?"

"Dammit Ivy, why are you slamming back drinks like they're made outta water—are you *trying* to get loaded? How come you're flirting with my date? And *why*, for the love of God," Jaz demanded in disgust, "are you *giggling*? My God, the last time I heard you giggle, you must have been in junior high."

"Well *excuuuse* me," Ivy replied to the latter statement with a throaty laugh. She conveniently chose to ignore the rest.

"What's gotten into you, Ive—why are you acting like a rebellious thirteen-year-old all of a sudden?"

Jaz studied her cousin carefully, as if she might somehow read the reasons for Ivy's aberrant behavior on her face. Then abruptly, speculatively, her eyebrows shot up and she said, "No, wait; don't tell me; let me take a wild stab here. Could it be that you and the Italian Stallion had a big fight?"

Ivy's good humor vanished in a flash. "Don't call him that," she snapped and then immediately wondered at her instinctive defense. Hell, considering some of the names she'd been mentally calling Vincent herself since the moment she'd stalked from their apartment, she certainly had no rational grounds to object to Jaz's sarcastic sobriquet.

That was the thing, though. *She* was allowed to cut him to ribbons; no one else was. Her eyes brimmed with tears.

She resolutely blinked them back and straightened her spine. Damned if she was going to bawl over that no-good, suspicious . . . Abruptly swivelling the stool around, she leaned into the mirror and made a small production over inspecting her makeup.

"I'm sorry, Ive," Jasmine promptly apologized, catching a glimpse of the very real pain in her cousin's eyes. She reached out to gently touch a finger to Ivy's bare shoulder and their eyes met in the mirror. "Listen, don't pay me any mind. Hell, it's no big secret how jealous 1 am of your relationship with D'Ambruzzi—"

Ivy exhaled expressively through her nose. Some swell relationship.

"—but I'll try to put a lid on the sarcasm, okay?" At Ivy's nod, she employed a purposefully neutral tone and inquired gently, "So . . . *did* you guys have a fight?"

Ivy nodded.

"A serious one, I take it. Care to talk about it?"

Holding her cousin's gaze with an overt show of

indifference, Ivy wet a finger and studiously smoothed her eyebrows. She shook out her hair. "No," she finally retorted flatly. Then her eyes slid past Jaz's to her other cousin. "Sher, you got any lipstick? I look like the walking dead here." She accepted the tube her cousin handed her and applied it carefully. Leaning back a bit, she inspected the results critically. "Tha's better." Fresh out of valid excuses to look elsewhere, she finally met Jaz's eyes in the mirror, and silently wondered at the dynamics going on here. She had to admit she didn't understand this at all. Sherry was the one she would have thought would have a problem with the dissolution of her romance. Jasmine she would have expected to cheer. Yet here it was *Jaz* going on and on at her, while Sherry just leaned against the wall, not saying word one. It was confusing.

"Oh, for heaven's sake; what's the big deal?" she blurted, and then was exasperated at the compulsion she felt to explain, "I just wanna have a little fun tonight, okay? Maybe indulge in a harmless l'il flirtation. Vincent's a jerk, your boyfriend's handy, and, Jaz, you tol' me yourself there isn't any real chemistry between you guys."

"There isn't; that's not the point, Ivy."

"Hey, I'll butt out though, Jazzy, if tha's what you want me to do. It's just. . . I didn't think he was a serious contender."

"He's not." Watching Ivy's growing distress, Jaz assured her gently, "It never occurred to me that you were out to steal my man, Ive."

"As if I could even if I wanted to," Ivy said gloomily. Then she brightened. "But it's not like I wanna sleep with the guy or anything. All I wanna do is have a few laughs."

Jaz asked gently, "But what about Vincent, Ivy?"

"What about him?" was the snapped response.

The frigidity in Ivy's voice bothered Jaz. She drew a deep breath, silently let it out and shook her head. "My God, I never thought I'd hear myself defending the man, but Ivy, it was pretty damn clear when I saw the two of you together that D'Ambruzzi thinks you're the greatest thing to sashay down the pike since Marilyn Monroe."

"Yeah, right," Ivy said bitterly.

"It's true, Ive," Sherry agreed, speaking up for the first time. "Anyone can see he's crazy about you."

Then why is he so damn willing to believe I'll sleep with the first man I meet? Ivy wondered with desperate unhappiness, and the ache inside her expanded. Her expression gave away nothing as she watched her cousins' reflections in the mirror, and finally Jasmine sighed.

"I give up," she said. "Fine, flirt with Tyler if it makes you feel better. Whatever floats your boat. But knock off the drinking . . . and don't lead him on, okay? It turned out that he's not The Prince; but neither is he the troll. So don't let your actions be misconstrued, Ivy Jayne . . . and I'm not talking for his sake here. You don't wanna do anything you can't live with come morning when you've sobered up."

"Yes, Mommy."

Jaz and Sherry exchanged troubled glances, but in the final analysis they knew there wasn't anything else they could do. Ivy was a grown woman. If she was hell bent on finding trouble then the best they could do was keep their eyes peeled, and hope for an opportunity to head off the worst of it.

Tyler was feeling invincible. It was exactly—no, dammit, it was even *better*—than he had imagined it would be. Sitting right across the table from the Doc, talking to her, basking in her admiration . . . Christ, he felt such a surge of power, he was amazed the lights hadn't dimmed all over the city.

She was crazy about him, just as he'd known she would be. Their minds were atuned. She might not yet fully comprehend who he was, exactly, but she felt the mystic connection, same as he. Her approval was such that the voice in his head hadn't merely faded into the background; it had disappeared altogether.

And if that wasn't cause for celebration, he didn't know what was.

Everything else faded to insignificance beside the glistening fact of her approbation. It no longer chafed that Jaz had taken forever to come through for him, or that she was glaring daggers at him tonight. Hell, the former simply didn't matter any more; and the latter . . . well, she was simply jealous because another woman found him attractive, and probably because she could sense that any chance she might have once had to be screwed by him was now history. Neither did he care that the cousin called Terry studied him as though he were an exotic species under a microscope. The Doc liked him; that was all that mattered.

He hadn't felt peace like this in weeks, months . . . years. Hell, he probably hadn't felt it in his entire lifetime. Nothing on earth could possibly destroy his euphoria.

Or so he sincerely thought—right up until the moment he looked up to see the same cop who had been at the hospital the first time he'd ever laid eyes on Ivy Pennington walk through the door, pause, and look around.

Then head straight for where he was seated.

* * *

Vincent scanned everyone seated around Ivy's table. It was a gesture as automatic to him as breathing . . . and yet in this particular instance it was also a fruitless one, as he then dismissed them in approximately the same instant that his mind's eye firmly fixed them in place. As he strode across the lounge his eyebrows drew together and formed a formidable scowl. He didn't know what the hell he was doing here.

But he hadn't been able to stay away.

When she'd first stormed out of the apartment, he had merely shrugged, righteous in the certainty of being on moral high ground, and then stonily put her from his mind. He'd concentrated instead on the case surrounding her.

By compartmentalizing and blocking out all else—skills he had long ago honed to a fine finish—he'd focused all his efforts into creating a flow chart. It displayed every fact concerning this case that he could dredge up. Unfortunately, there were damn few facts that were concrete enough to merit inclusion, an acknowledgment that had left a bitter taste and forced him to take it one step further and admit to himself that had it not been for Ivy's involvement, this was a case he would have been obliged to place on the back burner some time ago.

Setting aside a case wasn't an option he ever enjoyed exercising, but unfortunately he didn't always have a choice. His caseload was jammed beyond an acceptable capacity, an unalterable fact that forced him to prioritize. His time, of necessity, must be devoted to those cases he had an actual prayer of solving. Though that never stopped him from hoping that while he worked the top priority cases something would also break on the tough ones: those that garnered so few leads.

Sitting on the couch, hunched over to study the sparse evidence so neatly documented on the chart he had propped up on the coffee table, he'd racked his brain for inspiration. Ultimately, however, it had merely brought his thoughts right back to the one person he most wanted to avoid thinking about.

Ivy Jayne Pennington.

When he'd accused her of seeking an excuse to sleep with another man, he hadn't for a second doubted the accusation's veracity. Why should he? Lack of trust was conditioned into his personality by the major contributing factors of his life: an isolated adolescence, the type of work he did, and of course his disasterous marriage to the faithless LaDonna.

And yet . . .

He couldn't quite dismiss the words that had popped into his mind immediately when she'd turned to him and said that as long as he believed she had the name anyway, then tonight she was going to have the game as well. His instinctual reaction hadn't been the surge of jealousy that one might expect. Rather, he'd thought . . . Yeah, right, Ivy.

Bullshit.

He'd tried to disregard that gut response, and for quite a while he'd been successful. But in the end it had refused to be ignored. In fact, the harder he worked to put it out of his mind, the larger it had seemed to grow.

Big threat, no doubt about it. But an idle one. He knew it on an instinctive level, a level so deep it brooked no arguments. Ivy had too much honesty, too much integrity, to ever sleep with one man while she was committed to another.

It was a revelation that should have made him happy, and it did, of course . . . in a distant corner of his mind or heart where the knowledge was absorbed without quite taking in the full ramifications. But then again, it didn't. It made him squirm. He hated being in the wrong, especially in such a big way, and this was big. Huge. It shed a whole new light on some of his recent actions that made them appear pretty damn stupid.

He'd been acting like a complete ass.

His pride had kicked in hard on the heels of that thought and he'd assured himself he wasn't about to hotfoot it over to her uncle's bar for any big apology. Hell, no. He'd catch her when she came home.

Famous last words.

He still didn't know what the hell he was doing here.

But he did know that he wasn't able to stay away.

Terry intercepted him before he was halfway across the lounge. Stopping in front of him, barring his way by standing chest to chest, he advised flatly, "I don't think you want to go over there just yet."

"Get out of my way, Pennington."

"I'm serious, D'Ambruzzi. Ivy's a little drunk—she's not at her most receptive." He shouldered Vincent in the direction he wanted. "It must have been one helluva fight. C'mon over to the bar and I'll buy you a drink."

Shooting a glance across the room, only to feel, even from this distance, the chill that emanated from Ivy as she studiously ignored him, Vincent shrugged and acquiesced. He silently claimed a bar stool, greeted Ivy's uncle with a level look and a nod, and ordered a club soda.

Terry waited until Mack had returned to the

other end of the bar before he turned to Vincent. "I'd rather Uncle Mack not realize there's a problem here," he said in a low voice.

"Hey, I can sure as hell live with that." Vincent raised his glass and drank half the contents in one gulp. Setting it down with a thump, he turned his head and looked at Terry. "Just what do you want, Pennington?"

"Well, for starters, I'd sure like to know what you found out on Griffus."

"Who?"

"Dammit, D'Ambruzzi! You forgot, didn't you?"

"Jasmine's boyfriend!" He had forgotten. Refusing the guilt that wanted to color his apology, he shrugged with a show of indifference. "Sorry. It slipped my mind entirely."

"I think you're gonna wish you'd remembered," Terry informed him dryly, "considering the way Ive's been flirting with the guy all night."

Vincent spun around on his stool so fast he nearly fell off. A song had just ended, and as he stared across the room the man seated across from Ivy leaned over and said something. It made her laugh. Vincent's stomach churned violently and he came halfway off the stool, all his positive thoughts of trust forgotten.

Terry's hand on his arm stayed him. "There's something about that guy that's off," he said grimly. "I can't put my finger on what it is, but it's there. And this is not just jealousy at work here, Vincent. I feel it in my gut."

"He's flirting with Ivy? How the hell can he flirt with Ivy if he's here as another woman's date?" Vincent demanded.

"You got me, bud. It doesn't seem to be bothering Jaz any, though. And as much as I hate to defend the guy, I gotta tell you that Ivy started the whole thing. She's in a dangerous mood tonight, man. My sister and Jaz dragged her off to the ladies' at one point—I assumed to try and straighten her out—but the minute they got back she picked up right where she'd left off and frankly, Jasmine doesn't seem to give a shit. Jesus, D'Ambruzzi, I've honest-to-God never seen Ivy quite like this. What the hell did you two fight about anyhow?"

"None of your goddamn business."

Terry shrugged and took a sip of his beer. "You musta screwed *somethin'* up big time to send her running out looking for a lot of booze and a little admiration."

"Yeah, I did. But I can fix it right now. And I will." He stood up and flexed his hands, which had been balled up into fists on his thighs. "Just as soon as I finish rearranging that bastard's face for him."

Jesus, what were they talking about? Tyler Griffus's attention was divided, and it threw him off balance. He wanted to maintain a calm facade around the Doc but at the same time was afraid to take his eyes off the cousin and the detective. Every time the detective's dark, cold gaze turned his way, Tyler's stomach took a sickening dip. Fucking cop.

How the hell had the cop found him? He'd been so careful. Or—giving due credit to what appeared the more likely scenario—how had the cousin caught on to who he was? The son of a bitch. Tyler hadn't done *anything* to give himself away and yet every indication pointed to the Doc's cousin as the one who had called the friggin'' cops.

He had to get out of here.

Yeah, and go where, stupid? The voice was back, roaring through his brain like a flash flood through a dry culvert, rage rising to reach immediate saturation levels and then threatening to overflow, testing the boundaries of his control. *If they've somehow figured it all out—Christ, how have they figured it out?—then your anonymity is shot. And if the pigs know your name, then they're gonna know where you live; they're gonna know where your shop, your only source of livelihood, is located. You can run, you dumb shit, but you cannot hide.*

Still functioning on automatic, he said something to the Doc that made her laugh and that small proof of his ability to remain operational on two levels at once made the virulent hatred of the predator within subside to a more manageable proportion.

Okay. What you can do, however, is bluff, it advised him, calming down to the extent that Tyler felt the imminent threat of its trying to take control recede. *Bluff like hell. Knowing isn't the same as proving, after all. And maybe, maybe, it's something else entirely anyway.*

Which was exactly what it turned out to be. He simply had no way of projecting that the hoped-for something else would prove to be even less welcome and more damaging to the fragile hold he had on his inner demon than the situation he had assumed was already at its very worst.

"Whoa, whoa there, cowboy," Terry said, grabbing hold of Vincent's arm and jerking him back to his bar stool. "Let's not go off half cocked here."

Vincent snapped his arm free. The eyes he turned on Ivy's cousin were cold and hard and a vicious sort of toughness emanated from him in waves. Terry suffered some serious qualms when he observed the way Vincent's right hand kept straying to touch his gun—which was in a flat leather holster clipped to the waistband of his jeans—every time his attention shifted away from him to the man across the room who was flirting with Vincent's woman. Feeling responsible for starting this whole sorry mess, Terry thought he'd better do some fast talking here before the situation escalated entirely out of control. He never would have blurted everything out the way he had—with absolutely no care for finesse—except he'd just sort of taken it for granted he was speaking to a cop. Trouble was, although he could see the street cop's wary readiness for trouble in Vincent's very posture, it was clearly the man who was reacting to every thoughtless word he had uttered.

Terry was racking his brain for something to say that would defuse the situation when Vincent suddenly sank back onto the bar stool, that killer tenseness draining from his expression. He shoveled unsteady hands through his hair. "Jesus," he muttered hoarsely. "I came here in the first place because I thought I owed her an apology. Hell, she won't even look at me. Imagine how receptive she's gonna be if I bust the guy's chops for him." He scrubbed his hands over his face. "God Almighty, what's happening to my professionalism? It's getting so I don't even recognize myself anymore."

"Considering what a tight-ass you were the first day you showed up on Ive's doorstep, that ain't necessarily a bad thing," Terry observed.

Vincent merely snorted, a sound that almost managed to sound amused. "Thank you, Pennington; that's just what I needed to hear." He shrugged. "Still, I'll concede that you might have a point."

Abruptly, he rose to his feet. "Well, much as I've enjoyed our little man to man talk, sitting here isn't accomplishing much. I gotta go talk to Ivy."

He half expected her cousin to hold him back

once again, but Terry merely nodded. "Yeah, I suppose you do," he said. He looked at him soberly. "Good luck, D'Ambruzzi."

Ivy straightened her shoulders when she saw Vincent purposefully cross the floor towards her. It was about time.

For a while there she'd derived a masochistic sort of thrill out of silently baiting him. It was kind of like twisting the tiger's tail. She had known full well he was angry, could feel his frustration from clear across the room. It hadn't stopped her, however, from flaunting her flirtation with Tyler. On the contrary, she had gained a vindictive satisfaction from it, experienced a surge of power knowing her actions were impacting so strongly upon Vincent's emotions.

But it had palled. She was feeling confrontational and this was too passive. It was also a strain to pretend he wasn't even there while at the same time she tried to surreptitiously gauge his every reaction from the corner of her eye.

She wished to heaven she hadn't had so much to drink. She was spoiling for a fight but didn't want to make a fool of herself, and she was just sober enough to acknowledge that the prospect wasn't exactly beyond the realm of possibility, considering how madly her emotions were fluctuating. They were all over the place, which was unfortunate, for right now of all times she needed to present in a rational manner whatever arguments were going to ensue. She wanted to be calm and articulate. What she was very much afraid she was instead going to be, was hysterical and shrill.

She sat stiffly as she watched him approach. She had just damn well better not cry. She'd kill him if he made her cry.

*   *   *

Shit. Shit! Tyler Griffus took a deep breath and then straightened his spine, watching the detective's approach with a fatalistic sort of resignation. How the *hell* had it come to this?

Well, never mind; the important thing was that it had. And he was determined that if he had to go down then he would do so with a little dignity. Racing out the door wasn't going to do him any good. He simply wasn't designed to live life on the run, so why make a spectacle of himself? Sternly, he squelched the faint rumblings of the predator within. *Just, for once, shut the fuck up.*

He tried not to think about what they were going to do to him in prison. It was an undisputed fact that inmates did not like rapists. About the only form of life that they considered to be lower were men who sexually or physically abused children.

Dammit, they ought to understand that the women always asked for it. He'd *make* them understand. Somehow, he would.

His face impassive, he straightened his spine and raised his chin, meeting the detective's gaze dead on as he walked up to the table. Black eyes full of animosity, the cop planted his hands, palms flat, upon the table top and leaned heavily on them, staring at him. A muscle in his jaw jumped, and his heavy brows gathered over the bridge of his nose. His distaste was clear. There was a rage deep in his eyes, a desire to dish out some pain that was even clearer. But then he turned away.

And reached out to cup Ivy's chin in his long fingers. He gently turned her head, which had been averted, up to face him.

"We gotta talk, Ivy," he said. "Let's go home."

Chapter 18

Home? It was a word with connotations that electrified several of the people sitting at the table.

Ivy was the first to recover. "And just whose home might that be, Vincent," she demanded belligerently, knocking his hand away. *"Yours?"*

Vincent flushed. "It was wrong of me to get snide with you about that," he admitted in a low voice and would have elaborated if her cousins hadn't interrupted him before he had the chance.

"Home?" Sam and Davis said almost simultaneously. It was Davis who went on to demand, "What's the deal, Ivy? You *livin'* with this clown?"

"Yes!" Vincent's response was immediate and aggressive. He turned on Ivy's cousin in a manner that had *What're you gonna do about it* written all over it.

"Not any more I'm not," Ivy snapped almost on the heels of his assertion.

"Ah, c'mon, Ive," Vincent protested, redirecting his attention exclusively back to her. "Don't be like that. I know I behaved like a jerk earlier, and I'm sorry. But don't just shut me out entirely. If you aren't ready to go home yet, then can't we at least go somewhere a little more private? We've got to talk."

"I think you've said it all already, D'Ambruzzi."

"Oh, I haven't said the half of it, Pennington," he promptly retorted, and gave her a sardonic smile that nevertheless held vestiges of tenderness. A little amazed himself at the way all his doubts had just abruptly disappeared, he reached out to gently trace the smooth contour of her cheek. "And if you prefer it said publicly, then public it'll be. I love you, Ivy Jayne."

She felt as though someone had just reached inside and given all her vital organs a hard yank. Throat constricted, head swimming—with distress, with confusion and alcohol, with hope—she could barely catch her breath.

Then she realized that there were no longer any songs being sung in the lounge, looked around her, saw they were the focus of every eye in the bar, and was engulfed in a scalding fury. She pushed to her feet. Vincent didn't budge an inch and by the time she'd stood to her full height they were standing nose to nose. She swayed slightly as the abrupt movement and too much alcohol conspired to shift her center of balance, but Vincent prevented her from staggering when he reached out and grasped her arms. Ivy shook off his steadying hands.

"Is this some big *joke?*" she demanded. "You find it *funny* to make me the butt of it?"

"What, you think I'm ridiculing you?. he snarled back incredulously. "This is no joke, Ivy."

"Damn right it's not! I don't find this amusing at all. Three hours ago—"

"—I was a damn fool," Vincent interrupted her

in a more moderate tone, praying she wouldn't inform the entire bar—particularly her uncle, who disliked him enough already—of just how big a fool he had been. He might deserve it, but he prayed she wouldn't. "And I wish to hell I could take it all back, Ivy. I wish I'd never hurt you that way."

"You don't love me," she stubbornly insisted. "So don't say you do."

"Damn it to hell, I do!" Suddenly as angry as she, he gripped her upper arms, pulled her up onto her toes and demanded, "You think this is easy for me? I'm sorry for what I said, Ivy, sorrier than you can imagine. Hell, I thought I meant it—thought in fact I had it all figured out just how you'd act in any given situation. But as soon as you said . . . that thing you said before you left, well, I knew I was dead wrong. You've got more integrity than any ten men I've ever known, and I was an idiot."

Looking into her slightly unfocused, stubbornly shuttered green eyes, Vincent could see he wasn't getting through to her. She was still furious and in no frame of mind to hear what he had to say. So with a sigh he released her and stepped back. "This was a mistake," he admitted. "I'll, uh, just wait for you at home." Turning, he spotted Terry a few feet away, standing with his hands in his pockets, observing them. "She's had way too much to drink," he said. "See that she gets home safely, okay?"

"Yeah."

"Thanks. And see her into the apartment. She's had some unwanted attention from a deviant lately." Recalling that Terry already knew that, he shook his head impatiently. Turning back to Ivy, he reached out to touch her face but let his hand drop back to his side when she made a slight movement of withdrawal. "I do love you," he insisted quietly.

Then he turned and walked away.

Deviant? Tyler was thunderstruck as he watched Ivy sink, head bowed, back into her seat across the table. She thought he was a *deviant?* Rage burst forth, utterly past containment this time, expanding and swelling nearly beyond his capacity to disguise. Fortunately a song, raggedly begun, began to pick up tempo all across the lounge. It gave cover to the pure animal growl of blood-lust rage that escaped him.

The goddamn, duplicitous cunt. Butter wouldn't fucking melt in her mouth, would it? Pretending she understood. Pretending they were *alike,* when all along she'd been calling him a deviant behind his back. Bad-mouthing him, living with a friggin' cop, and probably *laughing* at him, too. She was no better than the rest of her kind, after all. No better than the rest of the lying, scheming bitches.

Oh, no, dammit, she wasn't getting off that easy. Because she was worse. A thousand times worse. And she was going to pay.

They *all* were going to pay.

"Are you sure you wouldn't rather be dropped off over there?" Terry inquired gently when Ivy stopped in front of her door.

She looked up from fitting her key in the lock. Turning her head to stare consideringly at the door he indicated, she wished she could give her cousin a resoundingly unequivocal "no." But the truth was . . .

She pulled her key out of the lock, fumbled for

the next one on the ring and walked one door down. She let herself into the apartment, but then came to an abrupt stop just over the threshold. Except for wavery bars of illumination across the hardwood floor, which the nearly full moon slanted through the blinds, Vincent's apartment was dark inside.

"Well, so much for all those heartfelt protestations of love," she said flatly, trying not to show how much it hurt.

Terry bulled his way past her. "Vincent!" he called out, even though it was obvious the apartment was empty. When to no one's surprise there was no answer, he turned back to Ivy. "Most likely he just wasn't expecting you home so soon," he said, and he truly believed that was the most likely scenario. Still, it didn't stop him from silently cursing his cousin's lover and all his ancestors, too. "You weren't exactly receptive to his overtures tonight," Terry continued. "He probably thought you'd stay out half the night just to show him that no one can push Ivy Pennington around." And in truth, considering her attitude earlier in the evening, it had surprised Terry just how fast Ivy had decided she wanted to go home after Vincent left the bar. All her rebellious flirtatiousness had simply vanished the moment he was out of sight. She hadn't even argued about having someone drive her home.

"Give him the benefit of the doubt, Ive," he coaxed now. "It's plain to anyone with eyes in their head that he's crazy about you."

But he found himself talking to thin air. She had already turned on her heel and stalked back to her own apartment. Before he could even attempt to catch up, the door had slammed closed behind her.

* * *

"Good God, what a night." Jaz kicked off her heels and headed straight for the kitchen. She chugged down several gulps of orange juice straight from the bottle, studied the meager contents in her refrigerator, and then closed the door.

What a night, she silently repeated. First Ivy getting loaded and acting like some headstrong, over-aged Lolita, then the Italian Stallion—oh hell, she'd said she wouldn't call him that any more— then *Vincent* showing up and saying all that stuff in front of God and everybody. That had taken a lot of balls; not that *cajones* were something she'd ever doubted for a moment that D'Ambruzzi had in plenty. Still, she had to confess she'd been impressed with the man in spite of herself. Too bad the same couldn't be said for the one person he'd wanted to impress.

And just to top off the evening, if Jaz ever saw Tyler Griffus again she would be one surprised woman. Something had obviously been chewing on him and he had practically *dumped* her at the front door. She'd actually been pretty relieved to see the back of him, truth to tell. They hadn't been getting along all that splendidly in recent days anyhow, and there had been something kind of funny in his eyes the latter part of this evening. Ever since D'Ambruzzi's unexpected arrival at the bar, as a matter of fact. Jeez, was it possible he had taken Ivy's flirtation seriously? Well, if he had, she simply couldn't bring herself to care. And wasn't that the real shame?

She never heard the key in the door, or its silent opening and near-closing. One minute she was alone, the next she had walked unsuspecting from her kitchen into her living room, to find herself suddenly face to face with a masked stranger. He reached out and gripped one of her arms, silently raising a surgically gloved hand to display his gleaming knife. Her eyes tracked its movements as it weaved back and forth below her nose. No words were necessary.

The threat was understood.

Terry banged on Ivy's door and demanded without result to be let in, until an irate neighbor finally stuck his head out in the hallway and told him to knock it the hell off or he was calling the cops. Swearing, Terry smacked the closed portal one last time in frustration before he turned away. Jesus! He didn't *believe* the way everyone was acting tonight.

He didn't need this on top of his damn jumpiness over Jaz's good friend Griffus. There was something just not right about that guy. It was a feeling which, if anything, had only grown stronger as the evening had progressed. Mere minutes from home, Terry impulsively made the U turn just before the Montlake Cut and got back onto 520. He wasn't going to be able to sleep if he didn't have a little talk with Jaz tonight, that was for damn sure. If it was a bit on the late side for a drop-in visit, too bad. Why should she get to sleep peacefully if he couldn't?

The first thing he noticed as he climbed out of his car and started up the walkway was that her front door was ajar. Heart slamming up against his ribcage, he broke into a run but then pawed cautiously just outside her door. Listening hard, not hearing anything, he let himself in. Except for the light burning in the kitchen and a bar of light from her bedroom spilling across the hallway where the door was cracked open, it was dark inside. He eased down the hallway. Was he making too much of this? Perhaps she simply hadn't pushed the door securely closed behind her.

Then he heard her whimper.

Bursting into her bedroom, Terry reeled back in shock at the sight that greeted him. Jasmine was spread-eagle on her back, her clothes in shreds around her, teeth clenched and face white as a man in a ninja mask straddled her chest, brutally gripping a fistful of hair to hold her still while he tried to force his erect penis into her mouth. She was resisting despite the knife point pressed beneath the curve of her jaw.

"NO!" Terry launched himself at the man. But his hesitation at the shock of what he'd beheld cost him; the element of surprise was lost. Jasmine's attacker twisted in one fluid motion and slashed out, and Terry's own momentum ended up working against him. Unable to halt his forward impetus, he felt a searing pain explode across his chest and one arm.

He fell back, grasping his wound. He could feel warm blood spilling between his fingers but he didn't have time to inspect the damage. Looking around frantically, he grabbed the first likely weapon he saw, an umbrella in the stand next to her dresser, and swung it with all his might at the assailant.

Dumb luck, he decided much later, but somehow he nevertheless managed to hit the man's right arm, causing the knife to tumble from his grasp. Jaz snatched it up and made a stabbing motion with it at her would-be rapist.

The man roared his rage and charged Terry. Pain exploded in Terry's chest at the impact, but the assailant didn't stay around to take advantage of his incapacitation. He stumbled to his feet and disappeared out the door.

Jaz scrambled across the bed and launched herself into Terry's arms. He nearly passed out at the impact, but gamely wrapped his good arm around her and held on tightly. He breathed openmouthed into her hair as she clung to him and sobbed.

"Shh, shh now," he whispered. "You're okay now. Everything's gonna be okay." Then he tipped his head down in sudden alarm, trying to see into her face. "That is . . . he didn't . . . ?"

"No," she sobbed and clung tighter. "No. Oh, God, Terry, th . . . ank you for getting here when you did. Oh God, oh God, I was so sc—scared; I've never been so scared in my entire life."

"Shh," he kept whispering. He kissed her hair. And her temple. Then he slid his lips down onto her cheekbone. Suddenly aware of her nakedness beneath his hands, long suppressed desire ignited in him and he tipped her chin up with an insistent finger. His mouth rocked over hers as he kissed her with explosive passion.

Jaz acquiesced for about three seconds. Then she shoved him away in scandalized astonishment. *"Terry Pennington!"* Terry groaned and stared at her with dull eyes, and her shock at being kissed that way by her *cousin* gave way to petrified concern when she noticed his condition for the first time.

He was pale as death and covered in blood. Hands covering her mouth, Jaz stared at him with wide eyes. Oh, God, he probably hadn't even realized who she *was* when he'd . . . She pulled a blanket off the bed and wrapped him in it. "I'm going to call 911."

"Yeah, I think that's prob'ly a good idea," Terry agreed in a weak voice. "I don't feel so hot. And call Ivy, Jaz. See if D'Ambruzzi's come home yet. He'd better be told what happened here."

*   *   *

Ivy nearly failed to answer the phone at all when it rang. Indulging in some extreme alcohol-fueled self-pity, she wanted only to be left alone. Because she was already dealing with a sense of guilt over the way she'd treated Terry earlier, however, she snatched up the receiver before the answering machine could get the call. "What?" she snarled ungraciously.

"Ivy? It's me." Ivy recognized her cousin's voice and rolled her eyes impatiently. Now what? A shuddery little exhalation came down the line. "Ivy, someone just tried to rape me."

"Jaz?" Ivy bolted upright, her tone changing instantly. She suddenly felt entirely sober. "When? How? Oh, God, are you all right?"

"Yeah. But, Ive? Is D'Ambruzzi there?"

"Oh, Jasmine, I'm sorry, he isn't. I don't know where he is, but I'll try to find him, okay? Are you sure you're okay?"

"Terry got here. He stopped the man before he, before he could . . . but Terry's hurt, Ivy. I think he's hurt pretty bad. The man who tried to rape me—he cut Ter with a knife and he's bleeding like crazy."

"I'll be right over."

"No, you don't have to do that. I called 911 and they're sending the cops and the paramedics. Terry said you'd offer, but he also said to tell you you've had too much to drink to be out on the road on your own."

"My God. Who *did* this?"

"I don't know. And isn't that funny, considering the way I've scoffed all these years at those inept witnesses they're always showing on cop shows? I always thought I'd make the greatest witness ever. But it's all a blur. He was wearing one of those

ninja things on his head and all I can remember
with any clarity is his hands. He wore surgical
gloves. And he had the biggest damn knife I've
ever seen." Her teeth started clattering so hard Ivy
could hear them on her end of the line. Then she
heard a knock on Jasmine's door and Jaz was saying,
"Ivy, I gotta go. The paramedics are here and Terry
needs attention."

And before Ivy could ask at what hospital she
could find her cousins or if Jasmine wanted her to
notify her parents for her, Jaz had disconnected.

She had tried the precinct without success and
was dialing Keith's number when her front doorbell rang. Reseating the receiver without completing the call, she went to answer it.

It was Tyler Griffus.

"Oh, thank God," she said, pulling him into the
apartment. "Did Jaz send you? I about went crazy
when she hung up without telling me what hospital
they were taking Terry to."

His veneer of civilization was paper thin. The
predator within had taken over entirely, swallowing
up the tiny bit of conscience he'd still possessed.
It had been close at Jasmine's house—too damn
close. Having fled that scene, he'd come straight
over here, where he'd lucked out getting into the
building. But then his luck had deserted him.

He hadn't been able to think of a way to get past
the Doc's front door without identifying himself.
He wasn't a damn housebreaker—he was accustomed to forcing his way in behind women who
had just *unlocked* their doors. So he had simply
knocked. But that meant that now his anonymity
was shot to hell. He was going to have to kill her.
He wasn't looking forward to it exactly, but he
didn't see a way around it.

And it was the Doc's own goddamn fault.

It was good of her to hand him the perfect excuse for getting her away from here, though. Maybe he wouldn't hurt her *too* much before he offed her, because the truth was, he'd been surprised not to find her at the cop's apartment next door, which was where he had gone first. He hadn't had a clue how he was going to handle the cop, so this was a bit of luck, finding her all alone. If he wanted to extend that luck, however, he'd better hustle her along, better put as many miles as possible between him and the long arm of the law.

He proffered his hand. "Come," he urged. "Jaz needs your support, but she didn't want you driving yourself."

"Yes, of course." Ivy reached out to take the hand he extended to her, and the glance she gave it was automatic and cursory, nothing more. Until she noticed the faint rimming of white beneath his fingernails, along his cuticles, and coating the fine cracks of his knuckles. Then her heart seemed to stop pumping for an instant.

When it recommenced, it pounded so hard she feared he would actually hear it. Oh God, Oh God. She'd been a med student and then a doctor for too many years not to instinctively recognize that powder for what it was.

Then her stark terror was superceded by fury. The son of a bitch—what arrogance! It wasn't as if you had to use a nail brush or anything to insure the damn powder's removal. It was clear *he* hadn't bothered to do more than perfunctorily slap his palms together, for it only took the slightest effort and a little running water to wash away the fine talc that remained on one's hands once the surgical gloves were removed.

*   *   *

Vincent's plan, when he walked out of Mack 'N Babe's, was to go straight home and await Ivy's arrival. The instant he hit the street, however, he realized he was much too wired to be cooped up in a small apartment—not if he didn't want to end up doing some serious damage to the place before she finally got there. And, hell, what was the rush? It was pretty much assured she was going to keep him waiting until the wee hours of the morning, anyhow, just for drill.

The sidewalks along Pioneer Square's First Avenue were exceptionally wide, but the abundance of sidewalk tables congesting them when the weather was nice rendered the pedestrian flow into a kind of catch-as-catch-can affair. It was a warm summer evening and despite the lateness of the hour, the streets were crowded. Vincent utilized his shoulders with perhaps a little more strenuousness than was absolutely necessary to forge a path through tourists, street people, and revelers as he worked his way past funky, neon-lit taverns and exotic rug stores. He stopped under the South End Steam Bath sign and ignored the young barker who sat on a stool next to him, bawling out, "Seven clubs for seven bucks!" as he tried to decide what to do next.

Triple globed turn-of-the-century street lamps illuminated every corner. Competing with multi-hued neon and a nearly full moon, they dappled the leafy trees that lined the meridian up and down the avenue, and highlighted the overflowing baskets of flowers attached to the light standards. Soulful rhythm and blues poured out onto the street, wafted along on a cloud of smoke that escaped every time the door leading to the clubs opened and closed behind him. Uncharacteristically, Vincent didn't even notice. Heeding only a debate taking place inside his head, he failed to appreciate the sweet young things in their abbreviated summer attire as they made their way along the crowded sidewalk; neither did he have a glance to spare for their counter-culture counterparts, clad equally skimpily but mostly all in black, and sporting the ubiquitous nose-ring and colorfully spiked hair. Tourists juggled packages and cameras, panhandlers courteously requested handouts, beat cops walked in pairs, talking quietly, occasionally laughing or twirling a nightstick.

Vincent saw none of it.

He couldn't quite figure out how his life had come to this. If someone had told him six months ago that he'd fall in love with a woman involved in one of his cases, he would have split a gut laughing. Yeah, right, Jack—pull the other one. It was improbable he was ever again going to fall in love, period. And with someone who could compromise the integrity of one of his cases? Not bloody likely— *that* had to be the height of unprofessionalism. While he might not be able to claim much else, when it came to his work he could honestly say he was the consummate professional.

Yet he had. And unprofessional or not, he wasn't giving her up. So where did that leave him? Well, one thing he could do was remove himself from the case involving her. He'd talk to his captain first thing Monday morning and have him assign it to someone else. As for tonight . . . well, there wasn't a hell of a lot he could do tonight.

Except stop by the unit and run Jasmine's boyfriend through the computer.

For a man who prided himself on abiding by his word at all times, he'd somehow managed to let that promise slide and he simply couldn't justify putting it off until Monday.

The Public Safety building wasn't that far away—it was close enough, at any rate, to make collecting his car only to have to turn around and look for another parking place several blocks away more of a hassle than it was worth. He set out on foot.

Two detectives he'd known in Vice hailed him when he walked through the door. He spent ten minutes listening to the gossip from that division before he finally excused himself. It was dark in Special Assaults when he let himself in.

He didn't expect to find anything, and when he tapped out G-R-I-F-F-I-T-H, T-Y-L-E-R on the keyboard, that's exactly what came up. Good enough. He reached for the power switch. He could call Terry Pennington and tell him with a clear conscience that he'd run a check and the man was clean.

Then his hand hesitated. No, wait a sec. That wasn't the guy's name. What the hell was it—Griffin, Griffis? Griffus, that was it! He tapped in the correction.

And slammed into action, whispering, "Oh, sweet Jesus," when words began to scroll onto the screen.

Chapter 19

It didn't take more than an instant for Ivy to figure out that anger wasn't the wisest emotion to display before a rapist. She'd had years of experience submerging her emotions before arrogant surgeons and other senior medical personnel of various temperament. Unfortunately, never before had she been forced to do so while in the grip of an almost overpowering terror. *Oh God, girl,* act, she ordered herself sternly. *Give him a performance that'll leave Bernhardt and Streep in the dust. 'Cause if you're not entirely convincing, you're going to end up raped . . . or worse.*

And then wondered somewhat hysterically what in hell could *be* worse. She eased her hand out of his. "Let me just grab my purse," she said coolly. "I'll be right back. If you want to save time," she tossed back over her shoulder as she headed for the bedroom—where the nearest private telephone was located—"you can go on down and start up the car. I'll be with you in a sec."

Ivy didn't really expect Tyler to take her up on her offer and he didn't. She was halfway down the hall when her predicament fully sank in . . . and then it hit her like a sledge hammer and nearly brought her to her knees. This was the man responsible for Jasmine's near rape and Terry's injuries, this guy standing in her living room right now. God alone only knew how she was supposed to extricate herself unscathed from this situation—she was trained as a doctor, after all, not a commando warrior, and from all appearances she was entirely on her own. Her step faltered and she reached out to brace an unsteady hand against the wall as a wave of nauseating dizziness turned everything white before her eyes and rose in a sour tide up her throat.

She took several slow, deep breaths and resumed an erect posture, continuing down the hallway. Once in her room, she headed straight for the nightstand where she'd placed the scalpel she'd been packing around for weeks now. It felt as though she'd had it secreted on her person in one pocket or another forever.

With her usual disregard for orderliness, she had simply tossed it next to her cousins' housewarming vase, with its by-now seriously depleted supply of condoms, as soon as she'd arrived home. For once in her life grateful for her sloppy personal habits, she picked it up again and slid it back into her skirt pocket. She still didn't know if she could bring herself to actually *use* the thing as a weapon . . . but she was by-God going to have it on her in the event she worked up the wherewithal.

Oh, God, where was Vincent? How could he have told her he loved her and then just disappeared—leaving her to face this on her own? She'd believed him when he said that—in spite of what her attitude at the time may have suggested, despite the unforgivable things he'd said earlier in the evening. That garbage he'd spewed had infuriated her almost beyond endurance and *still* she'd believed his protestations of love, because deep down inside she knew Vincent, and he simply wasn't a man to bare his soul in public . . . but where the hell *was* he? She needed him so desperately.

And damn his hide, he was nowhere to be found.

Silently, Ivy picked up the phone and punched out 911. It rang one time, two times. Oh, please, please. Pick it up. *Pick . . . it . . . up.* It began to ring a third time . . .

Then she let out a terrified screech and dropped the receiver. For an arm had suddenly clamped across her chest like a vise, the hand on the end of it gripping her shoulder with iron fingers, and a knife appeared, its wicked point waving mesmerizingly back and forth in front of her eyes.

Then it was gone, lowered from sight. But not forgotten—not forgotten at all. She felt its cool steel pressing the soft underside of her jaw at the carotid artery.

"Hang up the phone," Tyler instructed into her left ear in a flat, deadly voice.

Ivy reached down and groped blindly until she snagged the receiver by its spiral cord. Pulling it hand over hand until she had hold of it, she replaced it gently in its cradle. And very carefully refrained from swallowing.

"Oh, man, I've really got to hand it to you, you deceptive twat," he rasped. "You're good. That bit about warming up the car was a masterpiece—you almost had me fooled into thinking I might be wrong about you after all. Too bad you stumbled going down the hall. It was like watching one of those cartoons where the lightbulb suddenly flashes on over a character's head." The knife left her throat and he raised the hand that gripped her shoulder to her jaw, grasping her face and roughly jerking it around until she was looking at him over her shoulder, her head twisted to an awkward angle. "What gave me away, Doc—you suddenly remember seeing me in that bar of your uncle's?"

So he *had* been in Mack 'N Babe's after all. When? And then out of the blue—now that it was too late to do anyone a damn bit of good—she remembered. Of course: the guy who'd been checking her out only to turn to Jaz the moment she had noticed him. The one who'd gone all moon-eyed over her cousin. Oh, talk about *good*, she thought bitterly. Did the guy have a degree in psychology or something? He'd certainly zeroed right in on one of her rattier little hangups.

"The talc on your hands from the surgical gloves," she retorted in a voice designed to let him know he wasn't so damn smart, and the fingers grasping her cheeks squeezed warningly at her tone, causing her lips to purse. He kissed her roughly, insolently, and Ivy nearly gagged. Then he shoved her away.

"I forgot that a doctor would be bound to notice something like that," he admitted with a careless shrug, watching as Ivy gingerly worked her jaw back and forth. His expression turned black when he saw her wipe the back of her hand across her mouth. "Don't pretend you didn't like it, bitch," he snarled. "You know you want it—they *all* want it."

"Now that's where you're wrong, Hart," Ivy responded with immediate aggression and then winced at her own stupidity. *Damn* it, Ivy, shut up, shut up, shut up! *Use your head—you don't try to score points in an argument with a madman . . . you do your damndest to placate. God's sake, girl, and you call yourself smart?* "But I'm curious," she queried in a gentler tone. "What would make you say something like that?"

"Because, it's what I *know*," he retorted with flat finality. "It's what *She* taught me."

Ivy had been surreptitiously glancing around her. Tyler stood between her and the door and the phone was much nearer to him than it was to her. About the only thing she had going for her, she realized, was a chance to keep him talking . . . and hope to hell Vincent deigned to show up while she was still in one piece. God but she wished she'd been more receptive to his overtures at Mack 'N Babe's this evening! "Who is 'She,' Tyler?" she asked.

"None of your damn business—I don't want to talk about her!" Tyler looked Ivy up and down. "Take off your top," he snapped arrogantly. "I want to see your tits."

"No!" Ivy slapped her hands with instinctual protectiveness over her breasts.

For that instant she had forgotten all about his knife. But suddenly it was there, slicing up the front of her tank top until it snagged on the wire that formed the little notched V. Gripping the blade between his teeth, he reached for the shredded material with careless hands and yanked, baring her breasts. His fingernails left angry red scratches in their wake.

Ivy instinctively spread her fingers and palms across the area he'd exposed, trying to cover as much of herself as possible.

"Put your fucking hands to your side," he ordered her roughly, and when she balked he made a menacing gesture with the knife. Ivy lowered her hands slowly, fisting them in futile rage at her sides.

Tyler smiled with icy pleasure. Yes. This was the part he loved: the women's fear, his own power.

And what a rush it was to face a woman unmasked for a change, so she could see the full extent of his contempt.

He inspected Ivy's exposed flesh with a thoroughness he knew she would despise but was helpless to prevent. "Nice," he commented insolently. "I bet the cop spends all his time sucking on them." He watched in satisfaction as her eyes filled with sick horror and made obscene kissing noises just to prolong her agony. "So, how does he fuck a big girl like you, anyhow?" he asked, reveling in the hot color that washed like a tide from chest to forehead. "I bet he likes it doggie style, doesn't he? Yeah, I bet he likes to wrap your hair around his fists and pull on it like reins on a horse while he rams his c—"

"Shut up!"

Tyler reached out and grabbed Ivy's breast, squeezing it cruelly. "Don't tell me to shut up, you bitch! I'll say what I want, when I want, and no redheaded cunt is going to tell me otherwise." He ran the back of the knife down her throat, from jaw to collarbone, slapping the flat side of the blade with a snap against the top of her breast. He grinned with relish when she jerked. Then he leaned down suddenly and bit savagely at the nipple protruding between his clenched fingers and thumb. Ivy screamed, and satisfied, Tyler shoved her away.

She stumbled, just barely catching herself by planting her hand on the edge of the mattress. Before she could push herself upright, Tyler had knocked the back of her knee with one of his own. Ivy's leg buckled beneath her. With his hand to the back of her head, he shoved her face into the mattress, leaving her bent over the bed, and she felt him, hard and erect, rubbing obscenely between her buttocks. "I'll bet you like it doggie style, too," he muttered. "That's how I'm gonna do you."

Ivy whimpered. Never had she felt so vulnerable and exposed.

Never had she known such fear.

And then suddenly he was no longer pressing against her; the hand holding her head down was removed and he stepped back. Coughing, Ivy rolled over and pushed herself to her feet.

"Don't tell *me* to shut up," he muttered and reached for his belt buckle. "You want something to occupy your mouth, I'll give you something," he threatened. Then he paused, his hand rubbing at the bulge behind his fly but leaving the zipper fastened. "But first, let's see your pussy. I've never seen a red haired pussy before." When she didn't move, he snapped, "Show me, slut. I want all your clothes off, now. Every last stitch."

"Please," she whispered, tears filling her eyes and spilling over. She couldn't quite bring herself to believe that anyone could be so obscene, so indecent.

"Now!"

Her hand crept into her skirt pocket and curled around the scalpel. She thumbed off the cap, knowing then that she would have to use it. It was against everything she believed in, in direct opposition to everything for which she stood, but she could not let him defile her. It was awful enough hearing him spew his vile theories about Vincent's sexual proclivities. Yes, Vincent had made love to her every way there was, but this monster was trying to take something that was inherently beautiful, something that was special between the two of them, and turn it into an act that was ugly and coarse. She was damned if she was going to let him use her like some no-account receptacle . . . incidental to him only for the purpose of depositing his filth. The man was sick. Sick and foul.

She clumsily unbuttoned her skirt and then finessed the scalpel from its pocket as she bent over to pick it up off the floor. Concealing it amidst folds of abandoned material, she straightened.

"Now the panties, bitch," he snapped.

Oh God, how was she supposed to take off her underwear and still hold onto the scalpel? Less concerned for an instant with exposing her nudity to this monster of depravity than in the logistics involved in saving her skin, she hesitated uncertainly.

But, terrified he'd use his knife and simply cut them off of her, in the end Ivy awkwardly wrestled the narrow string of silk-covered elastic down her hip with her free hand, then pushed the corresponding piece over her opposite hipbone and slowly straightened. The silky material slithered down her thighs and calves to pool around her ankles.

She felt completely exposed standing there stripped to the skin in front of a man who clearly exulted in her humiliation.

And exult the predator ruling Tyler Griffus did. He had forgotten all about the need to get the Doc out of the apartment, forgotten the necessity for haste. Instead, he savored his power and her debasement, conjuring up even sweeter scenarios that featured her at her most helpless. Images of slow, sweet domination filled his imagination. He began to actually savor the thought of killing her, for she was worse by far than those other bitches had ever dreamed of being ... worse, perhaps, even than *Her*. At least *She* had never pretended to be his friend the way the Doc had when in reality she had actually been laughing at him behind his back all the while.

But dying quickly would be too merciful and he wasn't about to let her get off without paying full price. He longed to drag out the humiliation; he wanted to hurt her in every way there was.

"So what do you think the 'ol pigmeister will think if he comes in here and finds you stripped to your pretty white skin, doin' to me what a whore like you does best?" Tyler inquired, reaching for his zipper again. "Think he'll believe you didn't ask for it?"

Oh, God, the bastard was good at psychological warfare, Ivy thought in bitter despair. That hadn't even occurred to her, but what *would* Vincent believe, given what she'd threatened earlier this evening before she'd stormed out of his apartment and the way he'd seen her flirt with this very man with his own two eyes?

Oh God, given his own damnedable black suspicions concerning woman's ability to be faithful in the first place?

Was she going to hold off this obscene rapist long enough for Vincent to come galloping to the rescue, only to have him turn around and slam out again the second he laid eyes on the two of them? Hopelessness began to weigh down her extremities and when Tyler approached her, clutching his exposed phallus in one fist, waving it at her as menacingly as he had his knife and ordering her to "get down on your knees, bitch," her knees actually sagged beneath her.

Then in her mind's eye she pictured Vincent's dark eyes; she heard his voice. "I love you Ivy Jayne," it resonated within .the confines of her brain. "You've got more integrity than any ten men I've ever known, and I was an ass to say what I did." Her legs regained their strength and she rose to her full height.

"I said down on your knees, slut!"

With an enraged howl, Ivy shoved at her tormentor with her entire strength, which years of arduous emergency room wrestling of bodies had made considerable. Caught off guard, Tyler stumbled back. She slammed the blunt end of her scalpel into his funny bone, the bundle of nerves that ran alongside his elbow, and his knife dropped with a clatter to the floor. Snatching it up, screaming at the full capacity of her lung power, Ivy ran hell for leather for the door.

He brought her crashing to the floor in a flying tackle at the end of the hallway. Rolling her onto her back, Tyler quickly straddled her and swung his hand once, twice, across her face with a strength that caused her head to snap from one side to the other. He didn't even see the scalpel in her left hand as he grabbed onto her right wrist and banged her hand repeatedly against the hardwood floor. The knife flew out of her hand and skittered along the hallway. It stopped well within Tyler's reach, but he ignored it as he viciously kneed her legs apart and lowered himself between her thighs. "You've been beggin' for this, you duplicitous twat."

There was a commotion in the hallway outside the apartment but Ivy didn't hear it. She whipped her left hand up, pressing the scalpel's surgical steel blade against Tyler's jugular. *"Breathe* funny, you sick son of a bitch," she whispered harshly, "and I swear I'll slice you open faster'n you can whistle Dixie"—and knew in that instant she wasn't going to be able to do it.

Oh God, oh God, *now* what did she do? *Damn* her scruples—this was not the time or the place for them. She'd better come up with an alternate plan pretty damn quick, for she knew perfectly well she could only hold him off for so long before he came to the realization that she didn't actually have the guts to use the scalpel against him.

Aware of his erection withering against her inner thigh, she expelled a tiny breath of relief. At least the threat of rape was temporarily shelved. For a moment the temptation to taunt him with his inability to sustain it was sweet, but she retained just enough good sense to swallow the mockery before it could pass her lips. Right this minute *she* had the upper hand; she would be wise to hang onto it. This was a madman she was dealing with here. Ordinary men had ego problems in this area; set *this* guy off by mocking his manhood and he'd probably consider a slit throat small payment for the opportunity to kill her as slowly and painfully as possible before he ultimately bled out.

The thought of which sparked vindictive inspiration. This son of a bitch had put her through hell; she was constitutionally incapable of taking it lying down without at least trying to retaliate. "Do you know how long it takes a body to bleed itself dry?" she queried him in a conversational tone and smiled in satisfaction to see the color drain from his face. Good. She hoped the bastard messed his pants.

It was nice to know that two could play this terror by psychology game. She might not be as good at it as he was, but she was nothing if not a fast learner. "The trick, of course, is to keep calm so your heart won't beat so fast," she informed him with relish, feeling his pound against her chest. "But that's sorta hard to do, isn't it, Tyler, especially when you can feel it gushing away with every heartbeat? So usually it only takes about—"

The front door crashed open and Vincent's voice roared her name with a volume that seemed to consume every available airwave. All of Ivy's strength deserted her.

"Vincent?" she whimpered. She could hear his crashing progress throughout the apartment and fresh tears flooded her eyes. Her hand faltering in its steady pressure against Tyler's throat, she craned her head backward in time to see him race into the living room. "Oh, God, *Vincent!*"

In her split second of inattention, Tyler snarled, pinned down her left hand, and snatched his knife up off the floor. He wasn't going to jail. He'd been there once and didn't like it and he was never going back. He saw the pig, saw the piglet in blue who accompanied him, and decided if they were going to take him out, he wasn't going alone. He'd take the bitch-whore Doc with him.

He raised the knife.

"NO!" Vincent shouted and brought up his pistol in a two-handed stance. But it was the rookie patrol cop, just nine months out of the academy, who shot Tyler Griffus down.

The noise was deafening, roaring and echoing in the small, enclosed, wooden-floored hallway. Ivy screamed, clawing frantically at the body that dropped like a bag of wet cement onto her chest and face. Animal sounds emanating from deep in her throat, she wrestled Griffus part way off her, freeing her upper body. The effort left her hands covered to the wrist in blood, and she stared at them with horror. This wasn't the emergency room, this wasn't some stranger in need of her professional help; this was *her*. It was entirely personal, entirely too close to home, and with growing hysteria, she began to push and shove and kick, trying to dislodge the corpse pinning her to the floor.

"Jesus get him off of her!" Vincent roared to the rookie who, although closer, was staring down at the messy corpse at his feet and looking as though he'd like to puke. Vincent kicked the body away and sank to his knees, pulling a screaming, fighting Ivy into his arms. He held her tight. "Shh, shh, shh, it's okay, it's okay, it's okay. It's going to be all right." Her nude flesh was cold beneath his hands and it slipped and slid with her struggles. He looked up at the rookie. "Give me your shirt."

The young officer dragged his eyes away from the man he had killed and met Vincent's eyes blankly. "Huh?"

"She's going into shock, man; get me something to cover her up! Gimme me your shirt, grab a blanket. And call the medics. *Move,* dammit!" He looked back down at the panicky woman in his arms. "Ivy," he said authoritatively, "can you hear me? Listen to me baby, I've got you now. You're safe, Ivy. Griffus is dead. You're safe now."

Her eyes suddenly seemed to focus on his. "Vincent?" As she ceased to fight him, great, wracking sobs took the place of her struggles. A little color returned to her cheeks, a little warmth to her skin. "Oh, dear God, *Vincent?* Oh God, where have you *been?* What took you so long?" Clutching fistfuls of his shirt, she buried her face in his abdomen and cried her heart out.

Vincent looked at the scratches on her chest and breasts, the teeth marks circling one nipple and bowed his head over hers. "I'm sorry, baby; God, I am so sorry." He raised his head as the rookie handed him the quilt off Ivy's bed, nodded his thanks, and gently wrapped her in its warmth. Then he sat down on the floor with his back against the wall and pulled her onto his lap. As the young patrolman started to straighten, Vincent reached out and touched his arm. "It was a righteous shoot," he told him quietly. "He didn't leave you any other option."

The eyes that met his had aged considerably in the less than twenty minutes since Vincent had conscripted his services outside the precinct. "So why do I still feel like shit?" he asked.

Vincent looked him dead-level in the eye. "Probably because you're a decent man." He nodded down at the crying woman in his arms. "But you saved her life and for that you've got my thanks. The guy was gonna kill her."

The rookie nodded. "Yeah. I know." Rising to his feet, he said, "I'll secure the area, sir."

Vincent looked back down at Ivy. She had calmed some, snuffling and breathing raggedly, her cheek resting heavily against his chest. Gently he touched his forefinger to a dribble of blood below her right nostril. He pulled up a corner of the quilt and dabbed it away, then cleared his throat. "Ivy, I've got to ask you some questions."

She moaned.

"I know, I know. I'm sorry, baby, but it's my job. Would you rather talk to a woman? I can call Suse McGill."

She shook her head. Silent for a long, tense moment, she finally sighed, sniffed, and wiped her runny nose with inelegant disregard against his shirtfront. "He didn't rape me, Vincent," she whispered.

She felt the hard thump of his heart beneath her cheek and slowly raised her head to look him in the face.

"He didn't?" Oh, sweet Jesus, thank you. Considering her condition and Griffus's position between her sprawled thighs when he'd come barreling into the living room, he'd thought for sure he'd been too late, if not to prevent the rapist from completing his act, then at least to have prevented penetration. Vincent felt as if someone had just removed a heavy weight from his heart. He tightened his arms around her and planted a tender kiss on her forehead. "Can you tell me what happened?"

She began to cry again. "Oh, God, Vincent, it was so awful," she wailed. Struggling for control, she stated gruffly, "He humil . . . humili . . ." She took a deep breath, held it for a second, and then blew it out hard. "He humiliated me. He called me a—a twat and a c-cunt. Made me take off all my clothes and then talked about my body and the way you . . . you and I, the way we . . ."

"Make love," Vincent supplied through his teeth. It was damn fortunate the man was already dead. He'd like to kill him himself for what he'd put her through.

"Except it wasn't making love the way he talked about it. He made it sound so filthy and nasty, and Vincent, he tried to, tried to . . ." Slapping a hand over her mouth, Ivy gagged several times. Finally she took a deep, cleansing breath—and lowered her hand. She forced herself to continue. "He tried to, wanted me to . . . Vincent, he told me to get down on my knees—" Yesterday it wouldn't have bothered her to say the words; today she simply couldn't bring herself to do it. She clutched his shirt harder and stared up at him pleadingly.

"He was going to orally sodomize you."

She nodded weakly. "He said you'd blame me."

Vincent jerked, knowing that given the way he'd been acting lately, it must have preyed on her. "No," he said firmly. His dark fingertip edged the comforter away from her breast and hovered just above the nail gouges in her chest and her abused right nipple. "And this . . . ?" He covered her back up.

Stuttering, she told him. Little by little, he got the entire story out of her. It was a new perspective for him, hearing the victim's tale from a woman with whom he had a personal relationship. There was no way on God's green earth he could remain objective about her terror, her pain. It took him by surprise when she told him about holding the scalpel to Griffus's throat, for it was a detail that had escaped his notice when he'd barged onto the scene. At first he couldn't understand why she hadn't simply slit the bastard's throat when she'd had the opportunity—the little deviant had given her ample reason to eradicate him from the face of the earth.

But then Vincent thought about everything he knew that made Ivy Jayne Pennington the person she was. He thought of her dedication to her profession, her personal integrity, and he was glad that she hadn't been the one to kill him. Because somewhere on a level much deeper than how this was affecting *him,* a level much deeper than his futile desire to wreak vengeance on a dead man for the terror he'd caused the woman he loved, Vincent understood what it would have meant to her.

It would have been a decision she'd have found nearly impossible to reconcile with her beliefs. Ultimately, that would have proven a larger obstacle to her recovery than what she already had to face.

Chapter 20

Ivy was released from the emergency room at 4:15 a.m. and the first thing she did when Vincent let them into his apartment was head straight for the shower. She didn't come out until the hot water had run tepid.

Vincent was sitting on the bathroom floor, his knees drawn up and his back against the wall, dozing, when she stepped from the stall. She smiled for the first time in a long while and nudged him with her toe. "Hey."

"Umph." His eyes blinked open. "Oh. Sorry. Guess I fell asleep for a minute." The sound of his fingers rubbing over a sandpaper jaw was magnified by the acoustics of the tiny steamy room. He extended a towel to her. "Here. I thought you might need this."

"Thanks," she answered.

Vincent stood in awkward silence as she dried herself off. He wanted to do something that would take away the nightmare Griffus had put her through but didn't know quite what that something should be. "Do you feel like talking about it some more?" he finally inquired.

The hand drying her hair stilled and her eyes, haunted and bleak, rose to meet his. "No. I'm all talked out."

"Maybe tomorrow then, huh?"

"Yeah." Ivy tossed the towel into a corner on the floor. "Maybe tomorrow." Crossing the few steps that separated her from Vincent, she wrapped her arms around his waist and bowed her head until her forehead rested against his neck. "You know what I'd really like?"

His fingers curled gratefully around her nape. "What's that, baby?"

"I'd like you to take me to bed and just hold me 'til I fall asleep."

Vincent expelled the air he hadn't even realized he'd been holding. Picking her up, he maneuvered her through the door. "Now that," he said as he carried her into the bedroom, "is something I can handle."

When Ivy awoke late the following morning, it was to find Vincent propped up beside her inspecting the orange wash of antiseptic that had been swabbed around the teethmarks on her right breast. "I should have been here," he said when he saw she was awake. Reaching out to gently stroke her slightly swollen jawline, he added contritely, "It's not the first time I've let you down, Ivy. I'm sorry."

"Where were you, Vincent?"

He told her and then tried to explain the reconciliation of his old need to find suspicion in her every move with last night's sudden faith. "I knew from practically the first time we made love that you were going to own me," he admitted, lying down beside her and gathering her in his arms. "Own me body and soul . . . and it scared the bejesus outta me, Ive."

"Uh huh." For a sound that was basically a non-word, she managed to invest it with a world of skepticism.

"What, you think I'm kidding? I never doubted for a minute that you had the power to destroy me. Hell, I've been holding my breath for such a long time now, waiting for you to do just that, that it rendered me totally stupid. Oxygen deprivation," he tried to joke, but the eyes regarding him when he turned his head to look at her were in no mood for levity. He blew out his breath and rolled his head back to stare up at the ceiling. "I suppose I thought attacking first was the way to protect myself. Instead I damn near drove you away." Vincent was silent for a moment before he finally raised up on one elbow, twisting onto his side to meet her eyes. "And then, last night, boom! Just like that, I *knew*. Knew you'd never cheat on me. Knew you'd never do me harm of any nature. No more doubts, Ive. Out of the blue I understood I'd been the worst sort of fool."

"Say it, D'Ambruzzi," she whispered fiercely. "Say it now that I'm sober and paying attention."

"I love you, Ivy Jayne."

She closed her eyes. When she opened them again, she said in a low, hoarse voice, "He changed my whole outlook on sex, Vincent."

Vincent's voice was equally low. . . and filled with frustrated fury. "That son of a bitch." He slid back down beside her, pulling her close, tightening his arms around her.

"Oh God." She expelled an unsteady little exhalation. "What if I'm never the same woman again? Will you still love me then?" He rushed to assure her that he would, but the victimized woman in her remained skeptical.

There was a large part of her that wanted nothing so much as to bury last night's ordeal and pretend it had never happened. Instead, she forced herself to recount everything that had transpired from the moment he'd walked out of the bar until he'd burst back onto the scene. Haltingly, she filled in all the gaps she'd been too traumatized to supply more than sketchily the night before.

"I'm so afraid that nothing will ever be the same again," she confessed. "Sex with you has always been something so special. We could be totally raunchy together and still it was a . . . well, almost a celebration. But Griffus made it seem so filthy, Vincent. I doubt I'll ever be able to let you love me from behind again. Not without thinking of the way he turned it all ugly and obscene."

"That's what rapists do, you know," Vincent informed her. "It's their most powerful weapon." He raised up on his elbow again in order to look her straight in the eye as he said with authority, "With them it's never about sex; it's all about power and anger and humiliation and control. I know that given the nature of the crime it sounds contradictory," he said in soothing tones when she made a slight movement of disagreement. "But it's the truth, Ivy. This crime is a goddamn oxymoron. Rapists hate women and that's a fact. And a rapist's penis to him isn't his . . . his . . ." Vincent grimaced as he searched for an appropriate word.

"Luv tool?" Ivy supplied with a slight smile.

He squeezed her. "Right. It's not his luv tool, it's a damn weapon. It's a means to wreak havoc in some unsuspecting woman's life by violating her in the most damaging way possible. I deal with these guys day in and day out. Trust me when I say that any one of them would probably be delighted to know he was able to destroy something his victim valued.''

"But how do I get past this?" Ivy demanded and Vincent could read the fear of failure in her eyes. "Do we simply jump right back in the sack and screw our brains out as if nothing happened?" He knew she envisioned a series of attempts that might culminate with her lying frozen and unresponsive in his arms.

Then her wording sank in and he said a bit indignantly, "We make love, doll baby; we don't screw our brains out." But when Ivy gave him a look that was nearly up to her old, ascerbic standards, he smiled crookedly. "Okay, okay," he conceded sheepishly. "So maybe we like it down and dirty occasionally."

"Frequently," she amended.

"Whatever. It's still making love. At least . . . it's never made you feel dirty before, has it?"

"No," she hastened to assure him, unable to bear seeing the sudden look of doubt on his face. "It's always made me feel glorious."

"Jesus, that's a relief. In any event, before we attempt sex in any of its guises I want you to do something for me," he said. "I'm going to give you the names of the same social services I give to every rape victim I come into contact with. I want you to get in touch with however many of 'em you need to."

"They aren't going to want to be bothered with me, Vincent; I wasn't actually raped."

"You might not have been actually penetrated, but for a while last night you were sure as hell in danger of being raped. Griffus toyed with your emotions, Ivy, preyed on your fears. He violated your home and fully intended to violate your body. Go. Talk to someone. The women who work for

these services don't assign degree of victimization.
They understand everything you've been through
because most of them have been through it themselves. They can help.'' He brushed her hair back.
"And if you don't want to go alone, then get your
cousin Jaz to go with you. She could probably stand
to talk to someone as well."

Ivy sat bolt upright. "Oh my God, my family!"

"Hey, now; easy, girl." Vincent pulled her back
down.

"Vincent, let me go. I've got to—"

Vincent silenced her by placing a long finger
over her lips. "Everything's under control," he
assured her. "I talked to Babe earlier and she told
me the paramedics took Terry and Jaz to University
Hospital last night. Jaz was released and she spent
the night with her parents. Terry was kept overnight because his condition was a little more serious, but he's stabilized now and I told your aunt
we'd stop by to see him at the hospital around
three." Rolling onto his back, his right arm still
around her, he stretched out his free hand to scoop
his watch up off the night stand. Peering at it, he
said, "Which gives me about three and a half hours
to get downtown, give my statement, fill out my
report, and get back here."

He gave her a quick kiss, pulled his arm out from
under her, and climbed from the bed. Ivy watched
his naked backside as he walked across the room.
"Vincent?"

He turned at the doorway. "Yeah?"

"I love you."

His teeth were pearly white against his swarthy,
stubble-shadowed face when he smiled at her. "Just
keep tellin' me that, doll baby. It's all I need to
hear."

* * *

Vincent watched Ivy's family surround her in the corridor outside Terry's hospital room. Arms hugged her; hands stroked her. Voices, scaled in volume to suit the environment, babbled questions and concern, expressed love and support. Vincent stood back and tried to sort everyone out in his mind.

Sherry and Jaz he knew. There had never been a formal introduction to Sam or Davis, but Ivy had identified them so many times through the pictures in her photo albums that it was a piece of cake to connect names and faces. The same was true for a couple of older cousins.

He watched the hullaballou for a few moments and then walked over to Jaz, who following the initial greetings had distanced herself from the crowd surrounding her cousin. She looked up at him with wary eyes.

"How are *you* holding up?" he inquired gently.

Inspecting his expression as if suspecting an ulterior motive, she finally replied dully, "I'm okay."

Vincent pulled his notebook from his hip pocket, fished a pen out of another pocket, and scribbled for several moments. Ripping the page out, he extended it to her. "These are the names of some social services that can help you deal with last night's trauma," he informed her. "I want you to go see them with Ivy; they'll do you both a lot of good."

She took the paper and stood gazing down at it for a moment. Then she slowly raised her eyes again. They were brimming with tears. "Why are you being so nice to me?" she demanded raggedly. "I know you don't like me and I brought that pig right into the middle of this family."

"No, Jasmine, you did not." Vincent was at his

most authoritative as he met her eyes. "You were used by a man who specialized in deception."

"Yeah, and because of my gullibility and my damn desperate desire for a relationship that might lead to a husband and family, Terry was carved up and Ivy was damn-near raped."

"And so were *you,* according to everything I've heard. Dammit, Jaz, don't do this to yourself. I can't tell you how many victims I've seen accepting the blame for some deviant's actions, and it's just not right. Griffus was a twisted individual, corrupt through and through, and he was completely single-minded. Once he made up his mind that Ivy was his soul-mate, nothing would have stopped him from finding a way to get closer to her. If he hadn't obtained his objective through you, he would have gained it some other way." Seeing the slight lessening of self-disgust in her eyes, he added, "As for the relationship thing, Ivy said he was a master at determining which buttons to push and then using a nuclear detonator to set them off. He did the same thing with her."

There was a flurry of activity before he could add that he didn't as yet know her well enough to like or dislike her. Terry's parents came out of his hospital room and Sherry and another relative went in. Ivy, after speaking to her aunt and uncle briefly, broke away from the group by the door and came over to wrap her arms around Jaz. She squeezed her tight. "I am so sorry I got you mixed up in this mess, Jasmine," she murmured, which made Vincent roll his eyes and mutter, "Oh, for Christ's sake," and caused Jaz to actually laugh. Ivy leaned back, her arms still around her cousin, and looked in confusion from Jaz's face to Vincent's. "What?"

"D'Ambruzzi just finished lecturing me on the perils of accepting responsibility for someone else's actions," Jaz retorted. "And he's right. It's not your fault that sicko pervert fixated on you. And I guess it's not mine either that he used me to get closer to you."

"Well, of course it's not your fault," Ivy agreed indignantly. "Who on earth would think such a thing?"

"Me," Jaz admitted. "You know how ambivalent I've been about Tyler the last few weeks. It's hard to accept how easily I was taken in by this guy. Hell, no one likes to admit what a breeze they are to manipulate." She expelled a deep breath. "It's even harder to know that I kept him around simply to save me from having to hunt up a new escort. I mean, Jesus, Ive."

Ivy looked her cousin over consideringly. "So chances are you're probably going to be a tad bit deeper with the next guy."

A bark of laughter escaped Jaz. "Oh right. Like I'm ever going to be able to trust in my judgement again. Can't you just picture it—" she adopted a sultry, flirtatious tone "—'What did you say your name was again? Charles Manson? I'd *love* to go to the movies with you. Mind if I call you Charlie?' "

They looked at each other and laughed. "We're gonna be all right, aren't we Ivy?" Jaz said wonderingly.

"Yeah. All told, I guess we were a lot luckier than his other victims, weren't we? We're going to be just fine."

Epilogue

So many changes had occurred in such a short period of time; had it actually been less than a month since that night? Ivy sat in the middle of the bed with her knees hugged to her chest, brooding about it.

Not, of course, that all the changes had been negative.

She'd given up her apartment as soon as the Crime Scene tape had come off the door. Not wanting to be reminded of events she already had a difficult enough time forgetting, she'd hired a service to clean away the last remaining vestiges of Tyler Griffus for her. Then she had moved in with Vincent permanently.

It now felt more as if this were her home too instead of just his as their possessions began to intermingle. Her couch and newly upholstered chair had taken over the living room since they were more attractive than the furniture Vincent had owned. They had kept Vincent's bed, however, because his mattress was worlds nicer than the ratty old hand-me-down she'd been using for the past six years.

But they hadn't made love on that mattress since before That Night.

Ivy winced. That was probably part of the problem right there: the way she couldn't seem to prevent herself from setting that night off in capitals. She had to quit investing Griffus with the kind of power that allowed him to continue disrupting her life even posthumously. It wasn't right.

Not that she was just lying back and taking it. No, she and Jaz were even now in the process of fighting back in their own way.

Neither had felt comfortable at the one group session they'd attended, but talking to each other and the private counseling each was receiving helped. Their discomfort in group had probably stemmed from knowing that neither of them had actually been penetrated. As far as Ivy was concerned the difference between attempted rape and rape itself was immense. She, for one, had felt extremely ill at ease trying to express the sense of violation her near-miss had left her with to other women whose violation had been complete. There had been no near-miss about it for them.

On the home front, Vincent had been the epitome of understanding; she couldn't complain about that. He seemed to understand that she couldn't handle the resumption of relations right now. Night after night, sliding into bed beside her, he'd done nothing more threatening than pull her into his arms.

But theirs was a relationship that right from the beginning had been imbued with a high degree of sexuality, and Ivy couldn't help but wonder how long Vincent's patience would last.

She understood that, of all the factors involved,

probably time would be her greatest ally when it came to scabbing over the fresh scars that Tyler's treatment had gouged in her psyche. But she hated that bastard for what he'd done to her. And she hated herself for allowing the experience to turn her into a coward.

She couldn't believe that for the first time since she was twelve years old, she had actually greeted the onset of her period last week with relief. "Thank God" had been the first thought to flash through her mind. Now I have a legitimate excuse to turn Vincent away should he choose this night to reach for me. Sweet Merciful Mary. Her self-disgust on the heels of that thought had known no bounds.

As always in times of stress, she'd clung to the stability of her family. If it had been somewhat to the exclusion of Vincent, she'd excused herself with the knowledge that they were the one constant in her life. It had been her experience that family was something that never changed—until this afternoon, when she had discovered that *nothing* remains the same.

Keith and Anna Graham were visiting when the telephone rang. Ivy got up to answer it. "Yes?"

"Ivy, it's me," Sherry said and even down the line Ivy could hear her impatience. "Let me in."

Ivy hit the door release button.

Moments later her cousin was ringing the door bell. She stalked right past Ivy when she opened the front door for her but then came to a dead halt in the entryway to the living room. "Oh, my God; you've got guests. I'm sorry, Ive; I should have called first."

"Don't be silly. You already know Keith." Ivy introduced her to Anna and then turned back to

Sherry. The distress emanating from her cousin was palpable. "What's the matter, Sher?"

"Terry's *leaving*," Sherry wailed softly and started to cry. Embarrassed to be falling apart in front of strangers, she turned her back on the small group in the living room. "Ivy," she said in a low, intense voice, "he's moving to San Francisco."

Ivy excused her cousin and herself and grasping Sherry's arm, escorted her down the hallway to the bedroom. Closing the door behind them, she directed her over to the bed. "Sit." Then afraid she already knew the answer she forced herself to ask the question anyhow, wondering what excuse he had given. "Why is Terry moving?"

"Oh God, who knows? He *says* it's a career opportunity."

"But you don't believe that?"

"No. Yes. Oh, hell, I don't know." Sherry dashed the side of her hand across her eyes and looked up at Ivy. "All I know for sure is I don't want my brother to move three states away."

Neither did Ivy, but unlike her cousin she understood Terry's motivation. "Sherry, I'm sorry. I don't know what to say. Except I know it's gonna be hard for you."

"Will you talk to him, Ivy?"

"Well . . . sure. But I doubt I can influence him one way or another. No one can, Sherry, not once he's made his mind up about something. You know Terry."

"Do I ever. But try for me anyway, will you?"

"I'll try," Ivy promised. And felt like a damn hypocrite.

Sherry was too upset to sit around trying to observe the social niceties with people she didn't know and so left a few moments later. She'd been gone less than five minutes when the doorbell rang again. Giving Anna and Keith an apologetic smile, Ivy went to answer it.

Terry lounged against the doorjamb. "Hi," he said. "Thought I'd save you the effort of having to track me down."

"Jeez, Terry, what'd you do, follow Sherry?"

"Yeah. She was pretty upset when I gave her the news."

"I'll say."

"Yeah, well." Terry shrugged uncomfortably. "I knew she'd let Ben try to comfort her for a while but that she'd eventually come running to either you or Jaz." His face was suddenly a mask, cleared of all expression. "I'm glad it was you."

"Come on in." Ivy stepped back. "And just out of curiosity, Ter, has our paltry little security system *ever* slowed you down?"

"I almost had to ring up here once. But then some sweet little old blue-haired lady let me in. Hey, Vince," he said in greeting as they entered the living room and then nodded in a friendly manner to the Grahams. "Sorry 'bout barging in here unannounced like this, folks, but I've got to borrow Ivy for a few minutes." He wrapped his hand around her elbow and pulled her out onto the balcony, sliding the door closed behind them. Ivy turned back to shrug helplessly at Anna and Keith. She mouthed a contrite, 'Sorry'."

Keith turned to Vincent. "The lady's husband?"

"Twin brother."

Keith whistled in admiration. "Son, your life sure has become a lot more interesting since you met Ivy."

"Yeah, it's a goddam soap opera sometimes." And being the macho law enforcement type that he was, he would cheerfully let someone pull his fingernails out with a pair of pliers before he'd admit he was dying to find out what the hell was going on with her family now.

Out on the balcony Ivy said unhappily, "Sherry asked me to try to talk you out of going, Terry."

"You can't." Plowing his fingers through his hair, he held it off his forehead as he looked off into the distance. Then his hand dropped to his side and he turned to look at her. "I've got to get away, Ive. I can't have her—" neither of them needed to hear the name said aloud to know to whom he referred "—and I can't go on the way I've been. I just . . . can't. It's too damn painful and it's never gonna get any better unless I make a new life for myself somewhere else."

"I know." Ivy's eyes filled with tears. "I honestly do understand, Terry. But, oh, God, I'm going to miss you so much!"

He reached out and pulled her into his arms, giving her a fierce hug. "I'm going to miss you too, babe. But I gotta do this. And you've got Vincent now." He held her at arm's length and flashed a crooked smile. "Besides, San Francisco is a great place to visit; you guys can come down and see me any time you want. Just . . ." His smile faltered for a second. "Don't bring Jaz with you for the first couple of years, okay?"

"Oh, Terry. I'm so sorry."

"No," he said firmly, "it's okay, Ive. I really believe I'm going to be all right if I can just go somewhere where I can start all over. This town's got too damn many associations and memories. San Francisco's a clean slate."

"Promise me something," Ivy demanded fiercely. "Promise me you'll start dating nice, regular, *intelligent* women instead of those bubble-heads you usually go out with."

"Yeah, I will. My life really is going to be different,

Ive; one way or another I'm gonna get all my shit together. I promise you.''

They discussed the particulars for a few moments longer before Terry insisted on leaving so she could get back to her guests.

And so here she was, in a rapidly darkening bedroom, brooding over all the changes that had occurred in less than a month. Not even family dynamics remained stagnant, it appeared. Well, change was growth, they said.

And she would keep telling herself that until she got it through her head.

Vincent came into the room. She felt the mattress depress as he knee-walked across the bed. Then he was kneeling behind her. Reaching out, he massaged the knots of stress in her neck and shoulders with strong fingers. ''You want to talk about it?''

For the first time, Ivy realized she'd been shutting him out lately in more ways than simply sexually. Feeling some of the knots dissolve beneath his hands, she rested her forehead on her kneecaps and began to talk.

Vincent widened his knees to encompass her hips. Snugging himself up behind her, he insinuated his arms between her updrawn legs and her stomach, getting her to change position, and for the first time since the night Griffus had terrorized her, he didn't feel her grow anxious at an approach from him from the rear.

Living with her this past month had been like an extended roller coaster ride. Intellectually he had understood her tension whenever he reached for her; emotionally, it had taken a toll. But, okay, the physical aspect he could at least reason out. It was the emotional barrier she'd brought down between them at odd moments that really hurt. She seemed to need the support of her family and he understood that. But where was he in all this? Shouldn't she need his support, too?

As if reading his thoughts, she whispered, "I'm sorry, Vincent." She rested her head back against his neck. "I've been shutting you out and I don't even know why. I *love* you."

His hands moved restlessly over her body, eager to touch her but exercising care not to do so in a sexual manner. Fingers skimming the sides of her breasts on their journey up and down her sides, he kept his palms carefully arched away so as not to cup their fullness; his touch lightly mapped her thighs as far as he could reach, but then jumped over her mound on their return journey to lightly trace the shape of her stomach and abdomen. He was willing to give her all the time she needed and didn't want to spook her by making a move before she was ready. The truth was he was scared to death of doing something that might be construed the wrong way.

"I love you too, Ivy," he whispered hoarsely. "God, I've *missed* you." Without conscious thought his hands continued moving over her, rubbing up and down her arms, splaying across her chest, plying her sides from her underarms to the indentation of her waist to the fullness of her hips to the outside curves of her thighs. It felt so good to have some contact with her again. "Don't shut me out again like that. It makes me crazy."

Ivy started to cry. "Oh, God, Vincent, I've been so messed up. One minute I'm fine and then the next I'm so tense and afraid I just want to climb into a dark closet and scream."

"Ah, baby, it's gonna be okay. Talk to me. Tell me what you're feeling so I know what's going on." Rolling to his side, he curled around her back and listened while she poured out her fears. And all the while he held her, rocked her, crooned to her.

Touched her.

His hands were beginning to get to her. She found her concentration focused less on his words and more on their progress over her body. It began to madden her, awakening for the first time in nearly a month her old sexual hunger for this man.

She held her breath when his fingers curved inward from the outside of her thighs and rubbed at a creeping pace upward. They were getting closer, closer, oh God, nearly there . . . then, *damn,* they were moving up over her stomach without having touched the good stuff at all. Next his fingertips just barely touched the underside of her left breast before they furrowed between both breasts without actually touching either. They ended up drawing lazy circles on the neutral territory of her chest.

She began to feel as if she were wearing way too many clothes.

On his next circuit over her thighs, she spread her legs slightly and was rewarded by a light brush of his fingertips along her cleft. When she tried to turn her breast more fully into his touch and had that invitation ignored, she snapped impatiently, "Oh, God, Vincent, *touch* me!"

Desire slammed through Vincent's veins and he eased his hips away from her, afraid if she felt him hard against her buttocks they'd land right back on square one. He grinned to himself at the sound of her old imperious tone. Hell, he hadn't even realized she was becoming aroused until she'd spread her legs for him when his fingers reached the tops of her thighs last time around—and then he'd been afraid to believe it wasn't simply his imagination. This wasn't exactly something he had set out to accomplish.

But his mama hadn't raised no fool and he would sure as hell take full advantage of it. He kept teasing her while he eased her out of her clothing. Then he played with her breasts, partially satisfying her desire to be touched. He didn't offer any real gratification, however, until his own pants were down around his ankles.

He turned her onto her hands and knees and immediately felt her tense. "No," she whimpered, looking at him over her shoulder. Vincent leaned forward and kissed her. "Yes," he insisted, drawing back, and reached between her legs to stroke her. He knew they were going to be all right when she widened her knees for more of his touch.

"It's okay," he whispered, lining himself up and entering her gently from behind, pressing forward until he was imbedded fully inside her. He wrapped himself around her, curving his chest to her back, wrapping one arm around her and reaching down to delve into her damp curls with his fingers. "I love you, Ivy. I'll never hurt you. I promise you I'll never hurt you." He began to stroke himself in and out. "God, I love you so much." He pressed hot, open-mouthed kisses into the side of her neck.

Small, gasping moans escaped from deep in Ivy's throat and she began to push back against his thrusts. "Oh, please," she whimpered, and she cried out, a low, shuddery sigh of satisfaction as she climaxed, clamping down on him with hard, fast contractions that carried him right along with her over the edge.

"Ivy," he said when he'd pulled out and rolled onto his back, pulling her with him, "I forgot to use a condom."

"That's okay," she said around a yawn. "This is a pretty safe time anyway." She was feeling malleable as warm wax, filled with relief and exhultation. They were going to be all right. Vincent had helped her clear the first and highest hurdle, had broken the psychological hold Griffus had continued to exert on her emotions.

"Yeah, and besides," he said, feeling pretty contented himself, "not that we don't need to discuss family planning and all that, but . . . you *are* going to marry me, aren't you?"

Ivy raised her head up off his chest. "You want to marry me?"

"Hell, yeah. I sort of thought that was understood. First we live together for a little while, then we get married." He had tilted his chin into his neck to see her better and now regarded her a little uncertainly. "Don't we?"

A slow smile spread across Ivy's face and she lowered her head until her cheek was nestled back on Vincent's furry chest. "Yes," she murmured. "We do."

His arm tightened around her. "Good."

They were silent for a few moments and then Ivy tentatively said, "Vincent?"

"Hmmm?"

"Why did you insist on doing it that way?"

"What way is that, babe?"

"You know . . . doggie style?"

He propped himself up over her. "Because I wanted you to know that I'm not him," he said firmly. "That I could *never* be like him. You and I love each other, Ivy Jayne, and nothing we do in this bed is wrong. I didn't want that asshole dictating our love life." He brushed gentle fingertips over her face and continued more moderately, "The only time sex is dirty between two people who care for one another is when one of them turns it into a weapon. I'll never do that to you."

She grasped his hand and brought it down to her lips, kissing each finger. "I know that. I'd trust you with my life, Vincent. More importantly, I'd trust you with my heart." She gave him a lopsided smile. "Speaking of which," she said, "how long is this 'little while' that we live together before we get married?"

"I don't know. I was kind of waiting for you to come back to the land of the living before I set a deadline. But I guess now that you're back . . ." He considered her thoughtfully for several seconds until she finally gave his side a pinch. "Ouch! Okay, okay, how 'bout two weeks?"

"Two weeks! Are you crazy?"

He just cocked an eyebrow at her and grinned.

"Dumb question; let me rephrase that. Do you have any idea how long it takes to arrange a wedding, D'Ambruzzi?"

Alarm flashed over his face. "God, you're not gonna insist on some huge, hoop-de-do-dah, social event, are you? Keep in mind that I'm just a simple farm boy from the Midwest."

"Oh, here, let me knock the hayseed out of your hair." She mussed his hair with vigorous fingers. Then she gripped it with both hands and tugged until he was looking directly into her eyes. "Listen, Farm Boy. Unlike you, I've never been married before."

Vincent sobered up quickly. "Is that going to be a problem between us, Ivy?"

"I don't know, Vincent; do you love me more than you've ever loved anyone else in your life?"

"Yes ma'am, I sure as hell do."

"Then it's not going to be a problem. But getting back to my wedding . . ."

"Excuse me? *Your* wedding?"

"Okay, our wedding. It doesn't have to be huge, but I do want my family to attend and I want a white satin wedding gown. It's going to take me more than two weeks to arrange it."

"Okay—two months, and that's my final offer.

Otherwise the deal's off. Go find yourself another sucker to marry."

"Ooh, big threat. I'm scared. Two months and two weeks," she counteroffered. "Or I'm forced to pull out the big gun."

"Oh yeah? And what is that?"

Ivy smiled up at him smugly. "I tell Uncle Mack you refuse to make an honest woman of me."

Vincent regarded her with awe. "Jeez, you're a pisser," he said in pure admiration.

"Thank you." She cocked an eyebrow at him. "So? What's it gonna be then?"

Vincent bent his elbows, kissed her hard, and then stiff-armed himself away again. "Lady," he said, "you've got yourself a deal."

Thrilling Suspense from
Beverly Barton

Available Wherever Books Are Sold!

Visit our website at **www.kensingtonbooks.com**

Nail-Biting Romantic Suspense
from Your Favorite Authors

More by Bestselling Author
Hannah Howell

__Highland Angel	978-1-4201-0864-4	$6.99US/$8.99CAN
__If He's Sinful	978-1-4201-0461-5	$6.99US/$8.99CAN
__Wild Conquest	978-1-4201-0464-6	$6.99US/$8.99CAN
__If He's Wicked	978-1-4201-0460-8	$6.99US/$8.49CAN
__My Lady Captor	978-0-8217-7430-4	$6.99US/$8.49CAN
__Highland Sinner	978-0-8217-8001-5	$6.99US/$8.49CAN
__Highland Captive	978-0-8217-8003-9	$6.99US/$8.49CAN
__Nature of the Beast	978-1-4201-0435-6	$6.99US/$8.49CAN
__Highland Fire	978-0-8217-7429-8	$6.99US/$8.49CAN
__Silver Flame	978-1-4201-0107-2	$6.99US/$8.49CAN
__Highland Wolf	978-0-8217-8000-8	$6.99US/$9.99CAN
__Highland Wedding	978-0-8217-8002-2	$4.99US/$6.99CAN
__Highland Destiny	978-1-4201-0259-8	$4.99US/$6.99CAN
__Only for You	978-0-8217-8151-7	$6.99US/$8.99CAN
__Highland Promise	978-1-4201-0261-1	$4.99US/$6.99CAN
__Highland Vow	978-1-4201-0260-4	$4.99US/$6.99CAN
__Highland Savage	978-0-8217-7999-6	$6.99US/$9.99CAN
__Beauty and the Beast	978-0-8217-8004-6	$4.99US/$6.99CAN
__Unconquered	978-0-8217-8088-6	$4.99US/$6.99CAN
__Highland Barbarian	978-0-8217-7998-9	$6.99US/$9.99CAN
__Highland Conqueror	978-0-8217-8148-7	$6.99US/$9.99CAN
__Conqueror's Kiss	978-0-8217-8005-3	$4.99US/$6.99CAN
__A Stockingful of Joy	978-1-4201-0018-1	$4.99US/$6.99CAN
__Highland Bride	978-0-8217-7995-8	$4.99US/$6.99CAN
__Highland Lover	978-0-8217-7759-6	$6.99US/$9.99CAN

Available Wherever Books Are Sold!

Check out our website at
http://www.kensingtonbooks.com

Books by Bestselling Author
Fern Michaels

___The Jury	0-8217-7878-1	$6.99US/$9.99CAN
___Sweet Revenge	0-8217-7879-X	$6.99US/$9.99CAN
___Lethal Justice	0-8217-7880-3	$6.99US/$9.99CAN
___Free Fall	0-8217-7881-1	$6.99US/$9.99CAN
___Fool Me Once	0-8217-8071-9	$7.99US/$10.99CAN
___Vegas Rich	0-8217-8112-X	$7.99US/$10.99CAN
___Hide and Seek	1-4201-0184-6	$6.99US/$9.99CAN
___Hokus Pokus	1-4201-0185-4	$6.99US/$9.99CAN
___Fast Track	1-4201-0186-2	$6.99US/$9.99CAN
___Collateral Damage	1-4201-0187-0	$6.99US/$9.99CAN
___Final Justice	1-4201-0188-9	$6.99US/$9.99CAN
___Up Close and Personal	0-8217-7956-7	$7.99US/$9.99CAN
___Under the Radar	1-4201-0683-X	$6.99US/$9.99CAN
___Razor Sharp	1-4201-0684-8	$7.99US/$10.99CAN
___Yesterday	1-4201-1494-8	$5.99US/$6.99CAN
___Vanishing Act	1-4201-0685-6	$7.99US/$10.99CAN
___Sara's Song	1-4201-1493-X	$5.99US/$6.99CAN
___Deadly Deals	1-4201-0686-4	$7.99US/$10.99CAN
___Game Over	1-4201-0687-2	$7.99US/$10.99CAN
___Sins of Omission	1-4201-1153-1	$7.99US/$10.99CAN
___Sins of the Flesh	1-4201-1154-X	$7.99US/$10.99CAN
___Cross Roads	1-4201-1192-2	$7.99US/$10.99CAN

Available Wherever Books Are Sold!
Check out our website at **www.kensingtonbooks.com**